BY JAMES LUCENO

The ROBOTECH series
(as Jack McKinney, with Brian Daley)

The BLACK HOLE TRAVEL AGENCY series
(as Jack McKinney, with Brian Daley)

A Fearful Symmetry

Illegal Alien

The Big Empty

Kaduna Memories

THE YOUNG INDIANA JONES CHRONICLES

The Mata Hari Affair

The Shadow

The Mask of Zorro

Rio Passion

Rainchaser

Rock Bottom

Star Wars: Cloak of Deception

Star Wars: Darth Maul: Saboteur (eBook)

Star Wars: The New Jedi Order: Agents of Chaos I: Hero's Trial

Star Wars: The New Jedi Order: Agents of Chaos II: Jedi Eclipse

Star Wars: The New Jedi Order: The Unifying Force

Star Wars: Labyrinth of Evil

Star Wars: Dark Lord—The Rise of Darth Vader

Star Wars: Millenium Falcon

Star Wars: Darth Plagueis

DARTH PLAGUEIS

DARTH PLAGUEIS

JAMES LUCENO

 Ballantine Books • New York

Copyright © 2012 by Lucasfilm Ltd. & ® or ™ where indicated. All Rights Reserved. Used Under Authorization.

Excerpt from *Star Wars: Shadow Games* by Michael Reaves and Maya Kaathryn Bohnhoff copyright © 2011 by Lucasfilm Ltd. & ® or ™ where indicated. All Rights Reserved. Used Under Authorization.

Published in the United States by Del Rey, an imprint of The Random House Publishing Group, a division of Random House, Inc., New York.

DEL REY is a registered trademark and the Del Rey colophon is a trademark of Random House, Inc.

ISBN 978-0-345-51128-7
eBook ISBN 978-0-345-53255-8

Printed in the United States of America on acid-free paper

www.starwars.com
www.delreybooks.com

2 4 6 8 9 7 5 3 1

First Edition

Book design by Elizabeth A. D. Eno

For Howard Roffman, whose intelligence, critical acumen,
and stalwart direction helped shape this story

The STAR WARS Novels Timeline

OLD REPUBLIC
5000–33 YEARS BEFORE
STAR WARS: A New Hope

Lost Tribe of the Sith*
Precipice
Skyborn
Paragon
Savior
Purgatory
Sentinel

3954 *YEARS BEFORE STAR WARS: A New Hope*

The Old Republic: Revan

3650 *YEARS BEFORE STAR WARS: A New Hope*

The Old Republic: Deceived

Lost Tribe of the Sith*
Pantheon
Secrets

Red Harvest

The Old Republic: Fatal Alliance

1032 *YEARS BEFORE STAR WARS: A New Hope*

Knight Errant

Darth Bane: Path of Destruction
Darth Bane: Rule of Two
Darth Bane: Dynasty of Evil

RISE OF THE EMPIRE
1000–0 YEARS BEFORE
STAR WARS: A New Hope

67 *YEARS BEFORE STAR WARS: A New Hope*

Darth Plagueis

33 *YEARS BEFORE STAR WARS: A New Hope*

Darth Maul: Saboteur*
Cloak of Deception
Darth Maul: Shadow Hunter

32 *YEARS BEFORE STAR WARS: A New Hope*

| STAR WARS: EPISODE I |
| THE PHANTOM MENACE |

Rogue Planet
Outbound Flight
The Approaching Storm

22 *YEARS BEFORE STAR WARS: A New Hope*

| STAR WARS: EPISODE II |
| ATTACK OF THE CLONES |

22-19 *YEARS BEFORE STAR WARS: A New Hope*

The Clone Wars
The Clone Wars: Wild Space
The Clone Wars: No Prisoners

Clone Wars Gambit
Stealth
Siege

Republic Commando
Hard Contact
Triple Zero
True Colors
Order 66

Shatterpoint
The Cestus Deception
The Hive*
MedStar I: Battle Surgeons
MedStar II: Jedi Healer
Jedi Trial
Yoda: Dark Rendezvous
Labyrinth of Evil

19 *YEARS BEFORE STAR WARS: A New Hope*

| STAR WARS: EPISODE III |
| REVENGE OF THE SITH |

Dark Lord: The Rise of Darth Vader

Imperial Commando
501st

Coruscant Nights
Jedi Twilight
Street of Shadows
Patterns of Force

The Han Solo Trilogy
The Paradise Snare
The Hutt Gambit
Rebel Dawn

The Adventures of Lando Calrissian
The Force Unleashed
The Han Solo Adventures
Death Troopers
The Force Unleashed II

*An eBook novella
**Forthcoming

THE STAR WARS NOVELS TIMELINE

NEW JEDI ORDER
25–40 YEARS AFTER
STAR WARS: A New Hope

Boba Fett: A Practical Man*

The New Jedi Order
Vector Prime
Dark Tide I: Onslaught
Dark Tide II: Ruin
Agents of Chaos I: Hero's Trial
Agents of Chaos II: Jedi Eclipse
Balance Point
Recovery*
Edge of Victory I: Conquest
Edge of Victory II: Rebirth
Star by Star
Dark Journey
Enemy Lines I: Rebel Dream
Enemy Lines II: Rebel Stand
Traitor
Destiny's Way
Ylesia*
Force Heretic I: Remnant
Force Heretic II: Refugee
Force Heretic III: Reunion
The Final Prophecy
The Unifying Force

35 *YEARS AFTER STAR WARS: A New Hope*

The Dark Nest Trilogy
The Joiner King
The Unseen Queen
The Swarm War

LEGACY
40+ YEARS AFTER
STAR WARS: A New Hope

Legacy of the Force
Betrayal
Bloodlines
Tempest
Exile
Sacrifice
Inferno
Fury
Revelation
Invincible

Crosscurrent
Riptide

Millennium Falcon

43 *YEARS AFTER STAR WARS: A New Hope*

Fate of the Jedi
Outcast
Omen
Abyss
Backlash
Allies
Vortex
Conviction
Ascension
Apocalypse**

*An eBook novella
**Forthcoming

A long time ago in a galaxy far, far away. . . .

DARTH PLAGUEIS

PROLOGUE

A tremor took hold of the planet.

Sprung from death, it unleashed itself in a powerful wave, at once burrowing deep into the world's core and radiating through its saccharine atmosphere to shake the stars themselves. At the quake's epicenter stood Sidious, one elegant hand vised on the burnished sill of an expansive translucency, a vessel filled suddenly to bursting, the Force so strong within him that he feared he might disappear into it, never to return. But the moment didn't constitute an ending so much as a true beginning, long overdue; it was less a transformation than an intensification — a gravitic shift.

A welter of voices, near and far, present and from eons past, drowned his thoughts. Raised in praise, the voices proclaimed his reign and cheered the inauguration of a new order. Yellow eyes lifted to the night sky, he saw the trembling stars flare, and in the depth of his being he felt the power of the dark side anoint him.

Slowly, almost reluctantly, he came back to himself, his gaze settling on his manicured hands. Returned to the present, he took note of his rapid breathing, while behind him the room labored to restore order. Air scrubbers hummed — costly wall tapestries undulating in the summoned breeze. Prized carpets sealed their fibers against the spread of spilled fluids. The droid shuffled in obvious confliction. Sidious pivoted to take in the disarray: antique furniture overturned; framed artwork askew. As if a whirlwind had swept through. And facedown on the floor lay a statue of Yanjon, one of four law-giving sages of Dwartii.

A piece Sidious had secretly coveted.

Also sprawled there, Plagueis: his slender limbs splayed and elongated head turned to one side. Dressed in finery, as for a night on the town.

And now dead.

Or was he?

Uncertainty rippled through Sidious, rage returning to his eyes. A tremor of his own making, or one of forewarning?

Was it possible that the wily Muun had deceived him? Had Plagueis unlocked the key to immortality, and survived after all? Never mind that it would constitute a petty move for one so wise—for one who had professed to place the Grand Plan above all else. Had Plagueis become ensnared in a self-spun web of jealousy and possessiveness, victim of his own engineering, his own foibles?

If he hadn't been concerned for his own safety, Sidious might have pitied him.

Wary of approaching the corpse of his former Master, he called on the Force to roll the aged Muun over onto his back. From that angle Plagueis looked almost as he had when Sidious first met him, decades earlier: smooth, hairless cranium; humped nose, with its bridge flattened as if from a shock-ball blow and its sharp tip pressed almost to his upper lip; jutting lower jaw; sunken eyes still brimming with menace—a physical characteristic rarely encountered in a Muun. But then Plagueis had never been an ordinary Muun, nor an ordinary being of any sort.

Sidious took care, still reaching out with the Force. On closer inspection, he saw that Plagueis's already cyanotic flesh was smoothing out, his features relaxing.

Faintly aware of the whir of air scrubbers and sounds of the outside world infiltrating the luxurious suite, he continued the vigil; then, in relief, he pulled himself up to his full height and let out his breath. This was no Sith trick. Not an instance of feigning death, but one of succumbing to its cold embrace. The being who had guided him to power was gone.

Wry amusement narrowed his eyes.

The Muun might have lived another hundred years unchanged. He might have lived forever had he succeeded fully in his quest. But in the end—though he could save others from death—he had failed to save himself.

A sense of supreme accomplishment puffed Sidious's chest, and his thoughts unreeled.

Well, then, that wasn't nearly as bad as we thought it might be . . .

Rarely did events play out as imagined, in any case. The order of future events was transient. In the same way that the past was reconfigured by selective memory, future events, too, were moving targets. One could only act on instinct, grab hold of an intuited perfect moment, and spring into action. One heartbeat late and the universe would have recomposed itself, no imposition of will sufficient to forestall the currents. One could only observe and react. Surprise was the element absent from any periodic table. A keystone element; a missing ingredient. The means by which the Force amused itself. A reminder to all sentient beings that some secrets could never be unlocked.

Confident that the will of the dark side had been done, he returned to the suite's window wall.

Two beings in a galaxy of countless trillions, but what had transpired in the suite would affect the lives of all of them. Already the galaxy had been shaped by the birth of one, and henceforth would be reshaped by the death of the other. But had the change been felt and recognized elsewhere? Were his sworn enemies aware that the Force had shifted irrevocably? Would it be enough to rouse them from self-righteousness? He hoped not. For now the work of vengeance could begin in earnest.

His eyes sought and found an ascending constellation of stars, one of power and consequence new to the sky, though soon to be overwhelmed by dawn's first light. Low in the sky over the flatlands, visible only to those who knew where and how to look, it ushered in a bold future. To some the stars and planets might seem to be moving as ever, destined to align in configurations calculated long before their fiery births. But in fact the heavens had been perturbed, tugged by dark matter into novel alignments. In his mouth, Sidious tasted the tang of blood; in his chest, he felt the monster rising, emerging from shadowy depths and contorting his aspect into something fearsome just short of revealing itself to the world.

The dark side had made him its property, and now he made the dark side his.

Breathless, not from exertion but from the sudden *inspiration* of power, he let go of the sill and allowed the monster to writhe through his body like an unbroken beast of range or prairie.

Had the Force ever been so strong in anyone?

Sidious had never learned how Plagueis's own Master had met his end. Had he died at Plagueis's hand? Had Plagueis, too, experienced a similar exultation on becoming a sole Sith Lord? Had the beast of the end time risen then to peek at the world it was to inhabit, knowing its release was imminent?

He raised his gaze to the ecliptic. The answers were out there, coded in light, speeding through space and time. Liquid fire coursing through him, visions of past and future riffling through his mind, he opened himself to the reconfigured galaxy, as if in an effort to peel away the decades . . .

PART ONE:
Enlistment

67—65 Years Before the Battle of Yavin

1: THE UNDERWORLD

Forty-seven standard years before the harrowing reign of Emperor Palpatine, Bal'demnic was nothing more than an embryonic world in the Outer Rim's Auril sector, populated by reptilian sentients who expressed as little tolerance for outsiders as they did for one another. Decades later the planet would have a part to play in galactic events, its own wink of historical notoriety, but in those formative years that presaged the Republic's ineluctable slide into decadence and turmoil, Bal'demnic was of interest only to xenobiologists and cartographers. It might even have escaped the notice of Darth Plagueis, for whom remote worlds held a special allure, had his Master, Tenebrous, not discovered something special about the planet.

"Darth Bane would appreciate our efforts," the Sith Master was telling his apprentice as they stood side by side in the crystalline cave that had drawn them across the stars.

A Bith, Tenebrous was as tall as Plagueis and nearly as cadaverously thin. To human eyes, his bilious complexion might have made him appear as haggard as the pallid Muun, but in fact both beings were in robust health. Though they conversed in Basic, each was fluent in the other's native language.

"Darth Bane's early years," Plagueis said through his transpirator mask. "Carrying on the ancestral business, as it were."

Behind the faceplate of his own mask, Tenebrous's puckered lips twitched in disapproval. The breathing device looked absurdly small on his outsized cleft head, and the convexity of the mask made the flat disks of his lidless eyes look like close-set holes in his pinched face.

"Bane's seminal years," he corrected.

Plagueis weathered the gentle rebuke. He had been apprenticed to Tenebrous for as many years as the average human might live, and still Tenebrous never failed to find fault when he could.

"What more appropriate way for us to close the circle than by mimicking the Sith'ari's seminal efforts," Tenebrous continued. "We weave ourselves into the warp and weft of the tapestry he created."

Plagueis kept his thoughts to himself. The aptly named Darth Bane, who had redefined the Sith by limiting their number and operating from concealment, had mined cortosis as a youth on Apatros long before embracing the tenets of the dark side. In the thousand years since his death, Bane had become deified; the powers attributed to him, legendary. And indeed what more appropriate place for his disciples to complete the circle, Plagueis told himself, than in profound obscurity, deep within an escarpment that walled an azure expanse of Bal'demnic's Northern Sea.

The two Sith were outfitted in environment suits that protected them from scorching heat and noxious atmosphere. The cave was crosshatched by scores of enormous crystals that resembled glowing lances thrust every which way into a trick chest by a stage magician. A recent seismic event had tipped the landmass, emptying the labyrinthine cave system of mineral-rich waters, but the magma chamber that had kept the waters simmering for millions of years still heated the humid air to temperatures in excess of what even Tenebrous and Plagueis could endure unaided. Close at hand sat a stubby treddroid tasked with monitoring the progress of a mining probe that was sampling a rich vein of cortosis ore at the bottom of a deep shaft. A fabled ore, some called it—owing to its scarcity, but even more for its intrinsic ability to diminish the effectiveness of the Jedi lightsaber. For that reason, the Jedi Order had gone to great lengths to restrict mining and refinement of the ore. If not the bane of the Order's existence, cortosis was a kind of irritant, a challenge to their weapon's reputation for fearsome invincibility.

It was to Tenebrous's credit that the Sith had learned of Bal'demnic's rich lodes before the Jedi, who by means of an agreement with the Republic Senate had first claim to all discoveries, as they had with Adegan crystals and Force-sensitive younglings of all species. But Tenebrous and the generations of Sith Masters who had preceded him were privy to covert data gleaned by vast networks of informants the Senate and the Jedi knew nothing about, including mining survey teams and weapons manufacturers.

"Based on the data I am receiving," the treddroid intoned, "eighty-two percent of the ore is capable of being purified into weapons-grade cortosis shield."

Plagueis looked at Tenebrous, who returned a nod of satisfaction. "The percentage is consistent with what I was told to expect."

"By whom, Master?"

"Of no consequence," Tenebrous said.

Strewn about the superheated tunnel were broken borer bits, expended gasifiers, and clogged filtration masks, all abandoned by the exploratory team that had sunk the shaft several standard months earlier. From the shaft's broad mouth issued the repeated reports of the probe droid's hydraulic jacks. Music to Tenebrous's auditory organs, Plagueis was certain.

"Can you not share your plans for this discovery?"

"In due time, Darth Plagueis." Tenebrous turned away from him to address the treddroid. "Instruct the probe to evaluate the properties of the secondary lode."

Plagueis studied the screen affixed to the droid's flat head. It displayed a map of the probe's movements and a graphic analysis of its penetrating scans, which reached clear to the upper limits of the magma chamber.

"The probe is running an analysis," the treddroid updated.

With the reciprocating sounds of the probe's hydraulic jacks echoing in the crystal cave, Tenebrous began to circle the shaft, only to come to a sudden halt when the drilling ceased.

"Why has it stopped?" he asked before Plagueis could.

The droid's reply was immediate. "The Em-Two unit informs me that it has discovered a pocket of gas directly beneath the new borehole." The droid paused, then added: "I'm sorry to report, sirs, that the gas is a highly combustible variant of lethane. The Em-Two unit predicts that the heat generated by its hydraulic jacks will ignite an explosion of significant magnitude."

Suspicion crept into Tenebrous's voice. "The original report made no mention of lethane."

The droid pivoted to face him. "I know nothing of that, sir. But the Em-Two unit is quite insistent. What's more, my own programming corroborates the fact that it is not unusual to find pockets of lethane in close proximity to cortosis ore."

"Query the probe about excavating around the lethane pocket," Plagueis said.

"The Em-Two unit recommends employing that very strategy, sir. Shall I order it to proceed?"

Plagueis looked at Tenebrous, who nodded.

"Task the probe to proceed," Plagueis said. When the hammering recommenced, he fixed his gaze on the display screen to monitor the probe's progress. "Tell the probe to stop," he said after only a moment had elapsed.

"Why are you interfering?" Tenebrous said, storming forward.

Plagueis gestured to the display. "The map indicates a more massive concentration of lethane in the area where it's drilling."

"You're correct, sir," the droid said in what amounted to dismay. "I will order the unit to halt all activity."

And yet the hammering continued.

"Droid," Plagueis snapped, "did the probe acknowledge your order?"

"No, sir. The Em-Two is not responding."

Tenebrous stiffened, narrowly avoiding slamming his head into one of the cave's massive crystals. "Is it still within range?"

"Yes, sir."

"Then run a communications diagnostic."

"I have, sir, and all systems are nominal. The unit's inability to respond—" It fell briefly silent and began again. "The unit's refusal to respond appears to be deliberate."

"Deactivate it," Tenebrous said. "At once."

The hammering slowed and eventually ceased, but not for long.

"The Em-Two unit has overridden my command."

"Impossible," Tenebrous said.

"Clearly not, sir. In fact, it is highly probable that the unit is executing a deep-seated subroutine that escaped earlier notice."

Plagueis glanced at Tenebrous. "Who procured the probe?"

"This isn't the time for questions. The probe is about to breach the pocket."

Hastening to the rim of the circular shaft, the two Sith removed their gloves and aimed their long-fingered unprotected hands into the inky darkness. Instantly tangles of blue electrical energy discharged from their fingertips, raining into the borehole. Strobing and clawing for the bottom, the vigorous bolts coruscated into the lateral corridor the probe had excavated. Crackling sounds spewed from the opening long after the Sith had harnessed their powers.

Then the repetitive strikes of the jackhammer began once more.

"It's the ore," Tenebrous said. "There's too much resistance here."

Plagueis knew what needed to be done. "I'll go down," he said, and was on the verge of leaping into the shaft when Tenebrous restrained him.

"This can wait. We're returning to the grotto."

Plagueis hesitated, then nodded. "As you say, Master."

Tenebrous swung to the droid. "Continue your attempts to deactivate the unit."

"I will, sir. To do that, however, I will need to remain here."

"What of it?" Tenebrous said, cocking his head to one side.

"Should I fail in my efforts, the ensuing explosion will surely result in my destruction."

Plagueis understood. "You've been useful, droid."

"Thank you, sir."

Tenebrous scowled. "You waste your breath."

Nearly knocked over by the swiftness of Tenebrous's departure, Plagueis had to call deeply on the Force merely to keep up. Retracing the inclined path they had taken from the grotto in which their starship waited, they fairly flew up the crystal-studded tunnel they had picked their way through earlier. Plagueis grasped that a powerful explosion was perhaps imminent, but was mystified by his Master's almost mad dash for the surface. In the past Tenebrous had rarely evinced signs of discomfort, let alone fear; so what danger had he sensed that propelled him with such abandon? And when, in the past, had they fled danger of any sort? Safeguarded by the powers of the dark side, the Sith could hardly fear death when they were allied to it. Plagueis stretched out with his feelings in an attempt to identify the source of Tenebrous's dread, but the Force was silent.

Ten meters ahead of him, the Bith had ducked under a scabrous outcropping. Haste, however, brought him upright too quickly and his left shoulder glanced off the rough rock, leaving a portion of his suit shredded.

"Master, allow me to lead," Plagueis said when he reached Tenebrous. He was only slightly more agile than the Bith, but he had better night vision and a keener sense of direction, over and above what the Force imparted.

His pride wounded more than his shoulder, Tenebrous waved off the offer. "Be mindful of your place." Regaining his balance and composure, he streaked off. But at a fork in the tunnel, he took the wrong turn.

"This way, Master," Plagueis called from the other corridor, but he stopped to surrender the lead.

Closer to the surface the tunnels opened into caverns the size of cathedrals, smoothed and hollowed by rainwater that still surged in certain seasons of Bal'demnic's long year. In pools of standing water darted various species of blind fish. Overhead, hawk-bats took panicked flight from their roosting places in the stippled ceiling. Natural light in the far distance prompted the two Sith to race for the grotto; but, even so, they were a moment late.

The gas explosion caught up with them just as they were entering the light-filled cavity at the top of the escarpment. From deep in the tunnel resounded a squealing electronic wail, and at the same time, almost as if the cave system were gasping for breath, a searing wind tore down from a perforation in the grotto's arched ceiling through which the ship had entered. A muffled but ground-heaving detonation followed; then a roiling fireball that was the labyrinth's scorching exhalation. Whirling to the tunnel they had just exited and managing somehow to remain on his feet, Tenebrous conjured a Force shield with his waving arms that met the fireball and contained it, thousands of flaming hawk-bats spiraling within the tumult like windblown embers.

A few meters away Plagueis, hurled face-first to the ground by the intensity of the vaporizing blast, lifted his head in time to see the underside of the domed ceiling begin to shed enormous slabs of rock. Directly below the plummeting slabs sat their starship.

"Master!" he said, scrambling to his feet with arms lifted in an attempt to hold the rocks in midair.

His own arms still raised in a Force-summoning posture, Tenebrous swung around to bolster Plagueis's intent. Behind him, the fireball's final flames surged from the mouth of the tunnel to lick his back and drive him deeper into the grotto.

The cave continued to spasm underfoot, sending shock waves through the crazed ceiling. Cracks spread like a web from the oculus, triggering collapses throughout the grotto. Plagueis heard a rending sound overhead and watched a fissure zigzag its way across the ceiling, sloughing layer after layer of stone as it followed the grotto's curved wall.

Now, though, it was Tenebrous who was positioned beneath the fall.

And in that instant Plagueis perceived the danger Tenebrous had foreseen earlier: his death.

His death at Plagueis's hands.

While Tenebrous was preoccupied holding aloft the slabs that threatened to crush the ship, Plagueis quickly reoriented himself, aiming his raised hands at the plummeting slabs above his Master and, with a downward motion of both arms, brought them down so quickly and with so much momentum that Tenebrous was buried almost before he understood what had hit him.

Stone dust eddying around him, Plagueis stood rooted in place as slabs interred the starship, as well. But he gave it no thought. His success in bringing the ceiling down on Tenebrous was proof enough that the Bith had grown sluggish and expendable. Otherwise, he would have divined the true source of the danger he had sensed, and Plagueis would be the one pressed to the floor of the grotto, head cracked open like an egg and chest cavity pierced by the pointed end of a fallen stalactite.

His race to Tenebrous's side was informed as much by excitement as charade. "Master," he said, genuflecting and removing his and Tenebrous's respirators. His hands pawed at the stones, removing some of the crushing weight. But Tenebrous's single lung was pierced, and blood gurgled in his throat. Ragged tears in the sleeves of the enviro-suit revealed esoteric body markings and tattoos.

"Stop, apprentice," Tenebrous strained to say. "You're going to need all your strength."

"I can bring help. There's time—"

"I'm dying, Darth Plagueis. There's time only for that."

Plagueis held the Bith's pained gaze. "I did all that I could, Master."

Tenebrous interrupted him once more. "To be strong in the Force is one thing. But to believe oneself to be all-powerful is to invite catastrophe. Remember, that even in the ethereal realm we inhabit, the unforeseen can occur." A stuttering cough silenced him for a moment. "Better this way, perhaps, than to perish at your hand."

As Darth Bane would have wished, Plagueis thought. "Who supplied the mining probe, Master?"

"Subtext," Tenebrous said in a weak voice. "Subtext Mining."

Plagueis nodded. "I will avenge you."

Tenebrous canted his huge head ever so slightly. "Will you?"

"Of course."

If the Bith was convinced, he kept it to himself, and said instead: "You are fated to bring the Sith imperative to fruition, Plagueis. It falls to you to bring the Jedi Order to its knees and to save the rest of the galaxy's sentients from themselves."

At long last, Plagueis told himself, *the mantle is conferred.*

"But I need to warn you . . . ," Tenebrous started to say and fell abruptly silent.

Plagueis could sense the Bith's highly evolved mind replaying recent events, calculating odds, reaching conclusions.

"Warn me about what, Master?"

Tenebrous's black eyes shone with yellow light and his free hand clutched at the ring collar of Plagueis's enviro-suit. "You!"

Plagueis pried the Bith's thin hand from the fabric and grinned faintly. "Yes, Master, your death comes at my bidding. You said yourself that perpetuation with purpose is the way to victory, and so it is. Go to your grave knowing that you are last of the old order, the vaunted Rule of Two, and that the new order begins now and will for a thousand years remain in my control."

Tenebrous coughed spittle and blood. "Then for the last time, I call you apprentice. And I applaud your skillful use of surprise and misdirection. Perhaps I was wrong to think you had no stomach for it."

"The dark side guided me, Tenebrous. You sensed it, but your lack of faith in me clouded your thoughts."

The Bith's head bobbed in agreement. "Even before we came to Bal'demnic."

"And yet we came."

"Because we were fated to." Tenebrous paused, then spoke with renewed urgency: "But wait! The ship—"

"Crushed, as you are."

Tenebrous's anger stabbed at Plagueis. "You've risked everything to undo me! The entire future of the Sith! My instincts about you prove correct, after all!"

Plagueis leaned away from him, nonchalant, but in fact filled with an icy fury. "I'll find a way home, Tenebrous, as will you." And with a chopping motion of his left hand, he broke the Bith's neck.

Tenebrous was paralyzed and unconscious but not yet dead. Plagueis had no interest in saving him—even if it were possible—but he was interested in observing the behavior of the Bith's midi-chlorians as life ebbed. The Jedi thought of the cellular organelles as symbionts, but to Plagueis midi-chlorians were interlopers, running interference for the Force and standing in the way of a being's ability to contact the Force directly. Through years of experimentation and directed meditation, Plagueis had honed an ability to perceive the actions of midi-chlorians, though not yet the ability to manipulate them.

Manipulate them, say, to prolong Tenebrous's life.

Looking at the Bith through the Force, he perceived that the midi-chlorians were already beginning to die out, as were the neurons that made up Tenebrous's lofty brain and the muscle cells that powered his once-able heart. A common misconception held that midi-chlorians were Force-carrying particles, when in fact they functioned more as translators, interlocutors of the will of the Force. Plagueis considered his long-standing fascination with the organelles to be as natural as had been Tenebrous's fixation on shaping the future. Where Bith intelligence was grounded in mathematics and computation, Muun intelligence was driven by a will to profit. As a Muun, Plagueis viewed his allegiance to the Force as an investment that could, with proper effort, be maximized to yield great returns. True, too, to Muun psychology and tradition, he had through the decades hoarded his successes, and never once taken Tenebrous into his confidence.

The Bith's moribund midi-chlorians were winking out, like lights slowly deprived of a power source, and yet Plagueis could still perceive Tenebrous in the Force. One day he would succeed in imposing his will on the midi-chlorians to keep them aggregate. But such speculations were for another time. Just now Tenebrous and all he had been in life were beyond Plagueis's reach.

He wondered if the Jedi were subsumed in similar fashion. Even in life, did midi-chlorians behave in a Jedi as they did in a devotee of the dark side? Were the organelles invigorated by different impulses, prompted into action by different desires? He had encountered many Jedi during his long life, but he had never made an attempt to study one in the same way he appraised Tenebrous now, out of concern for revealing the power of his alliance with the dark side. That, too, might have to change.

Tenebrous died while Plagueis observed.

In Bane's age a Sith might have had to guard against an attempt at essence transfer by the deceased—a leap into the consciousness of the Sith who survived—but those times were long past and of no relevance; not since the teachings had been sabotaged, the technique lost. The last Sith possessed of the knowledge had been inexplicably drawn to the light side and killed, taking the secret process with him . . .

2: THE INNER LANDSCAPE

Plagueis wasn't certain how long he remained at Tenebrous's side. Long enough, though, that when he rose his legs were quivering and some of the dust from the explosion had settled. Only when he took a few backward steps did he realize that the event had not left him unscathed. At some point, probably when he was focused on murder, a rock or some other projectile had pulped a large area of his lower back, and now the thin tunic he wore beneath the enviro-suit was saturated with blood.

Despite the swirling dust, he inhaled deeply, eliciting a stab of pain from his rib cage and a cough that spewed blood into the hot air. Drawing on the Force, he numbed himself to the pain and tasked his body to limit the damage as best it could. When the injury ceased to preoccupy him, he surveyed the grotto, remaining anchored in place but turning a full circle. Littering the hard ground, injured hawk-bats were chirping in distress and clawing through circles of their own. Far above him, a beam of oblique and dust-moted daylight streamed through the dome's large oculus—itself the result of an earlier collapse. Close to the jumble of stones the collapse had piled on the grotto floor sat Tenebrous's small but priceless starship—a Rugess Nome design—alloy wings and snubbed nose poking from the artless mausoleum the explosion had fashioned. And finally, not meters away, lay Tenebrous, similarly interred.

Approaching the ship, Plagueis scanned the damage that had been inflicted on the deflector shield and navigation arrays, coolant ducts, sensors, and antennas. Tenebrous would surely have been able to effect repairs to some of the components, but Plagueis was out of his depth, lacking not only the Bith's fine motor skills but his knowledge of the ship's systems. Though unique, a marvel of engineering, the ship couldn't be traced to Tenebrous, since both the registry and title were counterfeit. It was possible that the rescue beacon was still functional, but Plagueis was reluctant to activate it. They had arrived on Bal'demnic in stealth, and he intended to depart in like manner.

But how?

Again he squinted into the light pouring in through the oculus. Not even his power in the Force was enough to carry him from the floor and up through the grotto's unblinking eye. Nothing short of a jetpack would do, and the ship didn't carry one. His gaze drifted from the oculus to the grotto's curving walls. He supposed he could spider his way along the arched underside of the dome and reach the eye, but now he saw a better way.

More, a way to accomplish two tasks at the same time.

From a spot mid-distance between the ship and rubble pile beneath the oculus, he immersed himself in the Force and, with gestures not unlike those he and Tenebrous had used in arresting the ceiling collapse, began to levitate slabs from the ship and add them to the rubble heap, stopping only when he had both exposed the hatch of the ship and was confident he could Force-leap through the oculus from atop the augmented pile.

When he tried springing the hatch, however, he found that it wouldn't budge. He was ultimately able to gain entry to the cockpit by assailing the transparisteel canopy with a series of Force blows. Worming his way inside, he retrieved his travel bag, which contained a comlink, his lightsaber, and a change of clothes, among other items. He also took Tenebrous's comlink and lightsaber, and made certain to erase the memory of the navicomputer. Once outside the ship, he peeled out of the enviro-suit and blood-soaked tunic, trading them for dark trousers, an overshirt, lightweight boots, and a hooded robe. Affixing both lightsabers to his belt, he activated the comlink and called up a map of Bal'demnic. With scant satellites in orbit, the planet had nothing in the way of a global positioning system, but the map told Plagueis all he needed to know about the immediate area.

He took a final look around. It wasn't likely that an indigene would have reason to investigate the grotto, and it was even less likely that another interstellar visitor would find this place; even so, he spent a moment regarding the scene objectively.

A partially crushed but costly and salvage-worthy starship. The decomposed body of a Bith spacefarer. The aftermath of an explosive event . . .

The scene of an unfortunate accident in a galaxy brimming with them.

Satisfied, Plagueis leapt to the top of the pile, then through the roof into the remains of the day.

The radiant heat of Bal'demnic's primary beat down on his exposed skin, and a persistent offshore wind tugged at the robe. West and south as far as his eyes could see was an expanse of azure ocean, curling white where it pounded the coastline. Rugged, denuded hills vanished into sea mist. Plagueis imagined a time when forest had blanketed the landscape, before the indigenous Kon'me had felled the trees for building materials and firewood. Now what vegetation survived was confined to the steep-sided gorges that separated the brown hills. A somber beauty. Perhaps, he thought, there was more to recommend the planet than deposits of cortosis ore.

A resident of Muunilinst for most of his adult life, Plagueis was no stranger to ocean worlds. But unlike most Muuns, he was also accustomed to remote, low-tech ones, having spent his childhood and adolescence on a host of similar planets and moons.

With that hemisphere of Bal'demnic rotating quickly into night, the wind was increasing in strength and the temperature was dropping. The map he had called up on the comlink showed that the planet's primary spaceport was only a few hundred kilometers to the south. Tenebrous had intentionally skirted the port when they had made planetfall, coming in over the northern ice cap rather than over the sea. Plagueis calculated that he could cover the distance to the spaceport by evening of the following day, which would still give him a standard week in which to return to Muunilinst in time to host the Gathering on Sojourn. But he knew, too, that the route would take him through areas inhabited by both elite and plebeian Kon'me; so he resolved to travel at night to avoid contact with the noisome and xenophobic reptilian sapients. There was little point to leaving dead bodies in his wake.

Cinching the robe around his waist, he began to move, slowly at first, then gathering speed, until to any being watching he would have appeared a dazzling blur; an errant dust devil racing across the treeless terrain. He hadn't run far before he chanced upon a rudimentary trail, impressed in places with the footprints of indigenes, and he paused to study them. Barefoot, lower-class Kon'me had left the prints, probably fisherfolk whose thatched-roof dwellings dotted the shoreline. Plagueis reckoned the size and weight of the reptilians responsible for the tracks, and estimated the time elapsed since they had passed. Drawing himself up, he scanned the dun hills, then sniffed the wind, wishing he were imbued with even a touch of Tenebrous's olfactory acuity. Up ahead he was bound to encounter elite Kon'me as well, or at the very least their cliff-side dome dwellings.

Night fell as he resumed his pace. The ocean shone silver under starlight, and night-blooming flora scented the humid air with heady aromas. Predators of any size had been hunted to extinction on the northern island continents, but the deep gorges were home to countless varieties of voracious insects that set upon him in clouds as he picked his way through the dense underbrush. Lowering his body temperature and slowing his breathing to alter the mixture of gases in his exhalations did little to dissuade the insects, so after a while he ceased all attempts at warding them off and surrendered to their thirst for blood, which they drew freely from his face, neck, and hands.

Let them devour the old Plagueis, he thought.

In the dark wood of that remote world, with a salted wind whistling through the trees and a distant sound of waves like drumming, he would take flight from the underworld in which the Sith had dwelled. Awakened from a millennium of purposeful sleep, the power of the dark side would be reborn, and he, Plagueis, would carry the long-forged plan to completion.

Through the night he ran, sheltering inside a shallow cave while the morning mist was evanescing from the hollows. Even that early the blue-scaled indigenes were about, appearing from their huts to cast nets

into the crashing surf or paddle boats to stretches of reef or nearby is-
lets. The best of their catch would be carried into the hills to stuff the
bellies of the wealthy, with whom rested responsibility for Bal'demnic's
political and economic future. Their guttural voices stole into the cave
that fit Plagueis like a tomb, and he could understand some of the
words they exchanged.

He chased sleep, but it eluded him, and he deplored the fact that
he still had need for it. Tenebrous had never slept, but then few
Bith did.

Awake in the oppressive heat, he replayed the events of the previous
day, still somewhat astounded by what he had done. The Force had
whispered to him: *Your moment has come. Claim your stake to the dark
side. Act now and be done with this.* But the Force had only advised; it
had neither dictated his actions nor guided his hands. That had been
his doing alone. He knew from his travels with and without Tenebrous
that he wasn't the galaxy's sole practitioner of the dark side—nor Sith
for that matter, since the galaxy was rife with pretenders—but he was
now the only Sith Lord descended from the Bane line. A *true* Sith, and
that realization roused the raw power coiled inside him.

And yet . . .

When he reached out with the Force he could detect the presence
of something or some being of near-equal power. Was it the dark side
itself, or merely a vestige of his uncertainty? He had read the legends of
Bane; how he had been hounded by the lingering presences of those he
had defeated in order to rid the Sith Order of infighting, and return the
Order to a genuine hegemony by instating the Rule of Two: a Master
to embody power; an apprentice to crave it. To hear it told, Bane had
even been hounded by the spirits of generations-dead Sith Lords whose
tombs and manses he had desecrated in his fervent search for holocrons
and other ancient devices offering wisdom and guidance.

Was Tenebrous's spirit the source of the power he sensed? Was there
a brief period of survival after death during which a true Sith could
continue to influence the world of the living?

It was as if the mass of the galaxy had descended on him. A lesser
being might have heaved his shoulders, but Plagueis, wedged into his
clandestine tomb, felt as weightless as he would have in deep space.

He would outlive any who challenged him.

*   *   *

Hours later, when the voices had faded and the insects' feeding frenzy had started anew, pain roused Plagueis from tortured slumber. The tunic was adhered to his swollen flesh like a pressure bandage, but blood had seeped from the wound and soaked through to the robe.

Slipping silently into the night, he limped until he had suppressed the pain, then began to run, beads of perspiration evaporating from his hairless head and the dark robe unfurling behind him like a banner. Famished, he considered raiding one of the local homes and feasting on the eggs of some low-caste Kon'me, or perhaps on the blood of her and her mate. But he reined in his impulses to strike terror, his appetite for destruction, sating himself instead on bats and the rotting remains of fish the waves had washed ashore. Hurrying along the black sand beach, he passed within meters of dwellings built from blocks of fossilized reefstone, but he glimpsed only one indigene, who, on leaving his hut naked to relieve himself, reacted as if he had seen an apparition. Or else in hilarity at the figure Plagueis must have cut in robe and boots. On the cliffs high above the beach, artificial lights glimmered, announcing the homes of the elite and the proximity of the spaceport, whose ambient glow illuminated a broad area of the southern littoral.

His destination close at hand, each incoming ocean wave reverberated inside him, summoning an unprecedented tide of dark energy. The knotted tendrils of time loosened and he had a glimpse into Bal'demnic's future. Embroiled in a multifronted war, a galactic war, in part because of its rich deposits of cortosis, but more as a pawn in a convoluted game, the subservient Kon'me turned against those who had mastered them for eons . . .

Lost in reverie, Plagueis almost failed to notice that a massive breakwater now followed the curve of the beach. Stone jetties jutted into a broad, calm bay, and behind the wall a city climbed into a surround of deforested foothills. Kon'me of both classes were about, but interspersed among them were offworlders of many species, most from neighboring star systems but some from as distant as the Core. The spaceport formed the city's southernmost outskirts, made up of clusters of modular buildings, prefabricated warehouses and hangars, illuminated landing areas for cargo and passenger ships. To a being unfamiliar with isolated worlds, a tour through the spaceport would have seemed closer to time travel, but Plagueis felt at home among the cubicle hotels, dimly lighted tapcafs, and squalid cantinas, where entertainment was costly and life was cheap. Raising the cowl of the robe over his head, he kept to the shadows, his height alone enough to draw attention. With security lax he was able to circulate among the grounded vessels without difficulty. He ignored the smaller, intersystem ships in favor of long-haul freighters, and even then only those that appeared to be in good condition. Muunilinst was several hyperspace jumps distant, and only a ship with adequate jump capability could deliver him there without too much delay.

After an hour of searching he found one to his liking. A product of Core engineering, the freighter had to be half a century old, but it had been well maintained and retrofitted with modern sensor suites and subspace drives. That it bore no legend suggested that the ship's captain wasn't interested in having the ship make a name for itself. Longer than it was wide, LS-447-3 had a narrow fantail, an undermount cockpit, and broad cargo bay doors, which permitted it to take on large freight. With the registry number stored in his comlink, Plagueis angled his way to the spaceport authority building. At that time of night the dilapidated structure was all but deserted, save for two thick-necked Kon'me guards who were sleeping on duty. Loosening the robe's sash to provide ready access to his lightsabers, Plagueis eased past them and disappeared through the main doors. Faint light from unoccupied offices spilled into the dark hallways. On the second floor he found the registrar's office, which overlooked the largest of the landing zones and the silent bay beyond.

A comp that had been an antique twenty years earlier sat atop a desk in a smaller private office. Plagueis placed his comlink alongside the machine and an instant later had sliced into the spaceport control network. A search for the freighter revealed that it did indeed go by a name—the *Woebegone*—out of Ord Mantell. Scheduled to launch the following morning, the ship with her crew of eight, including one droid, was bound for several worlds in the Auril sector, carrying cargos of fresh sea life. According to the manifest, the cargo had already cleared customs and was housed in a refrigerated hangar awaiting transfer to the ship. The good news was that the *Woebegone*'s ultimate destination was

Ithor, on the far side of the Hydian Way. A side trip to Muunilinst, therefore, might not strike the crew as too great a detour.

Plagueis called up an image of the freighter's captain, whose name was given as Ellin Lah. Opening himself fully to the Force, he studied the image for a long moment; then, exhaling slowly, he stood, erased all evidence of his technological intrusions, and returned the comlink to his robe's inner pocket.

The *Woebegone* had been waiting for him.

3: WOEBEGONE

Plagueis's instincts about Bal'demnic were correct. The planet's rugged beauty was of a sort that appealed to the hedonistic side of human nature and would one day draw the wealthiest of that species to bask in the warm light of its primary, toe its pristine sands, swim in its animated waters, and dine on the toothsome fish that filled its vast oceans. But in those days, humans were still relatively scarce in that part of the Outer Rim, and most visitors to Bal'demnic hailed from Hutt space or the far reaches of the Perlemian Trade Route. And so Captain Ellin Lah was Togruta, and her first mate, a Zabrak named Maa Kaap. The *Woebegone*'s pilot was a Balosar; her navigator, a Dresselian; and her three crew members Klatooinian, Kaleesh, and an Aqualish, of the Quara race. "Near-humans" all, to use the term favored at that time in the Core, where chauvinism had been raised to an art form. The only nonsentient was a bipedal, multi-appendaged droid called "OneOne-FourDee", after its model number.

Bal'demnic was but one of their planetary haunts. As often as not they could be spotted on Vestral, Sikkem IV, or Carlix's Folly. But all were similar in that Captain Lah and her shipmates rarely saw anything more of the planets than what lay within a radius of five kilometers from the principal spaceports, and their contact with indigenes was limited to spaceport functionaries, merchants, information brokers, and those in the pleasure professions.

Theirs was a precarious business, at a time when pirates plied the intersystem trade routes, hyperspace beacons were few and far be-

tween, and a lapse in judgment could result in disaster. The cost of fuel
was exorbitant, corrupt customs officials had to be bribed, and import–
export taxes were subject to change without notice. Delays meant that
cargoes of foodstuffs could lose the freshness that made them desirable,
or worse yet spoil altogether. Dangers were manifold and the earnings
were meager. You had to love the work, or perhaps be on the run—
from the law, yourself, or whoever else.

As a consequence of having imbibed too much local grog and gam-
bled away too many hard-earned credits—and perhaps as atonement
for so much carousing—concerns about the coming trip had bobbed
to the surface of Captain Lah's mind like an inflated balloon held under
water, then released.

"No oversights this run," she was warning the crew in a gentle way,
as they made their way across the landing zone to their waiting ship.

The fact that she had used the same euphemism Blir' had to mini-
mize the impact of the near catastrophe he had caused made all of them
laugh—except the Balosar, who lowered his head in mock shame, his
twin antenepalps deepening in color.

"We take your meaning, Captain," Maa Kaap said. "No inoppor-
tune omissions—"

"Ineradicable errors," the Kaleesh, PePe Rossh, interjected.

"Dumbass mistakes," Doo Zuto completed, his close-set, inward-
curving tusks in need of a thorough scaling.

The captain allowed them a moment of merriment.

"I'm serious," she said as they approached the *Woebegone*'s lowered
boarding ramp. "I'll say it again: this ship operates as a democracy.
I'm your captain because knowing who's good at what is just something I have a talent for." She looked at Blir'. "Do I ever tell you how
to pilot?" Then at Semasalli. "Do I ever question your decision about
jump points?"

"No, Captain," the two said, as if by rote.

"So I'm simply speaking as a member of what should be a compe-
tent team, and not as a commander." She blew out her breath in a way
that shook her trio of striped head-tails. "Either we turn a profit on this
run, or we think about going to the Hutts for another loan."

Even Wandau, who had had more dealings with various Hutts than
anyone else, bemoaned the mere prospect.

"That's right," Lah told the tall Klatooinian. "And don't any of you fool yourself into thinking that we can float an honest loan. Because no bank worth its assets is going to accept the *Woebegone* as collateral."

Maa Kaap and Blir' traded quick glances before the Zabrak said, "Excuse me for saying so, Captain, but you didn't seem particularly concerned about credits last night—"

"Watch what you say," Lah told her first mate, barely restraining a smile.

"I thought you were ready to give that young thing the ship," PePe said, joining the tease.

Lah waved a hand in dismissal. "I was just toying with him."

"*Toy* being the operative word," Maa Kaap said. "Since he was young enough to still play with them."

The captain planted her hands on her hips. "I can be convincing when I want to be."

"Oh, that you were," Zuto said, reigniting a chorus of laughter that accompanied them into the *Woebegone*'s main cabin space, where 11-4D was waiting.

"Everything in order?" Lah asked the droid.

The droid raised three of its appendages in an approximation of a salute. "Shipshape, Captain."

"All the cargo is aboard and accounted for?"

"Aboard and accounted for, Captain."

"You checked the thermo readouts?"

"In each bay, Captain."

She returned a satisfied nod. "Well, all right then."

The shipmates split up, each with duties to perform. Blir' and Sema-salli to the cockpit; Zuto, Wandau, and PePe to check that the cargo had been properly stowed; Maa Kaap and 11-4D to seal the ship; and Captain Lah to get clearance from Bal'demnic spaceport control.

Without fanfare the ship left the warm world behind and jumped from cold ether into the netherworld of hyperspace. Lah was still seated at the communications console when Blir' radioed her from the cockpit.

"We need your input on something."

"Since when?" she said.

"Seriously."

She headed forward, and had no sooner ducked into the cockpit than Semasalli indicated a flashing telltale on the ship's status display suite. A small metal plate below the telltale read: CARGO BAY 4 AMBIENT.

"Too hot or too cold?" Lah asked the Dresselian.

"Too cold."

Lah flicked her forefinger against the telltale, but it continued to flash. "Funny, that usually works." She studied Semasalli's frown. "What do you think?"

He sniffed and ran a hand over a hairless, deeply fissured head that mirrored the appearance of the convoluted brain it contained. "Well, it could be the bay thermostat."

"Or?"

"Or one of the shipping containers could have opened?"

"By itself?"

"Maybe during the jump," Blir' said from the pilot's chair.

"Okay, so we go check it out." She glanced from Blir' to Semasalli and shook her head in ignorance. "What aren't you telling me?"

Blir' answered for the two of them. "Remember the Zabrak that Maa was talking to in the cantina?"

"Which cantina?" Lah said; then added: "No, I remember him. He was looking for a lift."

Semasalli nodded. "He'd been booted from his last freighter. He didn't say why, but Maa thought he smelled trouble, and said we couldn't take him aboard."

Lah followed the clues they were giving her and nodded. "You're thinking we have a stowaway."

"Just a thought," the Dresselian said.

"Which is why you wanted to check with me before going aft."

"Exactly."

Lah's face grew almost as wrinkled as Semasalli's. "The ship would have told us if anyone had tampered with the anti-intrusion sys."

"Unless he came in with the cargo?" Blir' said.

"You mean inside one of the containers?"

Blir' nodded.

"Then he'd be stiff as an icicle by now." Lah turned to Semasalli. "Does bay four have a vid feed?"

"On screen," Semasalli said, swiveling his chair to face the status displays.

Lah put her palms flat on the console and leaned toward the screen while the Dresselian brought up grainy views of the cargo bay. Finally the remote cam found what they were looking for: an opened shipping container, wreathed by clouds of coolant, with its cargo of costly meat-fins already defrosting.

"Spawn of a—" Lah started when the next view of the cargo bay stunned her into slack-jawed silence.

Blir' blinked repeatedly before asking, "Is that what I think it is?"

Lah swallowed hard and found her voice. "Well, it sure isn't the Zabrak."

Plagueis was seated atop one of the smaller shipping containers when the hatch began to cycle. Fully awake since the *Woebegone*'s jump to hyperspace, he had sat still for the various scans the crew had run, and now lowered the hood of the lightweight and bloodied robe. When the hatch slid to, he found himself confronted by the ship's Togruta female captain, along with a muscular male Zabrak; a mottled Klatooinian as tall as a normal Muun; an Aqualish of the two-eyed variety; and a scarlet-hued, scaly-skinned Kaleesh, whose face resembled those of the bats Plagueis had consumed on Bal'demnic, and who was emitting an olio of potent pheromones. All five carried blasters, but only the Klatooinian's was primed for fire and leveled at Plagueis.

"You're not listed on the shipping manifest, stranger," Captain Lah said as she stepped into the bay, breath clouds emerging with the words.

Plagueis spread his hands in an innocent gesture. "I confess to being a stowaway, Captain."

Lah approached guardedly, motioning to the open container a few meters away. "How did you survive in there?"

Plagueis mimicked the wave of her hand. "Those sea creatures make a comfortable bed."

The Zabrak surged forward, his stippled cranium furrowed in anger. "Those creatures are how we make our living, Muun. And right now they're not worth a karking credit."

Plagueis locked eyes with him. "I apologize for spoiling some of your cargo."

"The coolant," Lah said more harshly. "How did you survive that?"

"We Muuns have three hearts," Plagueis said, crossing one leg over the other. "Two of them are under voluntary control, so I was able to keep my blood circulating and my body temperature close to normal."

Standing by the open container, the Quara said, "Speaking of blood, you're leaking some."

Plagueis saw that some of the sea creatures were coated with congealed blood. "The result of an unfortunate accident. But thank you for noticing."

Lah shifted her gaze from the container to Plagueis. "We have a medical droid. I'll have it take a look at your injury."

"That's very kind of you, Captain."

"You're a long way from the Braxant Run," the Kaleesh said. "And probably the last species we'd expect to find stowing away in a cargo container."

Plagueis nodded in agreement. "I can well imagine."

"Kon'meas Spaceport has passenger flights to Bimmisaari," the Zabrak added. "You couldn't wait, or you're out of credits?"

"To be honest, I wished to avoid the common spaceways."

Lah and the Zabrak traded dubious looks. "Are you a fugitive?" she asked. "Wanted?"

Plagueis shook his head. "I do, however, value my privacy."

"Well you might," the Quara said. "But you have to admit—" He motioned to the bloody sea creatures. "—this undermines your credibility some."

"What brought you to Bal'demnic, Muun?" the Klatooinian asked before Plagueis could speak.

"I'm not at liberty to divulge the nature of my activities."

"Banking Clan investments," the Klatooinian said with a sneer. "Or lawyering. That's all the Muuns do, Captain."

Lah appraised Plagueis. "Is he right?"

Plagueis shrugged. "Not all of us are bankers or lawyers. No more than all Togrutas are pacifists."

"Be better for you if you *were* a financial wizard," the Zabrak said, "to avoid being jettisoned from our ship."

Plagueis kept his eyes on Lah. "Captain, I appreciate that you and your crew have many questions about me. But perhaps for the sake of simplicity, the two of us could speak privately for a moment." When she hesitated, he added: "Strictly in the interest of facilitating an agreement."

Lah glanced at everyone, then set her jaw and nodded. "I won't be long," she told the Zabrak as he was exiting the bay. "But keep us on vid anyway."

The Zabrak shot Plagueis a gimlet stare as he spoke. "If you are long, we'll be returning soon enough."

Plagueis waited until he and Lah were alone. "Thank you, Captain."

She scowled. "Enough of the polite jabber. Who are you, and why didn't you leave Bal'demnic aboard whatever craft brought you there?"

Plagueis loosed an elaborate sigh. "Before we go into any of that, suppose we assess the present situation squarely. I've stowed away aboard your vessel in the hope of arranging quick passage to Muunilinst." Speaking in Basic, Plagueis pronounced the word with the second *n* silent. "Fortunately for both of us, I'm in a position to reward you handsomely for transport—and of course I'll cover the cost of whatever precious cargo I've ruined. You need only quote a reasonable price and the deal can be concluded. I assure you, Captain, that I am a Muun of my word."

Her eyes narrowed in misgiving. "Leaving aside your identity for the moment—you know, the important things—your onward passage is a matter I'll have to take up with the crew."

Plagueis blinked in genuine confusion. "I'm not sure I understand. You are the *Woebegone*'s captain, are you not?"

"We're equals aboard this ship," Lah said. "I don't make any major decisions without at least hearing everyone out—whether those decisions involve the cargo we transport or where we deliver it. And while you're trying to make up your mind whether I'm noble or simply foolish, let me add that I don't care what you think of the arrangement. As you said: it's the situation."

Plagueis smiled without showing his teeth. "In that case, Captain, I await the results of the summit."

Lah relaxed somewhat. "You're going to have to sit tight in the meantime."

Plagueis took the conditions in stride. "Take as much time as needed. The closer we get to Ithor, the closer I am to home."

The words stopped her cold. "How do you know we're bound for Ithor?"

"The same way I know that your name is Ellin Lah." Delighting in her confusion, Plagueis said: "I'm not a telepath, Captain Lah. After I selected your ship from among those on the field, I sliced into Bal'demnic's spaceport network."

She tilted her head in a mix of interest and unease. "Why the *Woebegone,* then?"

Plagueis sniffed. "I don't gamble, Captain, unless I know that the odds of winning are on my side."

She snorted. "That's not gambling."

In the main cabin space, 11-4D had been monitoring the conversation of the crew members since their return from cargo bay 4. The closest thing the *Woebegone* had to an actual medical specialist, the droid was responsible for the care and health of the crew, and so it had grown accustomed to eavesdropping on conversations whenever and wherever possible. Having created individual profiles based on heartbeat and breathing rates, body temperature and language, facial expression and vocalization, the droid understood that the discovery of a Muun intruder aboard the ship had significantly elevated Maa Kaap's stress level.

"When have you ever known a Muun to do that?" the Zabrak was saying.

"When have you ever known a Muun, period?" Wandau asked in kind.

"All right, then, when have you ever *heard* about a Muun doing that?"

Before Maa Kaap or anyone else could respond, the captain entered the cabin space, clearly confounded though doing her best to disguise it. 11-4D noted increased blood flow in her head-tails, which were themselves sensory organs, and a change in her pigmentation—a

Togruta response to nervous tension that sometimes prompted involuntary mimetic camouflage.

"So," Maa Kaap said, coming to his feet.

The crew members listened intently as Captain Lah summarized the short exchange she'd had with the Muun stowaway, who had refused to provide any personal details, not even his name. Nor had he offered explanation for his presence on Bal'demnic, or divulged the reason behind his wanting to depart in haste. Most important, he had revealed nothing about the cause or nature of his injury. Instead he had fixed on arranging a deal for passage to Muunilinst, a world on the distant Braxant Run and corporate headquarters of the InterGalactic Banking Clan.

"What's your gut telling you about him, Captain?" PePe asked, his pointed ears twitching in curiosity.

Captain Lah glanced back at the corridor that led to cargo bay 4. "He's as slick as they come and used to getting his way. But either we take him back to Bal'demnic—and put our cargo at risk—or we drop him at our first stop and make him someone else's problem."

"Or we just jettison him now," Wandau said.

Lah shook her head. "We don't know he didn't tell someone on Bal'demnic that he was stowing away. And if he did, his disappearance could put us in serious muck."

"What's it going be, then?" Maa Kaap pressed.

Lah made her lips a thin line. "I think we should get him off our hands as soon as possible."

Wandau and Zuto exchanged glances. "You don't want to even discuss coming up with a price for passage?"

"I've never been on the Braxant Run," Lah said. "Have any of you?" Heads shook.

"Is he willing to cover the cost of the spoiled cargo?" PePe asked.

"He said he would."

"Then maybe we take him to Ithor," the Kaleesh went on. "If he proves to be a cooperative passenger, we could consider taking him all the way to Muunilinst. Certainly wouldn't hurt to get familiar with that corner of space."

"I don't know . . ." Lah took her lower lip between her teeth.

"I'll go one step further," Zuto said, leading with his whiskered snout. "I mean, this Muun could be a jackpot that's fallen right into our laps. Weren't you just saying that no bank would ever grant us a loan against the *Woebegone*? Well, Muunilinst *is* the bank, and this Muun can provide all the collateral we'll ever need."

"Our reward for years of leading clean lives," PePe added.

Lah regarded the two of them. "Meaning what? We hold him for ransom?"

Zuto drew in his tusks and shrugged. "We don't have to call it that."

"Forget it," Lah said. "We've never done that—well, once, maybe—but we're not about to do it again."

"I agree," Maa Kaap said.

Wandau's head bobbed. "Same."

PePe withdrew somewhat. "Okay, so I was just thinking out loud."

"There's something else," Maa Kaap said. Raising his big hand, he beckoned to 11-4D. "Tell the captain what you were telling us."

The droid moved to where the crew members were gathered and swiveled its round head toward Lah. "Captain, I merely pointed out that Muuns are not known to travel unaccompanied without ample reasons for doing so. In fact, most Muuns are reluctant to leave Muunilinst for any purpose other than to transact business negotiations."

"That's exactly what I was saying about collateral," PePe interrupted. "There has to be some financial reason for his being on Bal'demnic—some major deal in the works we might be able to get in on. A construction project, maybe."

"Let FourDee finish," Maa Kaap said.

Lah looked at the droid. "Go ahead."

"It has yet to be determined just what the Muun was involved in. Suppose, however, that the nature of his business is going to impact Bal'demnic in a negative way. Should word spread that the crew of the *Woebegone* lent their support to the Muun's illegal departure, then what might become of the ship's reputation in the Auril sector? You may wish to include the worth of that in your calculations regarding an arrangement for onward passage."

Maa Kaap folded his arms across his barrel chest. "Is our stowaway going to offer to set each of us up for life, in case our services are no longer wanted in this sector?"

"What about what the Muuns can do to us if we *don't* take him," Zuto said. "They've got a reach as long as a galactic arm."

Wandau laughed without mirth. "What are they going to do—downgrade our portfolios? Freeze our assets? Ruin our credit rating? Our only assets are this ship and our reputation for doing what we say we're going to do."

"Mostly," Maa Kaap said quietly.

PePe slapped his hands on his thighs. "Goes back to what I said about asking for a lot more than what he might see as a fair price. These Banking Clan types hold on to every credit. But we've got ourselves a live Muun, and no matter who he is or what he's pretending to be, I guarantee you he's worth more than ten years of dealing in meattails and octopods."

Maa Kaap broke the short silence. "Captain?"

"I'm not swayed by any of this," she said after a moment. "I want him off our hands."

A look of puzzlement tugged at Zuto's features. "You think he's dangerous?"

PePe ridiculed the idea. "Muuns are cowards, the lot of them. They use credits as weapons."

Lah took a long breath. "You asked for my gut reaction. That's what I'm giving you."

"I've an idea," Maa Kaap said. "A kind of compromise. We drop out of hyperspace and comm the authorities on Bal'demnic. If this Muun's wanted, for whatever reason, we return him, cargo or no. If not, we decide on a figure for taking him to Ithor, and no farther." He looked at Lah. "Are you willing to take that deal to him? Captain?"

Lah responded as if her words had just caught up with her thoughts. "All right. That sounds reasonable." But she remained seated.

"Do you, uh, want backup?" Wandau asked after another long moment had passed.

"No, no," she said, finally getting to her feet.

I'm the captain, 11-4D could almost hear her remind herself. Focusing its photoreceptors, it observed her right hand move discreetly to the blaster holstered on her hip. And with a flick of her thumb, she primed the weapon for fire.

* * *

"We're going to have to keep you on ice for a bit longer," Lah said when she entered the cargo bay. Plagueis hadn't moved from the container that served as his seat, but his robe was parted and his hands rested on the tops of his knees.

"Does that mean you failed to reach a consensus?"

"I wouldn't go that far," Lah said. "We've decided we need to know who you are before we agree to provide you with passage. And since you seem reluctant to tell us, we're going to check with Bal'demnic."

Plagueis made his eyes dull with disappointment. "Captain, I've told you all you really need to know."

The *Woebegone* lurched slightly. "We're dropping out of hyperspace," Lah said.

In his mind Plagueis heard Darth Tenebrous say: *To we who dwell in the Force, normal life is little more than pretense. Our only actions of signifi-cance are those we undertake in service to the dark side.*

"I can't permit this, Captain," he told her.

Her expression hardened. "I'm afraid you'll have to."

He had been aware from the start of the conversation that her blaster was primed, and now her hand reached for it. Sharp canines glinted in her slightly open mouth. Had he truly believed that a deal could be arranged with the *Woebegone*'s hot-tempered and immature crew members? Their fates had been sealed from the instant Plagueis had glimpsed the ship on the landing field. The possibility of reaching any other conclusion was fictional. From that first moment, all of them had been locked into an inevitable series of events. The Force had brought them together, into conflict. Even Lah must have sensed as much.

Plagueis said: "Don't, Captain."

But by then the warning was nothing more than words.

4: THE MEANING OF DEATH

The *Woebegone* had just reverted to realspace when 11-4D's audio sensors registered unusual sounds from aft: an activation click, a prolonged hiss of energy, a dopplering slash, a stuttering exhalation of breath. The sounds were followed by a sudden outpouring of heat from the corridor that accessed the cargo bays and what might have been interpreted as a gust of wind. Only by adjusting the input rate of its photoreceptors was the droid able to identify the blur that raced into the cabin space as a male Muun dressed in a hooded robe, trousers, and softboots that reached his shins.

Maa Kaap, PePe, Wandau, and Zuto turned in unison as the Muun came to a momentum-defying stop a few meters from where the four of them were seated. Clenched in his right hand was a crimson-bladed energy device the droid's data bank recognized as a lightsaber—a weapon used almost exclusively by members of the Jedi Order. And yet the recognition prompted a moment of bewilderment. The Jedi were known to be guardians of peace and enforcers of justice, but the Muun's comportment—the set of his long limbs, the feral working of his jutting jaw, the yellow blaze in his eyes—suggested anything but peace. As for justice, 11-4D couldn't retrieve a single instance of the four crew members having performed an offense that warranted capital punishment.

The humming lightsaber dangling from his left hand, the Muun remained silent, letting his posture speak for his nefarious intent. In turn the crew members, realizing that they were being wrongly accused, clambered to their feet, reaching at the same time for the weapons strapped to their hips and thighs. That the Muun permitted them to do so furnished 11-4D with yet another mystery—at least until it realized that the Muun was merely courting combat.

The droid wondered what Captain Lah could possibly have said or done to arouse so much wrath in the Muun. It replayed the memory of her priming the blaster. Had she decided that the problems the Muun presented for the *Woebegone* could best be solved by killing him, only to have misjudged him entirely? Regardless, it was apparent that the Muun believed the entire ship complicit in Captain Lah's actions, and had decided to take it upon himself to mete out retribution of the cruelest sort. 11-4D assumed that this would include him, and instantly initiated a series of redundant routines that would back up and store data, in order to provide a record of what was about to occur.

The face-off tableau in the cabinspace had endured for only a moment when Wandau, who had served as a bodyguard for a celebrated Hutt, leapt into action, drawing and firing his blaster even as he raced for cover behind one of the bulkheads. A split second behind, Maa Kaap raised his weapon and fired a continuous hail of blaster bolts at the Muun. In the same instant Zuto and PePe, crouched low to the deck, sprang forward in an attempt to outflank their opponent and place him at the center of a deadly crossfire.

From the passageway that led to the cockpit came the rapid footfalls of the pilot, Blir', and the ship's Dresselian navigator, Semasalli. 11-4D knew that they had been monitoring cam feeds of the cargo bay, and thought it likely that they had witnessed whatever sentence the Muun had levied on Captain Lah.

The Muun's reaction to the barrage of bolts that converged on him required almost more processing power than the droid had at its disposal. By employing a combination of body movements, lightsaber, and naked right hand, the agile sentient evaded, deflected, or returned every shot that targeted him. Slowly surrendering energy, the bolts caromed from the deck and bulkheads, touching off alarms, prompting a switch to emergency illumination, and unleashing cascades of fire-suppressant foam from the ceiling aerosols. No sooner had the Balosar and the Dresselian entered the cabinspace than hatches sealed the corridors, preventing any escape from the melee. Only 11-4D's ability to calculate trajectories and react instantaneously to danger kept it from being on the receiving end of any of the numerous ricochets.

Spying Blir' and Semasalli, the Muun hurled the lightsaber in a spinning arc that took off the Balosar's antenepalps and scalp and most of the wrinkled Dresselian's left shoulder, misting the already agitated air with teal-colored blood. As alarms continued to wail and foam continued to gush, Blir' folded and fell face-first to the slickened deck, while Semasalli, screeching in pain, collapsed to one side, reaching futilely for his severed arm with the other.

The lightsaber had scarcely left the Muun's grip when Wandau flew from cover to bring the attack to the Muun, triggering his blaster as ceaselessly as Maa Kaap was still doing. This time, though, the Muun merely stretched out his right hand and *absorbed* the bolts. Traveling up the length of his arm and across his narrow chest, the energy seemed to fountain from the hand awaiting the return of the spinning weapon as a tangle of blue electricity that hissed from his tapered fingers, catching Wandau full-on and lifting him to the ceiling of the hold before dropping him to the puddled deck in a heap, as if his bones had turned to dust.

In strobing red light, Maa Kaap's eyes tracked the rise and fall of his broken comrade. His blaster depleted, the Zabrak drew a vibroblade from a belt sheath and launched himself at the Muun, his large right hand intent on fastening itself onto the Muun's spindly neck.

The Muun caught the lightsaber, but instead of bringing it to bear against Maa Kaap, he danced and twirled out of reach of the vibroblade and commenced parrying the Zabrak's martial kicks and punches, until a side-kick to the thorax drove Maa Kaap clear across the cabin and slamming into the bulkhead. OneOne-FourDee's audio pickups registered the snap of the Zabrak's spine and the bursting of pulmonary arteries.

Now Zuto and PePe dived at the Muun from both sides and actually managed to get a hold on him. But it was as if the Muun had turned to stone. The Kaleesh and the Quara attacked with teeth and claws, but to no perceptible effect. And when the Muun had had enough of it, he positioned the lightsaber directly in front of him and gyred in their grasp, taking off PePe's tusked face and Zuto's blunt, whiskered snout. OneOne-FourDee's olfactory sensors detected an outpouring of pheromones that signaled the death of the Kaleesh. Zuto, on the other hand—though gurgling blood and moaning in pain—could perhaps be saved if treated in time.

Straightening out of a wide-legged stance, the Muun deactivated the lightsaber and scanned the beings he had killed and those he had maimed with chilling exactitude. His yellow eyes fell on 11-4D, but only for an instant; then he fixed the lightsaber to his belt and went quickly to his nearest victim, who happened to be Doo Zuto. Dropping to one knee alongside him, the Muun gazed intently at the Quara's twitching body, but precisely at what the droid couldn't surmise. Zuto's bulging marine eyes seemed to implore his assailant for help, but the Muun did nothing to stanch the flow of blood or offer palliative aid.

He remained by the Quara's side for a few moments, then moved quickly to Maa Kaap, from whose crushed chest cavity blood bubbled with each shallow breath. Again, the Muun ran his eyes over his victim, from Maa Kaap's tattooed face to his large feet. Eyes closed, the Muun adopted a posture that suggested intense concentration or meditation, and Maa Kaap snapped back to panic-stricken consciousness. OneOne-FourDee tuned in to the Zabrak's pulse and found it regular—but only for a moment. Then the rhythm of Maa Kaap's heartbeat grew ragged and breaths began to stutter from his lungs.

Soon he was dead.

The Muun appeared to be frustrated, and his disappointment increased on finding that Blir' was deceased, as well. He spent only moments appraising Semasalli before going to Wandau, who was conscious though obviously paralyzed from the waist down.

"You dishonor your heritage and your weapon, Jedi," Wandau managed to say. "You could have used . . . the Force to compel us to do as you wished. I've not only seen that, but experienced it."

The Muun's face contorted in distaste. "If you've so little will," he said in the tongue of Wandau's species, "then you're of no use to me, Klatooinian." And ended Wandau's misery with a click of his thumb and middle finger.

Gradually the spray from the ceiling abated and the klaxons fell silent. His examinations completed, the Muun stood and turned slowly to the droid.

"What name do you respond to?"

"OneOne-FourDee, sir."

"Can you pilot this ship, OneOne-FourDee?"

"I can, sir." The droid paused, then asked: "Do you wish me to relocate the survivors to medbay or jettison any of the corpses?"

The Muun surveyed his handiwork. "Leave them." He shrugged out of his sodden robe and hung it over a chair, revealing a second lightsaber affixed to his belt. "Captain Lah remarked that you have medical capabilities."

"I do, sir."

Turning his back to 11-4D, the Muun stripped his bloodstained tunic from his distended lower back. "Are you capable of repairing this?"

The droid sharpened the focus of its photoreceptors and olfactory sensors. "The wound shows signs of infection and putrefaction, sir, but, yes, I can repair it."

The Muun lowered the tunic and retrieved a comlink from a pocket in the robe. Activating the device, he spent a moment inputting data, then turned the display so that 11-4D could read it. "Set a course for these coordinates, then attend to me in the captain's quarters."

"Anything else, sir?"

"Prepare food and drink. I'm famished."

With the *Woebegone* traveling through hyperspace, Plagueis lay prone on the captain's bunk, a bacta patch covering the wound on his back, contemplating the results of his attempts to prolong the lives of those crew members who had survived the altercation. Even where he had been successful in effecting repairs to damaged blood vessels and organs, the results had been temporary, as he had not been able to influence or appeal to the midi-chlorians to assist. Calling on the Force to mend ruptured arteries, torn muscle, or broken bone was no more difficult than levitating slabs of stone. But such refurbishments had little effect on a being's etheric shell, which was essentially the domain of the midi-chlorians, despite their physical presence in living cells.

Among the ship's crew, the Togruta, Captain Lah, had been the strongest in the Force, but she was beyond his help by the time he reached her. Had it not been for sloppiness on his part, owing to fatigue and blood loss, and lightning-fast reflexes on hers, the lightsaber might simply have pierced her neck and cervical spinal cord. But she had spun at the moment of impact, and the crimson blade had all but decapitated her. The Zabrak, too, had a slightly higher-than-normal midi-chlorian count, but not high enough to make him Force-sensitive. How different it had been to observe the behavior of the Zabrak's midi-chlorians compared with those of Darth Tenebrous, only two days earlier!

The Jedi routinely performed blood tests to verify the midi-chlorian counts of prospective trainees, but Plagueis had passed beyond the need for such crude measurements. He could not only sense the strength of the Force in another but also perceive the midi-chlorians that individualized Forceful beings. It was that dark side ability that had allowed generations of Sith to locate and initiate recruits. The dispersal of midi-chlorians at the moment of physical death was, for lack of a better term, inexorable. Analogous to his fated confrontation with the *Woebegone* crew, the moment of death appeared to be somehow fixed in space and time. According to his Sith education, since Captain Lah and the others had been in some sense dead from the moment Plagueis's gaze had alighted on the freighter, it followed that the midi-chlorians that resided in alleged symbiosis with them must have been preparing to be subsumed into the reservoir of life energy that was the Force long before Plagueis had stowed away. His attempts to save them—to prolong that state of symbiosis—were comparable to using a sponge to dam a raging river. And yet the Sith Lords of old were said to have been able to draw on the energies released during death to extend their own lives, as well as the lives of others. Unfortunately, much like the technique of essence transfer, that ancient knowledge had been lost.

Feeling the ship revert to realspace, Plagueis rose from the bunk, dressed, and walked forward, stepping over the corpses sprawled in the main cabin, the deck plates awash in fire-suppressant fluid and blackening pools of blood, and through passageways reeking of death. One of the crew members, the now one-armed Dresselian, was still alive but comatose.

In the ship's undermount cockpit the droid stood motionless at the control console. Beyond the transparisteel viewport myriad stars hung in space.

"Sir, we are approaching the coordinates supplied by your comlink," the droid said without turning from the view.

Plagueis settled into the pilot's chair, which barely accommodated his long body. "How do you come to be aboard the *Woebegone*, droid?"

"Formerly I served the needs of a medical facility on Obroa-skai."

"In what capacity?"

"Research, in addition to performing a wide range of surgeries on beings of diverse species."

Plagueis regarded the droid. "Thus, your many appendages."

"Yes, sir. But the ones I wear currently were retrofitted when I became the property of Captain Lah, so that I might better serve the needs of the *Woebegone*."

"And how did you become the captain's property?"

"I believe, sir, that I was awarded to Captain Lah in place of payments due for the receipt of certain merchandise. It is also my belief that the exchange was meant to be temporary—"

"But Captain Lah decided to keep you."

"Yes, sir. She decided to keep me. I'm sorry to say that I am at a loss to explain her reasons, and I never presumed to ask."

Plagueis nodded. "That's a good quality in a droid."

"I understand how it could be, sir."

"Tell me, droid, what is the possible consequence of low theloxin levels in a Pau'an?"

OneOne-FourDee didn't hesitate. "One possible consequence would be an elevation of the oxidation rate, leading to the growth of an exophthalmic goiter, which in turn would affect the production of roaamin from the anterior lobes of the lutiaary gland."

"And?"

"One result might be giantism, well beyond the Pau'an norm."

"If so?"

"The connecting ganglia making up the autonomic nervous system and controlling glandular secretion might induce an acceleration of the circular sphincter muscles of the digestive tract, resulting in xerophthalmia."

"So you are a diagnostician, as well."

"In a minor capacity, sir."

Beyond the viewport, growing larger against the backdrop of a behemoth ringed planet, a space station turned in fixed orbit near a heavily cratered moon. A hodgepodge of interconnected domed modules, the station featured two long, boxy arms to which ships of varying size were tethered. Plagueis called data to the display screen of his comlink and placed it in view of 11-4D.

"Transmit this code over the comm."

The droid performed the task and waited at the comm while the cockpit enunciators crackled to life.

"Unidentified freighter, Deep Space Demo and Removal is in reception of your request. Give us a moment to authenticate your transmission."

"Holding fast while you authenticate," Plagueis said.

"Freighter, you are cleared for docking," the voice returned a moment later.

"My ship," Plagueis said, leaning forward to take hold of the yoke.

As a precaution, the station directed them to a berth at the distal end of the larger of the two arms.

"You will accompany me into the landing bay," Plagueis told the droid when he had shut the ship down. "Raise the boarding ramp behind us and activate the anti-intrusion system. No one is to board the *Woebegone* unless I say otherwise."

"I understand, sir."

Waiting in the gloomy landing bay were a female Nikto and a russet-colored young male Dug, backed by a motley contingent of armed beings. Lowering the cowl of his robe as he approached, Plagueis saw the Nikto stiffen and signal those behind her to leave the area immediately.

"Magister Damask," she began in Basic, "I had no foreknowledge—"

Plagueis cut her off. "This isn't a social call."

"Of course, Magister. Regardless, do you wish me to apprise Boss Cabra of your visit?"

"Is he on station?"

"No, sir. But he can be reached by comm."

"That won't be necessary," Plagueis said. "I'll contact him myself."

"As you wish, Magister. What services can the station provide?"

Plagueis gestured in an offhanded way to the berthed freighter. "This ship is to be sealed and slagged."

"Without salvaging anything?" the Dug said.

Plagueis looked at him. "I said sealed and slagged. Do you need to hear it a third time?"

The Dug bared his teeth. "Do you know who you're talking to, Muun?"

Plagueis cut his eyes to the Nikto. "Who is this callow pup?"

"Pup?" the Dug repeated before the Nikto could intervene.

"Boss Cabra's youngest progeny, Magister," she said quickly, restraining the Dug with her extended left arm. "He means no disrespect."

Plagueis regarded the Dug again. "What are you called, pup?"

The Dug's rear legs were tensed for a leap, but the Nikto whirled rapidly, slapping him across his flewed and broad-nostriled snout and clamping a hand on his windpipe.

"Answer him!" she bellowed into his snarling face. "And with due respect!"

The Dug relented and whimpered, though certainly more out of humiliation than pain. "Darnada," he squeaked at last.

"Darnada," Plagueis repeated before addressing the Nikto. "Perhaps young Darnada should be muzzled to prevent him from endangering his father's business relationships."

"His brashness reflects his inexperience, Magister," the Nikto said in abject apology. She gave Darnada a menacing glance before continuing. "Trust that your orders regarding the ship will be honored in full, Magister."

"I will also need a change of wardrobe and a fueled, piloted ship."

"Can we provide the pilot with a destination beforehand?"

"Muunilinst."

"Of course, Magister. And what are your instructions regarding the droid?"

"Instructions?"

"Is the droid to be slagged along with the ship?"

Plagueis looked over his shoulder at 11-4D. "How much of your memory can be wiped without tampering with your medical protocols?"

"I'm modular in design," the droid said. "My memory storage can

be erased in its entirety or according to whatever parameters you establish."

Plagueis considered that. "Remain with the ship until it has been
liquefied. I will expect a complete audio-vid recording."

OneOne-FourDee raised its right-side appendages in a gesture of
acknowledgment. "At your service, Magister Damask."

5: HOMECOMING

Those fortunate enough to have visited Muunilinst in the decades preceding the Clone Wars often remarked that the planet had been blessed with the most beautiful skies in the galaxy. To maintain that pristine blue realm—to prevent it from being sullied by drop ships, shuttles, or landing craft—the Muuns had erected the most costly skyhook of its kind anywhere outside the Core. As efficient as it was luxurious, the skyhook, known affectionately as the Financial Funnel, linked the orbital city of High Port with the planetary capital, Harnaidan, which functioned as the nerve center of the InterGalactic Banking Clan. While the stately tower seemed to speak to the Muuns' high regard for aesthetics and ecology, its true purpose was to keep visitors from setting foot on Muunilinst, thereby safeguarding the planet's wealth of resources and keeping secret the lavish lifestyles of those who had ascended to the top of the food chain.

From its remote corner of the Outer Rim, Muunilinst exerted its influence across all of known space and halfway to the galaxy's nearest satellite star cluster. Dating back to the founding of the Republic, the Banking Clan had funded governments, supported settlements, and bankrolled countless commerce guilds, trade corporations, and shipping cartels. In a very real sense, the IBC dictated the ebb and flow of wealth from the Core to the Outer Rim. Scarcely a building was raised on Coruscant without the Banking Clan's approval; scarcely a starship left the yards at Kuat or Bilbringi or Fondor without the IBC having brokered the deal; and scarcely an election occurred on Corellia or Commenor without the Muuns having been consulted.

The Muuns accomplished all these things with a meticulous serenity that belied the frenzied workings of their mathematical minds. Save for when it came to collecting on overdue debts, the Muuns, on first acquaintance, appeared to be a stolid and lenient species, if somewhat arrogant, with an ascetic nature that was in full keeping with their willowy bodies and was reflected in the simple but harmonious architecture of their cities.

As pale as the Muuns themselves, High Port Space Center incorporated the design elements they favored most: domed interiors, arch-topped windows, fluted columns, and unadorned friezes and entablatures. Among these faux-stone building blocks large groups of Muuns maneuvered and mingled with unhurried if single-minded purpose, maintaining a conversational clamor that struck some visitors as reminiscent of the spoken language of thinking machines. Attending them were droids of all variety, and guest workers from the nearby worlds of Bescane, Jaemus, Entralla, and others. On any given day a visitor might spy envoys from Yagai, Gravlex Med, or Kalee, along with Hutts of the Drixo or Progga kin. But what one saw most, in overwhelming numbers, were members of the Banking Clan—financiers, accountants, lawyers—dressed in their signatory Palo fiduciary garb: formfitting green trousers and boots, round-collared green tunics, and flare-shouldered green cloaks. Some were accompanied by retinues of squat, dark-skinned, flat-nosed soldiers from the planet Iotra, sporting garish body armor and carrying ceremonial weapons.

That day, cutting through the verdant sea like some predatory sea creature came a wedge-shaped cluster of Muuns dressed in black cloaks and skullcaps, guarded by a contingent of towheaded Echani warriors whose silver eyes darted vigilantly, and whose metallic bodysuits masked the translucency of their skin. At the leading edge of the wedge marched an elder Muun with a whiskered chin and stooped shoulders, who was making directly for High Port's customs control station, where Hego Damask—as Plagueis was known to everyone but the late Darth Tenebrous—and 11-4D were waiting, amid a contingent of security personnel.

"We came as soon as High Port Immigration notified us," Larsh Hill said. "If you had contacted us from Deep Space Demolition, we could have sent a ship, rather than have you rely on Boss Cabra's specious hospitality."

"No one seems to believe that I'm capable of finding my own way home," Damask said.

Hill's long face wrinkled. "I don't understand."

"It's not important that you do. Suffice it to say that your dispatching a ship would only have resulted in further delay." Like Hill and his coterie of half a dozen, Damask's hairless head was encased in a tight-fitting bonnet, and the hem of his black cloak swept the polished floor.

"You were expected days ago," Hill said, with a note of exasperation.

"Events of an unforeseen nature prevented me from returning earlier."

"A successful journey, nevertheless, I assume."

"You assume correctly."

Hill relaxed somewhat. "We shouldn't tarry here any longer than necessary. Transport is waiting."

At Hill's gesture, the black-cloaked Muuns began to angle toward the skyhook turbolifts, four of the silver-suited warriors falling in to flank Damask and the droid, which walked behind him.

"You're limping," Hill said in hushed urgency. "Are you injured?"

"Healing," Damask said. "Make no further mention of it."

"We could postpone the Gathering—"

"No. It will take place as scheduled."

"I'm relieved to hear that," Hill said, "since several of your guests are already in transit to Sojourn."

The group was halfway to the turbolifts when a faction of Banking Clan officials deliberately cut across their path, forcing them to halt. The faction's obvious leader, a Muun of middle age, separated himself from the rest and moved to the front.

"Magister Damask," he said. "What a surprise to encounter you here, among the rabble."

Damask adopted a faint grin. "Excluding yourself, of course, Chairman Tonith."

Tonith stiffened. "We're simply passing through."

"As are we," Damask said, motioning to Hill and the rest.

"You've been traveling, Magister?"

"A business trip, Chairman."

"Of course." It was Tonith's turn to show a weak smile. "But in that case perhaps you haven't heard that the Senate is on the verge of creating additional free-trade zones in the Outer Rim Territories. Despite what I understand were considerable efforts on your part to the contrary, the shipping cartels face the danger of being broken, and even if not, will certainly have to deal with fierce competition from start-up companies. Both Core and Outer Rim worlds should benefit greatly from the arrangement, wouldn't you agree?"

Damask inclined his head in a bow of acknowledgment. "I hadn't heard, Magister. Whom can we thank for swaying the liberals to adopt the amendment?"

"Among others, the Jedi Order lobbied successfully."

"Then it must be for the best."

"One would think," Tonith said slowly. "Save for the fact that, in exchange, the Trade Federation will now enjoy full voting privileges in the Senate."

"Ah, well. Appeasements of one sort or another always figure into Senate affairs."

Tonith leaned slightly toward Damask. "Thank you, however, for suggesting that we invest in Outer Rim and trans-Perlemian shipping. The results provided a windfall."

"Where and when I can be of service, Chairman."

Tonith straightened. "Your clan father would be proud."

Damask looked Tonith in the eye. "I take that as a compliment."

"How else would I mean it, Magister?"

When the Banking Clan members had moved off and Damask's group was back in motion, Damask glanced at Hill. "Someday we will topple the Toniths from their lofty perch."

Hill smiled with his eyes. "I hope I'm alive to see that day. And just so you know, Hego, your father *would* be proud. Chairman Tonith's sarcasm notwithstanding."

"You would know better than most."

Having arrived at the skyhook turbolifts, Hill was motioning everyone but himself and Damask into a separate lift when Damask said, "The droid will ride with us."

Hill appraised 11-4D as the three of them entered the turbolift. "A new acquisition?"

"A door prize of sorts," Damask said.

Hill didn't pursue it. "You'll be going to your residence or to Aborah?"

"Directly to the island. The droid will accompany me."

"I'll make the necessary arrangements."

Damask lowered his voice to ask, "Are we secure in here?"

"Completely."

Damask turned to face the taller, elder Muun. "Rugess Nome is dead."

"The Bith?" Hill said in astonishment. "How? Where?"

"Of no relevance," Damask said, remembering. "Eventually Nome's estate will pass to us, but that won't be for some time to come, since it's unlikely that his body will ever be found."

Hill didn't bother asking for details. "We'll allow a standard year to pass. Then we'll petition the probate courts to render a decision—at the very least for whatever assets are contractually ours. You are the executor, in any case, are you not?"

Damask nodded. "Ultimately we'll be liquidating most of the estate. But there are several . . . antiques of a curious sort I plan to retain. I'll prepare an inventory. In the meantime I want you to familiarize yourself with a world called Bal'demnic. Once you have, you're to acquire mining rights for the entire northeast peninsula of the principal landmass. Purchase as much property as you can, from the shoreline to the central highlands. I'll provide you with specific coordinates."

Uncertainty tugged at Hill's strong features. "Are we venturing into the mining business now?"

"When the time is right. Use intermediaries who can't be traced to us. I suspect that you will have to go all the way to the top to secure what we need. The indigenes will be troublesome to negotiate with, but I'm confident they can be persuaded. Bargain like you mean it, but in the end spare no expense."

"Bal'demnic is that important?"

"A hunch," Damask said.

Descending rapidly, the skyhook turbolift pierced layers of pure white clouds, revealing a curved panorama of aquamarine ocean, pale brown plains, and evergreen forest. And directly below, the view that was said to take one's breath away: the city of Harnaidan, studded with Neo-Classical structures as towering as the volcanic spires that ringed it, and home to fifty million Muuns, living in an urbanscape that was an orderly masterpiece of art and design. To some, it was the antithesis of most planetary capitals: the anti-Coruscant; the anti-Denon.

"What can we expect at the Gathering?" Damask asked, turning away from the view.

"Gardulla has requested an audience."

"I'm not in the habit of sitting down with Hutts."

"She asks your help in mediating a dispute."

"With whom?"

"The Desilijic clan."

Damask nodded knowingly. "This has been brewing for some time. What else?"

"Representatives from Yinchorr will be there."

"Good. Holotransmissions have their limitations."

"Members of the Trade Federation and the Gran Protectorate will also be attending."

Damask snorted. "There's no pleasing any of them." He grew pensive, then said: "There's another small matter we need to settle. Extend a personal invitation to the owners of Subtext Mining."

Hill rubbed his whiskered chin. "I can't recall having engaged in dealings with them. Does this have anything to do with Bal'demnic?"

Damask ignored the question. "For a time they advised Nome. Make certain they understand that we operate in complete confidentiality."

"If the Bith partnered with them, they must come highly recommended."

"One would think." Damask turned his back to Hill to take in the view once more. "But, in fact, I don't see much future for them."

Unlike so many worlds that had been surveyed and settled by species from the Core, Muunilinst had given rise to its own brand of sentients. Farmers and fisherfolk, the ancient Muuns hadn't known how favored their planet was until interstellar travel had become commonplace, and precious metals the backbone of the galactic economy. Had those early millennia of expansion not been a time of peace, the Muuns might have lost what they had to military might; but as it happened they had resisted all attempts at exploitation and become masters of their fate. Still, what was an economic blessing eventually became a burden. Once the Muuns understood the value of what they had previously taken for granted, they held on to their riches with a ferocious tenacity, and developed an almost agoraphobic attachment to their homeworld.

In the midst of Muunilinst's shallow oceans, the same volcanic activity that had fertilized the vast plains belched new seabed and precious metals enough to fuel the growth of empires. Mountains heaped up through vents in the planetary crust were found to be repositories of extraordinary wealth. Lapped by warm waters teeming with shellfish, tubeworms, and bioluminescent flora, such "smokers," as they were known, became both the source and the financial vaults of Muunilinst's most powerful and prosperous clans.

More remote than some, Aborah, which had been the province of the Damask clan for several generations, was otherwise typical of the dormant smokers whose thickly forested conical peaks poked from the calm waters of the Western Sea. A maze of interconnected lava tubes ran deep into the mountain island; waterfalls plunged from the sheer heights; and incense trees scented the salty air of the lowland valleys. Conveyed by speeder to Aborah's north tower complex, Plagueis escorted 11-4D on a tour of the corridors and caverns that constituted his place of sacrosanct solitude.

Motioning to the many droids that were on hand to welcome the pair to Aborah, Plagueis said: "You will come to find yourself at home here, as I have."

"I'm certain I will, Magister Damask," 11-4D said, its photoreceptors registering a dozen different types of droids in a single glance. Memo droids, GNK power droids, even a prototype Ubrikkian surgical droid.

"In time we'll see to having your original appendages restored so that you can earn your keep."

"I look forward to it, Magister."

The tour began in the outermost rooms, which were appointed with furnishings and objects of art of the highest quality, gathered from all sectors of the galaxy. But Plagueis was neither as acquisitive as a Neimoidian nor as ostentatious as a Hutt; and so the ornamented chambers quickly gave way to data-gathering rooms crowded with audio-vid receivers and HoloNet projectors; and then to galleries filled to overflowing with ancient documents and tomes, recorded on media ranging from tree trunk parchment through flimsiplast to storage crystal and holocron. The Muuns were said to abhor literature and to loathe keeping records of anything other than loan notices, actuarial tables, and legal writs, and yet Plagueis was guardian of the one of the finest libraries to be found anywhere outside Obroa-skai or the Jedi Temple on Coruscant. Here, neatly arranged and cataloged and stored in climate-controlled cases, was a collection of treatises and commentaries accumulated over centuries by the Sith and their often unwitting agents. Ancient histories of the Rakata and the Vjun; texts devoted to the Followers of Palawa, the Chatos Academy, and the Order of Dai Bendu; archives that had once belonged to House Malreaux; annals of the Sorcerers of Tund and of Queen Amanoa of Onderon; biological studies of the ysalimiri and vornskrs of Myrkr, and of the taozin of Va'art. Certain long-lived species, like the Wookiees, Hutts, Falleen, and Toydarians, were afforded galleries of their own.

Deeper in the mountain were laboratories where Plagueis's real work took place. Confined to cages, stasis fields, bioreactors, and bacta tanks were life-forms brought to Muunilinst from across the galaxy—many from the galaxy's most remote worlds. Some were creatures of instinct, and others were semisentient. Some were immediately recognizable to 11-4D; others resembled creatures concocted from borrowed parts. Some were newly birthed or hatched, and some looked as if they were being kept at death's door. More than a few were the subjects of ongoing experiments in what seemed to be vivisection or interbreeding, and others were clearly in suspended animation. OneOne-FourDee noted that many of the animals wore remotes that linked them to biometric monitoring machines, while others were in the direct care of specialist droids. Elsewhere in the hollow of the mountain were sealed enclosures warmed by artificial light, aswirl with mixtures of rarefied gases and luxuriant with flora. And deeper still were test centers crammed with complex machines and glass-fronted cooling units devoted to the storage of chemical compounds, alkaloids derived from both plants and animals, blood and tissue samples, and bodily organs from a host of species.

Plagueis instructed 11-4D to wander about the galleries and laboratories on his own, and then report back to him.

Hours later the droid returned to say: "I recognize that you are involved in research related to species durability and hybridization. But I must confess to being unfamiliar with many of the examples of fauna and flora you have amassed, and few of the arcane documents in your library. Is the data available for upload?"

"Some portion of it," Plagueis said. "The remainder will have to be scanned."

"Then the task will require standard years, Magister."

"I'm aware of that. While there is some urgency, we are in no rush."

"I understand, sir. Is there specific data you wish me to assimilate first?"

From the breast pocket of his cloak, Plagueis withdrew a storage crystal. "Start with this. It is a history of the Sith."

OneOne-FourDee took a moment to search its memory. "I have multiple listings under that heading. One defines the Sith as an ancient sect devoted to the study of the Force. Similar to the Jedi, but guided by different principles."

"That's close enough for now," Plagueis said.

"Magister Damask, if I may be so bold as to inquire: what is our eventual goal?"

"The goal is to extend my life indefinitely. To conquer death."

The droid fixed Plagueis in its photoreceptors. "I have access to data on alleged 'elixirs of life' and 'fountains of youth,' Magister. But all living things ultimately die, do they not?"

"At present, OneOne-FourDee."

The droid thought harder about it. "I have experience in organ replacement surgery, telomere genotherapy, and carbonite suspension. But nothing beyond that."

Plagueis's smooth upper lip curled. "Then you've merely scratched the surface."

* * *

With 11-4D deep in processing mode, Plagueis withdrew a vial of his own blood and subjected it to analysis. Despite the recent amplification of his powers he sensed that his midi-chlorian count had not increased since the events on Bal'demnic, and the analysis of the blood sample confirmed his suspicions. Research had long ago established that blood transfusions from Force-sensitive individuals did not confer Force powers to recipients, though blood with a high midi-chlorian count could grant temporary strength and resiliency. Experiments in absolute transfusion had gone horribly awry for recipients, suggesting to some that the Force exacted a toll on those who attempted to tamper with it. An individual's midi-chlorians seemed to know to whom they belonged and become unresponsive outside their dedicated vessel.

While midi-chlorians appeared to resist manipulation of a sort that might imperil the balance of the Force, they remained passive, even compliant, in the case of a weak-willed being manipulated by one who was strong in the Force. Perhaps that explained why it was often easier to call on the Force to heal someone other than oneself. Extending life, then, could hinge on something as simple as being able to induce midi-chlorians to create new cells; to subdivide at will, increasing their numbers into the tens of thousands to heal or replace damaged, aging, or metastatic cells. Midi-chlorians had to be compelled to serve the needs of the body; to bestow strength when needed; to overcome physical insult, or prevent cells from reaching senescence.

If one accepted the tales handed down in accounts and holocrons, the ancient Sith had known how to accomplish this. But had Sith like Naga Sadow and Exar Kun genuinely been more powerful, or had they benefited from the fact that the dark side had been more prominent in those bygone eras? Some commentators claimed that the ability to survive death had been limited to those with a talent for sorcery and alchemy, and that the use of such practices actually predated the arrival of the Dark Jedi exiles on Korriban. But sorcery had been employed less to extend life than to create illusions, fashion beasts, and resurrect the dead. Powerful adepts were said to have been able to saturate the atmosphere of planets with dark side energy, compel stars to explode, or induce paralysis in crowds, as Exar Kun apparently did to select members of the Republic Senate. Other adepts used sorcery merely as a means to better understand ancient Sith spells and sigils.

Darth Bane had referred to sorcery as one of the purest expressions of the dark side of the Force, and yet he hadn't been able to harness those energies with near the skill as had his onetime apprentice Zannah. Bane's disciples, however, believed that he had experimented with a technique of even greater significance: that of essence transfer, which he had learned after acquiring and plundering the holocron of Darth Andeddu, and which involved the relocation of an individual's consciousness into another body or, in some cases, a talisman, temple, or sarcophagus. Thus had the most powerful of the ancient Sith Lords survived death to haunt and harass those who would infiltrate their tombs.

But none of this amounted to *corporeal* survival.

Plagueis had no interest in being a lingering, disembodied presence, trapped between worlds and powerless to affect the material realm except through the actions of weak-minded beings he could goad, coax, or will into action. Nor did he seek to shunt his mind into the body of another, whether an apprentice, as Bane was thought to have attempted, or some vat-grown clone. Nothing less than the immortality of his body and mind would suffice.

Everlasting life.

Sadly he could glean only so much from the texts, crystals, and holocrons stored in the library. Crucial knowledge had been lost during the brief mastery of Darth Gravid, and many of the most important elements of Sith training since had been passed from Masters to apprentices in sessions that had been left unrecorded. More to the point, Darth Tenebrous had had very little to say regarding death.

Alone in one of the test centers, surrounded by his experiments— these things Plagueis could say he loved—the enormity of what had occurred on Bal'demnic suddenly rose up before him like a monolith of immeasurable proportions. For the first time he could feel the Force of the dark side not as a mere supporting wind, fluffing the sails of a pleasure boat, but as a hurricane eager to loose a storm of destruction on the crumbling Republic and the indolent Jedi Order. A scouring storm that would lay waste to everything antiquated and corrupt, and pave the way for a new order in which the Sith would be returned to their rightful place as the stewards of the galaxy, and before whom all the diverse species would bow, not only in obeisance and fear, but in gratitude for having been drawn back from the brink.

The task before him was at once invigorating and daunting, and in the eye of that cycloning storm he could hear the faraway voices of all those who had laid the goundwork of the Sith imperative—the Grand Plan; those who had enlivened the hurricane with their breath and lives: Darths Bane and Zannah, and on down through the generations that had included Cognus, Vectivus, Ramage, and Tenebrous. One hundred years earlier, Tenebrous's Twi'lek Master had opened a small rend in the fabric of the Force, allowing the dark side to be felt by the Jedi Order for the first time in more than eight hundred years. That had been the inauguration, the commencement of the revenge of the Sith. And now the time had come to enlarge that rend into a gaping hole, a gaping *wound*, into which the Republic and the Jedi Order would to their own hazard be drawn.

6: THE HUNTERS' MOON

An afternoon breeze carried the scent of fresh blood. Shrieks of agony and death pierced tendrils of mist snagged by the gnarled branches of greel trees. The reports of weapons—old and new, projectile and energy—reverberated from the escarpment that walled the ancient fortress to the west, behind which the system's primary was just now disappearing. As if some fantastic statuary perched atop a place of worship, Magister Hego Damask stood on the uppermost rampart, his black cloak fluttering, attuned to the sounds of slaughter. And to the clamor of parties of beings returning from their separate hunts, blood of whatever color and consistency stirred by primal violence, voices lifted in ancient song or throaty chant, the gutted carcasses of their prey strapped to antigrav litters, ready for roasting over bonfires that blazed in the fort's central courtyard, or for preservation by skilled taxidermists. Veermok, nexu, mongworst; krayt dragon, acklay, reek. Whatever their preference.

A nod to the planet that had birthed it, the moon was known as Sojourn, a name whispered by those who knew it slightly, and even by those who had visited repeatedly over the centuries. The system could be found in the registries, but only if one knew where to look, and how to decipher the data that revealed its location.

Here, once every standard year, Damask and the dozen Muuns who made up Damask Holdings hosted a gathering of influential beings from across the galaxy. Their names might be known to a few, but they were largely invisible to the masses and could move among them unrecognized, though they were responsible—in no small measure—for events that shaped galactic history. They were conveyed to Sojourn in secret, aboard ships designed by Rugess Nome and owned by Hego Damask. None came without an invitation, for to do so was to risk immediate destruction. What they shared, to a being, was Damask's belief that financial profit mattered more than notoriety, politics, or vulgar morality.

Founded generations earlier by members of the InterGalactic Banking Clan, Sojourn had begun as a place of relaxation for the clan's wealthiest clientele. A perquisite for those of exalted privilege. Later, under the management of the elder Damask—Hego's biological father— on his retirement from chairmanship of the IBC, the moon had become something else: a place where only the most important players were brought together to exchange ideas. It was on Sojourn that the galactic credit standard had been established; the chancellorship of Eixes Valorum first proposed; the makeup of the Trade Federation Directorate reorganized. Then, under Hego Damask, Sojourn became something else again. No longer a resort or think tank, but an experiment in bolder thinking, in social alchemy. A place to plot and strategize and wrench the course of galactic history from the hands of happenstance. Where once Iotran Brandsmen had provided security, Damask's contingent of silver-suited Echani Sun Guards now held sway. At great expense, scarlet-wood greel tree saplings had been smuggled from Pii III and planted in Sojourn's modified soil. The forests had been stocked with cloned game and exotic creatures; the ancient fort transformed into a kind of lodge, with Damask's very important guests residing in purposefully crude shelters, with names like Nest, Cave, Hideaway, and Escarpment. All to encourage a like-mindedness that would end in partnerships of an unusual sort.

Damask remained on the rampart while the light waned and darkness crept over the forested landscape. In the grand courtyard below, the bonfire flames leapt higher and the odors of charred meat hung thickly in the air. Wines and other intoxicants flowed freely; Twi'lek and Theelin females entertained; and the crowd grew rowdy. Each hunting party was required to display and butcher its prizes; to get limbs and other appendages wet with blood. Not all beings were meat eaters, but even those who subsisted on grains and other crops were drawn into the debauchery. At midnight the guiding principles of the Republic would be mocked in skits, and prominent Senators—save for those present—would be subjected to ridicule. That Sith ceremonies and symbols had been incorporated into the ceremonies and the architecture of the fortress was Damask's secret alone.

Sensing the arrival of Larsh Hill and two other Muuns, he swung from the parapet view.

"The Hutt has been waiting since starfall," Hill said.

"The price of meeting with me," Damask said.

Hill gave him a long-suffering look. "If she didn't know as much, she would be long gone."

The Magister tailed the trio down a long flight of stone steps and into a yawning reception area warmed by colorful rugs, tapestries, and a grand fire. Gardulla Besadii the Elder, crime lord and notorious gambler, floated in on a palanquin appropriate to her great size, attended by an entourage that included her Rodian majordomo, bodyguards, and others. Damask's own guards were quick to usher everyone but the Hutt back into the waiting room. Larsh Hill and the two other dark-cloaked Muuns remained at Damask's side.

Curled upright on her powerful tail, Gardulla extended her bare, stubby arms toward the fire. "I've been admiring your entertainers, Magister," she said. "Particularly the Theelin singers. Perhaps you could help me procure some."

"We've a Twi'lek who supplies the females," Damask said from his armchair. "You'll have to speak with her."

Gardulla noted the sharp tone in his voice. "On to business then."

Damask offered a gesture of apology. "A busy schedule affords me scant time for pleasantries."

Unaccustomed to straight talk, the Hutt frowned, then said, "I plan to make a grab for Tatooine, Magister, and I've come to solicit your support."

"An arid world in the Arkanis sector of the Outer Rim," Hill supplied quietly from behind the armchair.

"By *support*, I presume we are talking about credits," Damask said.

Gardulla repositioned herself on the litter. "I'm aware that you disapprove of spice and slavery, but there are profits to be made on Tatooine by other means."

"Not moisture farming, then."

Gardulla glowered. "You mock me."

Damask motioned negligently. "I tease you, Gardulla. I know little about Tatooine, other than that the planet was heir to an ecological catastrophe in the dim past, and that its vast deserts now support a population of ne'er-do-wells, scoundrels, and hapless spacers of all species. I've heard it said that nothing pans out on Tatooine, and that beings who reside there age prematurely."

Damask knew, too, that the ancient Sith had once had an outpost on Tatooine, but he kept that to himself.

"Fortunately, longevity comes naturally to my species," Gardulla said. "But I don't want for enemies of a different sort, Magister. Enemies who would like nothing more than to see me in an early grave."

"The Desilijic clan."

"They are precisely the reason I wish to remove myself from Nal Hutta—and from the likes of Jabba Desilijic Tiure and the rest. With your financial assistance I can accomplish that. I know that you have befriended Hutts in your own planetary neighborhood."

"It's true that Drixo and Progga have done well for themselves on Comra," Damask said, "but their successes came at a high cost. What are you offering in return for our investment?"

A light came into the Hutt's dark, oblique eyes. "A Podrace course that will make those on Malastare and on your own Muunilinst seem like amateur runs. In addition, the renaissance of an annual Podrace event that will bring tens of thousands of gamblers to Tatooine and fill my coffers to overflowing." She paused, then added: "And I'm willing to take you on as a partner."

"A silent partner," Damask amended.

She nodded. "As you wish."

Damask steepled his long fingers and raised his hands to his jutting chin. "In addition to a percentage of the profits, I want you to arrange for Boss Cabra to operate freely on Nar Shaddaa."

Gardulla adopted an incredulous look. "The Dug crime boss?"

"You know the one," Hill said sharply.

The Hutt fretted. "I can't make promises, Magister. Black Sun is deeply entrenched on Nar Shaddaa, and the Vigos are grooming Alexi

Garyn to assume control of the organization. They may not appreciate or permit—"

"Those are our terms, Gardulla," Damask cut in. "Find some way to allow Cabra to reach an accommodation with Black Sun and we will support your takeover of Tatooine." He gestured toward the fortress courtyard. "This very night I can arrange for you to meet with officials representing the Bank of Aargau, who will advance whatever amount of credits you need."

After a long moment of silence, Gardulla nodded. "I accept your terms, Magister Damask. You will not be disappointed."

When the Hutt had steered her antigrav litter from the room, members of the Sun Guard showed in a group of tall reptilian sentients who stood on two thick legs and whose broad snouts curved downward at the tip. Damask's previous contact with the Yinchorri had been limited to holoprojector; now he leaned forward in keen interest as the spokesmember introduced himself in gruff Basic as Qayhuk—secretary of the Council of Elders—and launched immediately into a diatribe denouncing the Senate for refusing to admit Yinchorr to the Republic. With bellicose encouragement from his comrades, Qayhuk went on to say with fist-pounding emphasis that although their homeworld had been charted hundred of years earlier by the Republic, Yinchorr remained an underprivileged, backrocket planet deserving of far better treatment.

"Or someone will pay in blood for the ongoing injustice," the secretary warned.

Larsh Hill waited until he was certain that Qayhuk was finished to remark under his breath, "I'm not sure even the Senate is ready for them."

Holding Qayhuk's baleful gaze and motioning with his hand, Damask said, "You have no interest in seeing Yinchorr seated in the Senate."

Qayhuk took umbrage. "Why else would we have journeyed all this way?"

"You have no interest in seeing Yinchorr seated in the Senate," Plagueis repeated.

Qayhuk glanced at his green-skinned brethren, then looked at Hill. "Is Magister Damask deaf or in ill health?"

Hill turned to Damask in concern but said nothing.

Damask concealed his astonishment. As rumored, the Yinchorri were apparently *resistant* to Force suggestion! But how was it possible that midi-chlorians in a being of relatively low intelligence could erect an impenetrable wall against the influence of a Sith? Was this some sort of survival mechanism—the midi-chlorians' way of protecting the consciousness of their vessels by refusing to be manipulated? He would need to possess one of these beings to learn the secret.

"We might be willing to help you lobby for representation in the Senate," he said at last, "but the process could require standard years or even decades, and I'm not convinced you have the patience for it."

Qayhuk's wide nostrils flared. "What's a decade when we have been patient for a century? Are we not sentients? Or are we required to *embrace* the conditions along with accepting them?"

Damask shook his head. "No one is asking you to applaud the arrangement."

Qayhuk's expression softened somewhat. "Then we have an accord?"

"We will draw up a contract," Damask said. "In the meantime, I want some assurance that I can call on you for a personal favor should the need arise."

Qayhuk stared at him. "A personal favor? Of what sort?"

Damask showed the palms of his hands. "Of whatever sort I require, Secretary."

The Yinchorri and his brethren traded uncertain glances, but Qayhuk ultimately nodded in agreement. "Done, Magister."

"A favor?" Hill asked as the Yinchorri were being seen out.

"Nothing more than a test," Damask told him.

Next to be admitted for audience were two Gran; the larger of the pair, a Republic Senator named Pax Teem, represented the Gran Protectorate. Teem had scarcely taken a seat when he said, "Promise me, Magister Damask, that you haven't entered into a deal with Gardulla."

"Our dealings with the Hutts," Hill said, "are no less confidential than our dealings with you, Senator Teem."

The Gran's trio of stalked eyes twitched in anger. "Rumors abound of Gardulla's plans to refurbish the Podrace course on Tatooine and enter into direct competition with Malastare."

Damask regarded him blankly. "Surely you haven't come all this way to hear me address rumors."

Teem worked his big jaw. "Promises were made, Magister."

"And fulfilled," Damask said; then, in a calmer voice, he added, "As a means of offsetting losses in revenue derived from Podracing, the cost of Malastare's fuel exports could be raised."

The Gran ruminated. "That sounds more like a possibility than a guarantee."

Damask shrugged. "We will take it up with the steerage committee. But for now, consider it a starting point for discussion." Reclining in the chair, he appraised Teem before saying, "What else is troubling you, Senator?"

"The favoritism you show to the Trade Federation."

"We merely helped them secure full representation in the Senate," Hill answered.

Teem grew strident. "The directorate was doing perfectly well for itself without full representation. And in exchange for what— surrendering some of the shipping monopoly they enjoyed in the Outer Rim?"

"What's fair is fair," Hill said evenly.

Teem gave him a scathing glance. "Fairness has no part in it. You're interested only in having the directorate do your bidding on Coruscant." Abruptly, he got to his big feet and ground his square teeth. "Even a rate hike for Malastare's fuel will profit Damask Holdings and the Trade Federation more than it will me!"

The Gran showed the Muuns his back and began to stamp toward the door, leaving his aide to stir in confusion for a moment, before he, too, rose and hurried out.

Hill's mouth was open in surprise. "He can't—"

"Let him go," Damask said.

The elder Muun compressed already thin lips. "If we're to benefit from the power they wield in the Senate, we'll need to find some way to placate them, Hego."

"I disagree," Damask said. "We need to find a way to show Teem that he is expendable."

By the time the guards had ushered in the quartet of Gossams who managed Subtext Mining, his ire had risen so high in his throat he could taste it. Typical of their diminutive species, the three saurians had reverse-articulated legs, fish-shaped heads, and long necks Damask knew he could snap with two fingers—and perhaps would, for how they had double-crossed Tenebrous.

"We were stunned to receive your invitation, Magister," Subtext's chief operating officer said. "We had no idea we were even on your scanners."

Damask smiled thinly. "We keep a close watch on galactic events. I trust you've been enjoying our food and entertainment?"

"More than you know, Magister," the chief Gossam said with a meaningful laugh. "Or perhaps more than we care to admit."

Damask forced a kindred laugh. "More than I know . . . That's very funny indeed." He broke off laughing to add, "Allow us to show you how we execute some of the inner workings of the Gathering."

The Gossams looked at one another in surprise before their leader said, "We'd be honored."

Damask stood and nodded to four of the Sun Guards, who fell in alongside the Gossams as he, Hill, and two other Muuns led them to a bank of ancient turbolift cars.

"All the real action takes place below," Damask said, setting the car in motion with a wave of his hand.

In silence they descended two levels, and when the car's doors parted, they filed into a cavernous underground hall. Central to the dimly lighted space were several large square platforms that could be raised by means of hydraulic poles, operated by separate teams of sweating, snuffling snub-nosed Ugnaughts. One platform, burdened with a slag heap of metal, was just descending, to sounds of raucous cheering and wild applause entering through an opening in the towering ceiling. Secured by manacles and chains on an adjacent platform writhed a hissing, snarling, fanged beast the size of a bantha.

"We're directly beneath the central courtyard," Damask explained as the beast-laden platform was elevating. "Each cargo symbolizes an abhorrent aspect of the Republic—practices we all wish to see overturned."

By then the platform had been raised to the level of the courtyard. The crowd quieted for a moment, then, simultaneous with massive discharges of energy, erupted into ovation once more.

"Those discharges were the laser cannons doing their work," Damask said loudly enough to be heard as the platform dropped back into view, revealing that what had been the beast was now a smoking, foul-smelling husk of sinew and bone. He aimed a sinister smile at the Gossams. "It's all theater, you understand. Merriment for the masses."

"Obviously a real crowd-pleaser, Magister," one of the Gossams said, swallowing some of his words.

Damask spread his thin arms wide. "Then you must join in." Approaching, he nodded his chin toward one of the empty platforms, beside which the Sun Guards had positioned themselves. "Climb aboard."

The saurians stared at him.

"Go ahead," Damask said, without humor now. "Climb aboard."

Two of the guards brandished blasters.

The chief Gossam looked from one Muun to the next, terror widening his eyes. "Have we done something to displease you, Magister?"

"A good question," Damask said. "Have you?"

The chief Gossam didn't speak until all four had clambered up onto the platform. "Precisely how did we come to your notice?"

"A mutual friend brought you to our attention," Damask said. "A Bith named Rugess Nome. You recently supplied him with a survey report and a mining probe."

The platform began to rise and the Gossams extended their long necks in fear. "We can make this right!" one of them said in a pleading voice.

Damask eyed the ceiling. "Then be quick about it. The laser cannons fire automatically."

"Plasma!" the same one fairly shrieked. "An untapped reservoir of plasma! Enough to provide energy to a thousand worlds!"

Damask signaled one of the Ugnaughts to halt the platform's rise. "Where? On what world?"

"Naboo," the Gossam said; then louder: "Naboo!"

Hill elaborated, though unnecessarily. "Something of a hermit planet in the Mid Rim, and capital of the Chommell sector. Relatively close to Tatooine, in fact. Once a source for the veermoks we had cloned for use as game in the greel forests."

Damask allowed him to finish and looked up at the Gossams. "Who hired you to conduct a mining survey?"

"A faction in opposition to the monarchy, Magister."

"We swear it to be true," another said.

"This Naboo is ruled by a royal?" Damask asked.

"A King," the chief Gossam said. "His detractors wish to see the planet opened to galactic trade."

Damask paced away from the platform. He considered torturing the Gossams, to learn who had hired them to sabotage Tenebrous on Bal'demnic, but decided to leave that for another day, since the Bith was known to have had many adversaries. Turning finally, he ordered the Ugnaught to return the platform to the floor.

"This plasma reservoir is as enormous as you claim?" he demanded.

"Unique among known worlds," the leader said in relief as he and his comrades stood shivering in Damask's withering gaze.

Damask regarded them in silence, then swung to the commander of the Sun Guards. "Transport them to the most remote world you can find in the Tingel Arm, and make certain they remain there in the event I have further need of them."

Leaving his fellow Muuns to rest, Damask climbed the fort's eastern rampart for starrise. He was as weary as any of them but too dissatisfied with the outcome of the Gathering to find much comfort in sleep. On the chance that an untapped reservoir of plasma might be of interest to the disgruntled leadership of the Trade Federation—and ignoring for the moment the effect it could have on Malastare's energy exports—he had ordered Hill and the others to learn everything they could about the planet Naboo and its isolationist monarch.

Once the Gossams of Subtext Mining had been dealt with, Damask and the Muuns had devoted the rest of the evening to meeting with members of what they termed their steering committee, which was made up of select politicians, lobbyists, and industrialists; financiers representing Sestina, Aargau, and the Bank of the Core; elite members of the Order of the Canted Circle and the Trade Federation Directorate; and gifted ship designers, like Narro Sienar, whom Plagueis planned to support in his bid to become chief operating officer of Santhe/Sienar Technologies. The committee met periodically, though seldom on Sojourn, to assure the swift passage of corporate-friendly legislation; fix the price of such commodities as Tibanna gas, transparisteel, and starship fuel; and keep Senators in place on Coruscant as career diplomats, as a means of distancing them from what was really taking place outside the Core.

Not everyone agreed that the Muuns' strategy of "tactical astriction" was the best method for keeping the Republic off-balance and thus ripe for manipulation. But Damask had insisted that their common goal of oligarchy—government by a select few—would eventually be realized, even if attained as a result of actions and events few would observe, and about which some of the membership might never learn.

Starlight glinted from the hulls of the last of the departing ships. Damask took comfort in knowing that his guests believed they had taken part in something secretive and grand, and had been encouraged to execute campaigns that on the surface may have seemed informed by self-interest but were in fact bits of Sith business.

Movements in the symphony that was the Grand Plan—

Keening klaxons fractured the morning silence.

Damask's eyes narrowed and swept the surrounding forests for signs of disturbance. He had moved to the southernmost parapet when two Sun Guards hurried up the stairs in search of him.

"Magister, the eastern perimeter has been breached," one of them reported.

Outside the fort's walls, illumination was coming up and drone ships were beginning to meander through the treetops. Occasionally one of the imported beasts would lumber into the safe zone, touching off the alarms, but none of the remote cams were showing evidence of intrusion.

"It's possible that one of our guests may have overstayed his or her welcome," the second Sun Guard said. He stopped to listen to a message being relayed to his helmet earphones. "We think we have something." He looked at Damask. "Will you be all right, Magister, or should we wait with you?"

"Go," Damask told them. "But keep me informed."

Stretching out with his feelings, he began to scan the forest again. Someone was out there, but not in the area the guards were searching. He attended through the Force to the sound of movement in the trees. Had the Gran infiltrated an assassin? If so, had they found one clever enough to divert the Sun Guards into chasing an illusion? Damask and the other Muuns should have been the targets, but instead of moving *toward* the fort, the intruder was actually moving away from it.

He spent another long moment listening; then, like a wraith, he dashed down three flights of stone steps and out through the old gate into the waking forest, parting his cloak as he ran, his left hand on the hilt of the lightsaber. Lifting off in great numbers from their evening roosts and screeching in displeasure, the morning's earliest risers warned the rest that a hunter was on the loose. Of the most dangerous sort, Damask might have added: a hunter of sentients. In moments he was deep in a stand of old-growth greel trees well outside the security perimeter, when he sensed something that stopped him in mid-stride. Motionless, he drew inward in an effort to verify what he'd felt.

A Force-user!

A Jedi spy? he wondered.

They had tried repeatedly to penetrate Sojourn's defenses during previous Gatherings. But unless one had arrived in a ship designed and built by Darth Tenebrous, there would have been no way to reach the surface undetected. And yet someone had obviously succeeded in making it downside. Lifting his hand from the hilt of the lightsaber, Damask minimized his presence in the Force, surrendering his eminence and disappearing into the material world. Then he began to move deeper into the forest, winding his way through the trees, allowing the Jedi to stalk him even as he berated himself for having acted rashly. If it came to ambush, he would not be able to fight back and risk exposing himself as a Sith. He should have allowed the Sun Guards to deal with the intruder.

But why would a Jedi bother to trip the perimeter sensors only to retreat beyond their reach? They didn't make mistakes of that sort. And surely whoever was out there wouldn't have expected a Muun to respond, if for no other reason than Muuns didn't make mistakes of that sort. So what was this one after?

Ahead Damask heard the characteristic hiss and hum of a lightsaber, and saw the weapon's blade glowing in the mist. Emerging from behind a thick-boled tree, the wielder had the lightsaber in his right hand, angled toward the spongy ground.

A crimson blade in a crimson wood.

Instantly he called his own lightsaber to his left hand, igniting the blade as the figure in the mist revealed itself fully: a tall, thin, pink-skinned craniopod with large lidless eyes—

A Bith!

Tenebrous?

He faltered momentarily. No, that wasn't possible. But who, then? Tenebrous's offspring, perhaps—some spawn grown from his genetic material in a laboratory, since the species reproduced only in accordance with the dictates of a computer mating service. Was that why Tenebrous had declined to discuss midi-chlorians or ways of extending life? Because he had already found a way to create a Force-sensitive successor?

"I knew I could draw you out, Darth Plagueis," the Bith said.

Plagueis dropped all pretence and faced him squarely. "You're well trained. I sensed the Force in you, but not the dark side."

"I've Darth Tenebrous to thank for it."

"He made you in his image. You're a product of Bith science."

The Bith laughed harshly. "You're an old fool. He found and trained me."

Plagueis recalled the warning Tenebrous had nearly given voice to before he died. "He took you as an apprentice?"

"I am Darth Venamis."

"Darth?" Plagueis said with disgust. "We'll see about that."

"Your death will legitimize the title, Plagueis."

Plagueis cocked his head to the side. "Your Master left orders for you to kill me?"

The Bith nodded. "Even now he awaits my return."

"Awaits . . . ," Plagueis said. As astonishing as it was to learn that Tenebrous had trained a second apprentice, he had a surprise in store for Venamis. Inhaling, he said, "Tenebrous is dead."

Confusion showed in Venamis's eyes. "You wish it were so."

Plagueis held his lightsaber off to one side, parallel to the ground. "What's more, he died by my hand."

"Impossible."

Plagueis laughed with purpose. "How powerful can you be if you failed to sense the death of your Master? Even now, your thoughts fly in all directions."

Venamis raised his lightsaber over one shoulder. "In killing you I will avenge his death and become the Sith Lord he knew you could never be."

"The Sith he *wanted* me to be," Plagueis corrected. "But enough of this. You've come a long way to challenge me. Now make a worthy effort."

Venamis charged.

To Plagueis, lightsaber duels were tedious affairs, full of wasted emotion and needless acrobatics. Tenebrous, however, who had pronounced Plagueis a master of the art, had always enjoyed a good fight, and had clearly bequeathed that enthusiasm to his other trainee. For no sooner had the blades of their weapons clashed than Venamis began to bring the fight to him in unexpected ways, twirling his surprisingly limber body, tossing the lightsaber from hand to hand, mixing forms. At one point he leapt onto an overhanging greel branch and, when Plagueis severed it with a Force blow, hung suspended in the air—no mean feat in itself—and continued the fight, as if from high ground. Worse for Plagueis, Tenebrous had made Venamis an expert in Plagueis's style, and so the Bith could not only anticipate but counter Plagueis's every move.

In short order, Venamis penetrated his defenses, searing the side of Plagueis's neck.

The contest took them backward and forward through the trees, across narrow streams, and up onto piles of rocks that were the ruins of an ancient sentry post. Plagueis took a moment to wonder if anyone at the fort was observing the results of the contest, which, from afar, must have looked like lightning flashing through the forest's understory.

Realizing that the fight could go on indefinitely, he took himself out of his body and began working his material self like a marionette, no longer on the offensive, instigating attacks, but merely responding to Venamis's lunges and strikes. Gradually the Bith understood that something had changed—that what up until then had been a fight to the death seemed suddenly like a training exercise. Exasperated, he doubled his efforts, fighting harder, more desperately, putting more power into each maneuver and blow, and in the end surrendering his precision and accuracy.

At the height of Venamis's attack, Plagueis came back into himself with such fury that his lightsaber became a blinding rod. A two-handed upward swing launched from between his legs caught Venamis off guard. The blade didn't go deep enough to puncture the Bith's lung but scorched him from chest to chin. As his large, cleft head snapped backward in retreat, Plagueis brought his lightsaber straight down, tearing Venamis's weapon from his gloved hand and nearly taking off his long fingers, as well.

With a gesture of his other hand, Venamis called for his lightsaber, but Plagueis was a split second quicker, and the hilt shot into his own right hand. Sensing a storm of Force lightning building in the Bith, he crossed the two crimson blades in front of him and said: "Yield!"

Venamis froze, allowing the nascent storm to die away, and dropped to his knees in surrender as Sojourn's risen primary blazed at his back through the trees.

"I submit, Darth Plagueis. I accept that I must apprentice myself to you."

Plagueis deactivated Venamis's blade and hooked it to his belt. "You presume too much, Venamis. Around you I would always have to watch my back."

Venamis lifted his face. "Is it true, Master? Is Darth Tenebrous dead?"

"Dead, and deservedly so." He took a step toward Venamis. "The future of the Sith no longer hinges on physical prowess but on political cunning. The new Sith will rule less by brute force than by means of instilling *fear*."

"And what is to become of me, Master?" Venamis asked.

Plagueis studied him stonily. After a quick glance around, he snapped a yellow, horn-shaped blossom from a dangling vine and tossed it to the ground in front of Venamis. "Consume it."

Venamis's gaze went from the flower to Plagueis, and he let misgiving show on his face. "I know this plant. It will poison me."

"It will," Plagueis told him in a manner that held no sympathy. "But I will make certain you don't die."

7: THERE WHERE THEY USED TO STAND

In the depths of Aborah, Venamis hung suspended in a bacta tank, wireless sensors affixed to his narrow chest, neck, and fissured, hairless cranium.

"You may be Tenebrous's most important gift to me," Plagueis said as he watched the Bith's body bob in the thick therapeutic liquid.

"His brain continues to recuperate from the effects of the coma-bloom alkaloids," 11-4D remarked from the far side of the laboratory. "His physical condition, however, remains stable."

Plagueis kept his gaze on Venamis. The wound Venamis's lightsaber had inflicted to Plagueis's neck had healed, but the faint scar was a fresh reminder of his mortality. "That's good, because I'm not interested in his mind."

In salute, the droid's new appendages made a surgical slashing motion.

Blood analysis had revealed a high midi-chlorian count, which to Plagueis was further indication that a being could have great potential in the Force and yet still be inept. He wondered: was it Venamis he had felt through the Force after the murder of Tenebrous? A Jedi would have made for a more interesting experimental subject, but a Dark Side Adept was perhaps better suited to his purposes. And soon enough the adjacent bacta tank would contain a Force-resistant Yinchorri, as well.

Immediately following the contest on Sojourn, Plagueis had commanded members of the Sun Guard to locate the starship that had allowed Venamis to infiltrate the Hunters' Moon, then move it and the poisoned Bith to Aborah. Larsh Hill and the other Muuns had been apprised that an intruder had been captured and disposed of, but no more than that. An investigation of the ship had yielded data that might have surprised even Darth Tenebrous, who had provided the ship. It seemed that well before he had confronted Plagueis or learned of his Master's fate, Venamis himself had been scouting for potential apprentices. Plagueis could not help being impressed, though begrudgingly. The young Bith would have done well in Bane's era. Now, however, he was an anachronism, and by extension, Tenebrous also.

That Tenebrous had targeted him came as no shock to Plagueis. He and the Bith had reached an impasse decades earlier regarding execution of the Sith imperative. The product of one of the galaxy's most ancient civilizations, Tenebrous believed that victory could be achieved through a mating of the powers of the dark side and expert Bith science. With the aid of sophisticated computers and future-casting formulas, the varied beings of the galaxy could be provided for, and the Jedi Order would gradually dwindle and disappear. Tenebrous had tried to persuade Plagueis that the Force did not play games of chance with the galaxy; and that while the fated ascendancy of the dark side could be predicted, its rise could not be influenced or hurried by the Sith.

The Muuns believed in formulas and calculations as strongly as the Bith did, but Plagueis was not a fatalist. Convinced that Tenebrous's brilliant equations were missing an important factor, he had argued that future events—whether predicted by machines or glimpsed in visions—were often clouded and unreliable. More important, he had been raised to believe in the elimination of competitors, and viewed the Jedi as just that. The Order wasn't simply some rival corporation that could be secretly acquired; it had to be undermined, toppled, and dismantled. Deracinated. He had assumed that, given time, he would have been able to win Tenebrous over, but his former Master had obviously pronounced him unfit to don the mantle of Sith successor, and had looked elsewhere. The unbridled desires of sentients were a blessing to the Sith, for those desires birthed an abundance of zealous and audacious beings who could be used to further the cause. Plagueis had been instructed to be on the lookout for suitable beings, just as Tenebrous had been when he had discovered Venamis. Perhaps Tenebrous had regarded the sneak attack as beneficial, no matter the results. Had Venamis been victorious, he was deserving of the mantle; and if not, then Plagueis might come to accept the true nature of the Master–apprentice relationship.

An old story that had never made much sense to him.

But it did explain Tenebrous's curious behavior in the months and weeks preceding the events on Bal'demnic. It was impossible to know how long Venamis's attack had been in the planning, but Tenebrous, for all his cool detachment, had plainly worried over the decision. On Bal'demnic he had been distracted, and that inattention had cost him his life. But in those final moments, before he had fully grasped the role Plagueis had played, he had been on the verge of revealing the existence of Venamis. It made little difference now, and, in fact, Plagueis found the Bith's vacillation contemptible.

Like Plagueis, Tenebrous had obviously embraced the fact that Darth Bane's Rule of Two had expired. Precious few Sith Lords had honored it, in any case, and with good reason, as Plagueis saw it. The goals of the Grand Plan were revenge and the reacquisition of galactic power. But while most Sith Lords since Bane had in their own fashion helped to weaken the Republic, their efforts had owed less to selflessness and allegiance to the Rule than to weakness and incompetence. Driven to discharge Bane's imperative they might have been, and yet each had fallen prey to individual foibles and eccentricities, and so had failed to exact revenge on the the Jedi Order. Plagueis understood. He would never have been one to lay in wait or devote his reign merely to positioning a subsequent Sith Lord for success. Nor would he have been content to remain in Tenebrous's shadow as an apprentice had the Bith actually triumphed where others had failed.

How, in all his wisdom, had Tenebrous failed to grasp that *Plagueis* was the culmination of the millennium-long hunger for revenge? How had the Bith failed to grasp that destiny had called him?

In a rare moment of compliment, the Bith had even said as much.

In the same way that tectonic forces cause a boulder to plunge into a river, forever diverting its course, events give rise to individuals who, stepping into the current of the Force, alter the tide of history. You are such a one.

Was Plagueis now to believe that Tenebrous had also considered Venamis such a one?

If so, it demeaned him.

The data discovered aboard Venamis's starship failed to shed light on how old he'd been when Tenebrous found him, or reveal anything about his training. Set ways of training an apprentice were a thing of the past, regardless. Doctrine was for the Jedi. Where the Jedi courted power, the Sith lusted after it; where the Jedi believed they knew the truth, the Sith possessed it. Owned by the dark side, they ultimately *became* their knowledge.

For the past five hundred years, the Sith of the Bane line had eschewed selecting children as apprentices, finding it more advantageous to discover beings who had already been hardened or scarred by life.

Plagueis, though, had been an exception.

Muunilinst had not followed suit when, in the madness that was the Third Great Expansion, worlds of the Core and the Inner Rim had stretched out to settle and claim many of the planets surveyed and made available by the Colonization Act and the Planet Grant Amendment. The reason was simple: though the Muuns had wealth beyond the wildest dreams of many species and access to starships of the highest quality, they were unwilling to leave their holdings on Muunilinst unattended. Nor were they interested in colonization for its own sake—in spreading their seed—because the more Muuns the galaxy contained, the less wealth there would be to go around.

Eventually, though, autarky and isolationism ceded to a desire to make themselves essential to the galaxy, and the Muuns began to fund settlements established by other worlds, or by independent groups, self-exiled as often as not. And so colonies at the distal end of the Braxant Run became dependent on Muunilinst for support, borrowing against the promise of discovering rich veins of ore or precious metals. When, however, the purported treasures failed to materialize, or markets became saturated, resulting in lower prices, the careworn populations of those settlements found themselves hopelessly indebted to Muunilinst and were forced to accept direct oversight by the Muuns.

So it happened that Plagueis's clan father, Caar Damask, came to be administrator of the treasure world of Mygeeto.

Located in Muunilinst's own stellar neighborhood, and a fertile breeding ground for nova, artesian, and low-level Adegan crystals, Mygeeto—*Gem*, as it was known in the ancient Muun tongue—was also one of the least hospitable worlds the Muuns had acquired. Captive to snow and ice, the planet boasted few indigenous life-forms and was continually assailed by storms that mounded its surface into crystal spurs the size of mountains. Regardless, and at great expense, the Muuns had succeeded in constructing a few self-contained cities and storage vaults, powering them with energy derived from the crystals themselves. Even in the best of instances Mygeeto was a challenge to approach because of its asteroid ring, but the asteroids became secondary impediments once the InterGalactic Banking Clan assumed control of mining operations in the ice shelves and glaciers. Then even the Jedi were prohibited from visiting without prior authorization.

Already a member of long standing in the IBC, the elder Damask had accepted the assignment as a personal favor to Muunilinst's High Officer, Mals Tonith, but more in the hope of advancing a career that had stalled and kept him confined to middle management. Unrecognized for his genius and angry about it, Damask had left his primary wife and clanmates behind and had attempted to build if not a life then at least a career for himself on the remote ice world. Success in supervising the mining operations came in short order, but contentment, of any sort, proved elusive until the arrival—ten years after his own—of a lower-caste Muun female who would first become his assistant, then his codicil wife, in due course giving birth to a son they named Hego, after Caar's clan father.

His upbringing in a domed city in a perpetually frozen environment was in many ways the antithesis of the typical Muun childhood, and yet young Hego managed not only to endure but to prosper. His mother took what some considered to be an unhealthy interest in his development, recording every detail and encouraging him to share even his most furtive thoughts with her. She was especially interested in observing his interactions with playmates—of diverse species—which she was never at a loss to provide, interrogating him after every session about his feelings about this or that youngling. Even Caar found time enough from a demanding schedule to be a doting parent.

Hego was not yet five years old when he began to sense that he was somehow different. Not only was he more astute than his playmates, but he could often manipulate them, arousing laughter when he wished to, or just as often tears; comfort just as often as anxiety. He learned to read intentions and body language. When he sensed that someone didn't like him he would go out of his way to be generous, and when he sensed that someone liked him too much he would occasionally go out of his way to be difficult, as a means of testing the limits of the relationship. He divined tricks and deceits, and sometimes allowed himself to play the victim, the dupe, out of concern for arousing unwanted suspicion or being forced to reveal too much about his hidden talents.

As his abilities increased, other children became playthings rather than playmates, but with no loss of enjoyment on Hego's part. One afternoon a Muun youngster he had grown to dislike pushed his way past Hego in an effort to be first to reach a staircase that led down to the Damask home's lower-level courtyard. Grabbing his peer by the upper arm, Hego said, "If you're in such a rush to get downstairs, then jump out the window." Locking glances, Hego repeated the suggestion, and his victim took it to heart. Many questions were asked after the youngling's broken body was discovered in the courtyard, but Hego kept the truth from everyone but his mother. She made him go over his explanation in increasing detail, until finally saying, "I've long suspected that you have the gift your father and I share, and now I know it to be true. It's a strange, wondrous power, Hego, and you have it in abundance. Your father and I have spent our lives keeping our gifts a closely guarded secret, and I want your word that for the time being you will speak of it only to me or to him. Later in life this power will serve you well, but right now it must remain undisclosed."

Having lived a surreptitious life for so many years, Hego found the notion of sharing the secret only with his parents completely natural.

No one held him responsible for his playmate's plunge from the window, but, soon after, the steady stream of playmates began to dry up. Worse, his father began to grow distant—even while Hego found himself becoming more and more a part of Caar's world. He considered that his father might be lying about having the power, or had come to think of Hego as some kind of monster. And yet he observed his father employing his eldritch powers of persuasion and manipulation in business dealings.

Like Muunilinst, Mygeeto received many important visitors, and at times it struck Hego that, in lieu of his being able to explore the galaxy, the galaxy was coming to him. On several occasions, his father met with Jedi Knights and Padawans who came in search of Adegan crystals, which the Jedi Order used in the construction of training lightsabers. Hego had long since perfected his ability to mask his powers from others. Even without revealing his true nature to the Jedi he was able to sense in them a kind of like-minded power, though one that was clearly at cross purposes with his own. From early on he knew that he could never be one of them, and he began to abhor their visits, for reasons he couldn't grasp. Even more puzzling, he came to sense a power closer to his own in a Bith visitor named Rugess Nome. Nome wasn't a Jedi but a starship engineer, who arrived in a luminous vessel of his own design. Before long, however, Hego began to suspect that his mother was the reason for Nome's frequent visits. And the suspicion that there was something between them incited feelings of anger and jealousy in young Hego, and a kind of conflicted despondency in his father.

Hego had made up his mind to bring his power to bear on the intolerable situation when, during one of Nome's visits, he was summoned to his father's office, where Caar, his mother, and the Bith were waiting. Without looking at his wife, Caar had said, "You are of our blood, Hego, but we can no longer raise you as our progeny."

Hego had looked from his father to his mother in mounting distress, fearing the very words Caar added a moment later. With a nod toward Nome, he said, "In truth, and in ways that you will eventually come to understand, you belong to him."

A decade later, Hego would learn that while Caar had, in fact, done his best to keep his Force abilities to himself, he had come to the attention of Nome when the two had chanced to meet on High Port Space Center. Years would pass before Nome found Hego's mother, whom he had conscripted not as an apprentice—for she wasn't strong enough in the Force—but as a disciple, whose task it had been to romance Caar and bear the fruit of that seduction: a child whom Nome and Bith science predicted would be born strong in the Force. Hego's parents had safeguarded the secret until his power had begun to reveal itself. And then a deal had been brokered: Hego, in exchange for the realization of Caar Damask's lifelong dream of being accepted into the upper echelon of the InterGalactic Banking Clan.

Five years after the revelation in the office, Caar was recalled to Muunilinst to become director of the treasury branch of the IBC. Hego's mother vanished, never to be seen again by either husband or son. And Hego's apprenticeship to Sith Lord Darth Tenebrous commenced.

In addition to being widely respected as a savant engineer and starship designer, Rugess Nome headed a shadowy organization that over the decades had gathered intelligence on the dealings of nearly every criminal, smuggler, pirate, and potential terrorist who had left a mark on the galaxy. With young Hego masquerading as Nome's accountant, the two secret Sith had traveled widely, often conspiring with the galaxy's most notorious beings, and facilitating anarchy whenever possible.

We Sith are an unseen opposition, Tenebrous had told his young apprentice. *A phantom menace. Where the Sith once wore armor, we now wear cloaks. But the Force works through us all the more powerfully in our invisibility. For the present, the more covert we remain, the more influence we can have. Our revenge will be achieved not through subjugation but by contagion.*

As Tenebrous explained it, the Jedi had emerged strong from the war of a millennium earlier, and while Darth Bane and subsequent Sith Lords had done their best to disrupt the reborn Republic, they labored at a disadvantage. So eventually it was decided that the Sith should hide in plain sight, amassing wealth and knowledge, and securing contacts and alliances with groups that would one day form the basis of a galaxywide opposition to both the Republic and the revered Order that served it. By all accounts those early centuries had been challenging, watching the Jedi return to their eminent position. But the Sith had had the luxury of studying the Order from afar without the Jedi ever being aware that they had adversaries.

The rend that Tenebrous's Twi'lek Master had opened in the fabric of the Force had been felt by the Jedi, and already the Order was beginning to show signs of circumspection and languor. The Republic, too, had been similarly undermined, by encouraging corruption in the Senate and lawlessness in the Outer Rim systems, which had become the dumping grounds for the Core.

With the wretched of the galaxy being converted to the cause, the powerful would now need to be brought together, with Darth Plagueis as their leader, manipulating the actions of an important few to control the behavior of countless trillions.

8: VICTIMS OF THEIR OWN DEVICE

In training Venamis, Tenebrous had obviously believed that he was protecting the Grand Plan; Venamis, too, by keeping an eye on a handful of Forceful candidates he, or perhaps Tenebrous, had discovered. But now it fell to Plagueis to do something about those potential competitors, if for no other reason than to eliminate the possibility of another surprise attack.

Venamis's ship data banks contained information on six beings, but subsequent investigation by 11-4D revealed that one had died of natural causes, another was executed, and a third was killed in a cantina brawl. Two of the remaining three were unnamed, but Plagueis and 11-4D had succeeded in learning as much about them as Venamis knew, after cracking the complex code the Bith had used to safeguard the entries. How Venamis's candidates had escaped notice by the Jedi was something of a mystery, but one scarcely worth solving. Plagueis simply had to determine whether they posed a threat—to him or to the Grand Plan.

Muuns were seldom glimpsed quaffing Rywen's Reserve in exclusive tapcafs, sampling refined spice in members-only clubs, or challenging the house in marathon sabacc tournaments. HoloNet celebrity programs never showed them with Twi'lek dancers on their slender arms, or venturing into forests, seas or mountain ranges purely for sport or adventure.

But Plagueis was about to break with tradition, now that the first of Venamis's potential candidates had been traced to a casino in Lianna City, in the heart of the remote Tion Cluster.

Jowls quivering, limpid eyes reflecting concern, and flanked by Nikto security personnel, the pudgy Sullustan manager of Colliders Casino hurried across the carpeted lobby toward the concierge desk where Plagueis and 11-4D were waiting. A pair of broad-purpose utility arms—one of which concealed a laser weapon—substituted for the droid's normal surgical appendages, and Plagueis was attired in what most beings would assume was Banking Clan garb, though differently cut and paler green in color.

"Welcome, sir, welcome," the manager began in a flustered voice. "Colliders is honored to have you as a guest, though may I say that you are the first being from Muunilinst to have used the casino's public entrance. The private entrance—"

Plagueis raised a hand to cut him off. "I'm not here on bank business."

The Sullustan stared. "Then this isn't an impromptu audit?"

"I'm here regarding a private matter."

The manager cleared his throat and stood up straighter. "Then perhaps we could begin with your name."

"I am Hego Damask."

The Sullustan's jowls began to quiver again. "Magister Damask? Of Damask Holdings?"

Plagueis nodded.

"Forgive me for not recognizing you, sir. Were it not for your munificence, Colliders would be in bankruptcy. More to the point, Lianna City wouldn't be the hub it is today, and the pride of the Tion Cluster."

Plagueis smiled pleasantly. "Then if we might adjourn to your office . . ."

"Of course, of course." The Sullustan signaled the guards to form a phalanx, then waved courteously for Plagueis and 11-4D to follow. "After you, sir. Please."

A turbolift carried them directly into a large office that overlooked the casino's main gaming room, which was crowded with Mid and Outer Rim species patrons seated at tables and individual machines, or huddled around ovide and jubilee wheels and other gambling devices. The manager gestured Plagueis into an overstuffed chair and settled himself at a reflective desk. OneOne-FourDee stood quietly at Plagueis's side.

"You said something about a private matter, Magister Damask?"

Plagueis interlocked his hands. "It's my understanding that Colliders played host to a big winner a week ago."

The Sullustan gave his head a mournful shake. "Bad news travels fast, I see. But, yes, he nearly wiped us out. An uncanny run of luck."

"Are you certain it was luck?"

The Sullustan considered the question. "I think I understand what you're getting at, so allow me to explain. Species known to have telepathic abilities are barred from gambling at Colliders, as is the case at most casinos. In addition, we have always operated under the assumption that ninety-nine percent of beings strong in the Force belong to the Jedi Order, and that Jedi don't gamble. As regards the remaining one percent—those who may have fallen between the cracks, as it were—well, most of them are probably off somewhere doing good deeds or locked away in monasteries contemplating the mysteries of the universe."

"And the remainder?"

The Sullustan planted his elbows on the desk and leaned forward. "On those rare occasions—and I emphasize *rare*—when we have suspected beings might be using the Force, we have demanded that they subject themselves to a blood test."

"Have you ever unmasked a Force-user?"

"Not in the twenty years I've been the administrator of this facility. Of course, in this business you hear stories. For example, there's one about a casino on Denon that employed a Forceful Iktotchi as a cooler—someone capable of breaking a gambler's winning streak. But I suspect the story is apocryphal. Here at Colliders we rely on the standard methods of making certain that the odds are always in our favor. Regardless, from time to time, someone proves an exception to the rule." He paused for a moment. "But I'll admit that I haven't seen a winning streak like this last one in years. It could take us months to recuperate."

"Did you demand a blood test?"

"As a matter of fact we did, Magister Damask. But our resident analyst said that the winner's blood didn't contain . . . well, whatever it would have contained if the player was a Force-user. I confess to having a poor understanding of the chemistry involved."

"I myself wish I understood more," Plagueis said. "Would you happen to have an image of the winner?"

The manager frowned. "I don't want to pry, but may I ask why this is of personal interest?"

Plagueis sniffed. "It's a tax matter."

The Sullustan cheered up. "Then by all means." His small fingers flew across the desk input pad, and in seconds the image of a Weequay appeared on a wall screen.

Plagueis was both disappointed and mystified. Data aboard Venamis's ship had identified the potential candidate as a Quarren. The being from Mon Calamari had been using the Force to break the banks of casinos on a dozen worlds, from Coruscant to Taris, from Nar Shaddaa to Carratos. Apparently the Weequay who had won big at Colliders had simply been lucky. Plagueis was about to say as much to 11-4D when an intercom chimed and the manager inserted a transceiver into his large ear.

"Not again!" he said. "All right, send a security team to watch him."

Plagueis waited for an explanation.

"Another winning streak," the Sullustan said. "A Kubaz this time!"

Plagueis stood up. "I wish to accompany the security team to the floor. I won't interfere. I'm simply curious about your methods for detecting cheaters."

"Of course," the manager said, distracted. "Maybe you'll spot something we've missed."

Plagueis reached the turbolift simultaneously with the arrival of two Bothans dressed in business suits and remained with them as they weaved their way through the ground-floor gaming area to one of the casino's Collider tables. Players drawn to the action were clustered three-deep around the table, making it impossible to catch so much as a glimpse of the lucky Kubaz until Plagueis and the Bothans reached the croupier's pit. Pressed in among females of various species who were attempting without success to get his attention, the dark-skinned, long-snouted male insectivore was seated across from the croupier, behind several tall stacks of credit chits. The game was called Collider because players placed bets on the types and spiraling paths of high-energy subatomic particles created as a result of collisions occurring within the accelerator table and the random firings of deviating electromagnets surrounding it. Due to the unpredictable nature of the collisions, the house enjoyed only a small advantage—where the accelerators weren't rigged—but the Kubaz was overcoming the odds by betting solely on the particle paths rather than the particle categories.

With the table accelerator humming to life and the Kubaz sliding some of his chits across the gambling grid, Plagueis stretched out cautiously with the Force, sensing intense concentration on the part of the Kubaz, and then an extraordinary surge of psychic energy. The Kubaz was using the Force—not to steer particles along certain paths but to dazzle the electromagnets and significantly reduce the number of paths the created particles were likely to take.

The gathered crowd applauded and roared another win, and the croupier pushed yet another stake of credit chits across the table, adding to the millions of credits the Kubaz had already won. In an effort to see deeper into the Kubaz, Plagueis opened himself to the Force again, and realized at once that the Kubaz had perceived the intrusion. Rising from the chair so suddenly that the females to either side of him were nearly knocked over, he ordered the croupier to cash him out. Without looking around him, he accepted the redeemable winnings chit and hurried off in the direction of the nearest bar. The Bothan security team fell in behind, after promising to alert Plagueis if the Kubaz attempted to leave the casino.

Returned to the upper-tier office where 11-4D was still waiting by the chair and the Sullustan manager was recovering from a flop sweat, Plagueis asked if Colliders maintained a database of players who had earned a reputation by breaking the banks of casinos, not only on Lianna but on other worlds where gambling was a popular pastime. On the wall screen moments later ran images of male and female Ongree, Askajians, Zabrak, Togrutas, Kel Dors, Gotals, and Niktos. Even a Clawdite shape-shifter.

"These are the most notorious of the lot," the manager was explaining when the image of a Neimoidian came on screen. "The ones the Gaming Authority suspects of having developed surefire methods of cheating. Any who show up at Colliders will be denied entrance."

Plagueis studied the final images and turned to the Sullustan. "You have been most helpful. We won't trouble you any further."

The turbolift had just lowered him and 11-4D to the casino level when he asked the droid whether it had noticed anything telling about the winners' lineup.

"I find it curious that they are all, shall I say, Muunoid bipeds of roughly the same physical construction, and almost identical in height. One-point-eight meters, to be precise." OneOne-FourDee looked at Plagueis. "Is it possible they are the same being?"

Plagueis smiled in satisfaction. "Perhaps a Clawdite?"

"I was about to suggest as much. However, it is my understanding that the Zolan reptomammalian shape-shifters are only rarely successful at perpetuating species camouflage for more than a brief time without experiencing intense discomfort. What's more, the lineup featured a Clawdite."

"What if it was a being taking the form of a Clawdite."

OneOne-FourDee gave a kind of start. "A Shi'ido, Magister. The candidate Venamis was monitoring is a skinshifter!"

Little was known about the reclusive, telepathic species from Laomon, save that they were capable of imitating a wide variety of sentient species. The most gifted were said to be able to mimic trees or even rocks. A powerful female Shi'ido named Belia Darzu had been a Sith Lord in the pre-Bane era, creating armies of technobeasts she controlled using dark side energy.

"That would explain the negative blood test results," 11-4D was saying.

Plagueis nodded. "I suspect that this Forceful Shi'ido has learned how to alter his blood. Or perhaps he merely clouded the mind of the analyst, compelling him to ignore the midi-chlorian count findings."

They had just stepped down into the gaming area when one of the Bothans hurried forward. "Magister Damask, I've just received word that the Kubaz is leaving."

"Did the Kubaz ask to have his winnings transferred to an account?"

The Bothan shook his head. "He preferred a credit chit. Many winners do, hoping to protect their privacy."

Plagueis thanked him and swung to the droid. "Hurry, FourDee. Before he gets too much of a lead on us."

They headed out into the glittering ecumenopolis, where cloud-scrapers and monads towered above them, pedestrian walkways were jammed with beings from up and down the Perlemian Trade Route, and the sky was crowded with traffic. And almost everywhere they looked, they saw the name Santhe—above the doorways to buildings, in advertisements that ran on giant wall screens, emblazoned on the sides of airspeeders and ships. The prominent family all but owned Lianna and had, for the past thirty years, wrested a controlling interest in one of Lianna's principal enterprises: Sienar Technologies—representatives from which had been guests at the recent Gathering on Sojourn.

Maintaining a reasonable distance, Plagueis and 11-4D trailed the Kubaz from walkway to busy walkway, then across one of the ornate bridges that spanned the Lona Cranith River into Lianna's sister city, Lola Curich. Past the headquarters of the Allied Tion Historical Society, Fronde's Airspeeders, a cantina called Thorip Norr . . . All the while the Kubaz had been glancing over his shoulder and was now increasing his pace as he neared the entrance to a pedestrian tunnel.

"The Shi'ido behaves as if he is aware of being followed," 11-4D said, photoreceptors fixed on their quarry.

"He'll attempt to lose us in the tunnel. We'd do better to wait for him to exit." Plagueis stopped to take a look around. "This way, FourDee."

Hurrying through buildings undercut by the tunnel, they emerged just where the pedestrian bypass debouched into a public square fronted by restaurants and boutique shops. OneOne-FourDee sharpened his optical receptors and trained them on the mouth of the tunnel. "Based on the rate of speed at which the Shi'ido was walking when he entered the tunnel, he should have exited by now."

"And indeed he has," Plagueis said. "Direct your attention to the hefty Askajian who is passing by the Aurodium Spoon."

The droid's photoreceptors rotated slightly. "The Shi'ido skinshifted inside the tunnel."

"I suspected he might."

"Would that I had a tool comparable to the Force, Magister."

They resumed their clandestine surveillance, shadowing the Askajian now, who led them on a convoluted tour of Lola Curich that ended at an automated InterGalactic Banking Clan kiosk alongside a PetVac franchise. Plagueis relied on 11-4D to furnish an update on the skin-shifter's activities.

"He has deposited the credit chit," the droid said. "But I'm unable to provide the account number. Even my macrovision pickups have their limitations."

Plagueis gestured in dismissal. "That won't be a problem."

They waited until the Shi'ido had exited the kiosk to dart inside. With the help of IBC codes Plagueis supplied, 11-4D soon acquired not only the account number but also the identity of the holder.

"Kerred Santhe the Second," the droid said.

Plagueis was speechless for a moment. Santhe had inherited principal ownership of Santhe/Sienar Technologies from the elder Kerred—who had the distinction of being Plagueis's first murder under the tutelage of Darth Tenebrous. But that a wealthy industrialist like Santhe should have need of a gambler's winnings made little sense. Unless the Shi'ido was somehow in debt to Santhe. Did the circuitous connection to Tenebrous explain how the skinshifter had first come to Venamis's attention?

"How well versed are you in Shi'ido physiology?" Plagueis asked 11-4D.

"Shi'ido subjects participated in longevity studies conducted on Obroa-skai. They possess a very flexible physiology and anatomy, with reconfigurable tendons and ligaments, and thin but dense skeletal features that allow them to support their fleshy mass and extensive reserves of bodily fluids."

"Are your sensors capable of determining when a Shi'ido is about to skinshift?"

"If the Shi'ido is in close proximity, yes."

"Then we haven't a moment to lose."

Catching up with their quarry as he was entering the public square, they overtook him and hurried into the pedestrian tunnel ahead of him. A hundred meters along, they found themselves in an unoccupied, dimly lighted stretch that Plagueis surmised the Shi'ido would make use of to transform, and they waited.

The Shi'ido did not disappoint him. And the moment he began to shift—from Askajian to what might have been either an Ongree or a Gotal—11-4D activated the laser weapon hidden in its right arm and fired a tightbeam into the base of the Shi'ido's brain.

The momentarily monstrous medley of species loosed a tormented scream and collapsed to the floor of the tunnel, squirming in pain. Moving quickly, 11-4D dragged him deeper into the dimness, where Plagueis positioned himself behind the skinshifter's grotesquely bulging cranium, uneven shoulders, and hunched back.

"Why did you transfer your winnings to Kerred Santhe?" Plagueis asked.

The Shi'ido's twisted mouth struggled to form a response. "Are you with the Gaming Authority?"

"You only wish. Again: Why Kerred Santhe?"

"Gambling debts," the Shi'ido slurred, as slaver dripped to the ground. "He's in debt to a couple of Black Sun Vigos and other lenders."

"Santhe is one of the galaxy's wealthiest beings," Plagueis pressed. "Why would he need what you've been stealing from casinos from here to Coruscant?"

"He's *millions* in debt. He hasn't stopped drinking and gambling since his father was assassinated."

Brilliantly assassinated, Plagueis thought. "Even so, Black Sun would never target him."

The Forceful Shi'ido craned his lumpy neck in an effort to get a look at his inquisitor. "He knows that. But the Vigos are threatening to go public with the information. A scandal could persuade Santhe/Sienar's board of directors to oust him as chief operating officer and appoint Narro Sienar as his replacement."

Plagueis laughed shortly in a surprised but satisfied way. "As well they should, skinshifter." He stood and began to move off. "You've been most helpful. You're free to go."

"You can't leave me like this," the Shi'ido begged.

Plagueis came to a halt and returned to his victim. "If you were funding terrorism or purchasing weapons, I might have allowed you to continue fleecing the casinos. But by fattening Black Sun's coffers and protecting the reputation of an enemy of one of my friends, you become my enemy, as well." He lowered his voice to a menacing growl. "Consider this: you have one last chance to use your Force talents to win big before your horrid image becomes the centerpiece of the cheaters database on every gambling world. I suggest you use your winnings wisely to make a new life for yourself where the Gaming Authority won't be able to find you, and I won't come looking for you."

To say that the planet Saleucami was the bright spot of its system meant merely that it alone, among half a dozen airless and desolate worlds, was capable of supporting life. Its own bright spots were not, as one might suspect, those areas that hadn't yet been victimized by meteor bombardments, but rather some of the impact craters the ceaseless celestial storm had left behind. For there the meteor strikes had conjured mineral-rich underground waters to the arid surface, turning the craters into caldera lakes, and the environs into oases of orbiculate flora.

Blue-skinned, yellow-eyed bipeds from the far side of the Core had been the first to colonize Saleucami, which meant "oasis" in their tongue, for the world was just that among those they had visited during the long journey from Wroona. Since then had come hearty groups of Weequay, Gran, and Twi'leks, in flight from conflicts or in search of hardscrabble isolation, and up to the tasks of farming the colorless ground for moisture and subsisting on tasteless root crops that withered in the midday heat and froze solid at night. Eventually the planet had given rise to a city and a spaceport, constructed in the shadow of one of the calderas nourished by geothermal energy.

Saleucami's more recent immigrants were of a different sort: young beings from worlds as distant as Glee Anselm and Arkania, dressed in tattered clothing and carrying their possessions on their backs. Drifters and searchers arriving in the battered transports and tramp freighters that served the Outer Rim systems. Male and female, though three times the latter to the former, distinguished by what some saw as a restless gaze and others the look of the lost. At first the native colonists didn't know what to make of these feckless wanderers, but gradually an entire industry had grown up to cater to their simple if peculiar needs for shelter, food, and surface transport into the wastelands, where enlightenment awaited, delivered at the outsized hands of a being who was rumored to possess prophetic powers.

Among them that day was a Muun wearing a simple hooded robe and well-worn boots. Where normally the mere sight of a Muun might have generated rumors that Saleucami was about to be acquired by the InterGalactic Banking Clan, the youthful horde the Munn had fallen in with barely gave him a second glance. Not when the crowd already included Ryn and Fosh and other exotic species; and not when Saleucami itself was viewed as little more than a stepping-stone to a greater world.

Plagueis had left 11-4D on Sy Myrth and completed the journey by freighter in the hope of maintaining as low a profile as possible. Background data on the prophet was scant, though Venamis had noted that she had been born in the Inner Rim and had arrived on Saleucami only three years earlier. Saleucami's colonists were willing to tolerate her presence, as well as the camp followers she attracted, provided they confined their assemblies to the wastelands.

Wedged in among forty others in an overpacked speeder bus, Plagueis let his gaze sweep across a forlorn landscape of volcanic mountains and the sheer walls of impact craters. In a cloudless sky of pale purple, blinding light flashed intermittently, and the monotony of the five-hour trip was relieved only by the occasional settlement or lone moisture farm. Journey's end was a relatively small caldera lake, from the shores of which rose a communal sprawl of tents and crude shelters, populated by the dreamy veterans of previous assemblies.

The Selected, as they were called.

Climbing from the speeder bus, Plagueis joined the crowd of newcomers in a short trek to a natural amphitheater, where pieces of meteorite provided seats for some. Others sat on their backpacks or spread out on the uneven ground. Shortly, the sound of whining engines announced the arrival of a caravan of hybridized landspeeders, many in pristine condition, though covered with dust and bleached of color by the harsh light. Nearly everyone in the amphitheater stood up and a wave of anticipation moved through the crowd, building to a fervor as an Iktotchi female stepped from one of the vehicles, encircled by disciples dressed as plainly as she was.

Plagueis couldn't think of a being more suited to Saleucami or cult status: a hairless biped with downward-curving horns and a prominent brow, skin hardened to withstand the violent winds of her homeworld, and a contentious countenance that belied an emotional nature. But, most important, possessed of proven precognitive ability.

Alone, she mounted a slab of stone that was the amphitheater's stage and, once the crowd had quieted, began to speak in a solemn voice.

"I have seen the coming darkness and the beings that will visit it upon the galaxy." She paused briefly to allow her words to be felt. "I have witnessed the collapse of the Republic, and I have beheld the Jedi Order spun into turmoil." She aimed a finger toward distant mountains. "On the horizon looms a galaxy-spanning war—a conflict between machines of alloy and machines of flesh, and the subsequent death of tens of millions of innocents."

She paced on the slab, almost as if speaking to herself. "I see worlds subjugated and worlds destroyed, and from the chaos a new order born, buttressed by ferocious weapons the likes of which haven't been seen in more than one thousand years. A galaxy brought under the yoke of a ruthless despot who serves the forces of entropy. And finally I have seen that only those hardened by this ineluctable truth can survive." She scanned the audience. "Only those of you who are willing to turn upon one another and profit by the misfortunes of others."

The crowd sat in stunned silence. Iktotchi were said to surrender some of their precognitive abilities the farther they traveled from their homeworld, but that wasn't always the case. And certainly not, Plagueis told himself, in the case of an Iktotchi who was strong in the Force. It was no wonder that Venamis had been keeping tabs on her.

"I have been sent to overturn your most cherished beliefs in a bright future, and to help you wage war on good intentions and the deception of pure ideas; to teach you how to accept the fact that even in the midst of this seemingly blessed era, this wink of the eye in sentient history, our baser instincts hold sway over us. I have been sent to counsel you that the Force itself will become as if it had been but a passing fancy among the self-deceived—an antiquated illusion that will turn to smoke on the cleansing fires of the new age."

She paused once more, and when she next spoke some of the edge had left her voice.

"What this reordered galaxy will need is beings who are fearless to be arrogant, self-serving, and driven to survive at all costs. Here, under my guidance, you will learn to let go of your old selves and find the strength to recast yourselves as beings of durasteel, through actions you might never have believed yourselves possible of performing.

"I am the pilot of your future."

She opened her arms to the crowd. "Look, each of you, to the ones to your left and right, and to those in front and behind . . ."

Plagueis did as instructed, meeting innocent gazes and angry ones, frightened looks and expressions of loss.

". . . and think of them as stepping-stones to your eventual escalation," the Iktotchi said. She showed her hands. "The touch from my hands will set the current flowing through you; it will trip the switch that will start your journey to transformation. Come to me if you wish to be selected."

Many in the crowd stood and began to press toward the stage, pushing others out of the way, fighting to be first to reach her. Plagueis took his time, finding a place at the end of a meandering line. While the notion of having a ready-made army of dark siders available to him was not without a certain appeal, the Iktotchi was spreading a message that had doomed the Sith of old, the Sith who preceded Bane's reformation, and had allowed internecine fighting to propel the Order into oblivion. The appropriate message should have been that they relinquish their need to feel in control of their own destinies and accept the enlightened leadership of a select few.

Saleucami's primary was low in the sky by the time Plagueis reached the stone slab and stood facing the Iktotchi. Her broad hands took hold of his, and she tightened her thick fingers around his narrow palms.

"A Muun of wealth and taste—the first who has come in search of me," she said.

"You were selected," Plagueis told her.

She held his gaze, and a sudden look of uncertainty came into her eyes, as if Plagueis had locked horns with her. "What?"

"You were selected—though without your knowledge. And so I needed to meet you in person."

She continued to stare at him. "That's not why you are here."

"Oh, but it is," Plagueis said.

She tried to withdraw her hands, but Plagueis now had firm hold of them. "That's not why *you* are here," she said, altering the emphasis. "You wear the darkness of the future. It is I who have sought you; I who should be your handmaiden."

"Unfortunately not," Plagueis whispered. "Your message is premature and dangerous to my cause."

"Then let me undo it! Let me do your bidding."

"You are about to."

A fire ignited in her eyes and her body went rigid as Plagueis began to trickle lightning into her. Her limbs trembled and her blood began to boil. Her hands grew hot and were close to being set aflame when he finally felt the light go out of her and she crumpled in his grasp. Askance, he saw one of the Iktotchi's Twi'lek disciples racing toward him, and he abruptly let go of her hands and stepped away from her spasming body.

"What happened?" the Twi'lek demanded as other disciples were rushing to the Iktotchi's aid. "What did you do to her?"

Plagueis made a calming gesture. "I did nothing," he said in a deep monotone. "She fainted."

The Twi'lek blinked and turned to his comrades. "He did nothing. She fainted."

"She's not breathing!" one of them said.

"Help her," Plagueis said in the same monotone.

"Help her," the Twi'lek said. "Help her!"

Plagueis stepped from the slab and began to walk against a sudden tide of frenzied beings toward one of the waiting speeder buses. Night was falling quickly. Behind him, shouts of disbelief rang out, echoing in the amphitheater. Panic was building. Beings were wringing their hands, jiggling their antennae and other appendages, walking in circles, mumbling to themselves.

He was the only one to board the speeder bus. Those he had arrived with and the Selected who had built shelters above the lakes were running into the dark, as if determined to lose themselves in the wastes.

In a starship similar in design to the one that had delivered Tenebrous and Plagueis to Bal'demnic—a Rugess Nome craft—Plagueis and 11-4D traveled to the Mid Rim world of Bedlam, near the argent pulsar of the same name. A leak point in realspace and a playground for purported transdimensional beings, the luminous cosmic phenomenon struck Plagueis as the perfect setting for the sanatorium to which the last of Venamis's potential apprentices—a Nautolan—had been confined for the past five years.

Uniformed Gamorrean guards met them at the towering front doors of the Bedlam Institution for the Criminally Demented and showed them to the office of the superintendent, where they were welcomed by an Ithorian, who listened closely but in obvious dismay to the purpose of Plagueis's surprise visit.

"Naat Lare has been named as a beneficiary in a will?"

Plagueis nodded. "A small inheritance. As chief executor I have been searching for him for some time."

The Ithorian's twin-lobed head swung back and forth and his long, bulbous-tipped fingers tapped a tattoo on the desktop. "I'm sorry for having to report that he is no longer with us."

"Dead?"

"Quite possibly. But what I meant to say is that he has disappeared."

"When?"

"Two months ago."

"Why was he originally confined to Bedlam?" Plagueis asked.

"He was remanded by authorities on Glee Anselm, but ultimately sentenced to serve out his time here, where he could be looked after."

"What was his crime?"

"Crimes, is more apt. He has a long history of sadomasochistic practices—most often performed on small animals—pyromania, petty crime, and intoxicant use. Typically we see this in beings who have been abused or had an unstable upbringing, but Naat Lare had a loving family and is very intelligent, despite having been expelled from countless schools."

Plagueis considered his next question carefully. "Is he dangerous?"

The Ithorian drummed his spatulate fingers again before responding. "At the risk of violating patient confidentiality, I would say *potentially* dangerous, as he has certain . . . let us say, *talents*, that transcend the ordinary."

"Did those talents figure into his escape?"

"Perhaps. Though we think he may have had help."

"From whom?"

"A Bith physician who took an interest in his case."

Plagueis leaned back in his chair. *Venamis?* "Have you contacted this physician?"

"We tried, but the information he furnished regarding his practice and place of residence was fraudulent."

"So he may not have been a physician."

The Ithorian's head bobbed on his curving neck. "Sadly. The Bith may have been an accomplice, of sorts."

"Do you have any idea where Naat Lare may have disappeared to?"

"Assuming he left Bedlam on his own, the possibilities are limited, given the dearth of starships that serve us. His first stop would have to have been either Felucia, Caluula, or Abraxin. We notified the authorities on those worlds. Unfortunately, we lack the budget to undertake an extensive search."

Plagueis cast 11-4D a meaningful glance and rose from the chair. "Your cooperation is greatly appreciated, Superintendent."

"We're confident that the Jedi will locate him, in any case," the Ithorian added as Plagueis and the droid were about to exit the office.

Plagueis swung back around. "The Jedi?"

"Because of Naat Lare's peculiar gifts, we felt obliged to contact the Order as soon as he was discovered to be missing. They graciously consented to assist us in the search." The Ithorian paused. "I could contact you if I learn something . . ."

Plagueis smiled. "I'll leave my contact information with your assistant."

He and 11-4D returned to the ship in silence. While the boarding ramp was lowering, Plagueis said, "Beings like Naat Lare don't remain hidden for long. Search the HoloNet and other sources for news of recent events on the three worlds the superintendent named, and apprise me of any accounts that capture your interest."

The ship had scarcely left Bedlam's atmosphere when 11-4D reported to the cockpit.

"A morsel from Abraxin, Magister," the droid began. "Buried among stories of intriguing or bizarre occurrences. Reports of the recent killings of dozens of marsh haunts in the swamps surrounding a Barabel settlement on the southern continent."

Large, nonsentient bipedal creatures, marsh haunts hunted in packs and were known to use the Force to flush their prey into the open.

"The superstitious among the Barabels believe that the Blight of Barabel is responsible for the rash of killings."

Plagueis slapped the palms of his hands on his thighs. "Our Nautolan has moved on from torturing household pets to murdering Forceful creatures. And I'm certain that the Jedi will reach the same conclusion."

"If they haven't already, sir."

Plagueis caressed his chin in thought. "This one has more than a hint of the dark side. It's no wonder Venamis was visiting him. Have the navicomputer plot a course for Abraxin, FourDee. We're returning to the Tion Cluster."

A standard day later they had made planetfall close to the area where the marsh haunt killings had been occurring. By design, the Barabel settlement was remote from any of the planet's spaceports, at the dubious edge of an extensive swamp, the twisting shorelines of which were palisaded by dense stands of water-rooted trees. On a finger of high ground a few pre-form buildings rose among clusters of stilted, thatched-roof homes linked to one another by paths that weaved through the dry-season grasses. The scaled, reptilian natives wore just enough clothing to be modest, and a sickly sweet smell of rotting vegetation hung in the motionless air. Abraxin had been strong in the dark side during Bane's lifetime, when it had been aligned with Lord Kaan's Brotherhood of Darkness, but Plagueis could sense that the power had waned significantly in the intervening centuries.

He and 11-4D hadn't walked a kilometer from the ship when they came upon a group of Barabels hauling a quartet of slaughtered marsh haunts from the legume-soup-colored water. The foul-smelling, bipedal carcasses had been slashed and stabbed, and had lost their red eyes to the delicate work of a vibroblade. On first glance one might have thought that the creatures had been decapitated, as well, what with their small heads set low between hunched shoulders. Plagueis found the Barabels to be no more pleasant smelling than the butchered haunts, but they knew enough Basic to answer his questions about the recent spate of killings.

"Memberz of the same hunt pack, these four," one of the reptilians explained, "and done in only last night."

Another, whose shedded tail was just beginning to regrow, added: "It'z the Blight." His clawed paw indicated the black eye sockets of one of the limp haunts. "This one believes that only the Blight would take the eyes."

Continuing on the shaded path that led into the settlement, Plagueis shrugged out of his cloak and folded it over his right forearm. A turn in the path revealed that he wasn't the only visitor improperly dressed for the climate. Up ahead two Jedi layered in the Order's traditional brown robes were haggling with a Barabel over the rental price for a water skimmer. Plagueis anchored himself in the material realm as the younger of the two Jedi—a Zabrak—swung slowly around to watch him and 11-4D as they passed.

Responding to the Jedi's look with a nod of his head, Plagueis kept walking, deviating from the path only when they had reached a small market building, from which the pair of Jedi and the Barabel skimmer pilot could still be observed. Familiar with Barabel, Plagueis eavesdropped on conversations among the merchants, who sat behind trays of dead fish, birds, and insects the swamp had provided. The marsh haunt killings were on everyone's mind, as were superstitions about the Blight. But the arrival of the Jedi was viewed as a good omen, in that the Order was venerated for having helped settle a clan dispute on Barab I almost a millennium earlier.

Plagueis drew 11-4D to the market entrance and instructed him to sharpen his photoreceptors on the Jedi, who were in the midst of concluding their business with the skimmer pilot. He then allowed himself to call deeply on the Force.

"Both of them reacted," the droid said. "The Cerean directed a gaze at the market, but didn't focus on you."

"Only because he has his feelers out for a Nautolan rather than a Muun."

A short time later, while Plagueis and 11-4D were wandering through the settlement, someone called out in Core-accented Basic: "We appear to be the only strangers in town."

The voice belonged to the rangy Cerean, who had emerged from an eatery bearing a flagon of liquid. Following him outside, the Zabrak set two mugs on a table that enjoyed a pool of shade.

"Join us, please," the Cerean said, nodding his tall conical head toward the table's spare chair.

Plagueis stepped toward the table but declined the chair.

"A locally produced beer," the Zabrak said, pouring from the flagon. "But I saw a bottle of Abraxin Brandy inside, if that's more to your liking."

"Thank you, but neither at the moment," Plagueis said. "Perhaps after working hours."

The Cerean motioned to himself. "I am Master Ni-Cada. And this is Padawan Lo Bukk. What brings you to Abraxin, citizen—"

"Micro-loans," Plagueis cut in before having to provide a name. "The Banking Clan is considering opening a branch of the Bank of Aargau here as a means of shoring up the local economy."

The Jedi traded enigmatic looks over the rims of the mugs.

"And what brings the Jedi to Abraxin, Master Ni-Cada? Not the shellfish, I take it."

"We're investigating the recent killings of marsh haunts," the Zabrak said, perhaps before his Master could prevent him.

"Ah, of course. My droid and I saw the bodies of four of the pitiful creatures when we entered the settlement."

The Cerean nodded gravely. "This so-called Blight will be over by tomorrow."

Plagueis adopted a look of pleasant surprise. "Wonderful news. There's nothing worse than superstition to cripple an economy. Enjoy your drinks, citizens."

OneOne-FourDee waited until he and Plagueis were well out of earshot of the Jedi to say: "Are we departing Abraxin, Magister?"

Plagueis shook his head. "Not before I find the Nautolan. I've no choice but to attempt to draw him out of hiding."

"But should you call on the Force, you're likely to attract the Jedi, as well."

"The risk may prove worthwhile."

They spent the afternoon eavesdropping on conversations about the locations of the killings, and determined that Naat Lare, whether he realized it or not, had been following a pattern. In the darkness at the edge of the settlement, at a spot along the bloodsucker-plagued shore of the dark swamp, some six kilometers from the market, Plagueis peeled out of his leggings, tunic, and bonnet, and slipped naked into the murky water. With an aquata breather clamped between his teeth, he propelled himself to the bottom. There, squatting in the muck, he opened himself fully to the Force and summoned the Nautolan, whose Force and olfactory senses might suggest that the mother of all marsh haunts was at hand for killing. A tattooed female Nautolan named Dossa had once been deemed suitable to serve Sith Lord Exar Kun; who knew what gifts Naat Lare might possess?

Surfacing to the riotous stridulations of insects, Plagueis leapt to the muddy shore, dressed, and perched himself in starlight on the slippery roots of a leafy tree. Shortly, he sensed an echo in the Force and saw ripples in the water some distance away. In the dim light, a blue-green nest of head-tresses broke the surface, followed by a pair of lidless maroon eyes. Then the amphibious sentient from Glee Anselm appeared, pulling himself ashore like some devolved beast and fixing his attention on Plagueis.

At the same time, Plagueis heard the sound of a water skimmer approaching rapidly from deeper in the swamp, and sensed the presence of the two Jedi.

"You're not Venamis," Naat Lare said in Basic, one hand on the hilt of a vibroblade strapped to his muscular thigh.

"He helped you escape Bedlam and sent you here as part of your training."

Naat Lare's hand closed on the hilt. "Who are you?"

Plagueis stood to his full height. "I am Venamis's Master."

The Nautolan looked confused, but only momentarily. Then he genuflected in the mud. "Lord," he said, lowering his head.

The sound of the skimmer was closer now, just around a bend in the swamp. "Two Jedi have tracked you."

Naat Lare's tresseled head swung to the sound of the skimmer.

Plagueis began to retreat into the shadows, and into mundane nature. "Prove yourself worthy to me and Venamis by killing them."

"Yes, my lord." The Nautolan sprang to his feet and dived into the slime-covered water.

Deep in the leafy trees Plagueis waited. The skimmer's motor went silent; then water surged and shouts of alarm and sudden flashes of light erupted in the night.

"Master!"

A harsh guttural sound rang out, followed by a scream of pain.

"Stand aside, Padawan."

"Master, it's—"

Another scream, higher in pitch.

"Don't! Don't!"

The thrum of an angered lightsaber, a howl of pain, and something heavy struck the water.

"Is he alive? Is he alive?"

Someone moaned.

"Wait . . ."

Waves broke on the rooted shore close to where Plagueis had concealed himself.

"Master?"

"It's done. He's dead."

9: UNTAPPED RESERVES

For more than fifty years Damask Holdings had occupied one of Harnaidan's most magnificent superspires. If not as soaring or massive as those belonging to the InterGalactic Banking Clan and its numerous subsidiaries, the building had the advantage of being constructed close to the largest of the city's naturally heated lakes, which had been incorporated into the property as an exclusive spa. The company's boardroom overlooked the lake and surrounding hot springs from an architectural setback on the two-hundredth floor, where Hego Damask, Larsh Hill, and the chief officers and executives of Damask Holdings convened for twice-weekly meetings. That day a one-quarter-life-sized holopresence stood at the center of the room's enormous circular holotable, addressing the gathered Muuns in Basic from the far-removed world of Naboo.

A human of medium height, the speaker had dark brown hair combed straight back from a sloping forehead, a thick and lengthy beard and mustache, and bright blue eyes set in a symmetrical if unremarkable face. He was attired in layers of richly colored clothing, which included a vest embroidered with Futhork calligraphy and a brocade overcloak that fell to his knees, revealing tall, shiny, low-heeled leather boots. His name was Ars Veruna, and although he didn't hold a position in Naboo's monarchical government, he was speaking for the current pretender to the throne, Bon Tapalo, and was likely to be appointed governor of the city of Theed in the event of Tapalo's election.

"Our campaign has been stalled by recent allegations from the leaders of some of the royal houses," Veruna was telling the gathered Muuns. "Something has to be done to recapture momentum—and quickly. Counterallegations made public by an unknown benefactor went a long way toward undoing the initial damage of the nobles' media releases, but a new wariness has gripped the electorate, strengthening the position of our provincial opponents."

"Audio cancellation," one of the Muuns said toward the holosystem's pickups. Secure in the knowledge that conversation around the table had been muted, he went on. "Are all the Naboo as hirsute and elaborately costumed as this Veruna?"

Larsh Hill replied. "They are traditionalists—tonsorially as well as politically. The style of dress and facial adornments pay homage to the regalia of Queen Elsinore den Tasia of Grizmallt, who dispatched an expeditionary fleet of humans to the planet some four thousand years ago, and to whom some Naboo claim to be able to trace an unbroken ancestry."

"They are not, after all, as furry as Wookiees," said another.

Hill grunted affirmatively. "In addition to humans, Naboo supports a hairless amphibious species known as the Gungans. Perhaps indigenous, perhaps not, but in no position to represent the planet in galactic dealings, in either case."

Seated with his back to the scenic view beyond the window wall, Plagueis studied the holoimage of Veruna. Generally he loathed politicians for their pretensions and ill-informed belief that wealth and influence conferred true power. But politicians were a necessary evil, and, if nothing else, Veruna burned with greed and ambition, which meant that he could be manipulated if necessary.

The missions to Lianna, Saleucami, and Abraxin were still fresh in his thoughts. On a philosophical level he understood why the generations of Sith Lords that had preceded him had trained apprentices, to whom they had bequeathed their knowledge of the dark side of the Force in anticipation of an eventual challenge for superiority. But with the Grand Plan culminating, it made no sense to challenge or kill beings of equal power unless they posed a threat to Plagueis's personal destiny. The Sith line would continue through him or not at all. Thus the need for a partner rather than an underling; a cohort to help put into play the final stages of the imperative. It had long been his belief that the dark side would provide that one when the time was right.

Plagueis hadn't anticipated having to turn his attention quite so suddenly to Naboo, but with the Trade Federation still grumbling about his support for the Outer Rim free-trade zones, and the Gran worried about losing Podrace revenues to Gardulla the Hutt, there were ample reasons for getting down to business. More important, Plagueis had long sought a planet that Damask Holdings and the steerage committee members could use as a base of operations. The possibility of having a future King at their beck and call was an added bonus, and even such unlikely players as Boss Cabra stood to profit from the Muuns' securing of Naboo.

It was during his absence from Muunilinst that Larsh Hill and some of the others had made overtures to the group vying for the throne of Naboo. In exchange for financial and logistical support in the upcoming election, Damask Holdings had asked for exclusive rights to transport plasma from the as-yet-untapped reservoir the Subtext Mining Group had recently discovered deep beneath the plateau that supported the capital city of Theed. Not every Naboo, however, was in favor of involving the planet in trade of the sort that would result from making plasma energy available, and a cadre of nobles had thrown their support behind Tapalo's chief rival for the monarchy.

Reactivating the audio feed, Plagueis asked: "What was the nature of the allegations made by the royal houses?"

"First, they leaked word of the mining survey we had performed," Veruna said, "but the revelation failed to have the intended effect, because several members of the electorate favor opening Naboo to galactic trade. Then, when they learned of our initial talks with Damask Holdings, the nobles accused us of selling Naboo to the highest bidder—to, and I'll quote—'a shady, extra-system cartel of ruthless criminals.'" The human paused for a moment. "You should understand, Magister, that our world has yet to overcome a long history of forbidding outside influence. The royal houses realize that trade is a sensitive issue and are now advocating for Naboo to oversee the transport of plasma to other worlds. But frankly we lack both the funds and the expertise to make that a reality."

"How were the nobles able to learn of our overtures to you?" Plagueis asked.

"We haven't been able to determine the source," Veruna said.

Plagueis muted the audio feed and turned to Hill. "We need to consider that someone close to our organization may be responsible for this 'leak.'"

Hill and some of the others nodded in agreement.

"The royal houses need to be informed that a leap into the business of transgalactic shipping is ill advised," Plagueis said when he had reactivated the audio feed. "Naboo will need funding, logistical support, and perhaps even Republic legislation, and it is precisely in those areas where Damask Holdings can serve as an intermediary. Actual funding would come from the InterGalactic Banking Clan, and other conglomerates would be involved in assisting Naboo in tapping the plasma and in the construction of a spaceport of sufficient size to handle the ships needed to transport it."

Veruna stroked his tapered beard. "Bon Tapalo will certainly want to address these points with the electorate."

Plagueis liked what he was hearing. "You mentioned certain counterallegations released by an unknown party."

"Yes, and I confess that we were as surprised by the information as anyone. It seems that our group is not the first to seek the advice and support of offworld interests. Roughly sixty standard years ago, at the height of a war between the Naboo and the Gungans, our monarch was killed, and it has now emerged that some members of the very same royal houses that oppose Tapalo struck a secret deal with a mercenary group to intervene in the war should the Naboo suffer further setbacks. Fortunately, the conflict was resolved without the need for outside help. In fact, as a result of that conflict, the monarchy has since been an elected rather than hereditary post."

"You say that the information came as a surprise," Plagueis continued.

Veruna nodded. "The information had to have been provided by a source within the opposition."

It now fell to Larsh Hill to mute the feed.

"Veruna is correct. We were able to trace the release of the information to the young son of one of the nobles. In the hope of avoiding a scandal that could divide the electorate, the head of the royal house has perpetuated a lie that the Tapalo group chanced on the information and made it public, when actually only someone with access to the family archives could have discovered it."

His interest piqued, Plagueis said, "What is the name of the royal family?"

"Palpatine."

"And the son?"

"Just that. He goes by the cognomen alone."

Plagueis leaned back in the chair to consider this, then said, "We may have found a potential ally—someone willing to keep us informed of the royals' plans for the election."

"An agent," Hill said. "An inside man, as it were."

Plagueis canceled the mute function. "We wish to visit Naboo in order to discuss these matters face-to-face."

Veruna was clearly surprised. "A public appearance by you would allow us to refute any allegations of secret collusion."

"Then all of us have something to gain."

Veruna bowed at the waist. "It will be our great honor to welcome you, Magister Damask."

Later it would be said by Naboo and Gungan alike that they couldn't recall a colder winter than the one that followed Hego Damask's autumnal visit to their world. The rivers and even the falls below Theed froze; the rolling plains and tall forests were blanketed three meters deep with snow; plasmic quakes rocked the Gallo Mountains and the Lake Country, the Holy Places and the undersea city of Otoh Gunga; and many of the egresses of the underwaterways that hollowed the planet were blocked by ice floes.

Tapalo and Veruna had insisted on sending one of Naboo's signature starships to transport the Muuns from Muunilinst, and the sleek Nubian had set down at Theed spaceport, a small facility that would have to be enlarged twentyfold if Naboo hoped to one day become a player in galactic commerce. The city itself struck Plagueis as the very antithesis of Harnaidan; where the capital of Muunilinst was vertical, angular, and austere, Theed was low, convex, and condensed, dominated by rotundas crowned with verdigris domes or flat roofs and tiered towers supported by round-topped archways. A river and several tributaries ran through the place, spanned by filigreed bridges and plunging in a series of high falls from an escarpment to verdant flatlands below.

A cortège of air skimmers carried the black-robed Muuns through streets better suited to pedestrian traffic to the interior courtyard of an ancient palace, where pretender to the throne Bon Tapalo, Veruna, and several other human advisers and would-be ministers of both sexes were on hand to welcome them. Draped in shimmersilk robes and propped by boots with high heels, the bearded and blond-haired Tapalo already carried himself like a regent—albeit of a second-rate world—remaining seated while Hego Damask and the rest of the Muuns were introduced, and flanked by guards dressed in flare-skirted uniforms and armed with vintage blasters. Veruna, on the other hand, immediately fell into step alongside Damask as the Muuns were being escorted into the central building of the complex.

"As I said when we spoke weeks back, Magister Damask, we are honored by your visit."

"And as I told you then, we all have something to gain." Damask turned slightly to look down at him. "Especially you, I suspect."

Veruna gestured to himself in question. "I—"

"Not now," Damask said softly. "When the time is right, you and I will confer privately."

Under a broad arch and through a lobby of polished stone they moved as a group, ultimately arriving at a second small courtyard where several tables had been set up, some overflowing with food and drink, and the largest reserved for the Muuns. No sooner were they seated than servants appeared and began serving food, including various meats that the Muuns politely declined. The practice of consuming food while conducting business was one that Damask had grown to tolerate in his dealings with humans, but in secret he detested it.

For many years he had detested the company of humans, as well. Barbaric meat eaters that they were, humans were a highly evolved species. Given their native intelligence and shrewd faculties, they deserved to be treated with the same deference Muuns were afforded. And yet many of the galaxy's sapient species considered themselves to be equal to humans, who had only themselves to blame. Unlike Muuns, humans had no compunctions about lowering themselves to the level of less advanced beings—the slow-witted, disadvantaged, needy, and pitiful—making a pretense of equality and demonstrating a willingness to work and sweat cheek-by-dewlaps alongside them. Instead of celebrating their superiority, they frequently allowed themselves to be dragged down into mediocrity. A Muun would no sooner accept a position as a starship pilot or a smuggler than he would a career diplomat or politician unless required to do so for the greater good of Muuns everywhere. Humans, though, could be found in every occupation. But what made them especially intriguing was their seeming intent to spread themselves to the far reaches of the galaxy, without any sense of control or planning, at whatever cost, and using up world after world in their insatiable quest, as if their diaspora from the Core reflected some sort of species imperative. More important, the Force seemed not only to allow their unchecked dissemination but to support it. In human hands, Damask suspected, rested the profane future of the galaxy.

Naboo blossom wine was still being poured when the Muuns made their pitch to the Tapalo group, employing the courtyard's holoprojector to provide a virtual portrait of what Theed and other nearby cities might look like ten years on. Funding by the IBC would be allocated to tapping the plasma reservoir beneath the plateau. At the same time, Outer Rim Construction and Assembly—one of Cabra's companies—would build an enormous refinery on the site of what was currently parkland, overlooking the Verdugo Plunge, housing the technology inside a triple-domed structure of Neo-Classical design. The Muuns detailed how the cliff walls could be stabilized and the tributaries of the Solleu River rerouted without disturbing the existing architecture or Theed's network of underground tunnels. Below the cliffs, the Trade Federation would enlarge Theed's spaceport, constructing a massive landing platform that would follow the natural curve of the escarpment, and open a second commercial port at Spinnaker.

By the time the pitch concluded, Tapalo looked stricken.

"Clearly you've put a good deal of thought into this," he said to Larsh Hill, "but is there no room in your plans for Naboo firms?"

"The last thing we want is to have these construction projects be seen as signs of foreign occupation," Hill said. "Our partners wish to work closely with Naboo's own Plasma Energy Engineering and the

Theed Space Vessel Engineering Corporation to make certain that the improvements are viewed as a cooperative effort. When the construction phases are completed, the refinery and the spaceports will be under your full control."

Some of the color returned to Tapalo's face. "The opposition contends that Naboo will be forever indebted to the Banking Clan and the Trade Federation."

"Only until the plasma begins to flow," Damask said. "I understand your trepidation. But the question you need to ask yourselves is whether you can win the crown without our help."

Separate conversations erupted at every table.

"I suppose so, Magister," Tapalo said, signaling for quiet. "But perhaps it's better to run the risk of defeat rather than ascend to the throne in dishonor."

"Dishonor?" Hill repeated in aggrieved disbelief. "Have we crossed the galaxy to be insulted?"

"Wait," Veruna said, coming to his feet and gesturing for calm. "We meant no insult to Damask Holdings." He turned to face Tapalo and his handpicked team of ministers and advisers. "Yes, we must be mindful of the concerns of the present electorate, but we shouldn't allow the fearful voices of a few to cripple our chance of joining the galactic community and raising the profile of the entire Chommell sector. I suggest we act boldly. To avoid being perceived as having bowed to pressure, I say we use this unprecedented visit by Damask Holdings to announce publicly that we and we alone are capable of entering into an arrangement with the Banking Clan and others that will allow Naboo to restructure its debt, achieve favored-world status with the Core, and provide for tax cuts, lower interest rates, and endless opportunities for employment, both on- and offworld." He clenched his fist for emphasis. "We must seize this moment before it disappears."

Slowly, Tapalo and the others began to nod in agreement.

"Do you have anything to add, Magister Damask?" Tapalo said at last.

Damask spread his hands. "Only that we couldn't have stated our case any better than Theed's future governor already has."

"Hear, hear," one of Tapalo's advisers said, lifting his goblet of wine in a toast to Veruna.

The rest followed suit, and drank.

And Damask thought: *One day soon, Veruna will be the King of Naboo.*

The plan called for the Muuns to spend the night in Theed and re-sume talks in the morning. With Hill and the others being shown to accommodations, Plagueis excused himself and struck out on foot for the university building on the opposite side of the city. His route took him through leafy parks, over two bridges, past towers and obelisks, and through the heart of Palace Plaza, with its pair of triumphal arches. Crowned by a statue of a human figure, the university's central rotunda was set back from one of the Solleu tributaries, dominating a precinct of stately buildings and public places. Plagueis located the student cen-ter and went to the registration desk, which was staffed by a young fair-haired female who stared openly at him as he approached.

"I'm looking for a student named Palpatine," he said in Basic.

"I know him," she said, nodding.

"Do you know where I might find him just now? Is he perhaps attending a class?"

She blew out her breath. "He comes and goes. Maybe I saw him at the Youth Program Building."

"Maybe."

"I think it was him."

Humans, Plagueis thought. "Can you direct me there?"

Her answer was a flimsi map, which Plagueis used to weave his way across campus to the headquarters of the Legislative Youth Program—an organization that oversaw Naboo's mandatory public service cur-ricula. Young people of both sexes buzzed about him, some scarcely noticing him, others going out of their way to get a closer look. At vari-ous times he asked after Palpatine, and was able to narrow his search to a square that fronted the columned library, where he eventually recog-nized Palpatine from holos Hill had provided, walking briskly through the square in the company of a human male nearly twice his age, black-haired and wearing more formal attire. Palpatine himself was dressed in slacks, short boots, and a loose-fitting shirt that was closed at the collar. Of average height, he had wavy red hair, a prominent nose, and a nar-row face that humans would probably have found friendly. His back was straight, his arms were long relative to the length of his torso, and he moved with an easy grace.

For some time Plagueis observed him from a distance, approaching only after Palpatine had parted company with the older man. Palpatine didn't spy him until Plagueis was only steps away, and when he did he turned sharply and began to walk in the opposite direction.

"Young human," Plagueis said, hastening his own pace. "A moment of your time." When Palpatine failed to acknowledge him, he lengthened his stride and called: "Palpatine."

Slowing to a reluctant halt, Palpatine looked over his shoulder. "How do you know my name?"

"I know more about you than just your name," Plagueis said, coming abreast of him.

Interest and caution mingled in Palpatine's blue eyes. "Normally I take exception to people claiming to know something about me, but since I know something about you, as well, I'll restrain myself."

From doing what? Plagueis wondered. "What is it you know about me?"

Palpatine exhaled in mild impatience. "You're Hego Damask. The president—no, the 'Magister'—of Damask Holdings. My father said that you were coming to Naboo to meet with Bon Tapalo. Your group is shoring up his bid for the throne."

"Did your father say that I might be coming to meet with you also?"

"Why would he? And what exactly is it you want with me?"

"I believe we have something in common."

"I very much doubt that."

"Perhaps all the more reason to become acquainted, then."

Palpatine glanced around him, as if searching for an escape.

"Who was the man you were speaking with earlier?" Plagueis asked.

Palpatine started to say something, then cut himself off and began again. "My mentor in the youth program. His name is Vidar Kim. He's an aide to Naboo's Republic Senator, and will likely succeed her." He looked hard at Plagueis. "And not a supporter of Tapalo."

Plagueis weighed the response. "Are you interested in politics beyond your participation in the Legislative Youth Program?"

"I'm not sure what I want to do after university."

"But you've some interest in politics."

"I didn't say that. I said I wasn't sure."

Plagueis nodded and looked up at the library building. "I'm a stranger to Theed. Would you consider showing me around?"

Palpatine's jaw dropped a bit. "Listen, I'm—"

"Just a short tour."

Engaging in small talk, they walked along the river in the direction of the concert hall and Queen Yram's Needle, then crossed a footbridge and began to angle toward the palace complex. Aside from providing Plagueis with holos of Palpatine, Larsh Hill hadn't been able offer much information regarding the youth's background. Though he lacked an appellation, Palpatine's father was a wealthy, influential royal, with a reputation for advocating for Naboo's continued independence and isolation. The family name was thought to be an ancient name of state among hereditary noble families, or perhaps a name borrowed from an ancient region of Naboo.

"Theed is a beautiful city," Plagueis remarked as they emerged from a narrow lane into the Palace Plaza.

"If you like museums," Palpatine said offhandedly.

"You've no interest in art?"

Palpatine looked at him sideways. "I enjoy art. But I'm more of a minimalist."

"In all things?"

"I wish Theed weren't so crowded. I wish the winters were milder. I wish our King had fewer advisers and ministers."

"That sounds like a political statement."

"It's simply my personal opinion."

"They're not mutually exclusive."

Palpatine stopped short. "What are you attempting to draw out of me?"

Plagueis indicated a nearby bench. When Palpatine finally relented and sat down, Plagueis said, "It has come to my attention that you were responsible for the release of some information that has aided Tapalo's campaign."

Genuine surprise blossomed on Palpatine's face. "How—"

Plagueis held up a hand. "That isn't important right now. What *is* is that you did so against what would have been the wishes of your father, your mentor, and some of the other royals."

"Are you planning to divulge this?"

Plagueis searched Palpatine's face. "What might happen if I did?"

"To begin with, my father would murder me."

"Literally?"

Palpatine exhaled forcefully. "He would disown me."

"It's true, then. You and your father find yourselves on opposite sides of the issues that animate the coming election."

Palpatine lowered his gaze to the ground. "It would be far stranger to find ourselves on the same side of any issue." He looked up again at Plagueis. "I want to see Naboo break with the past. I want us to belong to the greater galaxy. Is it wrong to want to play an important role in the history of the Republic?"

Plagueis rocked his head. "Governments rise and fall."

"You have a better idea of how to govern the galaxy?"

Plagueis allowed a laugh. "I'm just an old Muun who wouldn't know about that."

Seeing through him, Palpatine snorted. "Just how old are you?"

"In human years I would be well over one hundred."

Palpatine whistled. "I envy you that."

"Why?"

"All the things you've done and can still do."

"What would you do?"

"Everything," Palpatine said.

They got up from the bench and began to amble back toward the university complex. Plagueis submerged himself deeply in the Force to study Palpatine, but he was unable to glean very much. Humans were difficult to read in the easiest of cases, and Palpatine's mind was awash in conflict. *So much going on in that small brain,* Plagueis told himself. So much emotional current and self-interest. So unlike the predictable, focused intellects of the Outer Rim sentients, especially the hive-minded among them.

Palpatine stopped alongside a brightly colored, triple-finned landspeeder with a pointed nose and a repulsorlift engine that looked powerful enough to raise a loadlifter droid.

"This vehicle is yours?" Plagueis asked.

Pride shone in Palpatine's eyes. "A prototype patrol-grade Flash. I race competitively."

"Do you win?"

"Why else would I bother racing?" Climbing into the speeder, Palpatine centered himself at the controls.

"I have just the thing to adorn your rearview mirror," Plagueis said. From his breast pocket he fished a coin of pure aurodium dangling from a length of chain, and dropped it into the palm of Palpatine's hand. "It's an antique."

The young human appraised the gift. "I've never seen anything like it."

"It's yours."

Palpatine showed him a questioning look.

"Who knows, perhaps you'll go into banking one day," Plagueis said.

Palpatine laughed in a relaxed way. "Unlikely, Magister Damask."

"I suppose there are better ways to earn credits."

Palpatine shook his head. "Credits don't interest me."

"I'm beginning to wonder just what does."

Palpatine bit back whatever he was about to say.

"Palpatine, I wonder how you would feel about working with us—Damask Holdings, I mean."

Palpatine's thick eyebrows beetled. "In what capacity?"

"To be perfectly blunt, as a kind of spy." He went on before Palpatine could speak. "I won't say that you and I want the same things for Naboo, because clearly—and notwithstanding your feelings about the architecture—you hold your world dear. My group, however, is less interested in Naboo's government than it is in Naboo's plasma and what it will fetch on the open market."

Palpatine looked as if the plain truth was something new to him. "If you had phrased that any differently, I would have rejected your offer out of hand."

"Then you accept? You're willing to update us regarding whatever political machinations your father's group may have in the works?"

"Only if I can report directly to you."

Plagueis tried once more to see him in the Force. "Is that your wish?"

Palpatine returned a sober nod. "It is."

"Then by all means, you'll report exclusively to me," Plagueis said.

"I'll see to it that the necessary arrangements are made." He stepped away from the speeder as Palpatine powered it up.

Palpatine fell silent for a moment. "I could take you for a ride to-morrow," he said at last, above the whine of the engine. "If you have time, I mean. Show you some more of Theed and the outskirts."

"If I have your word you won't go too fast."

Palpatine smiled wickedly. "Only fast enough to keep it interesting."

10: THE CYCLE OF VIOLENCE

Flying a meter above the ground, Palpatine's agile speeder skimmed over the plains below Theed plateau, leaving long curving trails in the tall grasses. The day was bright and clear, the warm air abuzz with insects and strewn with pollen.

"Exhilarating," Plagueis said from the passenger-side bucket seat when Palpatine's foot had eased off the accelerator.

"Maybe I'll become a professional racer."

"The Naboo might expect more of the eldest son of House Palpatine."

"I ignore the expectations of others," Palpatine said without looking at him.

"Was the speeder a gift from your father?"

Palpatine glanced at him. "A bribe—but one I accepted."

"Does he approve of your racing?"

Palpatine made a harsh sound. "My father hasn't ridden with me for years."

"He doesn't know what he's missing."

"It has nothing to do with my talents." Palpatine turned slightly in the driver's seat. "When I was younger I was responsible for the deaths of two pedestrians. At the time, my father threatened never to allow me to fly, but he eventually relented."

"What made him change his mind?"

Palpatine swung forward. "I wore him down."

"I'm sorry," Plagueis said. "I didn't know."

Although, in fact, he did know. With help from 11-4D he had learned that Palpatine's troubled past had seen him bounced from one private school to the next, following incidents of petty crime and offenses that would have landed a commoner in a correctional facility. Time and again his father, who shared with his son a penchant for violence, had used his influence to rescue Palpatine and avoid the specter of family scandals. To Plagueis, however, the youth's transgressions were only further indication of his exceptionality. Here was a youth who had already risen above common morality and had judged himself unique enough to create an individual code of ethics.

Palpatine pointed to the distant tree line. "There are some ancient ruins in there, but that's Gungan territory."

"Have you had any dealings with them?"

"Personally, no. But I've seen the ones that come into Moenia to trade for goods."

"What are your thoughts about them?"

"Aside from the fact that they are long-eared, slimy-tongued primitives?"

"Aside from that, yes."

Palpatine shrugged. "I don't mind them, so long as they keep to their submerged cities and waterways."

"Not get in the way."

"Exactly. Humans deserve to have the upper hand here."

Plagueis could not restrain a smile. "There are many worlds in the galaxy where the matter of who has the upper hand, as it were, is in dispute."

"That's because most beings are afraid to take charge. Think what the Republic Senate might accomplish under the leadership of a strong being."

"I have given thought to that, Palpatine."

"What does the Senate do in response to each and every crisis? It dispatches the Jedi to restore order, and moves on without addressing the roots of the problem."

Plagueis found the boy's youthful ignorance entertaining. "The Jedi could rule the Republic if they wished," he said after a moment. "I suppose we should be grateful that the Order is dedicated to peace."

Palpatine shook his head. "I don't view it like that. I think that the

Jedi have dedicated themselves to limiting change. They wait for the Senate to tell them when and where to intervene, and what to fix, when in fact they could use the Force to impose their will on the entire galaxy, if they wanted. I'd have more respect for them if they did."

"Do you grant your father respect when he attempts to impose his will on you?"

Palpatine's grip on the steering yoke tightened. "That's different. The reason I don't respect him is because he's not half as intelligent as he thinks he is. If he could admit to his weaknesses, I could at least pity him."

Bringing the speeder to a sudden halt, he turned toward Plagueis once more, his face flushed with anger. Between them, dangling from the rearview mirror, was the coin Plagueis had given him.

Before long, I will own this human, Plagueis told himself.

"House Palpatine is wealthy," the youth went on, "but not nearly as wealthy as some of the other houses, and not nearly as influential with the King and the electorate, despite my father's attempts to take a leadership position with the royals. He lacks the political acumen needed to elevate our House to a position of true entitlement, and along with it the awareness to recognize that the time has come for Naboo to exploit its matchless resources and join the modern galaxy. Instead, he and his cronies, in complete and utter political ineptitude, want to keep us caged in the past."

"Does your mother share his views?"

Palpatine forced a laugh. "Only because she espouses no views of her own; only because he has made her subservient to him—as he has my well-behaved brothers and sisters, who treat me like an interloper and yet, to my father, represent all I can never be."

Plagueis considered the remarks in silence. "And yet you honor your House by going by its name."

Palpatine's expression softened. "For a time I thought about adopting the name of our distaff line. I haven't rejected the dynasty I was born into. I've rejected the name I was *given*. But not for the grandiose reasons some think. Just the opposite, actually. I'm certain that you, of all beings, understand as much."

There it was again, Plagueis thought: the deceptive cadence; the use of flattery, charm, and self-effacement as if rapier feints in a duel. The need to be seen as guileless, unassuming, empathetic. A youth with no desire to enter politics, and yet *born* for it.

Tenebrous had told him from the start that the Republic, with help from the Sith, would continue to descend into corruption and disorder, and that a time would come when it would have to rely on the strengths of an enlightened leader, capable of saving the lesser masses from being ruled by their unruly passions, jealousies, and desires. In the face of a common enemy, real or manufactured, they would set aside all their differences and embrace the leadership of anyone who promised a brighter future. Could this Palpatine, with Plagueis's help, be the one to bring about such a transformation?

Again he tried to see deeper into Palpatine, but without success. The psychic walls the youth had raised were impenetrable, which made the young human something rare indeed. Had Palpatine somehow learned to corral the Force within himself, as Plagueis had concealed his own powers as a youth?

"Of course I understand," he said finally.

"But . . . when you were young, did you question your motivations, especially when they ran counter to everyone else's?"

Plagueis held his challenging gaze. "I never asked why this or why that, what if this or what if that. I simply responded to my own determination."

Palpatine sat back in the speeder seat as if a great weight had been lifted from him.

"Some of us are required to do what others cannot," Plagueis added in a conspiratorial way.

Without a word, Palpatine nodded.

Plagueis had no need to delve any further into whatever traumas had given rise to Palpatine's cunning, secretive nature. He simply needed to know: *Does this young human have the Force?*

Two standard days later, on Malastare—a world of varied terrain that occupied a prime position on the Hydian Way—even the deafening clatter and nauseating odor of speeding Podracers wasn't enough to distract Plagueis from thinking about Palpatine. Damask Holdings had requested a meeting with Senator Pax Teem, and the leader of the Gran

Protectorate had provided the Muuns with box seats for the Phoebos Memorial Run. They had arrived directly from Naboo in the expectation of discussing business matters, but the Gran, Dugs, Xi Charrians, and nearly everyone else in the city of Pixelito were more interested in sport and betting.

"Have you picked a winner, Magister?" Pax Teem asked after two Podracers ripped past the viewing stands.

Lost in his thoughts about Naboo, Plagueis said, "I believe I have."

His conversations with Palpatine seemed to have opened some sort of emotional floodgates in the human. The Muuns had scarcely left Naboo behind when the first of several holocommuniqués was received from Palpatine, regarding the royals' latest plans for undermining Bon Tapalo's bid for the monarchy. Plagueis had listened attentively, but, in fact, Palpatine had precious little to offer. Since the release of the information about the royals' actions during the Gungan conflict, Palpatine's father had been conducting his meetings behind closed doors at the family estate, and had forbidden his son from so much as discussing the coming election. Tapalo's campaign, by contrast, was on the upswing, as a result of having announced a pending deal with the InterGalactic Banking Clan. The urgency of Palpatine's transmissions suggested that he had formed an attachment to Plagueis and was reaching out to him not only as a secret employer but also as a potential adviser. In Hego Damask, Palpatine saw the wealth and power he had long sought for House Palpatine. Confident that the young human would continue to be useful long after Damask Holdings' plans for Naboo had been realized, Plagueis did nothing to discourage the attachment.

"Why is it that we never see humans competing in the races?" he asked Teem after a moment.

The Gran waved his six-fingered hand in dismissal. "They haven't the talent for it. The favorite to win today is the Dug at the controls of the blue racer."

Plagueis tracked the Podracer for a moment. In the stands below him, thousands of Dugs—standing on all four appendages, on hind legs, or supported on arms only—were barking encouragement.

Plagueis found Malastare's high gravity oppressive, and the Gran more so. They had arrived on the planet a thousand years earlier as colonists, and had proceeded to beat the native Dugs into submission. The protectorate had since grown to overshadow the Gran homeworld, Kinyen, and was a powerful force within the Republic Senate, with wide-ranging influence in the Mid and Outer Rims.

Seated alongside Plagueis, Larsh Hill leaned forward to address Pax Teem. "Perhaps Gardulla will be able to entice humans to pilot Podracers in the course she is refurbishing on Tatooine."

Teem honked in irritation. "So it's true: you support the Hutt."

"It's simply business," Hill said.

But Teem was not appeased. "Is this the purpose of your visit—to reopen wounds that have not yet healed?"

"Yes," Plagueis said flatly.

Teem's trio of eyestalks swung to him. "I don't—"

"Don't compound the offense," Hill interrupted.

Teem feigned incomprehension.

"From whom did you learn of our interests on Naboo?" Plagueis asked.

The Gran looked to his comrades, but found no support in their abrupt silence.

"From whom?" Plagueis repeated.

A low of resignation escaped Teem. "We were approached by Subtext Mining, following the unexplained disappearance of some of its members—the ones I encountered on Sojourn, I suspect."

"They were in fine health when they left the Gathering," Hill said.

Teem nodded. "I'm certain they were."

"Why did Subtext approach you?" Plagueis said.

Teem hesitated, then said, "To inform us that you are involved in a deal for the plasma."

"Trusting that you would try to subvert our efforts by making them public," Hill said.

The Gran snorted. "First you strike a deal with Gardulla that favors Tatooine over Malastare, and now Naboo's plasma captures your attention, despite your offer to increase the cost of Malastare's energy exports. So why shouldn't we have alerted your opponents on Naboo, when you would have done the same?"

Plagueis waited for him to finish, and for a group of Podracers to pass; then he fixed his gaze on the assembled Gran. "You harm your-selves by attempting to sabotage us. The Protectorate could have prof-ited from Naboo, as the Trade Federation will, but no longer."

Pax Teem's huge feet slapped the floor of the private box. "We refuse to be demeaned! Again I remind you, Magister, that promises were made."

Plagueis smiled inwardly. It was true that Tenebrous had had plans for the Gran. At one time Pax Teem had been put forth as someone the Sith could move into the chancellorship and manipulate from a dis-tance into making mistakes that would bring the Republic to its knees. But Plagueis had now begun to explore other options.

"We are not without allies and cronies in the Senate," Teem was say-ing in a huff. "We can crush any legislation you wish to see passed, or arrange for your bills and no-bid contracts to languish in procedure for years. We'll put one of our own into the chancellorship. We'll deny the Trade Federation shipping rights on Kinyen and along the Trade Spine. We'll turn the Dugs loose on the Muuns." He glared at Plagueis. "You'll never get what you want, *Magister.*"

"On the contrary," Plagueis said, as he and the other Muuns were rising. "I already have what I want."

A rousing cheer went up from the stands as a Toong pilot overtook the favored Dug.

Plagueis turned to Hill as they were exiting the private box. "Order the Sun Guard to retrieve the miners we marooned in the Tingel Arm. Execute them and have their bodies dumped at the gates of Subtext Mining's corporate headquarters on Corellia."

A freshly minted *Capital*-class starship returned Plagueis and Hill to Naboo. Manufactured by Hoersch-Kessel and Gwori, the vessel was shaped like an elongated pod with a flat underbelly. A lateral wing tran-sected the convex hull aft, in which were housed arrays of powerful hyperwave transceivers. On board along with the chief executives of Damask Holdings were several high-ranking members of the Banking Clan, including the nephew of Chairman Tonith, all of them dressed in full IBC regalia.

A month had passed since Plagueis's initial visit, and in the interim he and Palpatine had spoken by holo on many occasions. The intelligence the human provided, though scant, had allowed Plagueis and Hill to keep one step ahead of Bon Tapalo's detractors, and as a result he continued to enjoy a slight margin with the electorate.

The Muun groups were approaching Naboo's spaceport immigration stations when they were intercepted by a contingent of armed security personal wearing leather jerkins, tall boots, and brimmed hats. Ushered into a glass-walled holding area equipped with not much more than benches and refresher units, the Muuns waited for over an hour until two Palace Guards entered, demanding to know which of them was Hego Damask.

After identifying himself and assuring Larsh Hill that he needn't worry, Plagueis followed the guards outside the terminal to a waiting round-nosed Gian speeder. A uniformed guard seated at the controls ordered Plagueis into the open-topped speeder's rear bench seat, where one of the escort personnel joined him. He didn't have a clue as to where he was being taken, but refused to give the guards the satisfaction of telling him that he would soon find out, or words to that effect. Instead he sat silently in the cushioned seat, careful not to register even the slightest surprise when the pilot began to steer the speeder away from Theed and out across the rolling verdant terrain Palpatine had taken him through.

"You may as well make yourself comfortable," his seatmate said at last. "We'll be traveling for about two hours."

Plagueis nodded in response and allowed himself to drift into a light trance, in preparation for whatever lay in wait for him at their destination. Gradually the undulating plains began to rise and a ridge of mountains came into view, limned against Naboo's brilliant blue sky. The speeder followed a broad river valley into hills lush with foliage, where herds of short-limbed shaaks grazed and frolicked. As the speeder gained altitude, the river narrowed and quickened, fed by waterfalls and crystalline lakes. Pure white clouds were beginning to form at the summits of the higher peaks when the speeder slewed across a vast stretch of meadow and came to a halt in front of a majestic home built in the style of Theed's fat domes and graceful towers. Two of the guards led him up a wide flight of stone stairs into a cool and dimly lighted foyer. Abandoned there, Plagueis wandered past wall hangings and plinthed statuary to the opposite end of the foyer, where round-topped, floor-to-ceiling windows overlooked a veranda and a large lake beyond. Seated at a table were an aristocratic-looking female human of middle age and a sulking male youth of Palpatine's age or younger, engaged in what appeared to be serious conversation. Touched by a breeze coming down off the slopes of the mountains, the surface of the water sparkled like Mygeeto gemstones. As Plagueis turned his back to the lake, his attention was drawn to a tapestry depicting the same family crest he had observed on the pocket of Palpatine's jacket, and featuring a trio of creatures: veermok, aiwha, and zalaaca.

He became aware of someone approaching him from behind, but didn't budge.

"Beautiful work, isn't it?" a basso-voiced human said in Basic.

Plagueis turned to find a tall man of patrician bearing standing at the threshold to a larger room.

"As is the view," Plagueis said, gesturing broadly toward the lake.

Dressed casually, though in fine taste, the silver-haired man advanced into the foyer. "I'm so glad you decided to accept my invitation to visit, Magister Damask."

"The presence of armed guards suggested an absence of choice, Cosinga Palpatine."

"They were for your protection, Magister."

"I never thought of Naboo as a dangerous world."

"For some it is," the elder Palpatine said. "But now that you are here, allow me to show you around."

The tour took them through a dozen rooms adorned with plush carpets and works of art. Stonework predominated, but the furniture was constructed of the galaxy's most prized hardwoods. By the time they stepped down onto the veranda the woman and the youth were nowhere to be seen, but the breeze had picked up and a storm was threatening. Cosinga Palpatine indicated an island in the distance, and the stately house that rose from the shore.

"That is Varykino," he explained. "A prize of the Lake Country. Once owned by the poet Omar Berenko, and presently occupied by the Naberrie family." He glanced at Plagueis. "Are you perhaps familiar with Berenko's masterwork, *The Defense of Naboo*?"

"Sadly, no."

"I'll arrange for you to be provided with a translation."

"A copy in the original text would be fine. I'm fluent in your language."

Testing him, Cosinga Palpatine switched to Naboo to say, "Yes, I understand you've become quite the expert on Naboo politics." Before Plagueis could respond, he waved his hand in front of a sensor that summoned three servants onto the veranda, each bearing trays of food and drink.

Plagueis exhaled in a fatigued way. More food, he thought; more olfactory stimulation for human noses.

They sat opposite each other at the same table the woman and youth had occupied earlier, and remained silent while the servants laid out the repast.

"Fresh fruits, vegetables, and farinaceous dishes," Palpatine said, indicating the spread. "No shaak or other meats."

Plagueis forced a smile. "Perhaps you'll take up a study of the Muun language next."

His host frowned, then sat back in his chair to allow the servants to heap food on his plates. He didn't begin eating until the servants had exited, and stopped after only a few mouthfuls and set his utensils down with finality.

"Let me tell you a short story about Bon Tapalo and Ars Veruna," he began, glowering at Plagueis. "Seventy years ago, some two decades after our own conflict with them, the Gungans found themselves embroiled in a war for survival with a mercenary army. Fortunately the Gungans prevailed, though not without many deaths and the loss of some of their swamp cities. Very little was ever made public regarding the cause of the war or the source of the mercenaries, but I'm willing to let you in on one of Naboo's darker secrets, in the hope that you'll learn something from it. The reason for the war was plasma, and the Houses that contributed most to funding the mercenary army were House Tapalo and House Veruna. When my grandfather learned of this he challenged Tapalo's father to a duel of honor, and eventually succumbed to the injuries Tapalo's blade inflicted." He gestured to a lawn that bordered the veranda. "The duel took place just there."

Plagueis glanced at the spot. "How utterly romantic and human."

Cosinga Palpatine's handsome face took on color. "Perhaps you fail to grasp the point of the story, Magister. Tapalo, Veruna, and the rest of that group of thugs are interested only in power and wealth, at whatever cost to Naboo. The discovery of a plasma reservoir below Theed was the worst thing that could have happened. And now they mean to exploit it for all it's worth, with the aid of influential beings like yourself. This is why Tapalo must never be king."

Plagueis pretended to consider it, then said, "It would appear that the electorate disagrees with you."

Palpatine nodded. "For now, yes. But we have plans for bringing the electorate back into line. Beginning with an announcement that the deal Tapalo struck with the Banking Clan has fallen through."

"I wasn't aware that it had," Plagueis said evenly.

Palpatine became angrier as he spoke. "Why do you think we stopped your party from entering Theed? We still wield enough power to keep you from setting foot on Naboo. And you may as well hear the rest of it, Magister. The Republic Senate has been apprised of Muunilinst's attempt to meddle with and destabilize the sovereignty of our world." When Plagueis didn't respond, he added, "The Naboo have a legend about six impenetrable gates that hold back chaos. House Palpatine is one of those gates, Damask."

"And we Muuns represent chaos," Plagueis said, without making it sound like a question.

Palpatine leaned forward and spoke in a calmer voice. "We are not opposed to having Naboo join the galactic community when the time is right. But not now, and not like this. Tapalo's promise of tax cuts and trade with the Core . . . Those are the very tactics the Republic deploys to seduce primitive worlds into surrendering their resources." He shook his head as anger took hold of him once more. "The Naboo admire philosophers, not *bankers* and deal brokers. Tapalo's election to the throne would lead to catastrophe."

"*The Defense of Naboo,*" Plagueis said. "The poem you mentioned."

"What about it?"

"What ever became of the author—Berenko?"

Cosinga Palpatine's eyes narrowed to slits. "He was abducted by assailants and never found." He rose halfway out of his chair to add, "Are you threatening me—here, in my own home?"

Plagueis made a placating gesture. "I thought we were discussing history. I only meant to ask what might happen if you are unsuccessful in . . . restraining chaos, and Tapalo wins despite your best efforts?"

"I've already told you that that will not happen. And here is why: because you're going to tell your friends in the Banking Clan and the Trade Federation that you've lost interest in Naboo. That you've found better company among the Hutts, slavers, and spicerunners of the Outer Rim." He paused momentarily. "You're a very long way from Muunilinst, Magister Damask. I strongly suggest that you reboard your ship and leave the Chommell sector as quickly and as quietly as possible, lest anyone fall victim to an untoward event."

Plagueis stared at the lake. "I take your meaning, Cosinga Palpatine," he said, without looking at him.

"And one more thing," Palpatine said, emboldened. "I don't know precisely why you've taken such a keen interest in my son, or he in you, but you're to have no further dealings with him."

Plagueis turned to him. "Your son has great potential."

"Potential I don't wish to see despoiled by your kind. We're moving him out of your reach, in any case."

"I'd been given to believe that the Naboo were an open people. But then, the Gungans probably wouldn't agree, either."

Palpatine stood up sharply. "Enough of this. Guard!" he said. And when three of them hurried in: "Get him out of my sight."

11: AVATAR OF MORTALITY

The planet Chandrila sponsored a monthlong retreat for members of the Legislative Youth Program. Once a year young beings from a host of worlds arrived to participate in mock Senate trials in and around Hanna City and to tour Chandrila's vast agricultural projects, wilderness areas, coral reefs, and garden parks. It was in Gladean Park—a game reserve outside coastal Hanna—that Plagueis paid young Palpatine an unannounced visit. But it was Plagueis who was surprised.

"I knew you would come, Magister," Palpatine said when Plagueis and 11-4D turned up at one of the game reserve's viewing blinds.

"How did you know?"

"I knew, that's all."

"And just how often are your premonitions correct?"

"Almost always."

"Curious," 11-4D remarked while Palpatine was hurrying away to excuse himself from the company of two friends.

Plagueis recognized the older male as Palpatine's mentor in the youth program, Vidar Kim, and sensed that the comely black-haired female was Kim's paramour. At the conclusion of Palpatine's animated explanation, Kim turned his head to show Plagueis a look of disapproval before moving off with his companion.

"Your mentor doesn't care much for me," he said when Palpatine returned.

Palpatine dismissed it. "He doesn't know you."

Standard weeks had passed without any communication between

the two of them. Judging by Palpatine's mood, he knew nothing about the forced meeting in the Lake Country, and yet he was agitated just the same, possibly in reaction to something Cosinga had done to monitor or foil his son's offworld holotransmissions. With Damask Holdings' secret agent silenced, the royals had gained ground. Despite Tapalo's denials that the deal with the Banking Clan had dissolved, the travel ban imposed on the Muuns had planted seeds of doubt among the electors, and the contest for the throne was becoming more heated with each passing day. Worse, the Banking Clan's interest in Naboo was beginning to wane.

"We'll have to keep this meeting brief," Plagueis told Palpatine while they were following an elevated pathway that connected the viewing blind to one of the park's rustic lodges. "Your father may have dispatched surveillance personnel."

Palpatine ridiculed the idea. "He is monitoring my offworld communiqués—that's why you haven't heard from me—but even he knows better than to have me watched."

"You underestimate him, Palpatine," Plagueis said, stopping in the middle of the pathway. "I spoke with him at Convergence."

Palpatine's mouth fell open. "The lake house? When? How—"

Plagueis made a soothing gesture and explained in great detail what had taken place. Concluding, he said, "He threatened, too, to place you out of reach."

All the while Plagueis spoke, Palpatine was storming through circles on the narrow path, shaking his head in anger and balling his fists. "He can't do this!" he snarled. "He hasn't the right! I won't allow it!"

Palpatine's fury buffeted Plagueis. Blossoms growing along the sides of the pathway folded in on themselves, and their pollinators began to buzz in agitation. FourDee reacted, as well, wobbling on its feet, as if in the grip of a powerful electromagnet. Had this human truly been born of flesh-and-blood parents? Plagueis asked himself. When, in fact, he seemed sprung from nature itself. Was the Force so strong in him that it had concealed *itself*?

Palpatine came to a sudden halt and whirled on Plagueis. "You have to help me!"

"How can I help you?" Plagueis asked. "He's your father."

"Tell me what to do! Tell me what you would do!"

Plagueis placed a hand on Palpatine's shoulder and began to walk slowly. "You could use this incident as a means of emancipating yourself."

Palpatine frowned. "Naboo doesn't honor that practice. I'm in his sway until I'm twenty-one years old."

"The legalities of emancipation don't interest me, and they shouldn't interest you. I speak of *freeing* yourself—of completing the act of re-creation you began when you rejected your given name."

"You mean disobey him?"

"If that's as far as you're willing to go. And without thought to consequences."

"I've wanted to . . ."

"Uncertainty is the first step toward self-determination," Plagueis said. "Courage comes next."

Palpatine shook his head, as if to clear it. "What would I do?"

"What do you want to do, Palpatine? If the choice was yours and yours alone."

The youth hesitated. "I don't want to live as ordinary beings live."

Plagueis regarded him. "Do you fancy yourself extraordinary?"

Palpatine seemed embarrassed by the question. "I only meant that I want to live an extraordinary life."

"Make no apologies for your desires. Extraordinary in what way?"

Palpatine averted his eyes.

"Why are you holding back? If you're going to dream, then dream large." Plagueis paused, then added, "You hinted that you had no interest in politics. Is that true?"

Palpatine firmed his lips. "Not entirely."

Plagueis came to a stop in the middle of the walkway. "How deep does your interest go? To what position do you aspire? Republic Senator? Monarch of Naboo? Supreme Chancellor of the Republic?"

Palpatine glanced at him. "You'll think less of me if I tell you."

"Now you underestimate me, as you do your father."

Palpatine took a breath and continued. "I want to be a force for change." His look hardened. "I want to *rule.*"

There! Plagueis thought. *He admits it! And who better than a human to wear the mask of power while an immortal Sith Lord rules in secret!*

"If that can't happen, if you can't rule, then what?"

Palpatine ground his teeth. "If not power, then *nothing*."

Plagueis smiled. "Suppose I said that I would be willing to be your ally in the quest."

At a sudden loss for words, Palpatine stared at him; then he managed to say, "What would you expect of me in return?"

"Nothing more than that you commit to your intent to free yourself. That you grant yourself the license to do whatever is necessary to realize your ambitions, at whatever risk to your alleged well-being and in full expectation of the solitude that will ensue."

They had not yet reached the lodge when Plagueis steered them into a gazebo that occupied the center of a luxuriant garden.

"I want to tell you something about my past," he began. "I was born and raised not on Muunilinst but on a world called Mygeeto, and not to my father's primary wife but to a second wife—what Muuns call a codicil partner. So I was a young adult before my father was finally returned to Muunilinst and I had my first taste of the planet that gave rise to my species. Owing to Muunilinst's regulations governing population growth, no Muun of less influence than my father would have been allowed to import a nonindigenous offspring, let alone a half-clan. And yet the members of my father's family regarded me as a trespasser, lacking proper legality and the social aplomb that comes to those born and raised on Muunilinst. For if there is anything the Muun detest more than wasteful spending it is nonconformity, and I had it in abundance.

"They were model citizens, my fair brothers and sisters: insular, self-important, identical in their thinking, thrifty to a fault, given to gossip, and it angered me deeply to have been accepted by the galaxy's downtrodden only to be rejected by this hive of self-serving parochial beings. Much to their further displeasure, they were forced to accept that I was a fully bonded clan member, entitled to the same share of my father's vast wealth as the rest of them. But as is the case with all members of the elite clans, I had to prove myself worthy of the status by preparing successful financial forecasts and allowing myself to be judged by the ruling elect.

"I passed my tests and trials, but soon after, my father took ill. On his deathbed I sought his advice concerning my predicament, and he told me that I should do whatever I needed to do, as my very survival was in jeopardy. He said that lesser minds needed guidance, and punishment on occasion, and that I shouldn't hesitate to use whatever means necessary to protect my interests; that I owed as much to myself, my species, to life itself."

Plagueis paused.

"The cause of his premature death was determined to be a rare genetic abnormality that affected the tertiary heart, and one that all of my siblings had inherited, but I—having been born to a different mother—had not. Panicked by the thought of early death, my siblings launched a galactic search for the finest geneticists credits could procure, and ultimately one surfaced, claiming knowledge of a curative procedure. And so they underwent treatment, each and every one of them—my clan mother included—in full confidence that they had dodged the family curse and could soon return to their primary passion, which was to have me legally ostracized from the family."

He looked hard at Palpatine.

"Little did they realize that *I* had hired the geneticist, and that the treatments he provided were as phony as his credentials. And so, in due course, they began to grow ill and die, each of them, as I watched from afar, gloating, even entertaining myself by feigning sadness at their funerals and indifference at the allocation rituals that transferred portions of their accumulated riches to me. Eventually I outlived all of them and inherited everything."

His amalgam of fact and fiction concluded, Plagueis stood tall and folded his thin arms across his chest. In turn, Palpatine trained his gaze on the gazebo's wooden floor. Plagueis detected the quiet whir of 11-4D's photoreceptors focusing on the youth.

"You think me a monster," he said when a long moment of silence had elapsed.

Palpatine raised his head and said, "You underestimate me, Magister."

Hanna City Spaceport was chaotic with the launch of starships returning youth program trainees to their near and distant homeworlds. In the central passenger cabin of the Naboo vessel *Jafan III*, Palpatine and a young trainee from Keren were comparing notes on their experiences during the previous week. On a track to becoming close friends despite their political differences, the pair had segued into discussing Naboo's upcoming election when a flight attendant interrupted them to say that Palpatine needed to return immediately to the spaceport terminal. The attendant didn't know who had requested his presence or why, but no sooner had he entered the connector than he recognized the stern countenance of one of the security guards his father had recently hired.

"Palpatine won't be reboarding," the guard told the attendant.

Confused, Palpatine demanded to know why he had been removed from the ship.

"Your father is here," the guard said after the attendant had reentered the starship. He pointed through the connector's transparisteel viewport to the far side of the field where sat a sleek starship bearing the crest of House Palpatine.

Palpatine blinked in surprise. "When did he arrive?"

"An hour ago. Your mother and siblings are also aboard."

"They didn't say anything to me about coming here."

"I wouldn't know about that," the guard said. "You've already cleared Chandrila customs, so we can proceed directly to the ship."

Palpatine glared at him. "Just discharging your orders, is that it?"

Unruffled, the guard shrugged his broad shoulders. "It's a job, kid. That's the long and short of it."

Surrendering to the inevitable but angered by the sudden change in plans, Palpatine trailed the guard through a maze of similar connectors to one that accessed the family starship. The elder Palpatine was waiting in the entry air lock.

"Why wasn't I informed of this beforehand?" Palpatine demanded.

His father nodded for the guard to seal the hatch. "Your mother and siblings are aft. I'll join you there once we've completed the jump." Maneuvering around Palpatine, he slipped into the cockpit. Palpatine turned to the air lock hatch and considered leaving while he had the chance, but ultimately thought better of it and went aft, though into not the main compartment but a smaller one that housed the communications suite. Strapped into an acceleration chair, he stewed through the launch and the jump to hyperspace. Unfastening himself when the ship was between worlds, he stood up and began to pace back and forth in the cabin, and was still in motion when his father entered a few minutes later.

"Our course is set for Chommell Minor."

Palpatine stopped to stare at him.

"For the foreseeable future, you're going to be residing with the Greejatus family. Clothes and other items we thought you'd like to have with you are already aboard." When Palpatine said nothing, he continued. "You and Janus got along well the last time we visited. A change of scene will do you good."

"You decided this without conferring with me?" Palpatine managed to ask at last. "What about my university courses? What about my obligations to the youth program?"

"That has all been arranged. You can partner with Janus in Chommell Minor's program."

"The Greejatus's hatred of nonhumans meets with your approval, then."

"Their chauvinism notwithstanding, I approve of them a lot more than I do your current friends."

Palpatine began shaking his head. "No. No."

His father's tone turned harsh. "This is for your own good."

Palpatine's nostrils flared. "Father of lies," he muttered. "How would you know what's good for me? Have you ever even cared? This is about my friendship with Hego Damask, isn't it?"

The elder Palpatine snorted in derision. "Is that what you think it is? Damask is merely using you as a means of securing information about our strategies for the election."

"Of course he is."

Taken aback momentarily, Cosinga said, "And yet you continue to . . . befriend him."

"What you consider the rape of Naboo, I consider to be an essential step forward, and Hego Damask a blessing. He's powerful, influential, and brilliant—more so than any of my professors. Head and shoulders above you or any of your royal confederates."

Cosinga's lip curled. "It begins to sound to me that this confrontation goes beyond mere political differences."

"You know it does. You're using the situation as an excuse to put me under your thumb again."

"Which wouldn't be necessary if you showed even the slightest ability to conduct yourself appropriately."

Palpatine sniffed. "My social infractions and trespasses. I refuse to go over old ground."

"You're easy on yourself, considering the shame you've nearly brought on us."

"I've brought no more shame on the family than you have."

"We're not discussing me," Cosinga said.

Palpatine threw up his hands. "All right. Leave me on Chommell Minor—but I won't remain there."

"I can see to it that you do."

"By assigning some of your musclemen to keep me in line? I'm a lot smarter than them, Father."

Cosinga made his lips a thin line. "After what you already did to counter our plans for Tapalo, there can be no hint of scandal. Have you no idea what's at stake for Naboo?"

"And for you," Palpatine said, with a sly smile. "The brother of your mistress becomes king, and you attain the lofty position you've always desired but don't deserve."

Cosinga flung his words with cruel abandon. "It will be so good to have you gone."

"Finally you admit as much."

Cosinga was suddenly crestfallen. "You're as much a mystery to me now as you were when you were young."

Palpatine's smile bloomed. "Only because you lack the ability to understand me fully."

"Grandiose, as ever."

"Grandiose, in *fact*, Father. You have no idea what I'm capable of. No one does."

Cosinga exhaled deeply. "I know that you are of my blood, because I had you tested, just to be certain. But in truth, I don't know where you came from—who or what you're actually descended from." He glared at Palpatine. "Yes, there it is: that glower I have been on the receiving end of for seventeen long years. As if you want to murder me. Murder has always been in your thoughts, hasn't it? You've merely been waiting for someone to grant you permission to act."

A darkness came over Palpatine's face. "I don't need anyone's permission."

"Precisely. You're an animal at heart."

"King of the beasts, Father," Palpatine said.

"I knew this day would come. I've known it since the first moment I tried to swaddle you, and you fought me with a strength that was too powerful for your size or age."

Palpatine looked out from beneath his quirked brows. "I was born mature, Father, fully grown, and you hated me for it, because you grasped that I was everything you can never be."

"Hated you more than you know," Cosinga said, allowing his ire to rise once more. "Enough to want to kill you from the start."

Palpatine stood his ground. "Then you had better do it now."

Cosinga took a step in Palpatine's direction, only to be hurled back against the bulkhead separating the communications room from the main cabin. A female voice from behind the closed hatch asked in distress, "What was that?"

Nursing an injured shoulder, Cosinga looked suddenly like a trapped animal, his eyes wide with surprise and fear. He made a move to strike the handplate that opened the hatch, but Palpatine thwarted his effort without raising a finger. Twisting violently around, Cosinga fell over one of the acceleration chairs, bloodying his face as it struck the arm-rest.

A pounding began on the hatch.

"Guards!" Cosinga shouted, but the word had barely left his lips when the bulkhead against which he was slouched buckled inward, heaving him face-first to the floor and driving the breath from him.

Palpatine stood rooted in place, his hands trembling in front of him and his face stricken. Something stirred behind his incandescent eyes. He heard the pounding on the hatch and whirled.

"Don't come in! Stay away from me!"

"What have you done?" It was his mother's voice, panicked. "What have you done?"

Cosinga pushed himself to his knees and began a terrified retreat, leaving smears of blood on the deck. But Palpatine was advancing on him now.

"If the Force birthed you, then I *curse* it!" Cosinga rasped. "I curse it!"

"As I do," Palpatine growled.

The hatch began to slide to, and he heard the voice of the guard who had escorted him from the *Jafan III*. "Stop!"

"Cosinga!" his mother screamed.

Palpatine pressed the palms of his hands to his head, then in eerie calm streaked to the hatch, pulled the surprised guard through the threshold, and tossed him clear across the cabin.

Raising his face to the ceiling, he shouted, "We're all in this now!"

They could have been torturers: Plagueis and 11-4D, leaning over an operating table on Aborah that supported Venamis, still in an induced coma and now anesthetized, as well; the droid's appendages holding bloodied scalpels, retractors, hemostats, and Plagueis, gowned and masked and with eyes closed, his shadow puddled on the floor by the theater lights, but in truth nowhere to be found in the mundane world. Folded deeply within the Force, instead, indifferent to the meticulous damage 11-4D had done to the Bith's internal organs, but focused on communicating his will directly to the Force's intermediaries, the droid monitoring cellular activity for signs that Plagueis's life-extending manipulations, his thought experiments, were having their intended effect.

A sudden current of intense dark side energy snaked through Plagueis. Stronger than any feeling he had experienced since the death of Darth Tenebrous, replete with flashes of past, present, and perhaps future events, the disturbance was powerful enough to snap him completely out of his trance. A rite performed; a confirmation conferred. Half expecting to find Venamis sitting upright on the table, he opened his eyes to the sight of 11-4D shuffling toward him from the operating theater's communication console.

Plagueis's mouth formed a question: "Hill?"

"No. The young human—Palpatine. A deep-space transmission."

Plagueis hurried to the device. They hadn't spoken since the reunion on Chandrila, but Plagueis had been waiting, wondering if his manipulations had borne fruit. If not, then he might have to take personal action to solidify the Naboo gambit. Placing himself in view of the holocams, he took a moment to appraise the noisy image onscreen, Palpatine's face bathed in the flashing lights of an instrument panel, something new in his eyes—color that hadn't been there previously. A glance at the comm board's coordinate readout; then:

"Where are you?"

"I'm not sure," Palpatine said in clear distraction, his gaze shifting to something off cam.

"You're in a starship."

Palpatine nodded, swallowed, and found his voice. "The family ship."

"Read aloud the navicomputer coordinates."

When he had, Plagueis looked to 11-4D for elaboration.

"Rimward of Exodeen along the Hydian Way," the droid said.

Plagueis absorbed it. "Contact the Sun Guard. Have them ready a ship and prepare yourself to accompany them."

"Yes, Magister."

Plagueis swung back to the monitor screen. "Are you capable of maintaining your present course?"

Palpatine leaned to one side. "The autopilot is engaged."

"Tell me what happened."

The human took a deep breath. "My father arrived unexpectedly on Chandrila. He had me taken from the youth program vessel and brought to our ship. My mother and siblings were already aboard. After the launch I learned that I was being taken to Chommell Minor. Just as you warned. We fell into an argument . . . then, I'm not sure what happened—"

"Tell me what happened," Plagueis demanded.

"I *killed* them," Palpatine snarled back. "I killed them—even the guards."

Plagueis restrained a smile, knowing now that Naboo would be his. *Over and done with. Now to reel him in further, and ensure his continued usefulness.*

"Did anyone on Chandrila observe you board the family ship?" he asked quickly.

"Only the guard—and he's dead. Everyone's *dead.*"

"We need to return you quietly and covertly to Chandrila. I'm sending help, my droid among them. Offer no explanations of what occurred—even if asked—but follow every command without question."

"You're not coming with them?" Palpatine asked, wide-eyed.

"I will see you soon enough, Palpatine."

"But the ship. The . . . *evidence.*"

"I'll make arrangements for the ship's disposal. No one will ever learn of this event, do you understand?"

Palpatine nodded. "I trust you."

Plagueis returned the nod. "And Palpatine: congratulations on becoming an emancipated being."

Sleek as the deep-sea creature on which it was modeled, the passenger ship *Quantum Collosus* plied the rarefied currents of hyperspace. One of the finest vessels of its type, the *QC* made weekly runs between Coruscant and Eriadu, reverting at several worlds along the Hydian Way to take on or discharge passengers. Draped in muted-green shimmersilk, Plagueis had boarded at Corellia, but had waited until the ship made the jump to lightspeed before riding a turbolift to the upper tier and announcing himself at the entryway to the private cabin he had secured for Palpatine.

"You said *soon*," Palpatine barked the moment the hatch had pocketed itself in the bulkhead. "A standard week is not *soon*."

Plagueis entered, removed his robe, and folded it over the back of a chair. "I had business to attend to." He glanced over his shoulder at Palpatine. "Was I simply supposed to drop everything in service to the predicament you've gotten yourself into?"

Speechless for a moment, Palpatine said, "Forgive me for having allowed myself to believe that we were in this together."

"Together? How so?"

"Am I not your agent on Naboo?"

Plagueis rocked his head from side to side. "You did provide us with some useful information."

Palpatine studied him uncertainly. "I did more than that, Magister, and you're well aware of it. You share as much responsibility for what happened as I do."

Plagueis seated himself and crossed one leg over the other knee. "Has it really been only a week? For you seem greatly changed. Were the Chandrilan and Naboo authorities so rough on you?"

Palpatine continued to stare at him. "As you promised, where there is no evidence, there is no crime. They went so far as to enlist the aid of salvagers and pirates in the search, but came up empty-handed." His look hardened. "But it's you who have changed. Despite the fact that you saw this event in the making."

Plagueis motioned to himself. "Did I suspect that you and your father might reach an impasse? Of course. It would have been obvious to anyone. But you seem to be implying that I somehow divined that the confrontation would end in violence."

Palpatine considered it, then snorted in derision. "You're lying. You may as well have forced my hand."

"What an odd way to put it," Plagueis said. "But since you've grasped the truth of it, I offer a confession. Yes, I deliberately goaded you."

"You came to Chandrila to make certain that my father's spies would see us together."

"Once more, correct. You make me proud of you."

Palpatine ignored the flattery. "You used me."

"There was no other way."

Palpatine shook his head in angry disbelief. "Was any of the story about your siblings true?"

"Some of it. But that scarcely matters now. You asked for my help and I provided it. Your father attempted to thwart you, and you acted of your own free will."

"And by killing him I've rid you of an opponent." Palpatine paused. "My father was right about you. You are a gangster."

"And you are free and wealthy," Plagueis said. "So what now, young human? I continue to have great hopes for you, but before I could tell you everything I needed you to be free."

"Free from what?"

"From fear of expressing your true nature."

Palpatine's expression darkened. "You know nothing of my true nature." He paced away from Plagueis, then stopped and turned to him. "You never asked about the killings."

"I've never been one for grim details," Plagueis said. "But if you need to unburden yourself, do so."

Palpatine raised his clawed hands. "I executed them with these! And with the power of my mind. I became a *storm,* Magister—a weapon strong enough to warp bulkheads and hurl bodies across cabinspaces. I was death itself!"

Plagueis sat tall in the chair, in genuine astonishment.

He could see Palpatine now in all his dark glory. Anger and murder had pulled down the walls he had raised perhaps since infancy to safeguard his secret. But there was no concealing it now: the Force was powerful in him! Bottled up for seventeen standard years, his innate power had finally burst forth and could never again be stoppered. All the years of repression, guiltless crimes, raw emotion bubbling forth, toxic to any who dared touch or taste it. But beneath his anger lurked a subtle enemy: apprehension. Newly reborn, he was at great risk. But only because he didn't realize just how powerful he was or how extraordinarily powerful he could become. He would need help to complete his self-destruction. He would need help rebuilding those walls, to keep from being discovered.

Oh, what a cautious taming he would require! Plagueis thought. But what an ally he might make. *What an ally!*

"I'm not sure I know what to think of this, Palpatine," he said at last. "Have you always had such powers?"

Color had drained from Palpatine's face, and his legs were shaking. "I've always known I was capable of summoning them."

Plagueis rose from the chair and approached him warily. "Here is where the path bifurcates, young human. Here and now you need to decide whether to disavow your power or to venture courageously and scrupulously into the depths of truth—no matter the consequences."

He resisted an urge to grasp Palpatine by the shoulder, and instead paced away from him. "You could devote the rest of your life to trying to make sense of this power, this gift," he said, without looking back. "Or you could consider a different option." He swung to face Palpatine. "It's a dark path into a trackless wilderness from which few return. Not without a guide, at any rate. But it is also the shortest, quickest route between today and tomorrow."

Plagueis realized that he was taking a great gamble, but there was no turning back from it. The dark side had brought them together, and it would be the will of the dark side that decided whether Palpatine became his apprentice.

"In your studies," he said carefully, "have you ever learned of the Sith?"

Palpatine blinked, as if preoccupied. "A Jedi sect, weren't they? The result of a kind of family feud."

"Yes, yes, in some ways just that. But more: the Sith are the prodigal offspring, destined to return and overthrow the Jedi."

Palpatine cut his eyes to Plagueis. "The Sith are considered to be evil."

"Evil?" Plagueis repeated. "What is that? Moments ago you defined yourself as a storm. You said you were death itself. Are you evil, then, or are you simply stronger and more awake than others? Who gives more shape to sentient history: the good, who adhere to the tried and true, or those who seek to rouse beings from their stupor and lead them to glory? A storm you are, but a much-needed one, to wash away the old and complacent and prune the galaxy of deadweight."

Palpatine's lip curled in anger and menace. "Is this the wisdom you offer—the tenets of some arcane cult?"

"The test of its value is whether you can live by it, Palpatine."

"If I had wanted that I would have forced my parents years ago to surrender me to the Jedi Order instead of transferring me from school to private school."

Plagueis planted his hands on his hips and laughed without mirth. "And of what possible use do you think a person of your nature would be to the Jedi Order? You're heartless, ambitious, arrogant, insidious, and without shame or empathy. More, you're a murderer." He held Palpatine's hooded gaze and watched the youth's hands clench in fists of rage. "Careful, boy," he said after a moment. "You are not the only being in this plush stateroom with the power to kill."

Palpatine's eyes opened wide and he took a step back. "I can sense it . . ."

Plagueis grew deliberately haughty. "What you sense is a fraction of what I can bring to bear."

Palpatine appeared suitably chastened. "Might I be of some use to the Sith?"

"Possibly," Plagueis said. "Perhaps even likely. But we would have to wait and see."

"Where are the Sith?"

Plagueis allowed a smile. "Just now there is only one. Unless, of course, it is your will to join me."

Palpatine nodded. "I do wish to join you."

"Then kneel before me and pledge that it is your will to join your destiny forever with the Order of the Sith Lords."

Palpatine stared at the floor, then genuflected, uttering, "It is my will to join my destiny forever with the Order of the Sith Lords."

Plagueis extended his left hand to touch him on the crown of the head. "Then it is done. From this day forward, the truth of you, now and forever more, will be *Sidious*."

When Palpatine stood, Plagueis took him by the shoulders.

"In time you will come to understand that you are one with the dark side of the Force, and that your power is beyond contradiction. But just now, and until I tell you differently, abiding submission is your only road to salvation."

12: SEDUCED BY THE DARK SIDE OF THE FORCE

The obedient orphan stood shivering in swirling snow. Around him rose ice pinnacles shaped like jagged teeth; a glacial wind howled through them. Plagueis stood nearby, flakes of snow and ice gyrating around him but never lighting on him, melting before they reached him. Unlike Sidious, who was outfitted in a thin enviro-suit, the Sith Lord was wearing only a cloak, narrow trousers, and a skullcap.

"It was on this world that I first became aware of my Force powers and dark impulses," he said, loudly enough to be heard over the wind. "Compared with temperate Muunilinst, Mygeeto is ruthless and uncompromising, but I learned to adapt to its harsh conditions, and before the age of eight I could venture out into the most violent storm dressed in less than you wear now. But I haven't brought you here to acquaint you with my past, Sidious. If you were of a species acclimatized to these conditions, I would have brought you instead to a desert world. If you were an aquatic being, I would have stranded you on dry land. The divide between the ways of the Force as practiced by the Sith and the Jedi has less to do with the distinction between darkness or the presence of light than between—in your case—naked cold and the presence of warmth. Between distress and comfort, entropy and predictability."

Plagueis paused to regard Sidious. "Your blood is close to frozen. Too much time here and you will die. That is what you will think at the beginning, when the dark side has sniffed you out and sidled up to you. You will think: *I will die; the dark side will kill me.* And it's true, you will die, but only to be reborn. You must take deeply into yourself the knowledge of what it means to be removed; you must feel it in the marrow of your bones, because it will ever be thus."

Plagueis laughed shortly. "Perhaps I sound like some professor of philosophy in that fine college of yours in Theed. But this isn't a lecture, nor should you think of it as physical conditioning. We need instead to prepare you for what awaits you should the dark side opt to take an interest in you. The comingling of fear and joy; of being humbled and empowered; of being escalated while at the same time used, as if an instrument. To be singled out and yet subsumed by an overarching grandness."

A predatory look came to his wan face as he advanced on Sidious.

"Now tell me again, apprentice. And in greater detail."

Once more Sidious allowed his memories to unfold, and he relived the crime—the event, as he had at last come to think of it. His father's limp and bloodied body. The smashed skulls of the bodyguards. His hands clenched around his mother's slender throat—but not really, only in his mind, strangling her with his thoughts. The lifeless forms of his siblings, slumped here and there . . . In telling and retelling it, in reliving it, he had finally gained a kind of authority over it, the ability to see the event merely for what it was, without emotion, without judgment. It was as if the event had occurred years rather than months earlier, and as if someone else had authored the crime. When that defining moment had come, a transforming power had curled up inside him, as dark as space without stars, born of hated and fear but one he could now draw upon.

"Very good," Plagueis said, after the recounted tale had forced itself between Sidious's blue and trembling lips. "I can feel your remove, and sense your increasing power." He continued to appraise Sidious while the snow whirled between them. "I can't have your will tempered by feelings of regret or compassion. You were brought into being to lead. Therefore you must see every living thing as nothing more than a tool to elevate you, to move you to your destined place. This is our galaxy, Sidious, our reality.

"In this pitiless place, your power is forged.

"Propelled by fear or hatred, even a Jedi can pass beyond the constraints of the Order's teachings and discover power of a more profound sort. But no Jedi who arrives at that place, who has risen above his or her allegiance to peace and justice, who kills in anger or out of desire, can lay real claim to the dark side of the Force. Their attempts to convince themselves that they fell to the dark side, or that the dark side compelled their actions, are nothing more than pitiful rationalizations. That is why the Sith embrace the dark from the start, focusing on the acquistion of power. We make no excuses. The actions of a Sith begin from the self and flow outward. We stalk the Force like hunters, rather than surrender like prey to its enigmatic whims."

"I understand, Master," Sidious managed in a stuttering voice.

Plagueis showed him a malevolent smile. "I once said as much to my Master, when in fact I understood nothing. I merely wanted to put an end to the pain." In a blur of motion, he tore open the front of Sidious's enviro-suit. "I am your torturer, Sidious. Soon you will make every effort to appease me, and with each lie you tell, with each attempt you make to reverse our roles, you will make yourself as shiny as an aurodium coin to the dark side.

"So appease me, Sidious. Tell me again how you killed them."

Sidious steadied himself on the scree slope, the jagged stones beneath his bloody palms, elbows and knees quivering, as if yearning to immerse themselves in the frigid waters of the crystalline blue lake at the base of the near sheer incline. A few meters above sat Plagueis, cross-legged atop a flat-topped outcropping, his back turned to Sidious and his gaze seemingly fixed on the blinding snowfields that blanketed the mountain's summit.

"If you don't already want to murder me, you will before I'm through with you," he was saying. "The urge to kill one's superior is intrinsic to the nature of our enterprise. My unassailable strength gives rise to your envy; my wisdom fuels your desire; my achievements incite your craving. Thus has it been for one thousand years, and so it must endure until I've guided you to parity. Then, Sidious, we must do our best to sabotage the dynamic Darth Bane set in motion, because we will need each other if we're to realize our ultimate goals. In the end there can be no secrets between us; no jealousy or mistrust. From us the future of the Sith will fountain, and the diverse beings of the galaxy will be better for it. Until then, however, you must strive; you must demonstrate your worthiness, not merely to me but to the dark side. You must take the hatred you feel for me and transform it into power—the power to overcome, to forbid anything from standing in your path, to surmount whatever obstacle the dark side designs to test you."

Scarcely listening, Sidious moved with utmost care, his hands and knees seeking firm purchase on the stones. For weeks Darth Plagueis had deprived him of sleep, food, and water. Now if only he could reach the Muun, his thirst would be slaked, his hunger sated, his contusions healed. Countless times the broad expanse of rock debris had slipped and he'd had to ride the slide almost to the shore of the lake, tumbling, surfing on his front and back, abrading his ruddy skin, bruising nearly every part of himself. Only to have to pick his way back to the top.

Seething in silence, he managed to scale a meter more of the slope, calling on the Force to ensure his balance, to render him weightless.

"Fool," Plagueis derided him. "Success doesn't come from summoning help from the Force, but from taking control of it and generating the power from within yourself." He sighed theatrically. "Still, I'm somewhat encouraged by the progress you've made. Mere centimeters from me now, almost within arm's reach. Soon I'll be able to feel your breath on my neck and perceive the heat of your rage—your desire to kill me, as if by doing so, you could lay claim to the authority I embody." He paused but didn't move, much less glance over his shoulder. "You want to strangle me, like you did your poor, misunderstood mother; tear me limb from limb as you did the bodyguards. Fair enough. But to do so you will have to make a greater effort, Apprentice."

Like a feline, Sidious leapt from the scree, his curled fingers aimed for Plagueis. But instead of vising themselves around the Muun's slender neck, his hands went through thin air and met each other, leaving him to collapse face-first atop the outcropping. Off to one side he heard his Master laugh in scorn. Either Plagueis had moved faster than

Sidious could discern or, worse yet, he had never been there to begin with.

"So easily tricked," Plagueis said, confirming the latter. "You waste my time. More of this and the dark side will never take an interest in you."

Sidious whirled, flinging himself at Plagueis, only to meet an irresistible force and be hurled backward to the frozen ground.

The Muun's shadow fell over him. Arms folded across his chest, Plagueis loomed.

"If you're to succeed in inhabiting both realms, Sidious—the profane world and that of the Force—you need to learn how to use guile to your advantage, and to recognize when others are employing it." Without extending a hand, Plagueis tugged him to his feet. "If you can survive a few more days without sustenance or rest, I may be inclined to teach you."

Clawing his way across the tundra, his body rashed with lightsaber burns, Sidious looked up at Plagueis, imploringly.

"How much longer, Master?"

Plagueis deactivated his weapon's crimson blade and scowled. "Perhaps a moment, perhaps an eternity. Stop thinking of the future, and anchor yourself in the present. A Sith apprentice is the antithesis of a Jedi youngling nurtured in the Temple, battling a floating remote with a training lightsaber. A Sith acquaints himself with pain from the start, and inflicts it, as well. A Sith goes for the throat, just as you did on your family's starship."

Sidious continued to gaze at him. "I meant, how much longer will it take me to learn?"

The Muun sized him up with a look. "Hard to tell. Humans are their own worst enemies. Your body isn't meant to withstand real punishment. It is easily injured and slow to heal. Your olfactory and tactile senses are relatively acute, but your auditory and visual senses are extremely limited."

"Have I no strengths, Master?"

Plagueis dropped to one knee in front of him. "You have the Force, apprentice, and the talent to lead. More, you have the bloodlust of a serial killer, though we need to hold that in reserve unless violence serves some extraordinary purpose. We are not butchers, Sidious, like some past Sith Lords. We are architects of the future."

Sidious swallowed and found his voice. "How long?"

Plagueis stood, reigniting the lightsaber as he did so. "Not a standard day sooner than a decade."

PART TWO:
Apprenticed To Power

54—52 BBY

13: RIDERS ON THE STORM

In mad pursuit of their prey and all but taking flight, the two Sith, Master and apprentice for eleven years now, bounded across the grassy terrain, their short capes snapping behind them, vibroblades clenched in their hands and bare forearms flecked with gore; blood caked in the human's long hair and dried on the Muun's hairless brow. Twisting and swirling around them was a herd of agile, long-necked quadrupeds with brown-and-black-striped fur; identical and moving as if possessed of a single mind, leaping at the same instant, reversing direction, cycloning gregariously over the short-napped savanna.

"This is not a chase," Plagueis said as he ran, "this is a summoning. You need to get behind the eyes of your target and become the object of its desire. The same holds true when you summon the Force: you must make yourself desirable, fascinating, addictive, and whatever power you need will be at your command."

Blended into the herd, the animal Sidious had fixed his sight on would have been indistinguishable to normal beings. But Sidious had the animal in his mind and was now looking through its eyes, one with it. Alongside him suddenly, the creature seemed to intuit its end and tipped its head to one side to expose its muscular neck. The moment the vibroblade stuck, the creature's eyes rolled back and grew opaque; hot blood spurted but quickly ceased to flow—the Force departing, and Sidious drawing its power deep into himself.

"Now another one," Plagueis said in a congratulatory tone. "And another one after that."

Sidious felt himself shoved into motion, as if by a gale-force wind.

"Feel the power of the dark side flow through you," Plagueis added from behind him. "We serve nature's purpose by culling the herd, and our own by sharpening our skills. We are the predatory swarm!"

The low-gravity planet was known then as Buoyant, its bewildering jumble of flora and fauna the result of an experiment by a long-forgotten species that had tweaked the atmosphere, set the world spinning faster than nature had intended, and encouraged the growth of lush forests and expansive grasslands. The still-functioning machines of the ancients dotted the landscape, and millennia later the animals they had imported were thriving. Nothing moved slowly or ponderously on rapidly spinning Buoyant, even day and night, or the storms that scrubbed the atmosphere with violent regularity.

Elsewhere on the planet—in dense forests, in arid wastes, beneath the waves of inland seas—the two Sith had already taken the lives of countless creatures: culling, sharpening, marinating themselves in a miasma of dark side energy.

Kilometers from where the quadruped hunt had commenced, Plagueis and Sidious sat under the enormous canopy of a tree whose trunk was wide enough to engulf a landspeeder, and whose thick branches were burdened with flowering parasitic plants. Breathing hard and drenched in sweat, they rested in silence as clouds of eager insects gathered around them. The pulse-beats of the Muun's trio of hearts were visible beneath his translucent skin, and his clear eyes tracked the slaloming movements of the escaping herd.

"Few of my people are aware of just how wealthy I am," he said at last, "since most of my riches derive from activities that have nothing to do with the ordinary business of finance. For many years my peers wondered why I chose to remain unwed, and ultimately reached the conclusion that I was in essence married to my work, without realizing how right they were. Except that my real bride is the dark side of the Force. What the ancients called Bogan, as separate from Ashla.

"Even the Jedi understand that there is no profit in partnering with a being who lacks the ability to understand what it means to be in the grip of the Force, and so the Order restricts marriage by dogma, in service, so the Jedi say, to the purity of Ashla.

"But Ashla is a perversion," he went on, "for the dark has always preceded the light. The original idea was to capture the power of the Force and make it subservient to the will of sentient life. The ancients—the Celestials, the Rakata—didn't pronounce judgment on their works. They moved planets, organized star systems, conjured dark side devices like the Star Forge as they saw fit. If millions died in the process, so be it. The lives of most beings are of small consequence. The Jedi have failed to understand this. They are so busy saving lives and striving to keep the powers of the Force in balance that they have lost sight of the fact that sentient life is meant to evolve, not simply languish in contented stasis."

He paused to glance at Sidious. "No doubt the texts I've provided contain references to the so-called Potentium theory—that light and dark depend on the intention of the user. This is yet another perversion of the truth perpetrated by those who would keep us shackled to the Force. The power of water and the power of fire are entirely different. Glaciers and volcanoes both have the potential to transform landscapes, but one does so by burying what lies beneath, where the other spews forth new terrain. The Sith are not placid stars but singularities. Rather than burn with muted purpose, we warp space and time to twist the galaxy to our own design.

"To become one of grandiloquent power requires more than mere compliance; what's needed is obstinacy and tenacity. That's why you must always be receptive to the currents of the dark side, because no matter how nimble you are, or think you are, the Force will show you no pity. As you've learned, your body sleeps but your mind is never at rest."

Getting to his feet, Plagueis extended his long arms in front of him and loosed a storm of Force lightning that crackled over the landscape, igniting fires in the grass.

"A Jedi sufficiently strong in the Force can be trained to produce a facsimile, but not true Sith lightning, which, unabated, has the power not only to incapacitate or kill, but to physically transform the victim. Force lightning requires strength of a sort only a Sith can command because we accept consequence and reject compassion. To do so requires a thirst for power that is not easily satisfied. The Force tries to resist the callings of ravenous spirits; therefore it must be broken and made a beast of burden. It must be made to answer to one's will.

"But the Force cannot be treated deferentially," he added as a few final tendrils sparked from his fingertips. "In order to summon and use lightning properly, you will someday have to be on the receiving end of its power, as a means of taking the energy inside yourself."

Sidious watched the last of the brush fires burn out, then said, "Will I eventually be physically transformed?"

"Into some aged, pale-skinned, raspy-voiced, yellow-eyed monster, you mean. Such as the one you see before you." Plagueis gestured to himself, then lowered himself to the ground. "Surely you are acquainted with the lore: King Ommin of Onderon, Darths Sion and Nihilus. But whether it will happen to you, I can't say. Know this, though, Sidious, that the power of the dark side does not debilitate the practitioner as much as it debilitates those who lack it." He grinned with evil purpose. "The power of the dark side is an illness no true Sith would wish to be cured of."

On Hypori they were the prey, standing back-to-back in their black zeyd-cloth hooded robes at the center of concentric rings of droids, retrofitted by Baktoid Armor to function as combat automata. Two hundred programmed assailants—bipedal, treaded, some levitated by antigrav generators—armed with a variety of weapons, ranging from hand blasters to short-barreled burst-rifles. Plagueis hadn't allowed his young apprentice to wield a lightsaber until a few years earlier, but Sidious was brandishing one now, self-constructed of phrik alloy and aurodium, and powered by a synthetic crystal. Made for delicate, long-fingered hands—as much a work of art as a weapon—the lightsaber thrummed as he waved the blade from side to side in front of him.

"Every weapon, manufactured by whatever species, has its own properties and peculiarities," Plagueis was saying, his own blade angled toward the ferrocrete floor of the battledome's fabricated cityscape, as if to light a fuse. "Range, penetrating power, refresh rate . . . In some instances your life might depend on your ability to focus on the weapon rather than on the wielder. You must train yourself to identify a weapon instantly—whether it's a product of BlasTech or Merr-Sonn, Tenloss or Prax—so that you will know where to position yourself, and the several ways to best deflect a well-aimed bolt."

Plagueis put his words into action as the first ring of droids began to converge on them, staggering the attack and triggering bursts at random. Orbiting Sidious, the Muun's blade warded off every volley, returning the bolts to their sources, or deflecting them into the façades of the faux buildings surrounding them or into other droids. At other times Plagueis made no attempt to redirect the attacks, but simply twisted and torqued his rangy body, allowing the bolts to miss him by centimeters. Around the two Sith, the automata collapsed one after the next, gushing lubricants from holed reservoirs or exploding in a hail of alloy parts, until all were heaped on the ferrocrete floor.

"The next ring is yours," Plagueis said.

Rugged, uninhabited Hypori belonged to the Techno Union, whose Skakoan foreman, Wat Tambor, owed his seat in the Republic Senate to Damask Holdings. In exchange, the bionic humanoid had made Hypori available as a training ground for members of the Echani Sun Guard and provided the necessary battle droids. Calling in another favor, Hego Damask had requested a private session in the fabricated cityscape, so that Plagueis and his apprentice could be free to employ lightsabers—though only for the purpose of deflecting bolts rather than dismemberment or penetration.

When it came Sidious's turn to demonstrate his skill, Plagueis spoke continuously from behind him, adding distraction to the distinct possibility of inadvertent disintegration.

"A being trained in the killing arts doesn't wait for you to acquire him as a target, or establish him or herself as an opponent, as if in some martial arts contest. Your reactions must be instantaneous and nothing less than lethal, for you are a Sith Lord, and will be marked for death."

The droids continued to converge, ring after ring of them, until the floor was piled high with smoking husks. Plagueis issued a voice command that brought the onslaught to an abrupt end and deactivated his lightsaber. The pinging of cooling weapons, the hiss of escaping gas, the unsteady whir of failing servomotors punctuated the sudden silence. Alloy limbs spasmed and photoreceptors winked out, surrendering their eerie glow. The recycled air was rotten with the smell of fried circuitry.

"Feast your eyes on our handiwork," Plagueis said, gesturing broadly.

Sidious switched off his weapon. "I see nothing but ruined droids."

Plagueis nodded. "Darth Bane advised: *One day the Republic will fall and the Jedi will be wiped out. But that will not happen until we are ready to seize that power for ourselves.*"

"When?" Sidious said. "How will we know when the time is right?"

"We are close to knowing. For a thousand years the Sith have allowed themselves to be reduced to the stuff of folklore. Since it serves our purposes we've done nothing to counter the belief that we are perversions of the Jedi, evil mages, embodiments of hatred, rage, and bloodlust, capable even of leaving the residue of our malefactions and dastardly deeds in places of power."

"Why have we not yet visited those places, Master—instead of worlds like Buoyant and Hypori?"

Darth Plagueis gazed at him. "You are impatient. You see no value in learning about weapons or explosives, Force suggestion or the healing arts. You hunger for power of the sort you imagine is to be found on Korriban, Dromund Kaas, Zigoola. Then let me tell you what you'll encounter in those reliquaries: Jedi, treasure hunters, and legends. Of course there are tombs in the Valley of the Dark Lords, but they have been plundered and now draw only tourists. On Dxun, Yavin Four, Ziost, the same is true. If it's history that has caught your fancy, I can show you a hundred worlds on which esoteric Sith symbols have been woven covertly into architecture and culture, and I can bore you for years with tales of the exploits of Freedon Nadd, Belia Darzu, Darth Zannah, who is alleged to have infiltrated the Jedi Temple, and of starships imbued with Sith consciousness. Is that your wish, Sidious, to become an academic?"

"I wish only to learn, Master."

"And so you will. But not from spurious sources. We are not some cult like the Tetsu's Sorcerers of Tund. Descended from Darth Bane, we are the select few who refuse to be carried by the Force and who carry it instead—thirty in a millennium rather than the tens of thousands fit to be Jedi. Any Sith can feign compassion and self-righteousness and master the Jedi arts, but only one in a thousand Jedi could ever become a Sith, for the dark side is only for those who value self-determinism over all else that existence offers. Only once in these past thousand years has a Sith Lord strayed into the light, and one day I *will* tell you that tale. But for now, take to heart the fact that Bane's Rule of Two was at the start our saving grace, putting an end to the internecine strife that allowed the Jedi Order to gain the upper hand. Part of our ongoing task will be to hunt down and eliminate any Sith pretenders who pose a threat to our ultimate goals."

Sidious remained silent for a long moment. "Am I to be equally distrustful of the lessons contained in Sith Holocrons?"

"Not distrustful," Plagueis said gravely. "But holocrons contain knowledge specific and idiosyncratic to each Sith who constructed them. Real knowledge is passed by Master to apprentice in sessions such as this, where nothing is codified or recorded—diluted—and thus it *cannot* be forgotten. There will come a time when you may wish to consult the holocrons of past Masters, but until then you would do better not to be influenced by them. You must discover the dark side in your own way, and perfect your power in your own fashion. All I can do in the meantime is help to keep you from losing your way while we hide in plain sight from the prying eyes of our enemies."

"'What celestial body is more luminous than a singularity,'" Sidious recited, "'hiding in plain sight but more powerful than all?'"

Plagueis grinned. "You are quoting Darth Guile."

"He goes on to compare the Sith to a rogue or malignant cell, too small to be discovered by scans or other techniques, but capable of spreading silently and lethally through a system. Initially the victim simply doesn't feel right, then falls ill, and ultimately succumbs."

Plagueis locked eyes with him. "Consider the mind-set of an anarchist who plans to sacrifice himself for a cause. For the weeks, months, possibly years leading up to the day he straps a thermal detonator to his chest and executes his task, he has lived in and been strengthened by the secret he carries, knowing the toll his act will take. So it has been for the Sith, residing in a secret, sacred place of knowledge for one thousand years, and knowing the toll our acts will take. This is power, Sidious. Where the Jedi, by contrast, are like beings who, as they move among the healthy, keep secret the fact that they are dying of a terminal illness.

"But *true* power needn't bear claws or fangs, or announce itself with snarls and throaty barks, Sidious. It can subdue with manacles of shimmersilk, purposeful charisma, and political astuteness."

*   *   *

The location of the planet known to the Sith as Kursid had been ex-
punged from Republic records in distant times, and for the past six
hundred years had been reserved for use as a place of spectacle. Masters
and apprentices of the Bane lineage had visited with enough regularity
that a cult had come into being in that part of the world based on the
periodic return of the sky visitors. The Sith hadn't bothered to investigate what Kursid's indigenous humanoids thought about the visits—
whether in their belief systems the Sith were regarded as the equivalent
of deities or demons—since it was unlikely that the primitives had yet
so much as named their world. However, visiting as apprentice and—
more often than not—as Master, each Sith Lord had remarked on the
slow advancement of Kursid's civilization. How, on the early visits,
the primitives had defended themselves with wooden war clubs and
smooth rocks hurled from slings. Two hundred years later, many of
the small settlements had grown to become cities or ceremonial centers
built of hewn stone, with social classes of rulers and priests, merchants
and warriors. Gradually the cities had become ringed with ranged
weapons of a crude sort, and magical guardian symbols had been emblazoned on the sloping sides of defensive walls. At some point previous to Darth Tenebrous's visit as an apprentice, replicas of the Sith
ships had been constructed in the center of the arid plateau that served
as a battleground, and enormous totemic figures—visible only from
above—had been outlined by removing tens of thousands of fist-sized
volcanic stones that covered the ground. On Plagueis's first visit, some
fifty years earlier, the warriors he and Tenebrous faced had been armed
with longbows and metal-tipped lances.

That the Sith had never demanded anything other than battle hadn't
kept the primitives from attempting to adopt a policy of appeasement,
leaving at the ships' perpetual landing site foodstuffs, sacrificial victims,
and works of what they considered art, forged of materials they held
precious or sacred. But the Sith had simply ignored the offerings, waiting instead on the stony plain for the primitives to deploy their warriors, as the primitives did now with Plagueis and Sidious waiting.

Announcing their arrival with low runs over the city, they had
set the ship down and waited for six days, while the mournful calls
of breath-driven horns had disturbed the dry silences, and groups of

primitives had flocked in to gather on the hillsides that overlooked the battleground.

"Do you recall what Darth Bane said regarding the killing of innocents?" Plagueis had asked.

"Our mission," Sidious paraphrased, "is not to bring death on all those unfit to live. All we do must serve our true purpose—the preservation of our Order and the survival of the Sith. We must work to grow our power, and to accomplish that we will need to interact with individuals of many species across many worlds. Eventually word of our existence will reach the ears of the Jedi."

To refrain from senseless killing, they wielded force pikes rather than lightsabers. Meter-long melee weapons used by the Echani and carried by the Senate Guard, the pikes were equipped with stun-module tips capable of delivering a shock that could overwhelm the nervous systems of most sentients, without causing permanent damage.

"The next few hours will test the limits of your agility, speed, and accuracy," Plagueis said, as several hundred of the biggest, bravest, and most skilled warriors—their bodies daubed in pigments derived from plants, clay, and soil—began to separate themselves from the crowds. "But this is more than some simple exercise in proficiency; it is a rite of passage for these beings, as they are assistants in our rise to ultimate power, and therefore servants of the dark side of the Force. Centuries from now, advanced by the Sith, they might confront us with projectile weapons or energy beams. But by then we will have evolved, as well, perhaps past the need for this rite, and we will come instead to honor rather than engage them in battle. Through power we gain victory, and through victory our chains are broken. But power is only a means to an end."

To the clamorous beating of drums and the wailing of the onlookers, the warriors brandished their weapons, raised a deafening war cry, and attacked. A nod from Plagueis, and the two Sith sped across the plain to meet them, flying among them like wraiths, evading arrows, gleaming spear tips, and blows from battle-axes, going one against one, two, or three, but felling opponent after opponent with taps from the force pikes, until among the hundreds of jerking, twitching bodies sprawled on the rough ground, only one was left standing.

That was when Plagueis tossed aside the stun pike and ignited his crimson blade, and a collective lament rose from the crowds on the hillsides.

"Execute one, terrify one thousand," he said.

Hurling the warrior to the ground with a Force push, he used the lightsaber to deftly open the primitive's chest cavity; then he reached a hand inside and extracted his still-beating heart.

The keening of the crowd reached a fevered pitch as he raised the heart high overhead; then it ended abruptly. Following a protracted moment of silence, the fallen warriors were helped from the battle-ground and the crowds began to disperse, disconsolate but embold-ened by the fact that they had discharged their duty. Horns blew and a communal chant that was at once somber and celebratory was carried on the wind. In the principal city, a stone stele would be carved and erected for the dead one, and the day-count would commence until the return of the Sith.

Plagueis placed the still heart on the primitive's chest and used the hem of his robe to wipe the blood from his hand and forearm.

"At one time, though I recognized that Muuns are a higher class of beings, I puzzled over the fact that beings would relinquish their seats for me, or step into the muck to allow me to pass. But early on in my apprenticeship I came to realize that the lumpen species were mak-ing room for me not because I was a Muun, but because I was in fact superior to them in every way. More, that they should by all rights allow me to step not merely past them but *on* them to get where I needed to be, because the Sith are their salvation, their only real hope. In that we will ultimately improve the lives of their descendants, they owe us every courtesy, every sacrifice, nothing short of their very lives.

"But there are dark times ahead for many of them, Sidious. An era of warfare necessary to purge the galaxy of those who have allowed it to decay. For decay has no cure; it has to be eradicated by the flames of a cleansing fire. And the Jedi are mostly to blame. Crippled by empathy, shackled to obedience—to their Masters, their Council, their cherished Republic—they perpetuate a myth of equality, serving the Force as if it were a belief system that had been programmed into them. With the Republic they are like indulgent parents, allowing their offspring to experiment with choices without consequence, and supporting wrongheadedness merely for the sake of maintaining family unity. Tripping over their own robes in a rush to uphold a galactic government that has been deteriorating for centuries. When instead they should be proclaiming: *We know what's best for you.*

"The galaxy can't be set on the proper course until the Jedi Order and the corrupt Republic have been brought down. Only then can the Sith begin the process of rebuilding from the ground up. This is why we encourage star system rivalries and the goals of any group that aims to foment chaos and anarchy. Because destruction of any sort furthers our own goals."

Plagueis paused to take the warrior's heart back into his hands.

"Through us, the powers of chaos are harnessed and exploited. Dark times don't simply emerge, Sidious. Enlightened beings, guiding intelligences manipulate events to bring about a storm that will deliver power into the hands of an elite group willing to make the hard choices the Republic fears to make. Beings may elect their leaders, but the Force has elected us."

He glanced at his apprentice. "Remember, though, that a cunning politician is capable of wreaking more havoc than two Sith Lords armed with vibroblades, lightsabers, or force pikes. That is what you must become, with me advising you from the dark."

"Are we grand enough?" Sidious said.

"You should ask, are we crude enough?" Plagueis quirked a smile. "We're not living in an age of giants, Sidious. But to succeed we must become as beasts."

Taking a bite from the warrior's heart, he passed the blood-filled organ to his apprentice.

14: THE SHAPE OF HIS SHADOW

"You appear to be enjoying the steak, Ambassador Palpatine."

"Exquisite," he said, holding her gaze for a fraction longer than might have been called for.

Working on her third glass of wine since dinner began, she interpreted his ready smile as permission to turn fully toward him. "Not too gamy?"

"Scarcely a trace of the wild."

A dark-haired human beauty with big blue eyes, she was attached in some way to the Eriaduan consulate on Malastare—host of the gala at which the Dug winners of the Vinta Harvest Classic were being feted.

"Are you on Malastare for business or pleasure?"

"As luck would have it, both," Palpatine said, patting his lips with a napkin. "Kinman Doriana and I are members of Senator Kim's party."

He indicated the clean-shaven, slightly balding young man in the adjacent seat.

"Charmed," the woman said.

Doriana smiled broadly. "You're not kidding."

Her gaze moved to the neighboring table, where Vidar Kim sat with members of the Gran Protectorate and politicians from nearby Sullust, Darknell, and Sluis Van.

"Senator Kim is the tall one with the quaint beard?"

"No, he's the one with the three eyestalks," Doriana said.

The woman blinked, then laughed with him. "A friend of mine was asking about Senator Kim earlier. Is he married?"

"For many years, and happily," Palpatine told her.

"And you?" she said, turning to him again.

"Frequent travel forbids it."

She watched him over the rim of the wineglass. "Married to politics, is that it?"

"To the work," he said.

"To the work," Doriana said, raising his glass in a toast.

Just twenty-eight, Palpatine wore his reddish hair long, in the tradition of Naboo statesmen, and dressed impeccably. Many who encountered the ambassador described him as an articulate, charismatic young man of refined taste and quiet strength. A good listener, even-tempered, politically astute, astonishingly well informed for someone who had only been in the game for seven years. A patrician at a time when few could claim the title, and destined to go far. Well traveled, too, courtesy of his position as Naboo's ambassador-at-large but also as the sole surviving heir to the wealth of House Palpatine. Long recovered from the tragedy that had struck his family more than a decade earlier, but perhaps as a result of being orphaned at seventeen, something of a loner. A man whose love of periodic solitude hinted at a hidden side to his personality.

"Tell me, Ambassador," she said, as she set her glass down, "are you one of those men with a friend in every spaceport?"

"I'm always eager to make friends," Palpatine said in a low monotone that brought sudden color to her face. "We're alike in that way."

Taking her glossy lower lip between her teeth, she reached for her wineglass once more. "Are you perhaps a Jedi mind reader disguised in ambassadorial robes?"

"Anything but."

"I've often wondered whether they have secret relationships," she said in a conspiratorial voice. "Gallivanting around the galaxy, using the Force to seduce innocent beings."

"I wouldn't know, but I sincerely doubt it," Palpatine said.

She looked at him in a calculating way, and raised her hand to caress his chin with a manicured forefinger. "On Eriadu some believe that a cleft chin identifies someone the Force has pushed away."

"Just my luck," he said in mock seriousness.

"Just your luck, indeed," she said, sliding a flimsi-card across the table toward him. "I have hostess duties to attend to, Ambassador. But I'm free after midnight."

Palpatine and Doriana watched her walk away from the table, teetering slightly on high heels.

"Nicely played," Doriana said. "I'm taking notes."

Palpatine slid the flimsi-card toward him. "A gift."

"When you earned it?" Doriana shook his head. "I'm not that desperate. Yet, anyway."

The two of them laughed. Doriana's engaging smile and innocent good looks belied a sinister personality that had brought him to Palpatine's notice several years earlier. A Naboo, he had a troubled past and, perhaps as a consequence, talents that made him useful. So Palpatine had befriended him and clandestinely drawn him into his web, in accordance with Plagueis's instructions that he always keep an eye out for allies and would-be co-conspirators. That Doriana wasn't strong in the Force made no difference. In eleven years of Sith apprenticeship and of traveling far and wide in the galaxy, Palpatine had yet to encounter a single being whose strength in the Force had gone unrecognized or unexploited.

At the neighboring table, Vidar Kim and the rest were enjoying themselves, their privacy ensured by the table's transparent sound-muting umbrella. Envy gnawed at Palpatine while he watched Kim . . . the position he enjoyed in the Galactic Senate, the posting on Coruscant, easy access to the galaxy's elite. But he knew that he needed to bide his time; that Plagueis would move him to the galactic capital only when there was some good reason to do so.

As often as Plagueis maintained that the Rule of Two had ended with their partnership, the Muun remained the powerful one, and Palpatine the covetous one. Bane's dictum notwithstanding, denial was still a key factor in Sith training; a key factor in being "broken," as Plagueis put it—of being shaped by the dark side of the Force. Cruelly, at times, and painfully. But Palpatine was grateful, for the Force had slowly groomed him into a being of dark power and granted him a secret identity, as well. The life he had been leading—as the noble head of House Palpatine, legislator, and most recently ambassador-at-large—was nothing more than the trappings of an alter ego; his wealth, a subterfuge; his handsome face, a mask. In the realm of the Force his thoughts ordered reality, and his dreams prepared the galaxy for monumental change. He was a manifestation of dark purpose, helping to advance the Sith Grand Plan and gradually gaining power over himself so that he might one day—in the words of his Master—be able to gain control over another, then a group of others, then an order, a world, a species, the Republic itself.

Doriana's elbow nudged him out of his reverie.

"Kim's coming."

"Don't think I didn't see that," the Senator said when he reached Palpatine.

Palpatine let his bafflement show.

"The flimsi-card that woman slipped you," Vidar said. "I suppose you entertained her with the usual tall tales."

Palpatine shrugged in a guileless manner. "I may have said something about getting to know the galaxy."

"Getting to know the galaxy's women, he means," Doriana interjected.

Kim laughed heartily. "How is it that I come to have assistants who leave trails of conquests, and a son who meditates on the Force in the Jedi Temple?"

"That's what makes you so well rounded," Doriana said.

More than even Plagueis, Kim had been Palpatine's mentor in the sphere of mundane politics. Their relationship went back fifteen years, to when Palpatine had been forcibly enrolled in a private school in Theed, and Kim had just completed his stint in the Apprentice Legislator program. In the time since, Palpatine had watched Kim's family grow to include three sons, one of whom—Ronhar, six years Palpatine's junior—had been turned over to the Jedi Order as an infant. When Plagueis had learned of this, he had encouraged Palpatine to allow his friendship with Kim to deepen, in the expectation that sooner or later his and Jedi Ronhar's paths would cross.

Give order to the future by attending to it with your thoughts, his Master frequently told him.

"Come and join us at the table," Kim was saying.

Palpatine stood and fell into step beside Kim as he headed back to the larger table.

"One day you'll be replacing me at this job," the Senator said quietly, "and the sooner you grow accustomed to what goes on, the better." He sighed with purpose. "Who knows, a few hours of senatorial gossip might even be enough to deter you from going into galactic politics altogether."

Some dozen beings were grouped in a circle, all of them male but not all of them human. The prominent chairs were occupied by Gran Protectorate Senator Pax Teem and his aide, Aks Moe. To both sides of them sat Sullustan and Sluissi Senators. Also present were Eriaduan Senator Ranulph Tarkin and his aide, Bor Gracus; the Darknell ambassador; and Dugs, Boss Cabra—a Black Sun Vigo—and his son, Darnada, guests of the Podrace winners and attendees of the most recent Gathering on Sojourn.

By then Palpatine had made three visits to the Hunters' Moon, but only to observe and to familiarize himself with some of the galaxy's key players. Plagueis, as Hego Damask, had gone to great lengths to avoid being identified as Palpatine's benefactor. Only King Tapalo's chief minister, Ars Veruna, knew that Damask was grooming him for a career in galactic politics, and, as a personal favor to the Muun, had appointed Palpatine Naboo's ambassador.

"Ah, new blood," Pax Teem remarked after Kim had introduced Palpatine to everyone.

"I quite enjoyed the Podraces," Palpatine said as he sat down.

Teem's leaf-like ears twitched. "You're too young to have witnessed them in their glory days, Ambassador. Before Tatooine succeeded in capturing the fancy of race enthusiasts." The Gran pronounced *Tatooine* as if an execration.

Palpatine knew that Plagueis had been responsible for Tatooine's rise, as well for weakening Malastare's once-lucrative trade in fuel, by helping to make Naboo's plasma resources available to many worlds.

"Have your duties taken you to that horrible place?" Aks Moe asked.

Palpatine nodded as he sat. "Just two months ago."

"And how did you find it?" Cabra said.

Palpatine turned to the Dug crime boss. "Contentious. What with the Desilijic and Besadii Hutts vying for control."

The statement met with murmurs of concurrence.

Teem spoke to it. "Perhaps Gardulla's rivalry with Jabba Tiure will one day result in Malastare's resurgence." His eyestalks twisted toward the Dugs. "Though I'm certain Boss Cabra favors Gardulla, out of respect for the help she provided on Nar Shaddaa."

Young Darnada bristled at the remark. "Whatever mark we've made on Nar Shaddaa, we made on our own. Ask any Black Sun—"

Stopping him before he could go on, Cabra said, "We will always be indebted to Gardulla for her efforts on our behalf."

Kim watched the Dugs, then gestured negligently. "Tatooine is too remote and lawless to have an impact on galactic events, in any case. It's the activities of the Trade Federation that should concern the Republic. Look what the Federation has done to our own Naboo."

Kim became the object of everyone's gaze. An outspoken critic of King Tapalo and Ars Veruna, he continued to serve in the Senate only as an appeasement to those noble houses that were aligned against the regent.

"It is my understanding that Naboo embraced the arrangement," Ranulph Tarkin said.

"*Some* did."

"No can one deny that your world has prospered as a result," Teem interjected.

"Prospered, yes," Kim said, "but not nearly to the extent it should have. If not for the deals Hego Damask brokered with the Banking Clan, the Trade Federation, and—" He glanced at Cabra. "—Outer Rim Construction, Naboo would be as wealthy as Kuat or Chandrila."

The Dug remained silent while Kim continued. "Naboo's plasma is being sold for ten, sometimes twenty times what the Federation pays for it."

"A monster of our own creation," Tarkin muttered. "The Trade Federation didn't become powerful by exploiting the Outer Rim. It was supported by Eriadu's own House Valorum, and supported by Tagge and others."

"Then perhaps the time has come for us to make our dissatisfaction public," Kim said, glancing around the table. "The Muuns are merely avaricious, but the Trade Federation has the potential to become dangerous."

"I agree with the good Senator from Naboo," the Sullustan delegate said. "Even now the Trade Federation seeks to seat its client worlds in the Senate, as a means of fortifying its voting block. Mechis, Murkhana, Felucia, Kol Horo, Ord Cestus, Yinchorr . . . the list goes on and on."

The Sluissi Senator made a sound of disapproval, and a tremor seemed to snake through his humanoid upper torso. "Don't dismiss too lightly the part the Muuns play in all this. Yinchorr's Senate seat was Damask Holdings' doing." He looked at Cabra. "Is that not the case?"

The Dug's powerful shoulders heaved. "I'm not in a position to know."

Laughter from the others prompted Darnada to part his muzzle just enough to reveal the tips of his fangs.

The Sluissi looked at Kim and Palpatine. "Perhaps Black Sun is unaware that the son of Hego Damask's operating officer—Larsh Hill—is in line to replace Tonith as chairman of the Banking Clan."

Tarkin put his elbows on the table and leaned forward. "I've heard the rumors to the effect that Damask has been meeting with the heads of the guilds, the Corporate Alliance, and the Techno Union. What might become of trade—of any sort—if he brokered a deal between them and the Trade Federation?"

"Here's the point," Kim said. "If we're going to prevent the Trade Federation—and the Muuns—from tightening their hold on the Senate, we need to band together and vote to defeat the proposed legislation."

Before Kim could add anything, Tarkin said to Palpatine, "Do you agree that the Trade Federation needs to be taken down a notch, Ambassador?"

Palpatine glanced at Kim, who said, "Speak freely."

"Senator Kim and I are in complete accord on the issue, and have been for some time. No single corporate entity can be allowed to grow too powerful—especially at the expense of developing worlds. Naboo must safeguard its interests, just as Eriadu and Sullust and Sluis Van have safeguarded theirs."

Tarkin watched him closely. "Is Naboo prepared to assume control of transporting its plasma? Aren't you in danger of biting the proverbial hand that feeds you?"

"Naboo has no intentions of planetizing the Trade Federation's facilities. We're simply pressing for a renegotiation of the original contracts."

Tarkin thought about it. "So you feel that a defeat in the Senate might make the Trade Federation more . . . pliable, as it were?"

Palpatine vouchsafed a thin smile. "Only those bills that support well-reasoned regulation should win approval in the Senate."

"Well put," Tarkin said.

Palpatine waited for someone to point out that he had offered nothing of substance, but no one did. Even Kim failed to grasp that he was being undermined.

Pax Teem was about to speak when a Gran messenger intruded on the privacy canopy.

"Senator Kim, we are in receipt of an urgent communiqué from Naboo."

While Kim was excusing himself, Palpatine dropped into the Force. Conversation at the table grew faint, and the physical forms of Pax Teem and the others became indistinct—more like blurs of lambent energy. He kept himself still as a disturbing echo reached him. By the time an ashen Kim was returning to the table, Palpatine was already out of his seat and hurrying to meet him.

"What is it? What's happened?"

Kim stared at him as if from another world. "They're dead. Everyone. My wife, my sons . . ."

And he collapsed sobbing against Palpatine's shoulder.

The funeral for the Kim family was everything it hadn't been for the Palpatines. In keeping with tradition, the bodies of Kim's wife, two sons, and the ship's pilot and copilot had been returned to Theed from the crash site in seaside Kaadara and cremated in the Funeral Temple. A procession hundreds-strong led by King Tapalo and his chief advisers proceeded on foot from the Temple to the nearby Livet Tower, where everyone spent a moment gathered around the Eternal Flame, contemplating transience and the importance of living a harmonious life; then moved in solemn precision to the banks of the Solleu River, where the grief-stricken Senator scattered the ashes and wept openly as the current carried them over the Verdugo Plunge to the flatlands beyond.

Following the ceremony, mourners gathered to express their condolences to Vidar Kim, who wore a robe of deep green over a black tunic. When Palpatine's turn came, the two men embraced.

"I have only one hope for a family, Palpatine, one hope." Kim's eyes were red-rimmed and brimming with tears. "Ronhar."

Palpatine compressed his lips in uncertainty. "He is a Jedi Knight, Vidar. His family is the Order."

Kim was insistent. "I need him more than the Order needs him. Only he can carry the Kim line forward—just as you will someday carry on the Palpatine line."

Palpatine said nothing.

With vehicular traffic banned from Theed's narrow streets, the city seemed almost as it had a decade earlier, before antiquated laws had been repealed and wealth had worked its dubious magic; before Flash speeders and R2 astromech droids had become the rage, and fads and fashions—in dress, transport, and food—had poured in from the Core.

The murders of Cosinga and the others had left Palpatine emancipated and wealthy. Though interrogated by numerous officials, he had been absolved; his story, his alibi, accepted. Some of the influential nobles had their suspicions that Palpatine had furnished intelligence to Damask Holdings to secure the election of Bon Tapalo, but most Naboo had offered sympathy and support. On the heels of Tapalo's ascension to the throne, Palpatine had sold the Lake Country estate and taken an apartment in Theed, stocking it with extra-system art that had found its way to Naboo from Core and Mid Rim worlds. In the early years of his apprenticeship to Darth Plagueis he had remained in mandatory public service; he then spent five years in the Apprentice Legislator program before being appointed ambassador, following Tapalo's reelection.

Palpatine supposed he could have lobbied for a more prestigious position, but only at the risk of undermining Plagueis. Equally important, a high-status post might have interfered with his ability to rendezvous with his Sith Master on remote worlds, where they had been able to be observed together without consequence.

As he left Kim to the next mourner in line, he noticed Ars Veruna separating himself from a group that included Palpatine's allies Kinman Doriana and Janus Greejatus.

"A word, Ambassador," Veruna said when he drew near.

Palpatine allowed himself to be steered by the elbow into an unoccupied viewing area near the Solleu Bridge.

"My heart goes out to poor Vidar," Veruna began. Roughly the same
height as Palpatine, he wore a brocaded cloak and tall headpiece. "A
starship crash, of all things. One would have thought that a tragedy of
such nature might have compelled him to retire from politics, but that
doesn't appear to be the case." He rested his elbows on the stone balus-
trade and gazed at the fast-moving river. "Well, you of all people would
know better than most the effect of such unforeseen developments."

"Vidar is planning to return to Coruscant before the month is out."

"On Senate business?"

"Personal, I suspect."

Veruna grew pensive, then said, "The last time you and I stood together was at the inaugural ceremony for the plasma generator." He
turned to regard Palpatine. "You look well. Changed, I think. From
your travels."

"Broadened," Palpatine said.

"The very word I was searching for." Veruna paused briefly. "It has
reached my ear that you made quite an impression on Seswenna sector
Senator Ranulph Tarkin when you were on Malastare recently."

Palpatine shrugged. "I wasn't aware."

"He enjoyed hearing your views regarding the Trade Federation's
plan to seat some of its client worlds in the Senate. Would you care to
elaborate on what you told him?"

Palpatine smiled lightly. "I offered nothing substantive. In fact, I
was merely playing politics."

Veruna nodded knowingly. "I am greatly relieved to hear that." He
glanced around before continuing. "As you well know, the King and I
have our separate arrangements with the Trade Federation. Now, however, we're forced to take into account the discontent of our constitu-
ents. Unfortunately, the person largely responsible for Tapalo's election
and our party's continued popularity is not going to take kindly to
hearing that Naboo plans to vote against the very legislation Damask
Holdings has been lobbying to see enacted."

"I can appreciate your predicament," Palpatine said. "Why not order
Senator Kim to vote in favor of the Trade Federation?"

Veruna laughed shortly. "Would that it were as simple as that.

The problem is that Kim knows about our separate arrangements, and intends to use this opportunity to send a message to the Trade Federation—as well as to Tapalo's detractors—that Naboo will no longer allow itself to be exploited." He inhaled deeply. "Recalling him from Coruscant would be tantamount to admitting that Naboo remains at the mercy of the Trade Federation, and might jeopardize our standing with many of the trade worlds on whom we have come to depend."

Palpatine pretended to consider it. "Perhaps it will be worth the risk to vote *against* the Trade Federation."

Veruna studied him with sudden interest. "Go on."

"Whether the legislation is enacted or becomes embroiled in procedure, Naboo's contracts with the Trade Federation will remain binding and inalterable. The Federation will continue procuring our plasma for meager credits and marketing it for inflated prices. But Naboo will at least be on the public record as having stood up to the galactic conglomerates."

"More playing politics, is that it?"

Palpatine rocked his head from side to side but said nothing.

"And what about Magister Damask?"

"Apprise him of the plan beforehand. He's not unreasonable."

Veruna stroked his beard in thought. "That just might work." He smiled slyly. "It's a pity Naboo already has a voice in the Senate."

Palpatine sniffed. "Should the opportunity ever arise, I would, of course, accept. But until then, I'm content to serve in my own way."

"Serve Naboo."

"Who or what else?"

Veruna rubbed his hands together. "One day, if I have my way, our Space Corps will include a fleet of swift Nubian fighters capable of chasing the Trade Federation from our system."

"I, too, foresee the day," Palpatine said.

Veruna laughed again. "Ah, but when? How long will we have to wait, Palpatine?"

"Only until Hego Damask awards you the throne."

15: QUANTUM BEING

A gift to Damask from the Council of Elders on the occasion of Yinchorr's seating in the Senate, the towering reptilian condemned murderer shuffled to the center of the energy field that defined his cage on Aborah and, with confusion contorting the features of his beaked face, prostrated himself on the permacrete floor and mumbled in Basic: "I'm honored to be here and to perform whatever tasks you require of me."

Standing at the field's shimmering perimeter, 11-4D pivoted his head toward Plagueis. "Congratulations, Magister. At last he responds to your suggestion. You have undermined his resolve."

That *resolve*, Plagueis had learned after more than two years of experimentation on the Yinchorri, was in fact a kind of Force bubble fashioned by the turtle-like alien's limited number of unusually willful midi-chlorians. This suggested that the Yinchorri was actually strong in the Force, despite his pitifully low count. The discovery had come as a breakthrough, and Plagueis was still grappling with the implications.

The Force bubble itself was similar to those generated by creatures that drew on the Force to avoid predation by natural enemies. The relationship between the arboreal ysalamir and its adversary, the vornskr, provided a curious example, in that the latter was attracted to the former by the very mechanism the ysalamir employed as a defense. Where an extremely low midi-chlorian count might have bolstered the odds of survival, nature had instead made the ysalimir species strong in the Force. So strong, in fact, that several of the creatures acting in concért could create a Force bubble encompassing kilometers rather than meters. In a sense, the Jedi Order had done the same on a galactic scale, Plagueis believed, by bathing the galaxy in the energy of the light side of the Force; or more accurately by fashioning a Force bubble that had prevented infiltration by the dark side, until Tenebrous's Master had succeeded in bursting the bubble, or at least shrinking it. How the Order's actions could be thought of as *balancing* the Force had baffled generations of Sith, who harbored no delusions regarding the Force's ability to self-regulate.

The Yinchorri former convict wasn't the only new addition to Plagueis's island facility. In the eleven years that had elapsed since the capture of Venamis and the recruitment of Sidious, Plagueis had collected more than a dozen beings of diverse species and had been subjecting them to a wide range of experiments involving volition, telepathy, healing, regeneration, and life extension, with some promising results. As for the Bith would-be Sith Lord, he was alive and well, though kept comatose more often than not, and always under the watchful photoreceptors of 11-4D or a host of custodial droids.

Plagueis hadn't lost interest in Venamis by any means, but the Yinchorri's immunity to Force suggestion—an immunity the species shared with Hutts, Toydarians, and others—had provided him with a new line of investigation. Unlike ysalamiri, which created a Force bubble in the presence of danger, the Yinchorri were in a perpetual state of *involuntary* immunity to Force suggestion. The fact that immunity was in a sense hardwired into them meant that the ability was an adaptation, prompted by a past threat to the survival of the species. To Plagueis, it meant that the Yinchorri's midi-chlorians had evolved to provide protection to a species that was naturally strong in the Force. If that were indeed the case, then the Yinchorri were living proof that the Sith of the Bane line had been on the right path from the very start.

For while toppling the Jedi Order and the Republic was essential to the task of restoring order to the galaxy, that goal belonged to the realm of the ordinary—to the world that was nothing more than a by-product of the eternal struggle between the light and dark forces, both of which were beyond any concepts of good or evil. The greater goal of the Sith involved toppling the Force itself, and becoming the embodiment of the galaxy's animating principle.

It had been theorized by Jedi and Sith alike that balance between the light and dark sides was actually under the guidance of a group of discorporate entities—the ones called the Celestials, perhaps—who had merged themselves with the Force thousands of generations earlier, and had continued to guide the fate of the galaxy ever since. In effect, a higher order of intermediaries, whose powers were beyond the understanding of mortal beings. But many Sith viewed the notion with disdain, for the theoretical existence of such a group had little bearing on the goal of making the Force subservient to the will of an enlightened elite. Only the Sith understood that sentient life was on the verge of a transformative leap; that through the manipulation of midi-chlorians—or the overthrow of the Forceful group that supervised them—the divide between organic life and the Force could be bridged, and death could be erased from the continuum.

As evidenced by those few Lords who had managed to perpetuate their spirits after physical death—foremost among them Emperor Vitiate, who was said to have lived a thousand years—the ancient Sith had come halfway across that bridge. But those few had been so focused on worldly power that they had ended up trapping themselves between realms. That they had never provided the Order with guidance from beyond attested to the fact that their influence had been negligible, and had long since faded from the world.

In the same way that the pre-Bane Sith had been responsible for their own extinction, the great dark side Lords of the past had doomed themselves to the nether realm through their attempts to conquer death by feeding off the energies of others, rather than by tapping the deepest strata of the Force and learning to speak the language of the midi-chlorians. Plagueis was finally learning to do that, and was just beginning to learn how to persuade, prompt, cajole, and coax them into action. Already he could command them to promote healing, and now he had been successful in enticing them to lower their defenses. If he could compel a murderous Yinchorri to become peaceful, could he—with a mere suggestion—accomplish the opposite by turning a peaceful being into a murderer? Would he one day be able to influence the leaders of worlds and systems to act according to his designs, however iniquitous? Would he one day conquer not only death but life, as well, by manipulating midi-chlorians to *produce* Forceful beings, even in the

absence of fertilization, as Darth Tenebrous might have attempted to
do with gene-splicing techniques and computers?

Perhaps.

But not until the singular flame of the light side was extinguished
from the galaxy. Not until the Jedi Order was stamped out.

From the start of his apprenticeship with Plagueis, his Master had demanded to know what Palpatine regarded as his greatest strength, so
that he would know how best to undermine him; to know his greatest fear, so that Plagueis would know which to force Palpatine to face;
to know what Palpatine cherished most, so that Plagueis could take
that from him; and to know the things that Palpatine craved, so that
Plagueis could deny him.

Some combination of the strictures—or perhaps recognition
on Plagueis's part for his apprentice's unabated craving to visit Sith
worlds—had landed Palpatine on scenic Dathomir. Sparsely populated
and largely unexplored, Dathomir wasn't Korriban or Ziost, but it was
powerful in the Force, in part because of its fecundity, but mainly due
to the presence of groups of female adepts who practiced dark side
magicks.

He was meandering without clear purpose through one of Blue
Desert City's dustier quarters, far from the city center, when he became
aware of a faint pulse of Force energy, the origin of which was indistinct
but close at hand.

Calling more deeply on the Force, he allowed himself to be drawn
toward the mysterious source, as if he were a starship surrendering
to the embrace of a tractor beam. A tortuous series of turns delivered
him into a market area brimming with knockoff goods, ersatz jewelry,
and bits and pieces of junk that had found its way to Dathomir from
who knew where, and ultimately to a small square amid the hustle and
bustle, on one corner of which stood a human female, whose symmetri-
cally blemished face was the color of burnished durasteel, and whose
flamboyant clothing identified her as a visitor to the city, likely from
some remote village on the planet's far side. The hood of her crimson
robe was raised, and from one shoulder hung a soft bag the size of a
small suitcase.

Palpatine moved to the square's diagonal corner to observe her. She was eyeing individuals in the passing crowd, not as if searching for someone in particular, but with a gaze more in keeping with target acquisition. She didn't strike Palpatine as a thief or pickpocket, though she did exude a dark energy informed by equal measures of urgency and deceit. Abruptly he made himself discernible in the Force, and immediately she turned her head in his direction and began to hurry across the square in his direction.

"Good sir," she said in Basic as she drew near.

Feigning interest in the cheap wares of an itinerant trader, he pretended to be taken by surprise when she approached him from his blind side.

"Are you addressing me?" he asked, turning to her.

"I am, sir, if you've a moment to indulge a being in need."

Her oblique eyes were rimmed by dark blemishes that matched the tint of her thick lips; poking from the wide sleeves of her robe, the tapered fingers of her hands bore long, talon-like nails.

Palpatine pretended impatience. "Why single me out, among this crowd of more richly attired beings?"

"Because you've the look and bearing of a man of intelligence and influence." She gestured broadly. "The rest are rabble, despite their fine cloaks and headwear."

He made a decorous show of suppressing a yawn. "Save your adulation for the rubes, woman. But since you've correctly identified me as better than the rest, you're obviously aware that I've no time to waste on confidence games or tricks. So if its mere credits you're after, I suggest you widen your search for someone more charitable."

"I don't ask for credits," she said, studying him openly.

"What then? Come to the point."

"It's a gift I offer."

Palpatine laughed without merriment. "What could you possibly have to offer someone like me?"

"Just this." She opened the soft shoulder bag to reveal a humanoid infant of less than a standard year in age. The infant's hairless head was stippled with an array of short but still pliant horns, and its entire body had been garishly and ceremonially tattooed in red and black pigments.

A male Zabrak, Palpatine told himself. But not of the Iridonian sort;

rather, a Dathomirian. "How do you come by this newborn? Have you stolen him?"

"You misunderstand, good sir. My own child, this one is."

Palpatine glowered. "You say that he is a gift, and yet you dissemble. Have you had dealings that have led you into such deep debt that you would part with your own flesh and blood? Or perhaps you're addicted to spice or some other intoxicant?"

She stiffened. "Neither. I seek only to save his life."

Palpatine's expression changed. "Then speak honestly. You're a long way from your coven, Nightsister. And a practitioner of magicks more than sufficient to keep your child from harm."

Her eyes opened wide and bored into him, in search of explanation. "How—"

"Never mind how I know, Witch," Palpatine said sharply. "The child, whether yours or not, is a Nightbrother, conceived for the purpose of serving the sisterhood as a warrior and slave."

She refused to avert her gaze. "You're not a Jedi."

"Clearly I am not, as I suspect you have already intuited. But you still haven't answered my question. Why are trying to rid yourself of the infant?"

"To spare the one for the sake of the other," she said after a moment. "Half a clan pair, this one is. And I want one to live freely, since the other can't."

"Who poses the threat?"

"Talzin is her name."

"Who is Talzin?"

"The Nightsister Mother."

Palpatine filed the information away. "Where is the infant's father?"

"Dead—by tradition."

He snorted. "Will the infant not be missed?"

"Talzin knows only of the one, not the other."

"You delude yourself."

Gently, she pushed the shoulder bag toward him. "Then take him. Please."

"What would I do with him?"

"This one is strong in the Force. In the right hands, he can become a powerful asset."

"Servitude of a different sort."

She ignored the remark. "Take him. Save him."

Palpatine regarded the newborn again. "Have you named him?"

"Maul, he is called."

"Befitting the power you divine in him."

She nodded. "Take him."

Palpatine gazed at her and, motioning with his right hand, said, "You will forget this encounter."

She locked eyes with him. "I will try."

"For your own sake, I hope you do. Now, go. Before I change my mind."

Placing the bag in his hands, she turned and hurried off, disappearing into the crowd.

Palpatine studied the bundle of life he held. That the Force was strong in the infant was reason enough not to allow him to wander about unprotected, and perhaps fall into the hands of the Jedi.

Now Palpatine simply had to figure out what to do with him.

From a high turret in the old fort on Sojourn, Plagueis and Sidious observed the revelry in the courtyard below. There, amid the blazing fires, the smell of fresh blood and roasting meat, the cacophony of guttural chants, strident music, and screams of abandon, a Gathering was in progress. Returned from the hunts, beings of many species told tall tales and shared in vulgar laughter, while exotic dancers writhed atop tables laden with food and intoxicating drinks. Away from the roasting pits, beings huddled in the sultry night air, forming alliances, revealing hidden agendas, hatching plots. Passion, envy, and conspiracy were on the loose. From the high turret, the two Sith could see Damask's Sun Guards and Muuns circulating, Larsh Hill introducing his eldest son, San, to representatives of the Commerce Guild and the Techno Union. The Gotal Grand Mage of the Order of the Canted Circle was speaking with starship designer and Santhe/Seinar CEO Narro Sienar. Boss Cabra was making the rounds, as well, pressing the flesh, the scales, the rough hide of partners and potential allies. Members of the Trade Federation were in attendance, including a richly dressed Neimoidian. And for the first time in decades, representatives of various hive species were present—the Xi Charrian prelate, the Geonosian Archduke, even a couple of mistrustful and dangerous-looking insectoid Colicoids, from the Colicoid Creation Nest.

"We will not be denied," Plagueis was saying with unusual annoyance. "We will have our way in the Senate, regardless of what the Gran Protectorate, Black Sun, and the rest wish to see happen. Let the beings of the Hydian Way and Rimma Trade Route worlds go on thinking that the Trade Federation is seeking to tighten its grip on intersystem commerce. The real danger in seating the Federation's client worlds will emerge when the Senate ignores the needs of those worlds, and disenfranchisement begins to spread through the Mid and Outer Rims. Then the Republic will reap the whirlwind, and we will harvest the benefits."

He exhaled in disgust. "Pax Teem and the rest aren't acting out of concern for the Republic but out of fear that their entitlements might disappear if trade shifts to the outer systems. Half of them sit in the Rotunda only because *I* want them there. They've forgotten how effortlessly they can be replaced." He swung away from the view of the courtyard to face Sidious. "As for Veruna, you should encourage his plans to amass a Space Corps to defend Naboo against the Trade Federation. When we make him King, we will lead him by the nose into a morass that will appear to be of his own making."

Plagueis lowered his gaze to the courtyard. "The climate begins to shift, Darth Sidious. The body politic begins to show signs of contagion. The reemergence of anger, hatred, and fear signal a loss of faith in the Force. The light is waning, pushed into retreat by dark matter, and the universe begins to seem inimical rather than comforting. In such times, beings are wont to look for solutions in the enactment of harsh laws, the ostracism of strangers, and warfare. Once the Republic has fallen, the Jedi are but a memory, and beings have nowhere to turn but to us, we will provide them with a sense of stability and order: a list of enemies, weapons capable of decimating entire star systems, durasteel prisons in which they can feel secure." He gestured to the courtyard. "Look how they hunger for the dark."

A fierce light came into Plagueis's eyes. "We must demand the attention of the dark side to aid us in dictating the future. Together and separately we will see to that, and once we've put these Senate issues behind us, we will set the stage for the next act. With the promise of unlimited funding, guilds and unions will ally, and the hive species will turn pincer and claw to the manufacture of weapons, even in the absence of conflict, let alone all-out war."

Doubt tugged at the corners of Sidious's mouth. "The Jedi won't simply stand by and do nothing, Master. While I have no affection for them, I do respect their power. And weakening the Republic without weakening the Jedi could provide them with justification for attempting a coup. They have the numbers to succeed."

Plagueis took it under advisement. "Their time is coming, Sidious. The signs are in the air. Their Order might have already been decimated had it not been for the setback Darth Gravid dealt the Sith. But his apprentice carried the imperative forward, and each successive Sith Lord improved on it, Tenebrous and his Master most of all, though they wasted years attempting to create a targeted virus that could be deployed against the Jedi, separating them from the Force. As if there were some organic difference between the practitioners of the light and darks sides; as if we communicate with the dark side through a different species of cellular intermediaries! When, in fact, we are animated by the same power that drives the passion of these beings gathered below. Target midi-chlorians and we target life itself."

"An attack of that sort would fail, regardless," Sidious said, as if thinking out loud. "The Jedi are widely scattered, and it's unlikely that we would be able to act quickly enough to kill all of them in the same instant. We would need to assign an individual assassin to each, and there would be no way to still the tongues of that many assassins. Our plan would be revealed. We would be betrayed and become the targeted ones."

Plagueis paced away from the turret's window, his hands interlocked behind his back. "We don't want them to die too quickly in any case. Not, that is, until the Republic has been so ravaged, so weakened, that beings will willingly embrace the stability we impose."

"Are the weapons that will be produced by the Colicoids and the others meant ultimately to be used against the Jedi?"

"We shall see what comes to pass. Until such time we must accept the fact that no mere army can overwhelm the Jedi. The ancient Sith were tens of thousands strong and failed the test. Once the galaxy teemed with warriors and warships. Now we have only isolated bands of mercenaries and star system defense forces. That's why we must strive to return the galaxy to a state where barbarism is the norm."

"The Jedi will have to be felled from within," Sidious said, his eyes tracking Plagueis as the Muun paced the floor. "Lured into a trap of their own devising, as you said we will do with Veruna."

Plagueis stopped to regard him. "Follow that thought."

Sidious took a moment. "We will have to exploit their vanity and blind obedience to the Republic," he said with greater confidence, and as if the truth of it should be obvious. "They must be made to appear the *enemies* of peace and justice rather than the guardians."

"The *enemies* of peace and justice rather than the guardians," Plagueis repeated, in revelation. "Even the survivors of a purge would be forced into hiding . . ." Coming back to himself, he cut his gaze to Sidious. "Great care has to be taken not to turn them into martyrs, Darth Sidious—if in the end we want the beings of the galaxy to turn their backs to the light side of the Force."

"Forceful beings will continue to be born."

"In the absence of training and brainwashing, they will pose no harm to us. *You* will see to that, *Supreme Chancellor Palpatine.*"

Sidious looked at the floor and shook his head. "You should be the one, Master."

"No," Plagueis said firmly. "It must be you. You have the political skills, and more to the point, you are a human. In this era only a human is capable of rising to the top of Coruscant's biased political heap."

"Human or not, my knowledge of the dark side will never equal yours. The title, the crown, should be yours."

"And it will be, once you openly appoint me co-chancellor. Feared and respected by the galaxy's most powerful beings, Hego Damask will be seen as a windfall for the Republic. But even then I will advise only in secret from behind your throne."

Sidious bowed his head in deference. "In the annals of Sith history, you will be known as Plagueis the Wise."

Plagueis quirked a cunning smile. "You flatter me."

Star Wars: Darth Plagueis

"Whatever you ask of me, Master, I will do it."

Plagueis fell silent for a long moment, then said, "You need now to hear about the first mission I performed for Darth Tenebrous. The events transpired some twenty-five years into my apprenticeship. At the time, Tenebrous had sought to expand his network of influential beings by reaching out to a human industrialist named Kerred Santhe—"

"The former owner of Santhe Corporation."

"The same," Plagueis said. "Santhe Corporation had been designing freight vessels for generations, but had only limited success with its line of personal starships. My Master believed that he might entice Kerred into an alliance by offering him exclusive rights to a Rugess Nome ship. Santhe leapt at the opportunity, but only to manipulate Tenebrous into a situation where agents of Santhe Security were able to steal the plans."

Plagueis paused in narrow-eyed reflection. "It was one of the few times I saw my Master outmaneuvered. But he didn't set his sights on revenge—not immediately, at any rate. Once in production, the star-ship met with such success that Kerred Santhe was able to acquire a controlling interest in Sienar Technologies and Republic Sienar Systems. Only by agreeing to an arranged marriage between his youngest daughter was Sienar's president, Narro, able to retain his position as chief designer. By then, though, Narro had entered into a secret part-nership with Tenebrous, and the time had come to settle scores."

Plagueis moved as he spoke.

"Damask Holdings was in its infancy, but I had already earned a rep-utation among the galaxy's elite, and so received an invitation to attend a design conference on Corulag, which was then headquarters not only for Sienar Technologies but for Aether Hypernautics, Danthe Artifice, and a dozen other corporations. The guest speaker was the Senator representing the Bormea sector, and many luminaries from Coruscant, Corellia, and Kuat attended. From distant Lianna came Kerred Santhe and his young and unhappy wife, supported by an entourage of retain-ers and Santhe Security guards. I was seated at a table directly across from him, and the menu specialty that night was bloateel. Have you ever tasted it, Sidious?"

"As a teenager. At a gala hosted by House Palpatine."

"Then you know that the creature is one of the most poisonous to be found in the galaxy. The preparation is both dangerous and exacting, as the creature must be skinned while alive to guard against its toxins infiltrating the flesh. Needless to say, nothing enlivens a banquet like the prospect of near-instant death, and the hall could barely contain the anticipation as individual portions were served.

"I waited to act until I saw Santhe chewing his first bite."

Plagueis brought the thumb and forefinger of his left hand close together, and Sidious, taken by surprise, felt his throat close. He gasped for breath.

"Yes. Just so you have an understanding of what Santhe must have felt." Plagueis opened his fingers and Sidious inhaled deeply, his face flushed and his hands stroking his throat.

"Only then I kept the pressure on until his face began to turn red, his hands flew to his throat, his muted calls for help brought everyone around him out of their chairs. I think his bulging eyes might have found mine when I finally pinched his trachea closed completely. Of course, medtechs had been standing by in the event of just such an emergency—Ithorians, if I recall correctly, armed with doses of anti-toxin and medicines to counter the effects of anaphylactic shock. But none did the trick that night, for the dark side of the Force had Santhe in its grip and no drug or resuscitation technique was equal to the task of keeping him alive."

Plagueis touched his chin. "Many alleged that Rugess Nome and Narro Sienar had somehow engineered an assassination. Others, that Malkite Poisoners or a sect of the GenoHaradan had been contracted to carry out the kill. But in the end the chefs were held accountable, and given long prison sentences. Santhe Security squads made several attempts on my Master's life afterward, but we dealt with them. Much later we learned that Santhe's body had been placed in carbonite freeze, and that all his internal organs had been replaced by vat-grown ones. The surgical teams may even have been successful at restarting his body, but the Kerred Santhe they had known was irretrievable."

Plagueis said nothing for a long moment, then continued: "The circumstances will be different for you. You won't have the satisfaction of seeing our opponent die in person, because we want to ensure your deniability. A public assassination on Coruscant would be best for sending a message."

"Senator Pax Teem," Sidious said in a raspy voice, tinged with residual anger.

Plagueis shook his head. "Teem may yet prove useful. I'm referring to Senator Vidar Kim. His sentiments have made him a liability. More important, his death will allow us to position you where you've long yearned to be."

16: BOLD AS LOVE

The hood of his stylish robe raised against a chill wind, Palpatine hurried through the streets of Theed. The sudden turn in the weather abetted his desire to avoid making eye contact with strangers or, worse, encountering anyone he knew. As he grew stronger in the dark side, the profane world became a stranger and stranger place, swept by currents he'd had no previous awareness of and populated by vaguely outlined life-forms he saw as magnitudes of the Force. As Plagueis ordered, he had been living in the future, consorting with the dark side to execute the plans he and his Master had designed.

Vidar Kim's office was in the eastern portion of the city, a long walk from the apartment Palpatine had been renting for the past several years, and the quickest route required crossing and recrossing the Solleu tributaries that defined Theed's districts and neighborhoods. He had never had much fondness for the city, with its ancient buildings, public squares, its tens of thousands of residents going about their lives, and now Theed began to seem like some stage set in an elaborate theater production, and Naboo itself a node in a vast web being woven by the dark side, into which so many planets and species would ultimately be drawn.

At no time during the visit to Sojourn had Darth Plagueis asked to hear his feelings about the death order he had issued for Vidar Kim. And no wonder, since Palpatine had given his word to do anything Plagueis asked of him. But it was obvious that the Muun had sensed Palpatine's conflict. Fear and hatred had prompted him to murder his family in cold blood, but his relationship with Kim was as close as he had come to having a true friendship—even though, as Naboo's Senator, Kim stood between Palpatine and his immediate goal. On Sojourn, Plagueis's parting words to him were: *Remember why the Sith are more powerful than the Jedi, Sidious: because we are not afraid to feel. We embrace the spectrum of emotions, from the heights of transcendent joy to the depths of hatred and despair. Fearless, we welcome whatever paths the dark side sets us on, and whatever destiny it lays out for us.*

Clearly Plagueis knew that Palpatine had helped seal Kim's fate by encouraging him to take a stand against the Trade Federation, and therefore against Plagueis. That his Master hadn't said as much was perhaps his way of reminding Palpatine that he would have to be prepared to accept any and all consequences that sprang from his machinations. It was a subtle lesson, but one Palpatine took to heart. From then on, he would be careful to plan his moves meticulously; and more important, to allow the dark side to complete its lapidary work of transforming him into a powerful being. Recalling Plagueis's surprise Force choke, he pledged also never again to lower his guard. But he viewed the lesson as part of the process of their learning to rely on each other and forge themselves into a team. United in the dark side, they could keep no secrets; there could be no chance of one being able to act without the other being aware. They had to learn to see through each other.

Palpatine hadn't been attempting to flatter Plagueis when he had called him *wise*—not entirely, at any rate. The Muun was powerful beyond Palpatine's present understanding. The only being capable of guiding the galaxy into the future. A crescendo. At times it was difficult to grasp that they would see in their lifetime the fall of the Republic and the annihilation of the Jedi Order, and yet Palpatine seemed to know it to be true. A grand design was unfolding, in which he wasn't merely a player but an architect.

Resigning himself to Kim's death was easier than it might have been because Kim, too, had become a broken man in the wake of the deaths of his wife and younger sons. His reaching out to the son he had voluntarily surrendered to the Jedi was an act of desperation—and based on nothing more than a desire to assure that the Kim family line continued. How like the self-important royals among whom Palpatine had been raised. So fervent to be remembered by those who followed!

Rather than demand or ensure that Palpatine get his hands dirty once more, Plagueis had insisted on providing him with an agent to facilitate the assassination. Plagueis had said that they needed to guarantee Palpatine's deniability and make certain that no hint of scandal pursue him. But Palpatine had begun to wonder: Despite all the talks about partnership and disclosures, had Plagueis merely been making excuses for the fact that he harbored doubts about Palpatine's abilities?

Palpatine thought back to the story Plagueis had recounted about the murder of Kerred Santhe. Blame had fallen on the chefs who had prepared the bloateel. Kim's death, however, wouldn't result from food poisoning but public assassination. So who might emerge as having the most to gain from his death? Certainly not the Naboo, or the Gran Protectorate. The fact that fingers would point instead to the Trade Federation made him wonder why Plagueis would want to place the cartel in a position that jeopardized its chances of seating new worlds in the Senate. So once more he found himself wondering: Did Plagueis have an ulterior motive for *not* wanting the Trade Federation to succeed?

He wanted Kim's death to be viewed as a message. But by whom? Perhaps Palpatine was meant to be the recipient. When Plagueis said that many of the Senators were expendable, that they retained their seats only because of him, was he, in the same breath, saying that Palpatine, even as Sidious, was also expendable, easily replaced by another Forceful apprentice? While the Muun encouraged transparency in Palpatine, he sometimes made himself opaque. Would he at some point bequeath all his knowledge to his apprentice, or would he hold back, merely to keep the upper hand?

"Thank you for coming on such short notice, Palpatine," Kim said in a rush, ushering him into an office cluttered with data disks and flimsi printouts, and smelling of sweat, stale air, spoiling food. Tall windows opposite the hardwood entry doors overlooked the palace, including the new tower that Tapalo—in accordance with tradition—had constructed on being elected monarch.

"What I have to say will place you at some risk, but there's no one I trust more than you." Kim was in constant motion while he spoke, moving from his desk to the windows and back again. "I'm not entirely sure that this office is secure, but we have to take the chance."

Palpatine concealed a frown of misgiving and gestured to the couch. "Please, Vidar, sit and unburden yourself."

Kim came to a halt, exhaled wearily, and did as Palpatine suggested. His face was drawn, his hair in disarray, his normally neat beard and mustache in need of grooming.

"Palpatine, I have good reason to suspect that Tapalo and Veruna arranged the crash that claimed the lives of my family."

Palpatine's surprise was sincere. "Vidar, the crash was investigated and ruled an accident. Some problem with the antigrav—"

"Accidents can be faked—planned! You've piloted speeders ever since I've known you. You know that systems can be sabotaged."

Palpatine sat down opposite him. "What possible motive would they have for killing your family?"

Kim's bloodshot eyes fixed on him. "I know their dirty secrets, Palpatine. I know about the payments they've been receiving from the Trade Federation since Tapalo took office. The laws they've enacted to open all of Naboo to survey and plasma exploitation. I know about the deals they struck with certain members of the electorate to engineer Tapalo's unprecedented victory in the last election."

"Even so," Palpatine said after a moment, "why would they bring your family into this?"

Kim all but growled. "By relieving me of my plenary duties they risk angering many of the royals who support me. Instead they hope to *persuade* me to tender a resignation—out of grief, out of fear, out of I don't know what."

"Tapalo would know better than to attempt such a despicable act."

"You give him too much credit. The crash was meant to be a message to me. But it had the opposite effect."

. "How so?" Palpatine said, leaning toward him.

"I'm leaving for Coruscant this afternoon. And my first act will be to notify the Jedi Order."

Palpatine sat up straight. "Vidar, the Jedi listen only to the Senate and the Supreme Chancellor. You can't simply walk into the Temple—"

"I'll contact the members of the Council through my son. If I can convince Ronhar to leave the Order, the information will be my gift to the Jedi."

"And suppose Ronhar doesn't want any part of this." Palpatine crossed his arms across his chest. "Have you even been able to speak with him? It's my understanding that Jedi aren't permitted contact with their parents."

Kim scowled and studied the carpet. "Regardless, I was able to make contact."

"And?"

Kim's expression was cheerless when he looked up. "He told me that I'm a stranger to him, and that the Kim name has no significance for him."

Palpatine sighed. "Then that's the end of it."

"No. He has agreed to speak with me in person on Coruscant. I'm determined to convince him, Palpatine. Family *must* come first."

Palpatine bit back what he was about to say and began again. "Will you promise to keep me informed? Or at least let me know how to reach you?"

Kim went to the desk and sorted through the mess until he found the flimsi he was looking for. "This is my itinerary for the coming week," he said, passing the flimsi to Palpatine. "Palpatine, if something untoward should happen to me on Coruscant . . ."

"Stop, Vidar. We're getting way ahead of ourselves."

Kim ran a hand over his head. "You're right." He returned to the couch and sat. "Palpatine, we're too close in age for me to have thought of you as a son, but I do consider you the younger brother I never had."

Palpatine nodded without a word.

"If I fail to get through to Ronhar or the Jedi, I can at least alert my colleagues on the Senate Investigatory Committee."

Palpatine restrained an impulse to stand. "I think you're wrong about Tapalo and Veruna, Vidar. But I can say without hesitation that you will be risking your life by making such accusations public."

"I'm perfectly aware of that, Palpatine. But if Ronhar rejects my plea, what else will I have to live for?"

Palpatine placed his hand on Kim's shoulder.

The small part you will play in the revenge of the Sith.

* * *

By the time he left Kim's office the weather had turned sharply colder. Snow flurries were swirling around the palace towers, and the shallows to the Solleu tributaries were sheened with ice. The agent from Coruscant whom Plagueis had provided—Sate Pestage—was waiting in a small plaza behind the Parnelli Art Museum, warming his hands with his breath.

"The Naboo have never heard of climate control?" he commented as Palpatine approached.

Recalling his early conditioning sessions on glacial Mygeeto, Palpatine almost laughed at the man's remarks. Instead he said, "Radical change has always come slowly to this world."

Pestage cast a glance at the stately columns that enclosed the domed museum. "No doubt about that."

Slightly taller and older than Palpatine, he was sinewy and capable looking. His brown eyes were close-set and glistening, and his pointed nose and angular cheekbones were emphasized by black hair that had receded from his forehead and temple. Plagueis had mentioned that Pestage had been born in Daplona on Ciutric IV—an industrialized ecumenopolis outside of which Darths Bane and Zannah had once lived secret lives. Plagueis hadn't revealed how he had discovered Pestage— perhaps Damask Holdings had had dealings with Pestage's influential and extensive family—but he had said that Pestage was someone Palpatine might want to consider adding to his growing entourage of aides and confidants.

From the pocket of his robe, Palpatine prized the flimsi Vidar Kim had given him and handed it over. "His itinerary for Coruscant."

"Perfect." Pestage slipped the flimsi into his pocket.

"I want you to wait until his business on Coruscant is concluded."

"Whatever you say."

"He's threatening to alert the Jedi Order and the Senate Investigatory Committee about various deals that were made."

Pestage snorted. "Then he deserves everything that's coming to him." He scanned their surroundings without moving his head. "Have you made a decision about who to use from the data I supplied?"

"The Maladians," Palpatine said.

A group of highly trained humanoid assassins, they had struck him as the obvious choice.

Pestage nodded. "Can I ask why?"

Palpatine wasn't accustomed to having to justify his decisions, but answered regardless. "The Mandalorian Death Watch has its own problems, and the Bando Gora its own galactic agenda."

"I couldn't agree more," Pestage said. "Besides, the Maladians are known to honor all their contracts."

"How soon can you have them on Coruscant?"

Pestage looked at him askance. "Perhaps it's best that that remains on a need-to-know basis."

The man's audacity both impressed and bridled Palpatine. "There can be no mistakes, Sate."

A long-suffering look flared on Pestage's face, but his tone was compliant when he responded. "If there are, then I'm certain this will be our final conversation. I know fully well what Magister Damask and you are capable of, and I hope to make myself worthy of continuing to serve you. One day, perhaps, you'll begin to think of me as family, as I'm sure Senator Kim does you."

Just how much does this man know? Palpatine wondered.

"You've no qualms about living a double life, Sate?"

"Some of us are simply born into it," Pestage said, indifferent to Palpatine's penetrating gaze.

"You'll contact me here?"

"As soon as the work is completed. Just make sure to stay close to your comm."

"You'll also be contacting Magister Damask?"

Pestage rocked his head. "He gave me the impression that he would be unavailable for the next few weeks. But I suspect we're safe in assuming that the results won't escape his notice."

On a planet at the edge of known space, above the holo-well of a gleaming metallic table, a quarter-sized three-dimensional image of a tall biped rotated between graphs and scrolling lines of anatomical and physiological data. In a spoon-like seat suspended from the white room's towering ceiling sat Hego Damask, dwarfed by a trio of slender, tailed scientists—two crested males and a female whose complexion was more gray than white.

"This being is representative of the entire species?" the scientist called Ni Timor asked in a gentle, almost sussurant voice.

"This one murdered six members of his species," Damask said, "but he is otherwise typical of the Yinchorri."

Tenebrous had introduced him to the planet Kamino early on in his apprenticeship, but he hadn't visited in more than three years. In stocking Sojourn's greel forests with rare and in some cases extinct fauna, he had hired the Kaminoans to grow clones from biological samples he procured through brokers of genetic materials. The glassy eyes, long necks, and sleek bodies of the bipedal indigenes spoke to a marine past, though in fact they had been land dwellers for millions of years preceding a great flood that had inundated Kamino. With global catastrophe looming, most technologically advanced sentient species would have abandoned their homeworld and reached for the stars. But the Kaminoans had instead constructed massive stilt cities that were completed even while the oceans of their world were rising and submerging the continents. They had also turned their considerable intellect to the science of cloning as a means of ensuring the survival of their species, and along the way had taken genetic replication farther than any known species in the galaxy. Residing outside the galactic rim, the Kaminoans performed their work in secret and only for the very wealthy. It was unlikely, in any case, that they would have abided by the Republic's restrictions on cloning. Moral principles regarding natural selection seemed to be something they had left on the floor of what was now Kamino's planetwide ocean, which perhaps explained why they were no more reluctant about providing game animals for Sojourn than they were about supplying shovel-handed clones to work in the mines of inhospitable Subterrel.

Damask considered them to be one of the galaxy's most progressive species: almost Sith-like in their emotional aloofness and scientific objectivity.

The female scientist, Ko Sai, had highlighted an area of the Yinchorri's midbrain. "The lack of neural pathways to the forebrain indicates an innate proclivity for violence. Although the absence could be idiosyncratic."

The third Kaminoan, Lac Nor, called for an enhancement of the highlighted area. "The Yinchorri's violent nature could complicate matters, Magister. Without access to sociological studies, we have no means of determining to what degree the culture of violence shapes the beings born into it. A clone raised in a laboratory setting might exhibit feral behavior unless provided with some means to express aggression."

"An outlet," Ko Sai offered.

"Scientific studies are available," Damask said. "The question is, can compliance be bred into them without affecting their violent tendencies?"

"Probably not without disturbing the basic personality matrix," Ko Sai said. "We might produce a clone that is merely Yinchorri in aspect, but lacks the signature characteristics of the species."

Damask frowned. "That won't do."

"Have you considered using a more acquiescent species?" Ni Timor asked

"Which would you recommend?

"One of the placid species. Ithorians, for example. Or Caamasi."

Damask shook his head. "Neither species would suit my purposes. What about humans?"

"Our experience with humans is limited—though of course we have grown many replacement organs."

"Human emotionalism is somewhat problematic," Ko Sai added, "but not unsolvable."

Damask considered the comment, and then agreed with the Kaminoan's assessment.

Emotion in human beings was a fatal flaw. The same characteristic that fueled their need to form strong bonds and believe that all life was sacred made them compassionate to a fault. Only weeks earlier on Sojourn, he realized that even Sidious, for all his growing strength in the dark side, remained a prisoner of his emotions. That Sidious was feeling an urge to stretch out with his new powers was to be expected and encouraged, but he had to be taught the lesson every Sith needed to learn. With great subtlety Sidious had manipulated Vidar Kim into a position where he had become a liability, and therefore had to die. He hadn't bothered to address the issue directly because the time had come for Sidious to embark on the political career that would carry him to the chancellorship. Still, Sidious's reaction to the assassination orders—fleeting as it had been—had convinced Plagueis of the need for additional tests. Sidious didn't need to have his mistakes explained to him; he needed to experience the consequences.

"Perhaps, Magister," Lac Nor was saying, "if we understood your plans for the Yinchorri clones."

"I would expect them to serve as soldiers."

"Ah," Ni Timor said. "Then obedience, not mere compliance, must be a prime consideration."

"And yet the need for some measure of free will," Ko Sai was quick to point out. "Or else why not simply use combat automata?"

Lac Nor's large eyes fixed on Damask. "These Yinchorri appear to be ready-made for war, Magister. Are there so few of them in the galaxy that you need to clone an army?"

He had deliberately avoided mentioning Yinchorri immunity to Force suggestion because he should have no way of knowing about that, or indeed anything about the actions of midi-chlorians. But it was precisely the reptilians' capability to fashion Force bubbles that he hoped to explore.

"As you've already pointed out," he said after a moment, "their innate bellicosity interferes with their ability to follow orders."

Mostly to himself, Ni Timor said, "We would need to assure that their violent tendencies remained intact, while their behavior was less willful."

"Yes," Damask said.

Ko Sai craned her long neck. "Very challenging. Though perhaps if we could be supplied with a template for experimentation . . ." She gestured toward the 3-D images. "Is this specimen available for thorough evaluation?"

"I could have him delivered to Kamino," Damask said. "Assuming for the moment that you can discover some way to provide me with what I need, how much time would be required to grow a mature clone?"

The three scientists traded looks.

"In the case of the Yinchorri," Ni Timor said at last, "certainly no fewer than twelve standard years, to allow for both physical and mental development. As you know we have had some success in accelerating the growth rate of certain cloned creatures, but not yet with full sentients, owing to the plasticity of the youthful brain."

"More important," Lac Nor said, "while we might be able to grow a few clones, our facilities are at present inadequate to produce an army of any size."

"We would also need to consult with military specialists regarding programming," Ko Sai added.

"That can all be arranged," Damask said. "Would you have any objections to working with Rothana Heavy Engineering?"

"Of course not," Ni Timor said.

"Then Damask Holdings can provide whatever funding you need."

Ko Sai's eyes appeared to widen. "The Prime Minister will be very pleased to learn of this," she said with what passed for animation on Kamino.

In his apartment in snowbound Theed, Palpatine watched a HoloNet replay of Jedi Knight Ronhar Kim leaping from a Coruscant taxi in midflight onto a monospeeder piloted by the Maladian contracted to assassinate the elder Kim. At the same time Palpatine spoke by comlink with Sate Pestage.

"Is Naboo threading the story?" Pestage asked.

"On every network."

"*Breaking news, Coruscant,*" a female correspondent was saying. "*Chommell sector Senator Vidar Kim, of Naboo, was killed earlier today while en route to Mezzileen Spaceport, in what appears to have been an assassination. A hovercam stationed at Node SSJ in the Sah'c District captured the moment when a monospeeder approached Senator Kim's taxi from behind, and its helmeted pilot unleashed a salvo of blaster bolts, killing Kim instantly and barely missing a second passenger—an as-yet-unidentified Jedi Knight. The hovercam recording shows the human male Jedi, armed with an activated lightsaber, hurling himself from the taxi and knocking the pilot assassin from the seat of the monospeeder. Eyewitnesses state that the Jedi managed to steer the assailant to a pedestrian walkway close to where the speeder crashed and burned, but Realtime News has yet to learn whether the assassin survived the fall. Wounded in the attack, the pilot of the taxi was taken to Sah'c Med-Center, where his condition is listed as grave.*"

"Is the Maladian alive?" Palpatine demanded of Pestage.

"No. She spiked herself with a neurotoxin while Ronhar was trying to force information from her."

"You're certain?"

"Absolutely certain."

"The fool," Palpatine fumed. "Why didn't she wait until Kim had exited the taxi at Mezzileen?"

"You instructed me to make it public, which is exactly what I told her. She made a point of firing in full view of the security cam, but I haven't been able to determine whether or not she knew that Kim was riding with a Jedi. Based on the placement of the blaster bolts, I think she planned on taking out both of them."

"And if she'd succeeded, the Jedi would be conducting their own investigation."

"They are, regardless," Pestage said. "Because Ronhar issued a statement to the media that he may have been the target."

Palpatine directed a scowl at the comlink cam. "Why didn't you warn her about Ronhar?"

"I did warn her. Maybe she wanted to add another Jedi kill to her résumé."

"Another?"

"As I told you, the Maladians are very good at what they do."

Palpatine considered it. "If Ronhar is under the impression that he might have been the target, then Kim may not have revealed his suspicions about Tapalo and Veruna."

"He didn't. I had him under surveillance from the moment he arrived on Coruscant, and he didn't go anywhere near the Jedi Temple or meet with anyone on the Senate Investigatory Committee. I have recordings of the three meetings he had with Ronhar in his office in the Senate Annex, and at no time did he offer anything more than veiled references to intrigues on Naboo."

"Was he able to persuade Ronhar to leave the Order?"

"No. Ronhar said that he respected Kim for being his—what was the word he used?—*progenitor.* But that he considers the Temple to be his home and the Jedi to be his family."

Palpatine forced an exhale. "I warned him."

"Kim tried to convince him that family blood comes first, but Ronhar might as well have been listening to an episode of *Coruscant Confessions.*"

"Magister Damask will not be pleased. What rumors are circulating in the Senate?"

"That Kim may have been involved in shady business; that he double-crossed a group of lobbyists. You've got the Senate worried—if that was the idea."

Plagueis would be satisfied to learn as much, Palpatine thought. The *message,* he now realized, had been directed not to anyone in particular, but to the Senate itself. Beyond the goal of advancing Palpatine's political career ahead of schedule, the murder of Kim had spread apprehension in the galactic capital.

"It's done, in any case," he said finally.

"And without any leads for the police or the Jedi to pursue. You're completely in the clear."

Palpatine relaxed somewhat. "You've done well, Sate—the close call notwithstanding. There's a place for you among my support group if you're interested."

Pestage, too, sounded relieved. "Then I suppose I'll be seeing you on Coruscant. Senator Palpatine."

17: DAYS OF WINE AND IMPROPRIETY

Supreme Chancellor Thoris Darus was largely responsible for the heady atmosphere that prevailed on Coruscant. A human native of Corulag, Darus had brought a sense of style to the galactic capital that had been absent a decade earlier when Vaila Percivas held the position, and hadn't really been seen since the era of Eixes Valorum. Darus was unmarried, an incorrigible womanizer, an enthusiast of sport, opera, legitimate gambling, and high cuisine; his first term of office was characterized by a marked upswing in intemperance and, in the end, rampant corruption. Following the example set by the Supreme Chancellor, many of the tens of thousands who served in the Senate or lobbied on behalf of autocratic corporations and cartels had transformed Coruscant into a den of self-indulgence unrivaled anywhere in the Core or Inner Rim. From all areas of the galaxy had come beings eager to attend to the needs of the new political elite—from chefs to artists to specialists in pleasure. Courtesy of the Trade Federation and its numerous affiliates and corporate partners, goods flooded in from thousands of worlds, giving rise to new fashions, new foods, and novel forms of extravagance. Privileged Coruscanti, determined to enjoy life at the center, turned a blind eye to the storms that were brewing on the edges of civilization—intersystem rivalries, piratism, organized crime—and spiraling their way toward the Core. In three years the planet saw more immigration than it had seen in the preceding hundred, primarily from the Outer Rim, whose nonhumanoid species arrived in complete ignorance of the hardships that awaited them.

For Palpatine, Coruscant exceeded his expectations. Five years of travel and adventuring in the Expansion Region and Colonies had given him a taste for the high life, and here was a place not simply where his darkest desires could be fulfilled, but also where he could put his unique talents to the test. Its topography of cloudcutting edifices was a microcosm of the galaxy: swarming with beings who were willing to do whatever was necessary to claw their way from the depths, overseen by a tiered elite that nursed on their misery. If Coruscant was a magnet for those without skills or promise, it was also a paradise for those with credits and connections. And with assistance from many of the scions of wealth Palpatine had met while serving as Naboo's ambassador, along with Hego Damask's coterie of cronies and minions, he felt that he was on his way to the summit of the Senate Podium from the moment his boots touched the unnatural ground.

He grasped immediately that the only way the Republic might have saved itself was by removing the Senate to a world where temptation wasn't lurking at every traffic nexus; opportunity in every balconied café; vice in every canyon—although the racket that Supreme Chancellor Darus and the Senate had going was obvious only if one knew where to look, and that frequently required having unrestricted access to the private clubs and back rooms to which bribes gravitated. Even without the Force, Palpatine knew he would have succeeded. The task would prove no more challenging than gaining the full confidence of his peers. With everyone striving to outdo one another he need only ensure that he dress well, dine in the right places, associate with the proper company, and renew his season passes to the Galaxies Opera. At the same time, he understood that he could be almost as anonymous as he wished, simply by venturing up or down, dressing up or down, mingling with merchants rather than politicians, or consorting with the hucksters, shysters, con and scam artists that populated the lower levels.

His first apartment wasn't luxurious, but it was located in the government district, with room enough for his growing art collection, which now included a costly neuranium-and-bronzium sculpture of the ancient sage Sistros—appropriate for the affluent head of House Palpatine—and containing his original hand-built lightsaber, concealed in a cylindrical cavity undetectable by security scans.

The fact that his first official duty as Naboo's interim Senator was to attend a funeral—his second that year—seemed only appropriate, given the Sith's eventual plans for Coruscant.

Orders to attend Vidar Kim's funeral had come both from Naboo and from Plagueis, who said that he should use the opportunity to seek out Ronhar Kim and speak with him personally. Palpatine had yet to meet one-on-one with a Jedi, and a conversation with Ronhar would allow him to test his ability to conceal his true nature from another Force-user.

As wicked as Coruscant is, Plagueis had told him, *the Force is strong there because of the presence of so many Jedi. If you are successful in hiding in plain sight, you will be able to conceal your nature even from the most powerful among them. Take Ronhar into your confidence, and once you have, spend some of your time on Coruscant acquainting yourself with the spired headquarters of our enemy, and ask yourself: Is this not a fortress designed to hold the dark at bay?*

Otherwise, Plagueis's silence on the matter of Kim's assassination had been deafening. On learning that King Tapalo had appointed Palpatine interim Senator, Plagueis had offered his congratulations, but nothing more. After months of not seeing him, Palpatine had hoped to find Plagueis waiting for him on Coruscant, but Hego Damask and the Muuns who made up Damask Holdings were conducting unspecified business on distant Serenno.

The funeral service was held at Naboo's embassy, which was located below and to the west of Monument Plaza and the Senate. Dressed in a high-collared cape and purple robes, Palpatine arrived at the ornate monad in the company of Kinman Doriana, Sate Pestage, and Janus Greejatus, who had been dispatched to Coruscant by Tapalo, and whom Palpatine suspected had some strength in the Force. Kinman and Sate had forged an instant bond. The youthful Doriana was made for a world like Coruscant, and he couldn't have asked for a better guide to the galactic capital's titillating underbelly than Pestage, who seemed to know every nook and cranny of the place.

Ronhar Kim was among several dozen guests who were attending the service. Palpatine waited until the Jedi was alone in the viewing room before approaching him.

In concealing yourself, you will not be able to rely on your dark gifts, Plagueis said. *Instead you must be yourself, submerged in the unified pattern to which the Jedi are attuned; visible in the Force, but not as a Sith. Since you cannot allow yourself to be seen, you must make certain that you are taken for granted. Disguised in the profane; camouflaged in the routine—in those same realms from which you can attack without warning when necessary.*

A tall, muscular young man attired in black robes, Ronhar had thick black hair pulled into a bun behind, and with long strands in front dangling from temples to chin. In him, Palpatine could see Vidar, whose body was lying in state, supine on a massive rectangular stone bier. A simple blanket covered the corpse from shoulders to knees, and on the chest sat a shallow metallic bowel containing purple flowers and a lighted candle meant to symbolize the Livet Tower's Eternal Flame. Janus Greejatus would transport the cremation ashes to Naboo, where they would be scattered in the Solleu River.

"Jedi Ronhar Kim," Palpatine said as he entered the room, "please forgive the intrusion, but I wanted to offer my condolences in person."

Roused from his thoughts, Ronhar whirled on him, almost in defense, and scanned him head-to-toe. "Who are you?"

"Palpatine," he said. "I've been appointed to succeed Vidar Kim as Senator of Naboo. I knew your father well."

Ronhar's vigilance eased. "Forgive me for not knowing more about Naboo, Senator . . . Palpatine. But in fact, until several weeks ago I wasn't aware that Vidar Kim was my biological father, or even that Naboo was my homeworld."

Palpatine feigned understanding. "No need to apologize. I imagine that the Force is, in some sense, its own domain."

Ronhar nodded. "I scarcely knew the man. Were it not for the fact that he was a Republic Senator, the Jedi Council would not have granted dispensation for me to meet with him."

Palpatine allowed himself to stretch out with the Force, but only for a moment, and chiefly to gauge the Jedi's reaction, which proved to be indiscernible. "Excuse me for asking, but why then did you choose to attend the service?"

Ronhar grew pensive. "No doubt you know about the tragedy that claimed the lives of his wife and sons."

"I do."

"Vidar Kim contacted me to ask if I would consider renouncing my pledge to the Jedi, in order to become the bearer of the family name."

Palpatine moved closer to him and added compassion to his voice. "He told me, Ronhar. Does your presence here reflect doubt as to your obligations?"

"No," the Jedi said, perhaps more firmly than he intended. "I'm only here out of respect for the man. As you may also know, he died at the hands of an assassin while in my company." Ronhar's voice betrayed disappointment rather than anger. "If I had acted sooner, he would be alive, and at present I can't be certain that the assassin's blaster bolts weren't meant for me, rather than Vidar Kim."

"Who in their right mind would target a Jedi Knight?"

The Jedi sniffed and narrowed his dark eyes. "The Jedi do not lack for enemies, Senator. Doling out justice and ensuring the peace doesn't sit well with some beings."

"The world of politics is no safer, Ronhar. Not in this era, with so many in need. Thank the Force we have the Jedi."

"I wonder," Kim said.

Palpatine regarded him with interest. The Jedi was less interested in solving the murder of Vidar than he was in agonizing over his failure to prevent it. "You wonder about what, Ronhar?"

"What my life might have been had I not become a Jedi."

Palpatine adopted a look of shock. "The choice was not yours to make. You have the Force. Your destiny was a foregone conclusion."

Ronhar mulled it over. "And if Vidar Kim had elected not to surrender me to the Order?"

"A line of thought impossible to follow to any conclusion," Palpatine said.

The Jedi looked at him and squared his shoulders. "There are many forks in the path, Senator. Had I remained on Naboo I might have followed in Vidar Kim's footsteps and entered politics. Perhaps it's not too late."

Palpatine showed him a tolerant smile and came alongside him, confident now that his true nature was beyond detection. "I have to admit that the notion of a politician with Jedi values is not without its appeal. In fact, the Republic was once overseen by Jedi chancellors only. But I'm afraid you're something of an anachronism, Ronhar. The galaxy appears to have rejected the idea of enlightened leadership. The best politician presently is merely exceptional, where every Jedi is extraordinary."

Ronhar laughed shortly. "More and more, Senator Palpatine, you begin to sound like my former Master."

"Would that I had such talents," Palpatine said, making light of it. "But I do have a proposition, Ronhar. Not only am I new to the Senate, I'm new to Coruscant. And it would be good to have someone to count on as a friend. So what would you say to an alliance between a politician and a Jedi? Through me you could gain insight into the workings of the Republic, and through you I might better understand the Jedi, in their roles as peacekeepers."

Ronhar inclined his head in a bow. "I respect Vidar Kim all the more for bringing us together. May the Force be with you, Senator Palpatine."

On Serenno, remote from the Core along the Hydian Way, a female servant of Count Vemec, costumed in garb from an era long past, escorted the quartet of human Jedi into the castle's expensively modernized conference room. First to be introduced to those assembled—including dignitaries and politicians representing Serenno and nearby Celanon, and the Muun core of Damask Holdings—was Jedi Master and Council member Jocasta Nu, a pleasant-looking woman with straight hair, pronounced cheekbones, and brilliant blue eyes. Accompanying her were distinguished Jedi Masters Dooku and Sifo-Dyas, and a tall, powerfully built Jedi Knight named Qui-Gon Jinn, who remained standing while the rest took their designated seats at the circular table. The three men carried themselves with palpable self-assurance, and affected beards of different styles—Dooku's terminated in a stylish point; Sifo-Dyas's followed his strong jawline; Qui-Gon's was long and thick.

Plagueis, who rarely missed an opportunity to interact with Jedi, had planned to leave the business on Serenno to Larsh Hill and the others—until learning that Dooku would be present.

Fifty or so standard years old, Dooku was Serenno's native son, hailing from a noble lineage analogous to the Naboo Palpatines. Had he not been born strong in the Force, he would have been a Count, in the same way that Palpatine would have been a royal. But on the few occasions Plagueis had encountered Dooku, he had sensed something in him that warranted further investigation. Dooku was said to be one of the Order's finest lightsaber masters, and he had earned a reputation as a skilled diplomat, as well; but his passion and restlessness were what had captured Plagueis's attention. For all his decades in the Order, he seemed to have kept one foot anchored in the mundane. In place of the homespun brown robes worn by most Jedi—like the hale Qui-Gon Jinn—Dooku favored cloaks and robes more appropriate to a night at the opera on Coruscant. In addition, he was a candid critic of Supreme Chancellor Darus and the corrupt practices of the Senate.

Most important, perhaps, Dooku was linked to the Sith's Grand Plan in ways that went beyond circumstantial. Some twenty years earlier, in a scheme engineered by Tenebrous to replace human Senator Blix Annon with a young upstart named Eero Iridian, Dooku and his then-Padawan, Qui-Gon Jinn, were caught up in the events and had managed to send some of the principal players to prison. Dooku had also unwittingly sabotaged several of Tenebrous's plans to foster inter-system dissent in the Expansion Region.

In the aftermath of the near-disastrous assassination of Vidar Kim, Plagueis's interest in Dooku had assumed a new urgency. He felt certain that Sidious would evolve into a commanding Sith, but just now the young Naboo was drunk with power and prone to make mistakes. When the dark recognized one as a true ally, a novice could lose his or her way, as had almost happened to Plagueis following the murder of Kerred Santhe. Bane-adoring Sith Masters like Tenebrous might have used the meeting on Serenno as a means of threatening their apprentices with replacement. Plagueis, however, had no such intention, which was why he hadn't mentioned to Sidious that Jedi would be attending the meeting. Even so, he found himself wondering whether a dissatisfied Jedi like Dooku could be insurance against a reversal of fortune—some unexpected event that would rob him of Sidious—or perhaps turned to the dark without formal enlistment, and manipulated into instigating a schism in the Order.

As he had told Sidious, even a trained Jedi could succumb to the lure of the dark side on his or her own. One hundred thirty years earlier, on a former Sith world in the Cularin system, a Padawan named Kibh Jeen had been so strongly affected by the lingering power in a fortress on Almas that he submitted himself to the dark side and initiated a systemwide conflict. Perhaps, under Plagueis's influence, Master Dooku could be inspired to do something similar. The Jedi would bear closer observation.

One of Celanon's legal advocates was the first to speak when everyone had been seated.

"Celanon protests the presence of Jedi Master Dooku at this meeting, since it has come to our attention that he is Serennian by birth."

Serenno's arrogant Count Vemec started to respond when Dooku cut him off, addressing himself to the litigator. "If you had investigated further, you would also know that I renounced all ties to my family and Serenno on being accepted into the Jedi Order." He turned his penetrating gaze on Celanon's ambassador. "I assure you that I will be as impartial as any one of you."

Celanon's ambassador—a large, bumptious human—cleared his throat in a meaningful way. "Jedi Master Dooku's reputation for evenhandedness precedes him. We trust that he will be as fair in this matter as he is known to have been elsewhere."

"With that issue behind us," Vemec said, "I call for an official start to these proceedings."

The issue at hand involved the planned construction of an Aqualish-manufactured hyperwave repeater in Celanon space that would expand the reach of the HoloNet well into the Corporate Sector—a vast region of the Tingel Arm that had become an economic playground for the Banking Clan and the Corporate Alliance, through lucrative deals brokered by Damask Holdings. In compensation for the fact that placement of the repeater would necessitate changes in hyperspace trade routes, Celanon had announced that ships entering Celanon space from the systems of the upper Hydian would be required to pay substantial transit taxes. Plagueis had limited interest in the debate. Secretly he hoped that mediation would fail. Citing controversy, Damask Holdings could then withdraw, and the project would collapse, leaving systems in the Tingel Arm fuming over having been victimized by a foolish squabble between two wealthy Republic worlds.

After four hours of pointless back-and-forth, Plagueis began to feel like the victimized one. When Count Vemec finally called a break in the proceedings, and many of the participants headed to the food tables,

Plagueis found himself alone with Dooku, Sifo-Dyas, and Qui-Gon Jinn, and drew the cloak of the profane over himself.

"Bickering is becoming all too common," he remarked to no one in particular. "In the absence of resolution, it will be the outlying systems that will suffer most."

Dooku nodded sagely. "The hyperwave repeater should have been a Republic undertaking. The Senate erred in allowing the HoloNet to be privatized."

Qui-Gon Jinn's ears pricked up, and he glanced at Plagueis. "Discontent in the outer systems is in keeping with the aims of Damask Holdings, is it not, Magister?"

"On the contrary," Plagueis replied in a composed voice. "We advocate for the interests of neglected worlds when and wherever we can."

The tall Jedi wasn't persuaded to back off. "By supporting the likes of the Trade Federation and other cartels?"

"The Trade Federation has brought progress to many a backward world, Master Jinn."

"Through exploitation that leads ultimately to ruin."

Plagueis spread his hands. "Progress often comes at a cost. On occasion a world will go through growth pangs as a result, but to call the end result ruination is overstating the case." He studied Qui-Gon. "Surely the Jedi have had to ignore consequences of the same magnitude in enforcing the laws of the Republic."

Sifo-Dyas's dark brows formed a V. A short, muscular man, he had a broad nose, prominent cheekbones, and lustrous black hair cinched in a high topknot. His hands were large and callused, as if from physical labor. Concern shone in his brown eyes. "It is a misconception that we serve only the Republic, Magister. Our Order serves the greater good."

"As the Order defines it," Plagueis said, only to wave the remark away. "But then you have the advantage of being able to act in concert with the Force, where the rest of us are left to grope in the dark for what is just and right. Damask Holdings tries, nonetheless, to take the long view."

"As do the Jedi," Qui-Gon said. "But in several instances where we have had to resolve conflicts, it is your name that has surfaced."

Plagueis shrugged. "The wealthy are held to higher standards than the poor."

Dooku thought about it. "I blame the Senate for encouraging the galaxy to turn on credit."

Plagueis glanced from Dooku to Qui-Gon. "I'm willing to concede Master Jinn's point that the Muuns have cornered the market on finance, if he is willing to concede that the Jedi have cornered the market on ethics."

Qui-Gon granted Plagueis a dignified bow. "And so we find ourselves on different sides, Magister."

"Not necessarily. Perhaps we are after the same thing."

"Different paths to the same destination? It's a clever rationalization, but I refuse to accept it." Qui-Gon placed his hands in the opposite sleeves of his robe. "If you'll excuse me . . ."

Dooku smiled lightly as the tall Jedi sauntered off. "My former apprentice does not mince words."

"Frank talk is a rarity these days," Plagueis said. "The Senate could learn from beings like Qui-Gon Jinn."

Dooku made a glum face. "The Senate listens only to itself. Endlessly, and without purpose. If it and Supreme Chancellor Darus are going to perpetuate a climate where injustice can advance, then it will."

Sifo-Dyas grew uneasy. "The Rotunda is an arena even we don't enter," he said in a level voice, "except as spectators."

Plagueis could not restrain a smile. "But you have, from time to time, been known to lobby." He continued before Sifo-Dyas or Dooku could answer. "It can be a circus. One thing is certain, however: the Core is not holding. New leadership is needed."

"Darus will undoubtedly be elected to another term," Dooku said.

Plagueis pretended concern. "Is there no one who can defeat him, Master Dooku?"

"Frix, possibly. Kalpana—eventually. At present he isn't strong enough to overcome the special-interest lobbies."

Sifo-Dyas's unease increased. "We are sworn not to take an active role, in any case."

"Kalpana would certainly set a different tone," Plagueis said, "but perhaps an equally risky one. His stance against piratism, smuggling, even slavery is well known. Unfortunately, many of the outer systems survive only because of such practices."

"Then those worlds will have to find alternative means," Sifo-Dyas said.

Plagueis turned to him. "Without assistance from the Republic? It begins to sound to me as if the Jedi will have their work cut out for them."

Sifo-Dyas compressed his lips. "The Judicials and the Jedi will maintain peace."

"There's certainty in your voice," Plagueis said. "But let me pose a question: If discontent spreads and intersystem conflict breaks out—if member worlds threaten secession, as Serenno threatened in times past—would your loyalties not be divided?"

"The Republic will be preserved."

Plagueis grinned. "Again, that comforting confidence. But suppose the Republic's goals were not in keeping with the greater good? Suppose conflict grew to become actual schism?"

The two Jedi traded looks. "In the absence of armies there can be no war," Dooku said.

"Are the Jedi not an army—or at least capable of becoming one should the need arise?"

"We were an army at one time, but our enemies were vanquished," Sifo-Dyas said with deliberate vagueness. "No matter the extent of the conflict, we would attempt to forge a peace—and without becoming the ruling body you seem to fear."

Plagueis didn't reply immediately. Sifo-Dyas was proving to be even more interesting than Dooku, though in a different way. Only a misguided sense of loyalty to the Jedi Order kept him from giving voice to the real extent of his apprenhensions.

"And yet you say *forge* a peace. That has the ring of semantics to it, Master Sifo-Dyas. But for the sake of argument, what if the disaffected systems raised an army? Wouldn't the Jedi be obligated to serve and protect the Republic?"

Sifo-Dyas forced an exhale. "From where would these hypothetical armies arise? The outlying systems lack the resources . . ." Realizing his error, he trailed off.

Plagueis waited a moment, his satisfaction concealed. "I didn't mean to suggest that the Republic is *purposely* depriving the outlying systems of the right to self-determination. I'm merely speculating, because I do see a growing threat."

Dooku regarded him. "You are not alone in seeing it, Magister."

"Then one final question, if I may: If attacked, would you counterattack?"

"The Republic has pledged to remain demilitarized," Dooku said. "It would militarize only in the instance of a perceived threat."

"Once more, you've reframed your initial question, Magister Damask," Sifo-Dyas interrupted, a new fire in his eyes. "You're hypothesizing an attack on the Jedi Order itself."

"I suppose I am," Plagueis said self-deprecatingly. "I suppose I was thinking of the recent assassination of Senator Vidar Kim. A Jedi was involved, if I'm not mistaken."

"That matter is being looked into," Sifo-Dyas said in a controlled voice. "There's no evidence to suggest that the Jedi in question was targeted."

The silence that followed was broken by the voice of Jocasta Nu, who was summoning the Jedi to the far side of the conference room. Plagueis studied Sifo-Dyas peripherally. While Nu and the others conferred, he thought back to the conversation he'd had with Sidious on Sojourn.

We will have to exploit their self-righteousness and blind obedience to the Republic, Sidious had said at one point. *The Jedi must be made to appear the enemies of peace and justice, rather than the guardians.*

Mulling it over anew, Plagueis began to wonder whether he had taken the wrong approach on Kamino. Perhaps, he thought, it would be better to have the Kaminoans create an army capable of fighting *alongside* the Jedi rather than against them . . .

Sifo-Dyas was the first to return to Plagueis's corner of the room, as if eager to continue the conversation.

"Lest you're thinking of investing in military enterprises, Magister, I can assure you that the Republic will not reverse its stance on demilitarization." His words were forceful, but lacked certainty. "The Ruusan Reformations will not be repealed."

Plagueis showed the palms of his hands. "And I can assure you, Master Jedi, that my questions were in no means motivated by thoughts of profit. We—that is, I—don't wish to see the Republic caught off guard.

For now I'll place my faith in the Jedi, and in the belief that an army could be raised if necessary."

Sifo-Dyas's gaze faltered. "Out of thin air? Unlikely, Magister."

"Grown, then."

"Manufactured, you mean."

"No, I was being literal," Plagueis said. "But I know of only one group that might be up to the task. The group who grew laborers to work the mines of Subterrel."

Puzzlement wrinkled Sifo-Dyas's face. "I'm not familiar with Subterrel."

Plagueis was about to mention Kamino when he spied Jocasta Nu approaching, and a feeling from deep in the dark side rose up inside him, strangling his voice box, as if refusing to let the word escape.

"I apologize, Master Jedi," he said when he could. "The name of the group was on the tip of my tongue, but I seem to have swallowed it."

18: ARTFUL DODGING

Palpatine had been on Coruscant for just over two standard months when the Senate convened to vote on whether or not to seat Felucia, Murkhana, and half a dozen other planets considered by many to be client worlds of the Trade Federation. In the hope of generating public interest, Coruscant climate control had promised to provide perfect weather over the government district. Clouds had been swept aside and orbital mirrors had been positioned to provide maximum daylight. Maintenance droids had refreshed the paving stones of Senate Plaza and polished the thirty-meter-tall statues that lined the Avenue of the Core Founders. Police had cordoned off large areas of the district between levels 55 and 106, and deployed sniper units, squads of bomb detector automata, and three times the usual number of security hovercams. Reporters, documentarians, freelance journalists, and op-ed columnists were out in force, calling in favors in an effort to be as close to the action as possible. Limousine services were working overtime, and taxis were nearly impossible to find, which left aides and assistants to fend for themselves, arriving on foot or by mag-lev, ensembles freshly laundered, headpieces blocked, fur coiffed, boots buffed. Even the Jedi Knights and Padawans stationed throughout the plaza as a show of force appeared to be sporting their cleanest robes and tunics.

Analysts were touting the vote as landmark, though it had been an admittedly slow news week on Coruscant. More to the point, a vast majority of the capital's residents couldn't have cared less about the outcome, since most only knew of the Trade Federation through self-serving advertisements that streamed on the HoloNet. Local gossip was always more interesting than politics, in any case.

For weeks, however, opponents and supporters of the amendments that would revise the rules regarding member status in the Republic had been giving voice to their arguments in the great Rotunda, often vociferously enough to shake their repulsorlift platforms, jabbing fingers and other appendages in the air for emphasis or accusation, in defiance of calls by the vice chancellor for order and decorum.

Standing with Sate Pestage and Kinman Doriana beneath the abstract statue of Core Founder Tyler Sapius Praji, Palpatine felt one step closer to his destined place, even if the scene in the plaza struck him as more vanity fair than Senatorial assembly. Like many of the others, he had been out half the night, drinking and dining with lobbyists eager to win his favor. At tapcafs, cantinas, restaurants, and nightclubs throughout the entertainment districts, credits had flowed freely, whispered bribes had been proffered, promises made, deals struck. Now some of the players he had encountered during the long evening were shuffling bleary-eyed through the gaping entrances of the umbrella-shaped Senate Building: Senators and their top aides; commissioners of the investment sector and securities exchange; members of the Trade Federation delegation and the board of the InterGalactic Banking Clan.

Elsewhere on the broad avenue—at key intersections, taxi stops, and mag-lev exits—stood groups of Jedi, a few with the hilts of their lightsabers conspicuously visible. For Palpatine the sight of so many of them in one place was at once exhilarating and sobering. Though thoroughly cloaked in the everyday, he could feel their collective pride trickle into him through the Force. Only the baseness of Coruscant's populace, the almost sheer absence of anything natural, kept the world from being as strong in the light as Korriban was in the dark. While he accepted that he and Plagueis were more than equal to the most powerful of the Jedi Order, he understood that they were no match for their combined strength—the Sith imperative notwithstanding. The Jedi would fall only with the full collaboration of the dark side; that was, only when the dark side of the Force was ready and willing to conspire in their downfall.

His musings were interrupted by a sudden gust of wind, whipped up by a luxurious landspeeder that was alighting in the center of the avenue. Preceded by a vanguard of ceremonial guards wearing floor-length blue robes, Supreme Chancellor Darus emerged, waving to the crowd and for the hovercams that rushed in to immortalize his every expression. Palpatine studied him as the guards began to maneuver him through the throng, a train of handpicked journalists following dutifully in his wake: the easy way he carried himself; the way he made a point to stop and greet some while ignoring others; the way he laughed on cue . . .

He recalled the two coronations he and his father had attended in Theed, and could remember as if yesterday the envy that had wafted from Cosinga like sour sweat. How cravenly his inept father had desired to wield such power! And would that Cosinga could see his son now, standing so close to the center, surveying the Senate as Cosinga might have the Palpatine lands in the Lake Country, thinking: *Everything my gaze falls on will be mine: these buildings, these monads, these statues I will have slagged, this airspace whose use I will restrict to the powerful, that penthouse in 500 Republica, this* Senate . . .

Again his musings were interrupted, this time by the Gran Protectorate Senator Pax Teem, who was waddling briskly toward him, followed closely by the Senators from Lianna, Eriadu, and Sullust.

"Are you ready to make history, Senator?" Teem said, his eyestalks quivering in excitement.

"Rather than be a casualty of it," Palpatine told him.

The Gran grunted in amusement. "Well said, young sir. Needless to say, many are counting on you."

"Better many than all, because we cannot please everyone."

Teem grew serious. "Perhaps not. But we can strike a blow for utilitarianism. The greatest good for the greatest number."

Palpatine smiled in the way he had seen Darus smile. "And strike a blow we shall, Senator."

"Good, good," Teem chortled. "Then we'll see you inside where the galaxy's business is done."

Pestage snorted a laugh as Teem was moving away. "The greatest good for the greatest Gran."

It was true. Teem harbored no ill will toward the Trade Federation. He merely wanted to see Naboo blunder, Hego Damask cut down to size, and Malastare returned to its quondam grandeur.

The contingent of Senators had scarcely left when Palpatine heard his name called; turning, he saw Ronhar Kim in the company of two older human Jedi. Quietly he pulled his powers deeper into himself and adopted a mask of cordiality.

"Jedi Ronhar," he said, inclining his head in greeting.

The black-haired Jedi returned the nod. "Senator Palpatine, may I introduce Masters Dooku and Sifo-Dyas."

Palpatine was familiar with the former, but only by reputation. "A great honor, Masters."

Dooku appraised him openly, then arched an eyebrow. "Excuse me for staring, Senator, but Ronhar's descriptions of you led me to expect someone older."

"I disguise myself well, Master Dooku. My age, that is."

"Either way," Sifo-Dyas remarked, "a talent required by your position."

"An ignoble truth, Master Sifo-Dyas. But we strive to remain faithful to our conscience."

Dooku smiled with purpose. "Hold tight to that, Senator Palpatine. Coruscant will surely test your resolve."

Ronhar Kim had his mouth open to speak when another familiar voice rang out.

"I didn't realize that you were acquainted."

Over Dooku's shoulder Palpatine saw in surprise that Hego Damask, Larsh Hill, and two other black-robed Muuns were threading their way toward him. That he hadn't sensed his Master spoke to Plagueis's power to completely conceal himself, even from a fellow Sith.

"Magister Damask," Dooku and Sifo-Dyas said simultaneously, turning to greet him.

Damask looked at Palpatine. "Recently—on Serenno, in fact— Masters Dooku, Sifo-Dyas, and I engaged in a spirited discussion about the current state of the galaxy and our hopes for the future."

"Serenno," Palpatine said, more to himself and mildly confounded. Damask hadn't said anything about Jedi attending the meeting there. So what message was he sending now? Glancing at the trio of Jedi, he thought back to his Master's remark that even Jedi could be turned to the dark. Had the near-bungled assassination of Vidar Kim persuaded Plagueis to entice and recruit a Jedi to serve as his apprentice?

"Ronhar just introduced us to the Senator," Sifo-Dyas was explaining.

Dooku's eyes moved from Damask to Palpatine and back again. "May I inquire how it is that you and the Senator know each other?"

Damask motioned to Palpatine. "Senator Palpatine and Damask Holdings share a dream for Naboo . . ." He gestured inclusively to Hill and the other Muuns. "Palpatine was one of the few who early on saw the wisdom of ushering in a new era for his homeworld."

Palpatine sensed scrutiny from someone outside the circle the ten of them had formed. Just short of the Senate Building's Great Door, Pax Teem had stopped and was gazing at Palpatine, his eyestalks extended. And Palpatine could scarcely blame him, since even he had been caught off guard by Plagueis's eagerness to acknowledge him in public.

"How does it feel to have realized your wish for your homeworld?" Dooku said.

Palpatine came back to himself. "One can't very well stand in the way of destiny."

Again, Dooku glanced from Palpatine to Damask. "The will of the Force begets uncommon fellowships."

Chimes sounded, announcing that the session was beginning, and everyone began to file through the doors into the massive structure, going their separate ways from the atrium, some to spectators' boxes or media areas, and others, like Palpatine, Sate, and Kinman, to turbolifts that accessed Naboo's station in the Senate's middle tier—one of a thousand identical docking stations in the Rotunda, outfitted with a detachable repulsorlift platform and a suite of private offices. Central to the artificially lighted space was an elegant tower emblazoned with the seal of the Republic, at the summit of which rested the Supreme Chancellor's podium. Darus, the vice chancellor, and the administrative aide were already present, and after brief introductory remarks by the Supreme Chancellor, the vice chancellor called the matter to a vote.

A few Senators spoke, but most simply cast their votes, a tally of which was relayed to monitor screens at each station and projected overhead, along the inner curve of the dome. By the time the vice chancellor recognized the Chommell sector, the vote was tied. Though Palpatine's vote would break the stalemate, several systems had yet to weigh in.

Detached from the docking station, the platform carried Palpatine out over the lower tiers and deep into the kilometers-wide Rotunda. A hush fell over a portion of the Senate, and he inhaled the moment deep into himself. Still the platform continued to move toward the podium, as if even the Supreme Chancellor wanted a closer look at him, and it pleased him to know that his reputation had spread that far.

Then Palpatine spoke to them.

"The Trade Federation came to Naboo some ten years ago. It didn't arrive by force but by invitation, after a vast reservoir of plasma was discovered beneath Naboo's lush mantle—vast enough to supply clean energy to hundreds of disadvantaged worlds along the Hydian Way and, at the same time, introduce Naboo to the galactic community.

"Following months of reasoned debate, our newly elected monarch decided that Naboo should share its resources with the galaxy. Agreements were struck between Naboo and the Trade Federation, along with several construction conglomerates. Mining was begun, processing plants were constructed, and spaceports were enlarged to accommodate the fleet of shuttles needed to ferry the plasma to cargo ships parked in orbit.

"Three years later, plasma was flowing out into the galaxy and wealth was flowing into Naboo and the worlds of the Chommell sector, and an era of unprecedented prosperity had begun.

"That prosperity came with hidden costs, but Naboo was willing to absorb them, primarily for the sake of those beings who were benefiting from what nature had bequeathed to our small world."

He paused and turned slightly in the direction of the Trade Federation's platform.

"The Trade Federation has been accused of price fixing, exploitation, and monopolistic practices, but those matters are not at issue today. Today the Republic is being asked to widen its embrace to include several planets in the outlying systems many consider to be client worlds of the cartel. Many of you are concerned that seating these worlds will tip the balance of power by giving the Trade Federation and its corporate allies too strong a voice in the Senate. But was this matter not already settled when the Courts of Justice ruled that the Trade Federation should be treated as if it were a world? That decision opened the door to entities like the Commerce Guild, the Techno Union, and the Corporate Alliance, all of which enjoy their separate platforms in this hall. So the issue of *legality* is not up for debate.

"Instead, we must set ourselves to the task of deciding if the Trade Federation has become too aggressive in its pursuit of a louder voice."

Again he paused, this time to allow individual debates to come and go.

"Not three standard months ago," he said at last, "the Chommell sector's Senator of long standing was assassinated, here, on Coruscant. Senator Kim was known to many of you as an honest being, concerned about the growing influence of the cartels and the potential for a shift in power in the Senate. His tragic death provoked allegations and prompted investigations, and yet no progress has been made in determining the motive for his murder or identifying the agents behind it. This, despite inquires by Judicials, the Senate Investigatory Committee, even the Jedi Order.

"As a consequence of and, yes, in protest against the manner in which the investigation into Senator Kim's death has been handled, I am instructed by my regent, King Bon Tapalo, to announce that Naboo and the Chommell sector worlds are abstaining from the vote."

The hush that had fallen over a select section of the Senate spread to include the entire Rotunda. Then the outbursts that erupted—both damning and championing—were so clamorous and prolonged that the vice chancellor ultimately curtailed his attempts to restore order and let chaos reign.

19: THE TRIALS

In the aftermath of the Trade Federation victory in the Senate, Felucia, Murkhana, and other former client worlds became members of the Republic, unswerving in their allegiance to the needs of the Trade Federation. While Pax Teem and a handful of similarly disappointed Senators shunned Palpatine, accusing him—and Naboo—of having been bought by the cartel, most of the Senate dismissed the matter with a shrug. Palpatine was new to the game and, in fact, was merely expressing the wishes of King Tapalo. More important, the seating of new worlds meant new revenue and additional opportunities for graft. Ronhar Kim thanked Palpatine personally for not mentioning him in his address to the Senate. Moved by Palpatine's appeal, Supreme Chancellor Darus sent a personal message stating that he was instructing the Judiciary Committee to use its wide-ranging powers to unravel the Kim assassination.

Plagueis was pleased by the results, since it was only a matter of time before the newly seated worlds would find themselves caught between the Republic on the one hand and the Trade Federation on the other; taxed by the former, exploited by the latter—the perfect recipe for resentment. The two Sith did not meet in person, but Plagueis notified his apprentice that he and the other Muuns would be remaining on Coruscant for the foreseeable future, primarily to attend the induction of Larsh Hill into the arcane Order of the Canted Circle, many of whose members were regulars at the Gatherings on Sojourn.

For Darth Sidious, the weeks following the vote were a return to business as usual. With the Senate still in session, he spent most of his days in the Rotunda and most of his nights continuing to explore Coruscant, often in the company of Pestage and Doriana. In secret he continued his Sith training, accepting the absence of actual guidance from his Master as a sign that he was meant to stretch out on his own. And so he did, delving into many of the ancient texts Plagueis dismissed as worthless, including treatises on Sith sorcery and holocron construction.

Toward the end of the third week he was contacted by a lobbyist for an energy consortium known as Silvestri Trace Power. In several comlink exchanges, the lobbyist, a Sullustan, made it clear that Senator Palpatine stood to profit greatly by advocating for STP in the Senate, and suggested a meeting to discuss terms. Sidious probably wasn't supposed to dig too deeply into the origins of STP, or succeed in discovering ways around the roadblocks the consortium had constructed to thwart just such investigations, but he did, and was intrigued to learn that STP had once been a shell company created by Zillo Fuel Resources, which was based on Malastare.

Suspecting an attempt at entrapment, Sidious agreed to a daytime meeting, the location of which served only to further arouse his suspicions. Unlike the upper-tier restaurants patronized by the political crowd, the Shimmersilk was in a low-tier district known colloquially as POTU, which to most beings stood for "the periphery of the Uscru," but to the better informed meant "the peril of the Uscru"—a slowly gentrifying area accessed by the Deep Core Mag-Lev Line that had once been the haunt of turf gangs, serial killers, molesters, thieves, and other bottom feeders, on a world whose bottom was uncommonly deep. With residents preying mainly on one another, the police saw little reason to patrol, and even security cams were scarce, as they were frequently stolen and disassembled for parts. Still, the risk of mayhem or murder appealed to the Rotunda crowd, and it wasn't unusual to encounter a Senator or an aide slumming in the POTU, mingling with shady beings, indulging in proscribed substances, flirting with danger.

Sidious considered bringing Pestage and Doriana along, but ultimately rejected the idea. In the absence of undergoing any formal training with Plagueis, he was eager to see what he could do on his own.

Cramped and rattled by the frequent passage of nearby mag-lev trains, the Shimmersilk catered to what looked like a local crowd.

Dressed down for the meeting, as was Sidious, the Sullustan lobby-ist was waiting at a corner table, with his back to a wall adorned with cheap holoimages. Only six other tables were occupied—nonhuman couples in the main—and catered to by three clumsy human waiters and a Dug bartender. Instrumental jatz music, barely audible, wafted though air in sore need of recycling.

Sidious adopted a look of wide-eyed innocence as he sat down op-posite the Sullustan. They began to talk in a general way about current events and Senate business, before the lobbyist steered the conversation toward STP's need for Senate approval to expand its operations along the Rimma Trade Route. Drinks and appetizers were ordered and reor-dered, and before too long Palpatine's interest began to wane.

"I think you may have overvalued my worth to STP," he said at last. "I'm nothing more than the voice of Naboo's regent."

The Sullustan waved his small hand in a gesture of dismissal. "And I think you undervalue yourself. Your short speech to the Senate put you on the map, Senator. Beings are talking about you. STP believes that you can be of great service."

"And to myself, you said."

"Naturally—" the Sullustan started, but Sidious interrupted him.

"In fact, you're not here to recruit me." Motioning negligently, he repeated: "You're not here to recruit me."

The Sullustan blinked in confusion. "In fact, I'm not really here to recruit you."

"Then why are we here?"

"I don't know why we're here. I was instructed to meet with you."

"Instructed by whom?"

"I, I—"

Sidious decided not to press him too hard. "You were saying?"

Again the Sullustan blinked. "I was saying . . . Just what was I say-ing?"

They both laughed and sipped at their drinks. At the same time, Sidious used the Force to shift the apron of one of the waiters just enough to reveal the grip of a hold-out blaster the man was wearing at his waist. Lifting his glass for another swallow, he did the same to an-other of the waiters, whose apron concealed an identical weapon. Both had been manufactured by BlasTech, but not for common consumption. The E-series 1-9—the aptly named Swiftkick—was available only to elite members of Santhe Security, headquartered on Lianna.

"I had better slow down," he said with purposeful awkwardness. "I believe I'm becoming a bit light-headed."

The Sullustan's demeanor changed, though almost imperceptibly. "You just need some more food." He slid a menu across the table. "Choose whatever you wish. Cost is no issue." He stood. "If you'll excuse me for a moment, we'll order as soon as I return."

Sidious noted that the Sullustan wasn't the only one getting to his feet. Under low-voiced orders from the waiters, patrons were calling for their checks and exiting. In moments he would be the Shimmersilk's sole customer. As he swung slightly in his chair to stare into the corner of the room, a scenario began to emerge in his imaginings. The Sullustan, STP's link to Malastare, Santhe Security agents, even the Dug bartender . . . Their issues were not with him but with Damask Holdings. He wasn't being set up for an eventual allegation of corruption; a far more sinister deception was unfolding, and his interest was immediately renewed.

His first thought was that they had attempted to drug him. His investigations into Sith sorcery had taught him how to nullify the effects of many common poisons and venoms—a practice he had performed routinely before he'd even seated himself at the table. Perhaps, then, they were waiting for him to slump forward and lapse into unconscious or froth at the mouth and be shaken by spasms . . .

Just when he was thinking that it was his acting ability that was going to be put to the test, two of the waiters converged on him, now showing their discreet but powerful weapons.

"Someone wants a word with you, Senator," the taller of the pair said.

"Here?" Sidious said in apparent confusion.

The other one motioned to a door. "Through there."

Sidious masked his smile: the Shimmersilk had a back room.

He stood clumsily, leaning deliberately toward one of the security men, gauging his body temperature, heart rate, and respiration. "I'm slightly intoxicated. I may have to count on you for support."

The man made a sound of exasperation but allowed Sidious to place one arm on his shoulder.

How effortless it would be, he thought, as the dark began to rise in him, searing and hungry, yearning to assume control of his body and unleash itself, *to break the necks of both of them, to tear their beating hearts from their chests, to hurl and plaster them against the walls, to bring the entire sour-smelling place down on their heads . . .*

But he didn't. He needed to meet his abductor. He needed to learn the names of all those responsible. He needed to prove to his Master that he was adroit and capable—a true Sith Lord.

The back room had a second door that opened into a dark corridor leading to an ancient turbolift. Shoved forward by the guards, Sidious calculated the distance they had come from the Shimmersilk to the turbolift. He fell silent as they began to rise, and devoted his attention to calculating their rate of climb. He estimated that they had risen fifty levels when the turbolift came to a halt, depositing them in a corridor as aged as the first, though wider, tiled, and illuminated by wall sconces. Perhaps a maintenance corridor for the monads above, though still far below what would constitute the deepest of the sub-basements. The Santhe Security men guided him north across a stretch of stained permacrete floor to an intersection where a four-being speeder was idling, a heavily armed Rodian seated at the controls.

This one isn't Santhe, Sidious told himself. *A freelance mercenary or assassin.*

Shoved roughly onto the speeder's rear bench seat, he was reminded not to do anything foolish. Restraining an impulse to reveal that *they* already had, he continued to play the intimidated abductee, cowering in the seat, hands interlocked in his lap, avoiding eye contact. The speeder traveled east at a moderate speed until the first intersection, then turned in the direction of the government district and resumed the same speed for a longer duration. Sidious reckoned that they were twenty or so tiers beneath the outlying buildings of the Senate when the speeder swung west into an even broader corridor toward a district known as The Flats or The Works—a kind of industrial plain situated well below the governmental plateau, overlooked to the far north by the Jedi Temple and the horizontal landing fields of Pius Dea Spaceport, and to the south by the resiblocks and commercial towers of the Fobosi district.

Where Plagueis was attending Larsh Hill's induction into the Order of the Canted Circle.

The Rodian speeder pilot delivered them to an antigrav turbolift car.

While pretending to tremble in fear, Sidious had come to an additional conclusion: the fact that his abductors had gone to a lot of trouble to keep him out of public view meant that the plan called for him to be held for ransom or executed clandestinely rather than publicly.

The elevator carried them to a midlevel docking area of an abandoned factory, where several more guards were waiting. Oblique, particulate-suffused daylight streamed though massive windows yet to be smashed by the gangs that ruled The Works, falling on items that had been deemed worthless when the factory's owners had abandoned Coruscant for less costly worlds in the Mid or Outer Rim. Sidious's human handlers forced him to sit atop the boxy body of an overturned power droid. A portable holoprojector was moved into position in front of him, and a transmission grid placed under his feet.

One of the Santhe guards spent a moment activating the projector, then stepped aside as a faintly blue, life-sized image of Gran Protectorate Senator Pax Teem took shape above. Teem was dressed in a richly brocaded robe and a shimmersilk tunic banded by a broad cummerbund. The stable and sharply detailed quality of the image suggested that its source was Coruscant or a nearby Core world, rather than Malastare.

"We apologize for not having provided a seat more suited to your station, Senator. No doubt the head of House Palpatine is accustomed to more comfortable surroundings."

Sidious rejected outrage and intimidation for rankled curiosity. "Is this the point where I'm expected to ask why I've been abducted?"

Teem's eyestalks lengthened. "You're not the least bit interested?"

"I assume that this has something to do with Naboo's abstention in the vote."

"That's certainly part of the reason. You should have voted as your predecessor would have, Senator."

"Those were not my instructions."

"Oh, I'm certain of that much."

Sidious folded his arms across his chest. "And the rest of it?"

Teem rubbed his six-fingered hands together in eagerness. "This has less to do with you than with the beings you serve. In a way, it's simply your bad luck that you find yourself in the middle."

"I don't believe in bad luck, Senator, but I take your point to mean that my abduction is an act of retribution. And as such, you demonstrate that the Gran Protectorate is willing to employ the same tactics used by those who ordered the assassination of Vidar Kim."

Teem leaned toward the cam that was transmitting his image and allowed anger to contort his features. "You say that as if it's still a mystery, when we both know that the murder wasn't ordered by the Trade Federation but by your Muun master. By Hego Damask."

Sidious's expression didn't change. "He is hardly my *master*, Senator. In fact, I scarcely know him."

"He greeted you in front of the Senate Building like a close friend."

"He was extending his greeting to two Jedi Masters I happened to be standing with."

Teem's right forefinger jabbed the air. "Don't delude yourself into thinking that you can save yourself by lying. You and Damask have known each other for more than ten years. Ever since you were instrumental in helping him guarantee the election of Bon Tapalo."

Sidious gestured casually. "An old rumor that has no basis in fact, begun and perpetuated by rivals of House Palpatine."

"Again, you lie. Your treachery was to your father and his royal allies. In exchange for the information you released and the subsequent spying you carried out for Damask, he rewarded you by persuading Tapalo to appoint you ambassador."

Sidious hid his ruefulness. That his enemies on Naboo had reached out to Teem came as no surprise. But the revelation firmed his decision to have those enemies eliminated at the first opportunity. And to see to it, as well, that information regarding his past disappeared from the public record.

"The appointment as ambassador came years later," he said. "As a direct result of my political accomplishments on Naboo."

Teem snorted a laugh. "In the same manner in which the appointment to the Senate was a result of your accomplishments?"

"Speak plainly, Teem," Sidious said, his voice flat and menacing now.

Teem showed him a bitter smile. "Perhaps you had no direct hand in Kim's death, but I suspect that you were complicit." He paused, then added, "That little speech you gave in the Senate . . . I understand that it succeeded in attracting the attention of the Supreme Chancellor. Clearly you have all the makings of a career politician. Unfortunately, we plan to cut your career short."

Sidious brushed dust from the shoulder of his robe. "Release whatever allegations you have. They will provide gossip for the day and be forgotten the next."

Teem planted his large hands on his hips and laughed heartily. "You misunderstand me, Palpatine. We're not interested in besmirching your reputation or holding you for ransom. We intend to *kill* you."

Sidious took a moment to respond. It was odd to think now that he had once known fear. Though never incapacitating fear, and never for very long. But as a child, he'd experienced fear as a conditioned response to threat. Despite a reassuring voice inside him that had promised no harm could come, there had been, for a time, a *chance* that something terrible could happen. More than once his father's raised hand had made him cringe. Eventually, he had understood that he had conjured that voice; that he hadn't been fooling himself by exercising some infantile belief in invulnerability. And he understood now that it had been the dark side telling him that no harm could come to him, precisely because he *was* invulnerable. Since the start of his training, the voice had quieted by becoming internalized. Teem's belief that he had power over him might long ago have moved him to pity instead of stirring anger and loathing. Raw emotion was a consequence of leading a double life. While he relished his secret identity, he wanted at the same time for it to be known that he was a being who could not be trifled with; that he wielded ultimate authority; that merely to gaze on him was tantamount to glimpsing the dark matter that bound and drove the galaxy . . .

"What is it you hope to gain by killing me?"

"Since you ask: to rid the Senate of yet another useless crony, and to send a special message to Hego Damask that his days of influencing the Senate have come to an abrupt end. For ten years we've been waiting to execute this . . . *retribution,* as you call it. For some of us, even longer. Reaching back to Damask's partnership with a Bith named Rugess Nome."

The assassination of Kerred Santhe, Sidious thought. "I fear, Senator, that you have not given this matter sufficient thought."

Teem's face took on color. "Repercussions, Palpatine? Ah, but we have thought through the matter, and have taken the necessary precautions."

Sidious nodded. "I'll give you one final chance to reconsider."

Teem swung to someone off cam and loosed a belly laugh. "Tell that to the beings who hold your life in their hands, Palpatine. And do take heart in the fact that you accomplished so much in your brief career."

No sooner did the holoimage dissolve than two of the security men began to advance on him. Sidious readied himself for action. A Force blow to send them reeling back toward the holoprojector, then a leap, arms extended, hands curled into claws, one for each windpipe, which he would tear from their throats—

The Force intruded, drawing his attention to the windows in the upper walls.

At once, the sound of repeating blasters and pained cries echoed from adjacent rooms; then a nerve-jangling shattering of glass as Sun Guards crashed through the high windows and began to rappel to the filthy floor, firing as they slid down on their microfilament lines, catching the Santhe men and the Rodian with so many bolts that their bodies were left quartered by the volleys.

Other towheaded Echani rushed into the landing from both sides, some carrying force pikes, others blasters. Sidious had yet to move a muscle when a silver-eyed female hurried over to him.

"You're safe now, Senator Palpatine."

He smiled at her. "I can see that."

An Echani male standing alongside the holoproj was using a handheld device to extract information from it. A moment later, an image of Hego Damask dressed in a ceremonial robe genied into view where Teem's had been; the droid 11-4D stood behind him.

"We have the source, Magister," the Sun Guard said. "Panoply Orbital Facility."

Damask nodded. "Rendezvous with the rest of your team and execute the assault."

The Sun Guard nodded briskly. "Shall I leave personnel with Senator Palpatine?"

"No," Damask told him. "Senator Palpatine doesn't require your protection. Leave us."

Sidious could hear airspeeders hovering outside the factory. Without further word, the Sun Guards began to race from the room.

"You've obviously been keeping a close eye on me," Sidious said as he approached the projector.

Darth Plagueis nodded. "Your abduction has been in the planning stages for some time."

"Ever since you made it a point to greet me openly at the Senate."

"Even before that. Veruna alerted me to the fact that a group of disgruntled nobles had made contact with the Gran." Plagueis paused a moment. "You might consider using Sate Pestage to settle the score with them."

"The thought occurred to me."

"As for our public meeting, I needed to dangle you in front of them."

"Without my knowledge." The ruddiness that had come to Sidious's face deepened. "Another test?"

"Why should I need to test you?"

"Perhaps you thought I was becoming so enthralled with life on Coruscant that I wouldn't recognize danger."

"Clearly you weren't. I could see that you were aware from the start. You were determined to please me, and indeed you have."

Sidious inclined his head in a respectful bow.

"Even in partnership with Santhe Security, Teem and the other Gran are rank amateurs," Plagueis continued. "Our agents persuaded them to use the eatery in Uscru, and the factory in which you find yourself—owned by us, as it were, through a holding company called LiMerge Power. We were unable, however, to determine where the Gran would be taking refuge."

"And now you know," Sidious said. "But why go to such lengths to set them up? Why not simply kill them?"

"This isn't Sith business, apprentice. For the sake of appearances we need to justify what we are about to unleash on them. They failed to understand our message and now they must be taught a lesson. Still, other interests need to be convinced of our reasoning."

"How can I help?"

"You've already played your part. Now go about your usual business. We'll speak again when the ceremony at the Order of the Canted Circle is concluded."

Sidious fell silent for a long moment, then said, "Is there an end to these trials?"

"Yes. When there is no further need of them."

20: THE CANTED CIRCLE

The stage was set.

A perfect circle, twenty meters in diameter, had been cut from a single slab of imported stone and constructed so that one end touched the floor while the other was held ten degrees above it by concealed antigrav generators. This was the Canted Circle, known only to members of the order—which, throughout its long history, had never numbered more than five hundred in any given period—and was housed in the clear-domed summit of the esoteric society's monad in the heart of Coruscant's Fobosi district. Legend had it that the round-topped building—thought to be one of the oldest in that part of the planet—was built over an ancient lake bed and had been the sole survivor of a seismic event that had tipped it ten degrees to the southwest. A century after the quake, the structure had been righted to vertical, except for the central portion of the canted floor of its uppermost story, which later supplied the name for a clandestine organization founded by influential beings who had purchased the building sometime during the reign of Tarsus Valorum.

Just then, Larsh Hill, draped in black robes, was standing at the raised end of the circle, and Plagueis, 11-4D, and ten other Muuns—also wearing black garments, though different from the order's hooded garb—stood at the other. Scheduled to begin at the top of the hour, the initiation ceremony would commence with the high official joining Hill on the circle, initiating him, and placing around his neck the order's signature pendant. Plagueis had declined an offer of enrollment twenty years earlier, but had continued to do business with the Grand Mage and many of the order's most prominent members, several of whom were regulars at the Gatherings on Sojourn. The Order of the Canted Circle was content to serve as an exclusive club for some of the galaxy's most influential beings; its aims were narrow in focus and its rituals universally allegorical, replete with secret phrases and hand-shakes. Plagueis understood the need to instill members with a sense of furtive fraternity, but he couldn't risk having the high officials dig too exhaustively into his background. Larsh Hill's past, on the other hand, was exemplary—even the decades he had spent working with Plagueis's father. Once initiated, Hill would become Damask Holding's principal agent on Coruscant, and his son, San, would become Hego's right hand, in preparation for his eventual role as chairman of the Inter-Galactic Banking Clan.

Returned from the short holocommunication with Sidious, Plagueis was filled with a sense of triumph. Before night fell on the Fobosi dis-trict, the members of the Gran Protectorate would cease to be a con-cern. Pax Teem and the rest believed they had found shelter aboard one of Coruscant's orbital facilities, but the Sun Guards—save for a pair Plagueis had kept in reserve in the order's initiation room—were on the way to them now, in forces sufficient to crush whatever defenses Santhe Security might be providing. Sidious had played his part perfectly, and had redeemed himself fully in Plagueis's eyes. The time had come to bring his apprentice deeper into the Sith mysteries he had been inves-tigating for most of his life; to introduce him to the miracles he was performing on Aborah.

From a series of arch-topped doorways lining the circumference of the room came the sounds of solemn chanting as perhaps three dozen of the order's black-robed members began to file in and take their places along the perimeter of the Canted Circle. Last to emerge was the high official, who wore a mask and carried the circular, emblematic pendant draped over both hands, which he held as if in prayer. Rituals of a simi-lar sort had been enacted by the ancient Sith, Plagueis thought, as Larsh Hill genuflected before the high official.

At the same instant Hill's right knee touched the polished stone, a jangle of foreboding laddered up Plagueis's spine. Turning ever so slightly, he saw that 11-4D had rotated its head toward him in a gesture Plagueis had come to associate with alarm. The dark side fell over him like a shroud, but instead of acting on impulse, he restrained himself, fearful of betraying his true nature prematurely. In that instant of hesitation, time came to a standstill, and several events happened at once.

The high official gave a downward tug to the pendant he had placed around Hill's neck, and the old Muun's head toppled from his shoulders and began to roll down the tipped stage. Blood geysered from Hill's neck, and his body fell to one side with a thud and began to jerk back and forth as one after another of his hearts failed.

Yanking their hands from the roomy, opposite sleeves of their robes, the hooded members of the order made sidelong throwing motions, which sent dozens of decapitator disks screaming through the air. Muuns to both sides of Plagueis fell to their knees, their last breaths caught in their throats. A disk buried deep in his forehead, one of the Sun Guards twirled in front of Plagueis like a crazed marionette. Blood fountained, turning to mist. Struck in at least three places and leaking lubricant, 11-4D was trying to limp to Plagueis's side when another disk whirled into its alloy body, touching off a storm of sparks and smoke.

Plagueis pressed his right hand to the right side of his neck to discover that a disk had made off with a considerable hunk of his jawbone and neck, and in its cruel passing had severed his trachea and several blood vessels. He cupped the Force against the injury to keep himself from lapsing into unconsciousness, but he fell to the floor regardless, with blood pumping onto the already slick stone circle. Around him, slanted in his faltering vision, the assassins had drawn vibroblades from the other sleeves of the robes and were beginning a methodical advance on the few Muuns who were still standing. A hail of bolts streaked from the blaster cradled in the arms of the remaining Sun Guard, sweeping half a dozen hooded beings off the rim of the circle, before he himself was butchered.

Tricked, Plagueis thought, as pained by the realization as he was by the wound. *Outmaneuvered by a group of inferior beings who at least had had sense enough to place artfulness above arrogance.*

*　*　*

In his small but orderly Senate office, Palpatine gazed out on a sliver of Coruscant. On the far side of a ceaseless current of mid-tier traffic was the sheer cliff-face of a drab government complex.

Go about your usual business, Plagueis said. But how could he be expected to behave as if nothing had happened, even in the interest of establishing an alibi? Did Plagueis expect him to return to the Uscru and finish lunch? Go for a stroll in Monument Plaza? Keep his appointment to meet with the inconsequential Bothan who chaired the Finance Committee?

He stormed away from the office window, victim of his own unreleased rage.

This was not the life he had imagined for himself ten years earlier when he had sworn loyalty to the dark side of the Force. His hunger to be in closer contact with the Force, to be an even more powerful Sith, knew no bounds. But how was he to know when he had arrived at some semblance of mastery? When Plagueis told him?

He regarded his trembling hands.

Would his ability to summon lightning come more effortlessly? What powers had Sith Lord Plagueis kept to himself?

He was standing in the center of the room when he sensed someone in the corridor outside. Fists pummeled the door; then it slid to one side and Sate Pestage burst into the room. Seeing Palpatine, he came to a sudden stop, and the panicked look he wore on entering transformed to one of visible relief.

"I've been trying to reach you," he nearly screamed, running a hand over his forehead.

Palpatine regarded him quizzically. "I was occupied. What has happened?"

Pestage sank into a chair and looked up at him. "Are you sure you want to know?" He paused, then said, "In the interest of separating what I do from what you do—"

Palpatine's eyes blazed. "Stop wasting my time and come to the point."

Pestage gritted his teeth. "The Maladian commander I did business with during the Kim affair."

"What of him?"

"He contacted me—two, maybe three hours ago. He said that he felt humiliated because of the manner in which the Kim contract had been implemented, and wanted to make it up to me. He said he'd just received word that a Maladian faction had accepted a contract to carry out a major hit on Coruscant, involving someone closely affiliated with Damask Holdings." Pestage kept his eyes on Palpatine. "I feared it might be you."

Palpatine swung back to the window to think. Had the Santhe guards planned to turn him over to the Maladians following the holo-communication with Pax Teem?

He turned to Pestage. "Who took out the contract?"

"Members of the Gran Protectorate."

"It fits," Palpatine said, more to himself.

"What fits?"

"Where are these Gran now?"

"As soon as I heard from the Maladian, I asked Kinman to keep an eye on them. They're holed up in the Malastare ambassador's residence."

Palpatine blinked. "Here? On Coruscant?"

"Of course, here."

"It's not possible that they're offworld?"

"No, they're downside."

Palpatine paced away from Pestage. He opened himself fully to the Force, and was left staggered by an inrush of overwhelming malevolence. He planted his left hand on the desk for support and managed a stuttering inhale. Somewhere close by, the dark side was unspooling.

"Palpatine!" Pestage said from behind him.

"Hego Damask," Palpatine said, without turning around.

Pestage was too stunned to reply.

The Gran had turned the table on him! On *both* of them. Plagueis had been so fixed on executing his own plan that he had neglected to consider that the Gran might also have a plan. How, though? *How could he have been so blind?*

"Ready a speeder, Sate!"

He heard Pestage leap to his feet.

"Where are we headed?"

"The Fobosi. The lodge of the Canted Circle."

*   *   *

Slumped on his right side, knees drawn up to his chest, eyes open but unmoving, Plagueis watched the second Echani succumb to multiple stabs from the assassins' vibroblades. With blood welling out from under Plagueis's cupped right hand and glistening in a pool on the floor beneath his neck, they had taken him for dead. But now they were moving from the body of one fallen Muun to the next, checking for signs of life and finishing what they had begun. A few had lowered their black hoods, revealing themselves to be Maladians—the same group Sidious had employed to deal with Vidar Kim.

For an instant he wondered if Sidious had secretly taken out a second contract, but he immediately dismissed the thought—born as it was of his not wanting to admit to himself that the Gran had bested him. He wondered if the Maladians had actually been bold enough to kill the prominent Canted Circle members they were impersonating. Unlikely, given that the assassins were known and respected for their professionalism. The members had probably been rendered unconscious by gas or some other means.

Not a meter away stood 11-4D, five decapitator disks protruding from his alloy body and telltale lights blinking, in the midst of a self-diagnosis routine. Having run himself through a similar test, Plagueis knew that he had lost a great deal of blood, and that one of his subsidiary hearts was in fibrillation. Sith techniques had helped him perform chemical cardioversions on his other two hearts, but one of them was working so hard to compensate that it, too, was in danger of becoming arrhythmic. Plagueis moved his eyes just enough to fix the locations of some of the two dozen assassins that had survived the Sun Guards' counterattack; then he dug deep into the Force and catapulted himself to his feet.

The closest of the assassins swung to him with raised vibroblades and rushed forward, only to be flung backward off the canted stage and against the room's curved walls. Others Plagueis felled with his hands by snapping necks and putting his fists through armored torsos. Spreading his arms wide, he clapped his hands together, turning every loose object in the vicinity into a deadly projectile. But the Maladians were far from run-of-the-mill murderers. Members of the cult had killed and wounded Jedi, and in response to confronting Force powers, they didn't shrink or flee but simply changed tactics, moving with astounding agility to surround Plagueis and wait for openings.

The wait lasted only until Plagueis attempted to unleash lightning. His second subsidiary heart failed, paralyzing him with pain and nearly plunging him into unconsciousness. The assassins wasted not a moment, throwing themselves at him in groups, though in a vain attempt to penetrate the Force shield he raised. Again he rallied, this time with a ragged sound dredged from deep inside that erupted from him like a sonic weapon, shattering the eardrums of those within ten meters and compelling the rest to bring their hands to their ears.

In blinding motion his hands and feet smashed skulls and windpipes. He stopped once to conjure a Force wave that all but atomized the bodies of six Maladians. He spun through a turn, dragging the wave halfway around the room to kill half a dozen more. But even that wasn't enough to deter his assailants. They flew against him again, making the most of his momentary weakness to open gashes on his arms and shoulders. Down on one knee, he levitated a Sun Guard blaster from the floor and called it toward him; but one of the assassins succeeded in altering its trajectory by hurling himself into the path of the airborne weapon.

With nothing more than the Force of his mind, Plagueis rattled the floor, knocking some of the assassins off their feet, but others rushed in to take their places, slashing at him with their vibroblades from every angle. He knew that he had life enough to conjure one final counteroffensive. He was a moment from loosing hell on the Maladians when he sensed Sidious enter the room.

Sidious and Sate Pestage, in whose hands a repeating blaster fashioned a hell of its own, a barrage of light that separated limbs from torsos, hooded heads from cloaked shoulders. Hurrying to Plagueis's side, Sidious lifted him upright, and in unison they brought swift death to the rest.

In the stillness that followed, 11-4D, glistening with leaked lubricant, reenabled itself and walked stiffly to where the two Sith were standing, syringes grasped in two of its appendages.

"Magister Damask, I can be of service."

Plagueis extended his arm toward the droid and then lowered himself to the floor as the drugs began to take effect. He lifted his gaze to Pestage, then glanced at Sidious, who, in turn, showed Pestage a look that made abundantly clear he had become a member of their secret fraternity, whether he wanted to or not.

"Master, we need to leave at once," Sidious said. "What I felt, the Jedi may have felt, and they will come."

"Let them," Plagueis rasped. "Let them inhale the aroma of the dark side."

"This carnage is beyond explanation. We can't be here."

After a moment, Plagueis nodded and summoned a gurgling voice. "Recall the Sun Guard. When they're done here—"

"No," Sidious said. "I know where the Gran are. It won't be business as usual this time, Master."

The Malastare ambassador's residence occupied three mid-tier stories of a slender building located at the edge of the government district. The front of the residence looked out on the stand-alone Galactic Courts of the Justice Building, but the rear faced a narrow canyon that was more than fifty levels deep and off limits to traffic. Following directions furnished by Pestage, Sidious rode turbolifts and pedestrian walkways to a meager balcony ten levels above the upper story of the residence. His fury notwithstanding, he would have preferred to linger until nightfall, which came early to that part of Coruscant, but he was certain that the Gran were expecting word that the Maladians had satisfied the terms of the contract, and he couldn't risk having them flee for the stars before he got to them. So he lingered on the balcony until it and the walkway in both directions were unoccupied, then jumped from the overlook and called on the Force to deliver him safely to a narrow ledge that ran beneath the lowest floor of the residence. There he perched only for the time it took to activate the lightsaber he had retrieved from Plagueis's starship and use it to burn his way into a wide maintenance duct that perforated the building at each level.

Crawling to the first egress—a distance of scarcely ten meters—he lowered himself into a murky storage room and once more called the weapon's crimson blade from the hilt. Constructed to fit the Muun's large hand, the lightsaber felt unwieldy in Sidious's, so he switched to a two-handed grip. Moving with a caution that belied his murderous intent, and on the alert for cams or other security devices, he eased out of the room into a tight corridor and followed it toward the front of the building. There, in a formal entryway, two Dugs were standing guard in a desultory way. Moving quickly, a blur to human senses, he caught them by surprise, splitting open the chest and abdomen of one and beheading the other while the first was attempting to prevent his entrails from spilling onto the glossy mosaic floor. A brief scan of the foyer revealed the presence of cams installed in the walls and high ceiling. He wondered how the killings appeared to anyone monitoring a display screen. It must have seemed as if the two Dugs had been butchered by a phantom.

Still, all the more reason to hurry.

He sprinted up the stairs to the next floor, where he heard a cacophony of human voices muffled by the thick door to a nearby room. Blowing the door inward with a Force push, he took a wide stance in the shattered doorway and positioned the blade of the thrumming lightsaber vertically in front of him. Through the weapon's glow he saw a dozen or more Santhe guards in uniform seated around a table littered with food and drink containers gape at him in disbelief before reaching for weapons fastened to their hips or scurrying for others buried beneath the rubble of their celebratory meal.

Sidious waded into the room, returning volleys of blaster bolts from those first to fire, then attacked, raising his left hand to levitate two guards into midair before running his blade through each of them. Snarling like a beast, he whirled through a circle, ridding three guards of their heads and cutting a fourth in half at the waist. The blade impaled a guard who had flattened himself to the floor in abject terror, then went straight into the shrieking mouth of the last of them.

As that one collapsed in a heap, Sidious caught a glimpse of himself in an ornate mirror: face contorted in rage, red hair in electrified disarray, mouth webbed with strands of thick saliva, eyes a radioactive shade of yellow.

He flew back to the stairwell and raced to the top of the next flight, which opened into a large room filled with female Gran and younglings, along with Gran and Dug servants. Having heard the commotion from below, some were already on their huge flat feet; others, though, were too shocked to move.

All the better for him, and he left not a single one of them alive.

Then: through a warren of expensively appointed rooms to another set of closed doors, from behind which issued the sounds of a banquet in progress—one that had probably commenced hours earlier and wasn't meant to end until hours later, with the deaths of Senator Palpatine, Hego Damask, and the other Muuns an accomplished fact.

Now Sidious gave full vent to his ire. Crashing through the doors, he landed in the center of a table covered with plates of grains and grassy plants and surrounded by a herd of grazing Gran, whose boisterous laughs froze in their throats. From the head of the table, Pax Teem gawked at him as if he might be a creature escaped from his most horrifying nightmare. And yet he wouldn't be the first to taste Plagueis's blade but the last: once he had been forced to watch the rest of his party butchered, from hooves to eyestalks; the painted ceiling brought down by Sidious's Force pull; the flames of a gentle gas blaze in the room's fireplace incited to a blistering inferno that Sidious tugged behind him as he soared from the table to the floor and closed on his final victim.

In desperate flight from the Sith and the spreading flames, Pax Teem had backed himself to a tall window framed by floor-to-ceiling curtains. Entreaties of whatever sort tried to thrust themselves through his stricken voice box and past his square teeth, but none succeeded.

Deactivating the lightsaber, Sidious beckoned the flames with his fingers, encouraging them to leap from the table to the curtains. A bleating scream finally emerged from Teem's narrow muzzle of a mouth as the blazing fabric collapsed around him, and Sidious watched him roast to death.

21: INVESTITURE

Assassinations, murders, and other crimes were no match for the codes of silence that had governed the Order of the Canted Circle, the Gran Protectorate, Santhe Security, and the Jedi High Council almost since their inceptions. Had the elite members and private guards of the Canted Circle not been drugged and found unconscious in dressing rooms and other places, police investigators summoned to the head-quarters by two Jedi Knights would never have been allowed to enter the landmark building, let alone the order's vaunted initiation room, in which were discovered the bodies of two Echani, believed to be body-guards; a dozen Muuns, killed by decapitator disks and vibroblades; and three times that number of Maladian assassins dressed in borrowed robes, who had succumbed to blaster bolts, blunt-force injuries, and, in some cases, traumatic amputations. So scattered were the latter, in-vestigators initially suspected that an explosive device had been deto-nated, but no trace of a device was ever uncovered. The Muuns were quickly identified as top-ranking members of a clandestine financial group known as Damask Holdings, though its wealthy founder and chief operating officer, Hego Damask, was believed to have survived the sneak attack. The Jedi who had alerted the police never revealed what had drawn them to the Fobosi district to begin with, or why they expressed such interest in the case. As well, the members of the Order of the Canted Circle refused to answer any questions.

At the Malastare embassy in the heart of Coruscant the evidence was even more baffling, and complicated by a fire and ensuing gas explosion that had swept through the building. Fire marshals and forensics specialists were picking through the charred remains of the three-story resiblock when two members of the Jedi Council had paid an unannounced visit. Again, the Jedi had declined to explain their actions, but the police were able to make progress on their own. The amount of blood residue discovered at the scene led investigators to determine that, prior to the arrival of the police, several bodies had been incinerated on site, which suggested the work of elements of organized crime. In the wake of the recent assassination of Senator Vidar Kim, the Senate Investigatory Committee formed a special task force to look into the matter. Many beings were interviewed and interrogated, and many security cam recordings studied during the course of the investigation, but most of the principal players and witnesses hid behind their lawyers, even when threatened with imprisonment for obstruction of justice.

A standard month after the events on Coruscant, Plagueis summoned Sidious to Muunilinst. Sidious had visited the High Port skyhook but had never been invited downside, and now he found himself soaring over one of the planet's unspoiled blue oceans in a stylish airspeeder piloted by two Sun Guards. As the speeder approached Aborah, he settled deeply into the Force and was rewarded with a vision of the mountain island as a transcendent vortex of dark energy unlike anything he had ever experienced. It was something he would have expected to encounter only on Korriban or some other Sith world.

The droid 11-4D—fully repaired—was waiting for him on the landing zone and led him inside, leaving the guards to wait with the airspeeder.

"You appear to be in much better condition than when I last saw you, droid," Sidious remarked as a turbolift dropped them deep inside the complex.

"Yes, Senator Palpatine, Aborah is a restorative place."

"And Magister Damask?"

"I leave it to you to judge for yourself, sir."

Exiting the turbolift, the first thing to catch Sidious's eye was the library: rack after rack of texts, scrolls, disks, and holocrons—all the data he had been craving since his apprenticeship began. He ran his hands lovingly over the shelves but barely had time to revel in his excitement when 11-4D ushered him onto a descending ramp that led into what might have been a state-of-the-art medical research facility.

His eyes darting from one device to the next, he asked, "Is this new since the Magister's injuries?"

"Only some of what you see," the droid said. "For the most part this area is unchanged since I was first brought here."

"And when was that?"

"Approximately one standard year before I was introduced to you on Chandrila, sir."

Sidious considered it, then asked, "Is Magister Damask your maker, droid?"

"No, sir. He is simply my present master."

Deeper in the complex, they moved past cages containing as many creatures as could be found in a well-stocked zoo. OneOne-FourDee indicated a cluster separate from the rest.

"These are the Magister's most recent pregnancies."

"The Magister's?" Sidious repeated in bewilderment.

"His success rate has improved."

Sidious was still trying to make sense of the droid's statements when they entered a long corridor lined with windowless cells. Through the Force he could sense life-forms behind each locked door.

"Captives?"

"Oh, no, sir," 11-4D said. "Ongoing experiments."

As they turned a corner at the end of the corridor Sidious came to a dead stop. Centered in a kind of operating theater stood a towering bacta tank, in which floated a male Bith.

"That is Venamis," Plagueis said in a voice that wasn't entirely his.

Sidious pivoted to see his Master limp into the room, mouth, chin, and neck concealed behind a breath mask or transpirator of some sort. Most of the vibroblade wounds had healed, but his skin looked especially wan. Sidious had been wondering if Plagueis had been weakened by the attack, but he saw now that, for all the punishment his body had sustained at the hands of the Maladian assassins, the Muun was no less strong in the Force.

"Your thoughts betray you," Plagueis said. "Do you think that Malak's powers were weakened by Revan's lightsaber? Bane by being encrusted in orbalisks? Do you think Gravid's young apprentice was hindered by the prosthesis she was forced to wear after fighting him?"

"No, Master."

"Soon I will be stronger than you can possibly imagine." Plagueis forced himself to swallow, then said, "But come, we have much to discuss."

Sidious followed him into a cool chamber, furnished only with a bed, two simple chairs, a cabinet, and a square, exquisitely woven rug. Motioning Sidious into one of the chairs, Plagueis lowered himself with noticeable difficulty into the other. After a long moment of silence, he nodded in satisfaction.

"I am pleased to see how greatly you have changed—how powerful you have become, Lord Sidious. What happened on Coruscant was meant to happen, but I take consolation in the fact that the events have shaped you into a true Sith Lord. You are indeed ready to learn the secrets I have been safeguarding."

"What is this place, Master?"

Plagueis took a moment to gather enough strength to continue. "Think of it as a vessel that contains all the things to which I am devoted. All the things I love."

"This may be the first time I have ever heard you utter the word."

"Only because no other term exists that adequately expresses my unconditional attachment to the creatures and beings with whom I share this place. Love without compassion, however, for compassion has no part in this."

"The Bith—Venamis . . ."

"Dispatched by Tenebrous to test me—to eliminate me had I failed. But Venamis has been a gift; essential in helping me unlock some of the deepest secrets of the Force. Every creature you have glimpsed or sensed here has been a similar blessing, as you will see when I lead you into the mysteries."

"What did the droid mean when it said *the Magister's pregnancies*?"

Beneath the breath mask, Plagueis might have quirked a smile. "It means that the pregnancies were not achieved by normal means of conception, but rather through the Force."

Surprise and disbelief mingled in Sidious's blue eyes. "The Force?"

"Yes," Plagueis said pensively. "But I failed to exercise due caution. As we attempt to wrest the powers of life and death from the Force, as we seek to tip the balance, the Force resists our efforts. Action and reaction, Sidious. Something akin to the laws of thermodynamics. I have been audacious, and the Force has tested me the way Tenebrous sought to. Midi-chlorians are not easily persuaded to execute the dictates of one newly initiated in the mysteries. The Force needs to be won over, especially in work that involves the dark side. It must be reassured that a Sith is capable of accepting authority. Otherwise it will thwart one's intentions. It will engineer misfortune. It will strike back."

"The Maladians—"

"Perhaps. But in any case this is why the Jedi Order has descended into decadence and is dragging the Republic down with it. Because the Jedi have lost the allegiance of the Force. Yes, their ability to draw energy from the Force continues, but their ability to use the Force has diminished. Each of their actions engenders an opposite, often unrecognized consequence that elevates those attuned to the dark side; that buoys the efforts of the Sith and increases our power. Yet our use of that power requires delicacy. We must be alert to moments when the light side falters and openings are created. Then, and only then—when all the conditions have been met—can we act without fear of meeting resistance or repercussion.

"To say that the Force works in mysterious ways is to admit one's ignorance, for any mystery can be solved through the application of knowledge and unrelenting effort. As we had our way with the Senate, and as we will soon have our way with the Republic and the Jedi, we will have our way with the Force."

Silenced by awe, Sidious scarcely knew how to respond. "What would you have me do, Master?"

The transpirator emitted a series of tones, and Plagueis inhaled deeply. "I will relocate to Sojourn in order to devote myself fully to our investigations, to furthering the imperative, and to healing myself."

"What will become of Aborah?"

"For the time being it can serve as a repository."

"And Damask Holdings?"

"The group will not be re-formed, though I may continue to host annual Gatherings. And I will tutor San Hill personally, to prepare him for assuming chairmanship of the Banking Clan."

"Why do we need them?"

In a harsh whisper, Plagueis said, "Because war is now on the agenda, Sidious. But our actions must be circumspect, restricted to those star systems rife with petty conflicts, where appropriate beings can be encouraged, appropriate operations can be funded . . . We must arrange for worlds in the Outer Rim to suffer while the Core prospers. Pathetic as those worlds may be, we have no choice but to use what we have at hand.

"The IBC will be essential in financing the war we will slowly foment. We will need the Banking Clan to finance the manufacturers of weapons and to sustain an alternative economy for the eventual enemies of the Republic." Plagueis looked directly at Sidious. "Our success will be measured by signs and portents. There is much you need to learn regarding the Yinchorri and the Kaminoans. But all in due time. For now, Sidious, know that you are the blade we will drive through the heart of the Senate, the Republic, and the Jedi Order, and I, your guide to reshaping the galaxy. Together we are the newborn stars that complete the Sith constellation."

Sidious touched the cleft in his chin. "I'm relieved to learn that I didn't disappoint you, Master. But the Jedi summoned the police to the Fobosi district moments after we left. The plan is already endangered."

Color rose in Plagueis's cheeks. "The Jedi have long known that the dark side has been reawakened and cannot be checked by them. Now they have felt it on their own Coruscant."

"Even so, we can't continue to risk exposure," Sidious said carefully.

Plagueis studied him. "You have more to say about this."

"Master, would you consider training someone in the Sith arts to execute whatever missions are required?"

"Another Venamis? In defiance of our partnership?"

Sidious shook his head. "Not an apprentice; not someone who could ever aspire to become a true Sith Lord. But someone skilled in stealth and combat, who could be eliminated when no longer needed."

Surprise shone in Plagueis's eyes. "You already have someone in mind."

"You instructed me to keep an eye out for beings who might prove helpful. I found such a one on Dathomir not a year ago. A male Dathomiri Zabrak infant."

"Many Zabrak demonstrate strength in the Force. By nature, it would seem."

"This infant does. The mother birthed two and sought to save one from the clutches of the Nightsisters, especially from one known as Talzin."

"You purchased him?"

"Accepted him."

"Where is he?"

"I brought him to the accounting facility that Damask Holdings maintains on Mustafar, and left him in the care of the custodial droids."

Plagueis closed his eyes briefly. Mustafar had served as a place to dispose of enemies and evidence long before Boss Cabra's reclamation station had been made available to Hego Damask and others.

"And the mother?" he asked.

"Alive—for now."

"Might not this Talzin pursue the infant?"

Sidious looked inward. "She may."

Plagueis growled in irritation. "Then it will be your business if she does."

Sidious bowed his head in acceptance.

"Leave the infant on Mustafar in the care of the droids," Plagueis added at last, "but begin to train him. Inure him to pain, Lord Sidious, so that he will be able to serve us fully. Should his Force talents fail to mature, eliminate him. But if he measures up, relocate him at your discretion to Orsis. There you will find an elite training center operated by a Falleen combat specialist named Trezza. He and I have had dealings. Trezza will raise the Zabrak to be fierce but steadfast in his loyalty. You, however, will supervise his training in the dark side. Do not speak of the Sith or our plans until he has proven himself. And do not deploy him against any of our salient enemies until I have had a chance to evaluate him."

Sidious inclined his head. "I understand, Master."

"The Force provides, Sidious," Plagueis said after a moment. "As nature provides more male beings in the aftermath of war, the Force, ever mindful of balance, provides beings strong in the dark side when light has ruled for too long. This Zabrak bodes well."

"The Sith Lords who follow us will pay tribute to your wisdom, Master," Sidious said in earnestness.

Plagueis stood and touched him on the shoulder. "No, Lord Sidious. Because we are the end of the line." He gestured broadly. "Everything done here has been for a single purpose: to extend our reign indefinitely."

PART THREE:
Mastery

34—32 BBY

22: ORDINARY BEINGS

The crepuscular chill of the Senate Rotunda had a way of lulling many to sleep. Sharpening his senses, Palpatine could hear the gentle snoring of human and nonhuman Senators seated in hover platforms adjacent to his station; more clearly, Sate Pestage and Kinman Doriana, opposite him on the platform's circular seat, gossiping maliciously. For twenty years now Naboo and the Chommell sector had occupied the same place in the same tier in that immense mushroom of a building, though platforms had been added above and below and to both sides over those two decades to accommodate representatives of worlds newly welcomed to the Republic. Also in those twenty years, Palpatine had sat—and admittedly napped—through the orations, diatribes, and filibusters of countless beings, as well as State of the Republic addresses by four Supreme Chancellors: Darus, Frix, Kalpana, and Finis Valorum. The last was nearing completion of a second term of office that had been beset with challenges, most of which could be traced—but wouldn't be for decades to come—to the machinations of Hego Damask and his secret conspirator, Palpatine, in their guises as Sith Lords Plagueis and Sidious. But in fact, half the Senators in the Rotunda were leading double lives of one sort or another: pledging themselves to preserve the Republic while at the same time accepting bribes from the Trade Federation, facilitating slavery and the smuggling of spice and death sticks, or abetting the operations of pirates.

The words of the ancient Republic philosopher Shassium drifted into Palpatine's mind: *We are all two-faced beings, divided by the Force and fated for eternity to search out our hidden identities.*

From the Rotunda's tall pulpit, Supreme Chancellor Valorum was saying, "The crisis unfolding in the Yinchorr system offers further proof that, in our determination to maintain an era of prosperity in the Core, we have allowed the outer systems to become lawless realms, with pirates, slavers, smugglers, and arms merchants operating with impunity. Proscribed matériel and technologies find their way to species whose appeals for Republic aid have gone unanswered, and the outcome is antagonism and intersystem conflict. Brought together by mutual need, alliances of forgotten worlds turn to the galactic cartels to furnish what we have denied them: growth, protection, and security—along with weapons and combat training." He gestured broadly to near and distant Senatorial platforms. "While we sit in cool comfort, a confederacy of the disenfranchised expands in the Outer Rim."

Close by, someone yawned with theatrical exaggeration, eliciting a chorus of laughter from beings seated within earshot. The Senate should have been on vacation, but the crisis in the Expansion Region had forced Valorum to convene the governing body in special session.

Across the Rotunda from Naboo's station, Yinchorr's platform stood vacant—the result of the Yinchorri severing ties with the Republic six months earlier and recalling their diplomatic staff. Six months before that, and armed with weapons Darth Sidious had helped them procure, the Yinchorri had launched attacks on several worlds in neighboring systems. Supplied by a Devaronian smuggler, the clandestine shipments had included a cortosis shield from a secret mining operation on the planet Bal'demnic, and had factored into the deaths of a pair of unsuspecting Jedi. Plagueis had said that the Yinchorri could be incited with minimal provocation, but even Sidious had been surprised by their ferocity.

"Since Yinchorr became a member world twenty-five years ago," Valorum continued, "and notwithstanding the sanctions we attempted to impose, we have allowed the Yinchorri to transform themselves into a militaristic force that now threatens a vast region of Republic space. Just six months ago, when they augmented their navy with vessels commandeered from the Golden Nyss shipyards, we voted to censure them rather than intercede, in adherence to an antiquated belief that responsibility for policing the outer systems rests with the worlds that make up those systems. Ultimately, following Yinchorr's most recent attack on the Chalenor system, the Jedi were persuaded to intervene, but with grievous results."

Valorum halted briefly.

"As some of you already know, the mutilated bodies of Jedi Knight Naeshahn and her Padawan, Ebor Taulk, were transported to Coruscant and somehow delivered to *my* office in the chancellery building." He balled his fist for everyone to see. "This is when I say that enough is enough!"

Palpatine steepled his fingers. Valorum was trying hard to be stirring, but the sudden edge in his voice was blunted by the reaction of his audience, which was rote outrage at best.

A call for quiet by the Bothan vice chancellor was scarcely necessary.

Valorum composed himself for the hovercams, his flushed expression meant to convey indignation rather than embarrassment.

"The Jedi have since dispatched a larger force to bring to justice those responsible for this barbaric act, and to drive the Yinchorri back onto their own world. But I fear that their efforts won't be enough. Since we can't very well station Jedi or Judicials there as an occupying force, I am asking this body to sanction the use of private paramilitaries to enforce a technological blockade of Yinchorr that will prevent the Yinchorri from rearming and renewing their nefarious dreams of conquest."

The shouts of assent and condemnation that met Valorum's request were genuine, as were the Bothan vice chancellor's calls for order. Finally, Valorum raised his voice to be heard.

"Militant expansionism cannot be tolerated! Precedent for the use of paramilitaries was established under Supreme Chancellor Kalpana during the Stark Combine Conflict, as well as in the more recent Yam'rii crisis. In both cases, diplomatic solutions followed, and it is my belief that diplomacy will succeed in the Yinchorr system."

Valorum's political career had been forged during the Stark Hyperspace War. *Now,* Palpatine thought, *he begins to sound like his onetime rival Ranulph Tarkin.*

He waited for the Rotunda to quiet. "The events at Yinchorr speak to the greater challenge we now face. The Cularin system—our newest member—finds itself plagued by pirate attacks. The same is true at Dor-valla, in the Videnda sector. The so-called free-trade zones have become battlegrounds between defenseless worlds and corporate giants like the Trade Federation, or criminal cartels like Black Sun, which are squeez-ing these outlying systems dry."

In an act of what some deemed fair play and others political guile, the vice chancellor took that moment to allow the Trade Federation's platform to leave its docking station and hover into the dark chill of the Rotunda.

"With the Bothan's customary impeccable timing," Pestage remarked to Doriana.

The Trade Federation's Senator was an unctuous Neimoidian named Lott Dod, whose sussurant, snake charmer's voice wafted through the hall's enunciators. "I must protest the Supreme Chancellor's accusa-tions." His words didn't convey anger so much as the arrogance of wealth—a strategy he had learned from his predecessor, Nute Gunray. "Should the Trade Federation be expected to absorb the losses it has sustained because of pirate attacks? The Republic refuses to create a military to police those sectors while at the same time prohibiting us from protecting our cargoes with defensive weapons or droid soldiers."

"Now is not the time for this argument, Senator," Valorum said, showing the palms of his soft hands.

But a hundred voices overruled him.

"If not now, then *when,* Supreme Chancellor?" The question came from the wheedling, cranial-horned humanoid magistrate of the Cor-porate Alliance, Passel Argente. "How many cargoes will the Trade Federation or the Commerce Guild have to lose before we arrive at the proper moment to air this debate. If the Republic cannot protect us, then we have no recourse but to protect ourselves."

Again Valorum's face flushed. "In every crisis we have dispatched paramilitary forces—"

"With impressive results." The interruption came from Lavina Durada-Vashne Wren, the human female representative of the newly admitted Cularin system. "The Thaereian military made quick work of the pirates who were raiding our transports."

Raucous laughter drowned out the rest of her words.

"The only thing Colonel Tramsig did at Cularin was make himself more contemptible!" Twi'lek Senator Orn Free Taa bellowed from his platform. "The good Senator from Cularin was merely deceived by his dubious charms."

Argente spoke once more. "Does the Supreme Chancellor advocate that each system have a paramilitary force at its command? If so, then why not a pan-galactic military?"

Palpatine's eyes sparkled in sadistic delight. Valorum was getting everything he deserved. He had demonstrated some diplomatic skill during the Stark Hyperspace War, but his election to the chancellorship had more to do with a pedigree that included three Supreme Chancellors and deals he had cut with influential families like the Kalpanas and the Tarkins of Eriadu. His adulation of the Jedi Order was well known; less so his hypocrisy—much of his family wealth derived from lucrative contracts his ancestors had entered into with the Trade Federation. His election seven years earlier had been one of the signs Plagueis had been waiting for—the return to power of a Valorum—and had followed on the heels of a remarkable breakthrough Plagueis and Sidious had engineered in manipulating midi-chlorians. A breakthrough the Muun had described as "galactonic." Both of them suspected that the Jedi had sensed it as well, light-years distant on Coruscant.

"There will be no Republic military," Valorum was saying, having taken Argente's bait. "The Ruusan Reformations *must* be upheld. A military force has to be financed. Taxes imposed on the outlying systems would only add to their burden and lead to talk of secession."

"Then let the Core Worlds pay!" someone seated below Palpatine shouted.

"The Core has no need of a military force!" the Kuati Senator responded. "We know how to live in peace with one another!"

"Why are the Jedi unable to serve as a military?" the Senator from Ord Mantell asked.

Valorum turned to look at him. "The Jedi are not an army, and they number too few, in any case. They intercede at our request, but also at their own discretion. Furthermore, the Order has seen more deaths in the past twelve years than it saw in the previous fifty. Yinchorr is fast shaping up to be another Galidraan."

Palpatine took secret pleasure in Valorum's reference, since what had occurred at Galidraan had been clear evidence of the dark side acting in concert with his and Plagueis's subterfuges. Most important, for Plagueis the provincial conflict had had a devastating effect on Jedi Master Dooku, deepening his schism with the High Council regarding its decisions to deploy the Jedi as warriors.

"Once again we come full circle." Orn Free Taa's voice boomed through the Rotunda. "The Republic can find the credits to contract with private militaries but not to raise a military of its own. And yet the Supreme Chancellor sees fit to lecture *us* on antiquated thinking. Why not simply turn those credits over to the outlying systems and let them do their own contracting?"

"Perhaps the Senator from Ryloth has touched on something," Valorum said when the applause died down. "Better still, perhaps the time has come to impose a tax on the *free-trade zones* to supply the outlying systems with the funds they require."

Palpatine reclined in the platform's padded seat as angry rebuttals spewed from the stations of the Rim Faction worlds, as well as from those belonging to the Trade Federation, the Commerce Guild, the Techno Union, and the Corporate Alliance. How wonderfully and predictably the Senate had deteriorated over the course of twenty years. As had so many ordinary and extraordinary sessions, this one would end in chaos, with nothing resolved.

For the screens that filled the Rotunda, hovercams captured Valorum's sad expression of impotence.

Soon, very soon, it would fall to Palpatine to impose order on everyone.

Outside the curved walls of the Senate, the crises in the outlying systems had little effect on the lives of the billions who resided on Coruscant. Beings living in the lower levels continued to do their best to survive, while those living closer to the sky continued to spend lavishly on food, fine cloaks, and tickets to the opera, which Valorum had returned to fashion. Palpatine was an exception to the rule. In what sometimes seemed to him like perpetual motion, he met frequently with his peers in the Senate, listening carefully to what each had to say about galactic events, but not so carefully that any had reason to suspect him of being anything other than a career politician, fixed on enhancing his profile. If there was anything that set him apart, it was an impression he gave of taking his job perhaps too seriously. With just over a year remaining in Valorum's second term of office, the chancellorship was up for grabs, and those who knew Palpatine best suspected that he might actually pursue the position if asked. His equivocations on the matter only made him more desirable to those who thought he could bring something new to the mix—an authentic centrist viewpoint. Others questioned why, given the unprecedented challenges of the times, he or anyone else would aspire to the position.

Several days after the Senate met in special session, Palpatine violated the privacy he so valued to host an informal gathering in his suite in 500 Republica. The move to Coruscant's most exclusive address had coincided with Ars Veruna's ascent to the Naboo monarchy twelve years earlier. Veruna's victory had hinged on a renegotiated contract with the Trade Federation for Naboo's plasma, although it was widely believed that the King and his cronies had fared better from the deal than the citizens of Naboo. Unlike the apartment Palpatine had occupied when he first arrived on the capital world, this one had a dozen rooms and views of the government district surpassed only by those from the building's spacious penthouses. The neuranium-and-bronzium statue of Sistros—which still concealed the lightsaber he had constructed early in his apprenticeship—shared space with antiquities that had been procured from remote worlds.

Fashionably late, Finis Valorum was one of the last guests to arrive. Palpatine welcomed him at the door, while a contingent of cloaked and helmeted Republic guards took up positions in the corridor. The Supreme Chancellor's round face looked drawn, and perspiration beaded his clean-shaven upper lip. Clinging to his arm like an adornment was Sei Taria, ostensibly his administrative aide but also his lover. Just inside the threshold, Valorum hooked his thumbs in the wide blue cummerbund that cinched his robe and stopped to take in the suite and nod in appreciation.

"What the HoloNet newshounds would give to see this."

"It's hardly a penthouse," Palpatine said dismissively.

"Not yet, he means," Corellia's Senator remarked, causing several others to lift their drink goblets in a kind of toast.

Palpatine pretended to mask embarrassment. Once he would have been acting; now he wore the guise of Naboo's Senator as effortlessly as he wore his robes and cloak.

"Journalists are more than welcome to visit," he said.

Valorum cocked a silver eyebrow in doubt.

"Now that you've gotten them accustomed to transparency and accessibility," Palpatine added.

Valorum laughed without mirth. "For all the good it has done me."

Sei Taria broke an awkward silence. "You certainly make no secret of your favorite color, Senator." The lids of her oblique eyes were colored to match the burgundy of her septsilk robe; her dark hair was twisted into an elaborate bun behind her head, while in front, bangs bisected her flawless forehead.

"Scarlet figures prominently in the crest of my ancestral house," Palpatine explained evenly.

"And yet you favor black and blue in everything you wear."

Palpatine's thin smile held. "I'm flattered that you notice."

Taria's expression turned devious. "Many have taken notice of you, Senator."

Servants hurried over to take Valorum's and Taria's veda cloth cloaks.

"I hired them expressly for the evening," Palpatine said quietly. "I'm a solitary man at heart."

Taria spoke before Valorum could. "The title of the latest HoloNet piece about you, if I'm not mistaken. The Senator who turned his back on a vast fortune to devote himself to politics. Who worked his way up from Naboo's legislative body to the ambassadorship to the Galactic Senate . . ." She smiled without showing her teeth. "A heartwarming story."

"And every word of it true," Palpatine said. "From a certain point of view."

The three of them shared a laugh, and then Palpatine led them deeper into the press of guests, all of whom were well disposed toward Valorum. There was no one in the suite the Supreme Chancellor didn't know, and he greeted every one of them by name. The ability to make beings feel as if they mattered to him, personally as well as politically, was one of his few strengths.

A protocol droid delivered drinks on a tray, and Valorum and Taria helped themselves to glasses. When Valorum's trophy excused herself to make conversation with the wife of Alderaanian Senator Bail Antilles, Palpatine steered Valorum into the suite's main room.

"How is it that you manage to enjoy the support of both the Core and Rim Factions?" Valorum asked in genuine interest.

"A consequence of Naboo's location more than anything else. Mine is something of a displaced world—located in the Rim but sharing the sensibilities of many of the Core worlds."

Valorum gestured to a figurine in a wall niche. "Exquisite."

"Quite. A gift from Senator Eelen Li."

"From Triffis."

Palpatine reoriented the figurine slightly. "A museum piece, actually."

Valorum continued along the wall, indicating a second piece. "And this?"

"A ceremonial Gran wind drum. Over one thousand years old." He glanced out of the corner of his eye at Valorum. "A present from Baskol Yeesrim."

Valorum nodded. "Senator Ainlee Teem's aide. I didn't realize you were on good terms with the Gran Protectorate."

Palpatine shrugged. "For a time I wasn't—owing to a long-standing feud over Naboo's abstention in a Senatorial vote of some significance at the time, but ancient history now."

Valorum lowered his voice to ask, "Do you think you could bring Malastare over to my side?"

Palpatine swung to look at him. "Regarding the embargo of Yinchorr? Possibly. But not on the matter of taxing the free-trade zones. Both Ainlee Teem and Aks Moe have become allies of the Trade Federation."

"An even more bewildering reversal." Valorum sighed. "Friends become enemies; enemies, friends . . . I suspect I'm going to have to call in every political favor I'm owed to succeed at Yinchorr." He compressed his lips and shook his head. "I fear my legacy is on the line here, old friend. I've only one year left of my term, but I'm determined to see things though."

Palpatine conjured a compassionate tone. "If it's any solace, I support the use of a paramilitary force—even at the risk of escalating the crisis—if only to silence those who have accused the Republic of being spineless."

Valorum clapped Palpatine on the shoulder. "Your support is appreciated." He looked around the room, then asked even more quietly, "Whom can I count on, Palpatine?"

Palpatine's eyes scanned the crowd, alighting briefly on two human males, an Anx who wouldn't have fit in a room with lower ceilings, an Ithorian, and finally a Tarnab.

"Antilles. Com Fordox. Horox Ryyder. Tendau Bendon. Perhaps Mot-Not-Rab . . ."

Valorum eyed them in turn, then let his gaze settle on a Rodian. "Farr?"

Palpatine laughed to himself; Onaconda Farr thought of politics the way his Rodian brethren thought of bounty hunting: *Shoot first; ask questions later.*

"He's a militant, but I may be able to persuade him, as he enjoys close ties with House Naberrie, of Naboo."

"Tikkes?" Valorum asked, gazing covertly at the Quarren Senator, whose facial tentacles were manipulating snacks into his mouth.

"Tikkes will want something in return, but yes."

Valorum's pale blue eyes found Wookiee Senator Yarua.

Palpatine nodded. "Kashyyyk will support you."

Valorum drained his drink glass and set it aside. "And my opponents?"

"Aside from the obvious ones? The entire Ryloth group—Orn Free Taa, Connus Trell, and Chom Frey Kaa. Also Toonbuck Toora, Edcel Bar Gan, Po Nudo . . . Do you want me to go on?"

Valorum looked discouraged as they stepped out onto the balcony. A tone sounded, indicating that the noise cancellation feature had been activated. Valorum continued to the railing and stared off into the distance.

"A rare dark night," he said after a moment.

Palpatine joined him at the railing. "Weather control is brewing a storm." He turned slightly to adjust the noise cancellation system. "Listen: peals of thunder over The Works. And there," he added, pointing, "lightning."

"How unnatural it seems here. If only we might be as easily cleansed as this vast sky and these monumental buildings."

Palpatine glanced at him. "The Senate has obstructed you, but you've brought no dishonor to the office."

Valorum considered it. "I knew when my first term began that I would face opposition; that events had been spiraling out of control since the Stark Conflict. But since then I've sensed a darkness approaching from the outer reaches of the galaxy to shake Coruscant to its foundations. You would think, after a thousand years of peace, that the Republic would be unshakable, but that isn't the case. I've always placed my faith in the Force, believing that if I acted in accordance with its guiding principles, the galaxy would act in kind."

Palpatine frowned in the dark. "The Republic has grown unwieldy. We are coerced and cajoled into deals that compromise our integrity. We are criticized as much for what we do as what we don't do. Most beings in the Core couldn't point to Yinchorr in a star map, and yet the crisis there becomes your problem."

Valorum nodded in a distracted way. "We can't stand by and do nothing. The Jedi express as much in private, and yet even they are divided. If Master Dooku becomes any more vocal in his criticisms of the Senate and the Order, the Council may have to restrict him to the Temple." He fell silent, then said, "Well, I certainly don't have to tell you. People tell me you've become his confidant."

Instead of responding to that comment, Palpatine said, "And Master Yoda?"

"Inscrutable as ever," Valorum said. "But troubled, I think."

Palpatine turned away from him slightly. "The Jedi have faced down darkness in the past."

"True. But a study of history reveals that they have been defeated by it, as well."

"Then the outcome is not in our grasp."

Valorum raised his gaze to the night sky. "Whose, then?"

23: UNDER THE MIDNIGHT SUN

Just arrived on the Hunters' Moon, Sidious studied Plagueis as the Sith Lord and his droid, 11-4D, viewed a holorecording of a black-robed Zabrak assassin making short work of combat automata in his home on Coruscant, some hovering, some advancing on two legs, others on treads, and all firing blasters.

Twenty years had added a slight stoop to the Muun's posture and veins that stood out under his thinning white skin. He wore a dark green utility suit that hugged his delicate frame, a green cloak that fell from his bony shoulders to the fort's stone floor, and a headpiece that hewed to his large cranium. A triangular breath mask covered his ruined, prognathus lower jaw, his mouth, part of his long neck, and what remained of the craggy nose he'd had before the surprise attack in the Fobosi. A device of his own invention, the alloy mask featured two vertical slits and a pair of thin, stiff conduits that linked it to a transpirator affixed to his upper chest, beneath an armored torso harness. He had learned to ingest and imbibe through feeding tubes, and through his nose.

Seen through the Force, he was a nuclear oval of mottled light, a rotating orb of terrifying energy. If the Maladian attack had weakened him physically, it had also helped to shape his etheric body into a vessel sufficiently strong to contain the full power of the dark side. Determined never again to be caught off guard, he had trained himself to go without sleep, and had devoted two standard decades to day-and-night experimentation with midi-chlorian manipulation and attempts to wrest a few last secrets from the Force, so that he—and presumably his human apprentice—might live forever. His inward turn had enabled him to master the equally powerful energies of order and disorder, creation and entropy, life and death.

"You have made him fearsome," Plagueis remarked without turning from the recording, as the athletic Zabrak cleaved a Colicoid Eradicator droid down the middle and whirled to cut two others in half. The yellow-eyed humanoid's hairless head bore a crown of small horns and geometrical patterns of black and red markings.

"Fearless, as well," Sidious said.

"Still, they are only droids."

"He's even more formidable against living beings."

Plagueis looked over his shoulder, his eyes narrowed in question. "You've fought him in a serious way?" Reconstructed vocal chords and trachea imparted a metallic quality to his voice, as if he were speaking through an enunciator.

"I stranded him on Hypori for a month without food and with only a horde of assassin droids for company. Then I returned to goad and challenge him. All things considered, he fought well, even after I deprived him of his lightsaber. He wanted to kill me, but was prepared to die at my hand."

Plagueis turned fully to face him. "Rather than punish him for disobedience, you praised his resolve."

"He was already humbled. I chose to leave his honor intact. I proclaimed him my myrmidon; the embodiment of the violent half of our partnership."

"Partnership?" Plagueis repeated harshly.

"His and mine; not ours."

"Regardless, you allowed him to believe that he is more skilled than he actually is."

"Did you not do the same for me?"

Plagueis's eyes reflected disappointment. "Never, Sidious. I have always been truthful with you."

Sidious bowed his head in acknowledgment. "I am not the teacher you are."

Plagueis spent a long moment observing the holorecording. The Zabrak's fists and legs were as lethal as his lightsaber, and his speed was astounding. "Who applied the markings?"

"The mother did—in keeping with rituals enacted shortly after birth. An initiation, during which a Dathomirian Zabrak infant is submerged in an oily bath, energized with ichor conjured by the Nightsisters' use of magicks."

"A peculiar decision, given her hope to send the child into hiding."

"The Nightsisters rarely leave Dathomir, but Nightbrothers are sometimes sold into servitude. I believe the mother wished him to be aware of his heritage, wherever he ended up."

On seeing the Zabrak's lightsaber produce two blades, Plagueis drew in his breath. "A saber-staff! The weapon of Exar Kun! Did he construct that?"

"The prototype was two lightsabers he had welded pommel-to-pommel in imitation of the Iridonian zhaboka. I furnished the knowledge that allowed him to improve on the original design and construct the one he is using."

Plagueis watched as droid after droid was impaled on the opposing crimson blades. "It strikes me as unnecessary, but I won't deny his mastery of the Jar'Kai technique." Again, he turned to Sidious. "Niman and teräs käsi will never substitute for dun möch, but I appreciate that you have trained him to be a fighting machine rather than a true apprentice."

"Thank you, Master."

Plagueis's eyes wrinkled—in suspicion? In amusement?

"I agree with you that he should bear witness to the Yinchorri attack on the Jedi Temple."

"I will tell him. He already thinks of the Jedi as abominations. The sight of their sanctuary being violated will quicken his blood."

"Even so, hold him back. Let his anger and hatred fester."

Sidious bowed his head.

Plagueis deactivated the holoprojector. "The gift you requested for him is nearly complete. Raith Sienar has agreed to have the vessel delivered to Sojourn, and I will arrange to have it brought to the LiMerge Building." He made a beckoning motion with his fingers. "Come, Darth Sidious, there is much to discuss."

The ancient fort had never felt more forlorn. A company of Sun Guards still resided on Sojourn, escorting visitors to the surface and keeping the ground-based turbolasers in good working order. Authentication codes were still required for ships entering Sojourn space, but the moon's coordinates were no longer the secret they had once been. For the most part Plagueis had lived like a hermit among his droids, seldom venturing offworld, though continuing to use his vast wealth and influence to support those organizations that furthered the Sith cause and crush the plans of those he opposed. For the first year following the attack, rumors swirled that Hego Damask was dead, but word gradually began to circulate that he was merely living in seclusion on Sojourn. Four years later, the annual Gatherings had resumed, but only for five years, and now there hadn't been a Gathering in more than a decade. Fewer and fewer beings had attended the events in any case, many having distanced themselves from Damask in the wake of the murders on Coruscant.

During the long period between the Gran's sneak attack and the first Gathering of the new era, Sidious had spoken with Plagueis only by holo. Left to progress on his own, he had trained the Zabrak in secret on Mustafar, Tosste, and Orsis, visited several Sith worlds, and spent considerable time studying the Sith texts and holocrons that remained under guard on Aborah. From the Sun Guards, Sidious heard that Damask had locked himself away in the fort and was scarcely seen. On the few occasions Damask had summoned them, they had found the living quarters in shambles, some of the experimental subjects dead in their cages or cells, and many of the droids malfunctioning. Creatures from the surrounding greel forests had invaded and taken up residence in the place, making nests in the turrets and devouring anything edible. While Damask—unwashed, emaciated, erratic in his behavior— had seemed capable of speech, it was 11-4D who had communicated Damask's orders and requests to the guards. At one point, the guards had been ordered to install more than two hundred holoprojectors in what had been the fort's armory, so that Damask could both monitor current events and immerse himself in historical recordings, some of which dated back hundreds of years.

Sidious knew that his own powers had increased tenfold over the decades, but he couldn't be certain he had learned all of Plagueis's secrets—"his sorcerer's ways," as the Sun Guards referred to them—including the ability to prevent beings from dying. He sometimes wondered: Was he a level behind? Two levels behind? Such questions were precisely what had driven generations of Sith apprentices ultimately to challenge their Masters. The uncertainty about who was the more powerful. The need to test themselves, to face the definitive trial. The temptation to take the mantle by force, to put one's own spin on the power of the dark side—as Darth Gravid had attempted, only to set the Sith back countless years . . .

And so it had been left largely to Sidious to bring the same fervor to the manipulation of events in the mundane world that Plagueis brought to the manipulation of midi-chlorians. Instead of challenging each other, they had both dedicated themselves to executing the Grand Plan. Political mastery and mastery of the Force. Someday soon, the Sith would wield both, with Sidious the face of the former and Plagueis behind the scenes, advising him about the latter. Like Plagueis, Sidious had moved judiciously, for unintended repercussions in the real world could be as damaging to the Sith imperative as blowback from the Force. The fact that the Force had not struck back argued that their partnership was something unique and in accordance with the will of the Force. Plagueis's self-imposed isolation had taken a toll on some of the plans he and Sidious had engineered for the Trade Federation and other groups. But Plagueis had made what amounted to a full recovery from his injuries, and the dark side was no longer simply on the ascendant but risen and climbing toward the zenith.

The Yinchorri Crisis was the first time that Plagueis had sanctioned Sidious's direct involvement in galactic events. Until then, events manipulated by the Sith had been accomplished through the use of intermediaries. But when Sidious enlisted the aid of the Devaronian smuggler to instigate the Yinchorri, he had not only made contact by holoprojector—without revealing his Sith identity, of course—but also put him in touch with Pestage and Doriana, who had assisted in the dumping of the bodies of the dead Jedi on Valorum's threshold and had facilitated the insertion of the Yinchorri warriors tasked with infiltrating the Jedi Temple.

Initially the plan had been devised as a test, to see whether the Force-suggestion-resistant reptilian sentients could be fashioned into an anti-Jedi army. But in the same way that repeated attempts at replication by cloning had failed, all efforts to fashion them into an obedient army had proved futile. Custom-made for aggression they were, but also unpredictable and unruly. As a result, a redesigned stratagem had been put into motion to test Valorum's ability to manage a crisis and the Senate's resolve to end one. But neither Plagueis nor Sidious had expected the Supreme Chancellor to involve the Jedi, and now the modified plan was at risk, as well.

"It's well and good that Jedi have died," Plagueis was saying as he, Sidious, and 11-4D entered his cluttered study, "but we must guard against revealing our hand too soon. Was it wise to have the corpses shipped to Coruscant?"

"They had the intended effect on Valorum," Sidious said.

"Nevertheless, we may have misjudged him."

"He's more concerned about his legacy than he is about the Republic, but he may yet win a majority of the Senate over to his side, even at the cost of all his political cachet."

"We need to engineer a crisis from which he can't recover," Plagueis said.

"I have set just such events in motion."

Plagueis nodded in satisfaction. "Then perhaps there is a beneficial side to this. If the Senate approves an embargo, he will be indebted to you."

Sidious smiled tightly. "A blockade enacted for a blockade broken."

"To that end, we must begin to move Viceroy Nute Gunray and King Veruna into position. The Neimoidian was partnered with Valorum during the Stark Conflict. This time we will pit them against each other."

"I knew Gunray slightly when he served as a Senator. He is acquisitive and ambitious, but oddly immune to intimidation. We will need to win him over."

"And so we shall: with procurements that will earn him a position among the seven who make up the Trade Federation directorate."

"How should we approach him?"

"The gift you requisitioned for the Zabrak prompted an idea," Plagueis said. "Gunray is fond of pylats, which the Neimoidians associate with wealth. The avians are abundant on Neimoidia, but Sojourn's forests support a rare red-spotted white one, which the Kaminoans supplied. He will never identify it as a clone."

"A gift from Hego Damask or Senator Palpatine?"

Plagueis looked him up and down. "From Darth Sidious, I think."

Sidious stared at him in doubt. "By name?"

"Not merely by name, but by title, as well. It is time we make our presence known to a select few."

"Will the Sith title have any meaning for him?"

"When we make his dreams come true."

Plagueis began to pace the cool floor. "No Sith have ever been in the position in which we now find ourselves, Darth Sidious: in step with the reemergence of the dark side, fortified by the signs and omens, certain that revenge and victory are near at hand. If the Jedi would abide by their philosophy of acting in accordance with the Force, of doing what is right, they would roll over for the dark. But they resist. Yoda and the rest of the Council members will double their meditation sessions in an effort to peer into the future, only to discover it clouded and unknowable. Only to discover that complacency has opened the door to catastrophe.

"If indeed they have been acting in accordance with the Force, how could we be succeeding in tipping the balance? How could the dark side be gaining ground? In fact, the Jedi have fallen away from their self-assigned duty, their noble path. Could they have prevented it? Perhaps by having remained in control of the Republic, by electing and reelecting Jedi Supreme Chancellors. Or perhaps by absenting themselves completely from the affairs of the Republic, and attending to their arcane rituals in the belief that right thinking by them would keep the Republic strong and on course, the galaxy tipped into the light, instead of having allowed themselves to become marshals and enforcers."

He cast a questioning look at Sidious. "Do you see the grand error of their ways? They execute the Republic's business as if it were the business of the Force! But has a political body ever succeeded in being the arbiter of what is right and just? How easy it is for them to bask in self-assurance in their castle on Coruscant. But in so doing, they have rendered themselves ill equipped for the world we have spent a millennium bringing into being."

He cleared his throat.

"We're going to back them into a contradiction, Darth Sidious. We're going to force them to confront the moral quandary of their position, and reveal their flaws by requiring them to oversee the conflicts that plague their vaunted Republic.

"Only Dooku and a handful of others have grasped the truth. All those years ago when I first met him on Serenno, I thought: *What a blow it would be to the Order if he could be enticed to leave and embrace the dark side. What a panic it might incite.* For if one could leave, then ten or twenty or thirty could follow, and the hollowness at the center of the Order would be plain for all to see."

The Muun's eyes narrowed. "One can't be content to abide by the rules of the Jedi Order or the Force. Only by making the Force serve us have we prevailed. Eight years ago we shifted the galaxy, Darth Sidious, and that shift is now irreversible."

Approaching, he rested his bony hands on Sidious's shoulders. "On my first visit to your homeworld I recognized it as a nexus in the Force. And I remember thinking how appropriate it was that the dark side should be hiding on such a beautiful planet." He paused, straightened, then asked with sudden gravity, "Is Veruna ready, Sidious? I'm concerned that he might be as uncontrollable as the Yinchorri, and that a more malleable leader would better serve our interests."

Sidious considered the question. "It may not be necessary to remove him, Master. Like Gunray, he favors wealth over honor."

Plagueis nodded his head slowly. "Then nudge him, Darth Sidious. And let us see which way he leans before we decide his fate."

24: SITH'ARI

Their targets were only asteroids, but the chromium-nosed yellow starfighters attacked the microcratered rocks as if they posed a threat to Naboo itself. Products of the Theed Space Vessel Engineering Corporation and Nubian Design, and King Veruna's pet project since his coronation, the sleek, short-winged craft exemplified Naboo's infatuation with classic design and flagrant extravagance. The starfighters' engines were said to have set a new standard for emissions control, but for a world that prided itself on environmental awareness, the N-1s seemed entirely out of character and out of place.

"We're expected to have two additional squadrons ready for flight by the start of the year," Veruna told Palpatine as they stood at a dorsal viewport in the King's even more grandiose, mirror-finish Royal Starship. "All will feature twin laser cannons, proton torpedo launchers, and deflector shields, along with R-two astromech droids."

"A dream come true," Palpatine said. "Both for you and for the Nubian Design Collective."

Veruna arched a bushy, gray-and-white eyebrow. "Our deal with Nubian Design was mutually beneficial."

"Of course it was," Palpatine said, wondering how much Veruna and his cronies had pocketed on a contract most Naboo had opposed.

Palpatine had arrived with Pestage, and had met downside with Janus Greejatus before rendezvousing with Veruna and some of the members of his advisory council at Theed Hangar, including Prime

Counselor Kun Lago and the King's sharp-featured female security chief Maris Magneta. Conspicuously absent was Theed's teenage governor, Padmé Naberrie, whose appointment had been Veruna's compromise to an electorate that had been growing more oppositional with each passing year. Veruna, however, looked none the worse for wear. With his flaring eyebrows, long silver hair, and fussily pointed beard, he still cut a fine, swashbuckling figure. Lago and Magneta were considerably younger and more rough-cut, and had made their distaste for Palpatine and his party felt the moment they had boarded the gleaming starship.

Outside the viewport, strafing runs by Bravo Squadron were reducing asteroids to gravel and space dust.

"That's Captain Ric Olié in Bravo One," Veruna said. "Battle-hardened at Chommel Minor."

Pestage failed to restrain a short laugh. "Against that pirate group whose ships collided with one another?"

Veruna glared at Palpatine. "Your aide seems to have forgotten his place, Senator."

Palpatine flashed Pestage a look that said nothing and turned back to Veruna. "My apologies, Your Majesty."

If Veruna was unconvinced, he kept it to himself and fixed his gaze on the distant starfighter exercise. "I plan to end our partnership with the Trade Federation," he said after a long moment of silence, and without looking at Palpatine.

Palpatine moved slightly to place himself in Veruna's peripheral view, his eyes wide in genuine surprise. "Is that the purpose of this demonstration?"

The King turned to him. "If I had wanted it to be a show of force, I would have waited until the next scheduled plasma collection. However, since you seem to be asking, both Theed Engineering and Nubian Design assure me that the Federation's Lucrehulk freighters would be easy prey for our N-Ones."

Palpatine cut his eyes to Pestage and Greejatus and shook his head in dismay. "Then it's good you thought to invite me aboard, Your Majesty, because I bring news that may persuade you to rethink your position."

"What news?" Magneta demanded.

Palpatine ignored her by continuing to speak to Veruna. "This matter has yet to reach the Rotunda, but there is every indication that the Republic is eventually going to grant the Trade Federation permission to arm its ships."

Veruna's jaw dropped and he blinked. "With what?"

Palpatine pretended to become flustered. "I don't know precisely. Turbolasers, certainly, as well as droid starfighters. Whatever combat automata are being produced by Baktoid, Haor Chall, and the hive species." He gestured out the viewport. "Weapons that will prove to be a deadly match for those starfighters."

Veruna was still trying to make sense of it. "Why is the Republic doing this?"

"Because of what happened at Yinchorr. Because of persistent attacks by pirates and would-be insurrectionists. And because the Republic refuses to reverse its position on creating a military."

Veruna stormed away from the viewport, then stopped and whirled on Palpatine. "I don't believe it. Valorum was successful at Yinchorr. He would never bow to pressure from the Trade Federation."

"He isn't bowing to pressure. His strategy is to enter into a deal with the Federation: defensive weaponry in exchange for taxation of the free-trade zones."

Veruna was speechless.

"This is why I urge Your Majesty to keep Naboo on the proper side of this."

"Do tell us, Senator," Lago interrupted, "what it means to be on the *proper* side?"

Palpatine glanced from Lago to Veruna. "When the matter reaches the Rotunda, Naboo must vote in protest of taxation of the free-trade zones."

Veruna swallowed and found his voice. "In support of the Trade Federation? With my reelection approaching? You must be mad, Palpatine. Naboo has been under the yoke of the Federation for more than thirty years. The people would never forgive me."

"Your base remains strong," Palpatine said. "The people will gradually come to understand that you made the correct decision."

Veruna smoldered. "I don't like being put in this position, Palpatine."

Palpatine adopted a pensive pose, then looked at the King. "There may yet be a way . . . I'm certain that Hego Damask would be willing to broker a renegotiated deal with the Neimoidian bloc of the Trade Federation—"

"I don't need Damask to broker anything," Veruna snapped. "The Muun's time has come and gone. He's an anachronism. His enemies did us all a favor by forcing him into early retirement."

Palpatine's eyes narrowed imperceptibly. *And so, with a nudge, he reveals himself.*

"If I recall correctly, Damask's enemies paid dearly." He fell silent for a moment, repositioning himself in front of the viewport, so that Veruna would have the strafing starfighters in direct view while he listened. "Granted, Sojourn isn't the impregnable fortress it once was. But Damask's reach is as long as it ever was, and his ties to the Banking Clan have never been stronger."

"In case you haven't noticed, Senator," Magneta interjected, "Naboo's reach is now long, as well."

Palpatine glanced over his shoulder at the starfighters, then fixed his eyes on Veruna. "Your Majesty, Damask will not take kindly to being cut out of our dealings with the Trade Federation. He can make trouble."

Veruna's gaze wandered back to him. "Let him try. Naboo isn't the only world he has exploited. We would not want for allies. I'm more concerned about how the Senate would react to our voting against taxation of the trade zones."

Palpatine forced a breath. "It's a hopeless situation. The Rim Faction worlds rely on the Trade Federation for goods, so they will likely vote in the negative. The Core Worlds, on the other hand, will vote in favor of taxation, if only to bring revenue to the Republic and avoid having to support the outlying systems. Occupying the middle ground, the Trade Federation stands to win no matter what, in that it will finally be allowed to defend itself, and will force its clients to shoulder the increased costs that will result from taxation."

"What does all this mean for Valorum?" Lago said.

"I fear that he may not complete his term of office."

"Who will succeed him?" Veruna asked.

"That's difficult to say, Your Majesty. Ainlee Teem, I think. Though Bail Antilles enjoys some support."

Veruna thought about it. "What are the implications for Naboo should the Gran win over the Alderaanian?"

"Then, of course, you would have a friend in the chancellorship."

Veruna tugged at his beard. "I'll take your recommendations into account. But be forewarned, Palpatine, I will brook no deception. From you"—he fixed Pestage and Greejatus with a gimlet stare—"or any of your cabal. Remember: I know where the bodies are buried."

Time is short.

Vines and creepers had clawed their way up the walls and towers of the old fort, and lianas linked the crenellated parapets to the leafy crowns of nearby trees. Insects scurried underfoot, foraging for food or laden with bits of vegetation or scraps of splintered wood. The previous night's storms had left puddles ankle-deep on the walkway, and run-off cascaded through firing holes. The forest Plagueis had planted and stocked with rare and exotic game seemed determined to rid Sojourn of the fortress that had been erected in its midst.

From the tallest of the towers, he gazed over the treetops at the rim of the moon's parent world and the distant star they shared. Sojourn was running fast and the last light was fading. The air was balmy and riotous with the drone and stridulation of insects, the territorial cries of avians, the mournful waking howls of creatures of the night. Clouds of bats spilled from caves in the escarpment, devouring bloodsuckers born by the strong rains. A breeze rose out of nowhere.

Time is short.

Still in safekeeping on Aborah were texts and holocrons that recounted the deeds and abilities of Sith Masters who, so it was said and written, had been able to summon wind or rain or fracture the skies with conjured lightning. In their own words or those of their disciples, a few Dark Lords claimed to have had the ability to fly, become invisible, or transport themselves through space and time. But Plagueis had never succeeded in duplicating any of those phenomena.

From the start Tenebrous had told him that he lacked the talent for Sith sorcery, even though the inability hadn't owed to a deficiency of midi-chlorians. *It's an innate gift,* the Bith would say when pressed, and one that he had lacked, as well. Sorcery paled in comparison with Bith science, regardless. But Plagueis now understood that Tenebrous had been wrong about sorcery, as he had been wrong about so many things. Yes, the gift was strongest in those who, with scant effort, could allow themselves to be subsumed by the currents of the Force and become conduits for the powers of the dark side. But there was an alternative path to those abilities, and it led from a place where the circle closed on itself and sheer will substituted for selflessness. Plagueis understood, too, that there were no powers beyond his reach; none he couldn't master through an effort of will. If a Sith of equal power had preceded him, then that one had taken his or her secrets to the grave, or had locked them away in holocrons that had been destroyed or had yet to surface.

The question of whether he and Sidious had discovered something new or rediscovered something ancient was beside the point. All that mattered was that, almost a decade earlier, they had succeeded in willing the Force to shift and tip irrevocably to the dark side. Not a mere paradigm shift, but a tangible alteration that could be felt by anyone strong in the Force, and whether or not trained in the Sith or Jedi arts.

The shift had been the outcome of months of intense meditation, during which Plagueis and Sidious had sought to challenge the Force for sovereignty and suffuse the galaxy with the power of the dark side. Brazen and shameless, and at their own mortal peril, they had waged etheric war, anticipating that their own midi-chlorians, the Force's proxy army, might marshal to boil their blood or stop the beating of their hearts. Risen out of themselves, discorporate and as a single entity, they had brought the power of their will to bear, asserting their sovereignty over the Force. No counterforce had risen against them. In what amounted to a state of rapture they knew that the Force had yielded, as if some deity had been tipped from its throne. On the fulcrum they had fashioned, the light side had dipped and the dark side had ascended.

On the same day they had allowed Venamis to die.

Then, by manipulating the Bith's midi-chlorians, which should have been inert and unresponsive, Plagueis had resurrected him. The enormity of the event had stunned Sidious into silence and overwhelmed and addled 11-4D's processors, but Plagueis had carried on without assistance, again and again allowing Venamis to die and be returned to life, until the Bith's organs had given out and Plagueis had finally granted him everlasting death.

But having gained the power to keep another alive hadn't been enough for him. And so after Sidious had returned to Coruscant, he had devoted himself to internalizing that ability, by manipulating the midi-chlorians that animated him. For several months he made no progress, but ultimately he began to perceive a measured change. The scars that had grown over his wounds had abruptly begun to soften and fade, and he had begun to breathe more freely than he had in twenty years. He began to sense that not only were his damaged tissues healing, but his entire body was rejuvinating itself. Beneath the transpirator, areas of his skin were smooth and youthful, and he knew that eventually he would cease to age altogether.

Drunk on newfound power, then, he had attempted an even more unthinkable act: to bring into being a creation of his own. Not merely the impregnation of some hapless, mindless creature, but the birth of a Forceful being. The ability to dominate death had been a step in the right direction, but it wasn't equivalent to pure creation. And so he had stretched out—indeed, as if invisible, transubstantiated—to inform every being of his existence, and impact all of them: Muunoid or insec-toid, secure or dispossessed, free or enslaved. A warrior waving a ban-ner in triumph on a battlefield. A ghost infiltrating a dream.

But ultimately to no end.

The Force grew silent, as if in flight from him, and many of the animals in his laboratory succumbed to horrifying diseases.

Regardless, eight long years later, Plagueis remained convinced that he was on the verge of absolute success. The evidence was in his own increased midi-chlorian count; and in the power he sensed in Sidious when he had finally returned to Sojourn. The dark side of the Force was theirs to command, and in partnership they would someday be able to keep each other alive, and to rule the galaxy for as long as they saw fit.

But he had yet to inform Sidious of this.

It was more important that Sidious remain as focused on manipulat-ing events in the profane world as Plagueis was intent on dominating the realm of the Force, of which the mundane was only a gross and distorted reflection.

To be sure, the light had been extinguished, but for how long and at what cost?

He recalled a stellar eclipse he had witnessed on a long-forgotten world, whose single moon was of perfect size and distance to blot out the light of the system's primary. The result hadn't been total darkness but illumination of a different sort, singular and diffuse, that had confused the birds and had permitted the stars to be seen in what would have been broad daylight. Even totally blocked, the primary had shone from behind the satellite's disk, and when the moon moved on there had been a moment of light almost too intense to bear.

Gazing into Sojourn's darkening sky, he wondered what calamity the Force was planning in retreat to visit upon him or Sidious or both of them for willfully tipping the balance. Was retribution merely waiting in the wings as it had been on Coruscant twenty years earlier? It was a dangerous time; more dangerous than his earliest years as an apprentice when the dark side might have consumed him at any moment.

For now, at least, his full convalescence was near complete. Sidious was continuing to become more powerful as a Sith and as a politician, his most intricate schemes meeting with little or no resistance. And the Jedi Order was foundering . . .

Time would tell, and time was short.

The Dathomirian Zabrak sat cross-legged on the duracrete floor, recounting for Sidious the surveillance mission he had completed at the Jedi Temple, weeks earlier, at the height of the Yinchorri Crisis.

"It sickened me to see how easily the reptilian infiltrators were deceived, Master, even by the fair-haired human female sentry they thought they had taken by surprise outside the Temple. From where I watched I knew that she had feigned surprise when her lightsaber failed to penetrate her assailant's cortosis shield, and that she had merely been faking unconsciousness when the Yinchorri had yanked her to her feet and she impaled him on her activated blade." Maul snarled, revealing sharply filed teeth. "Their stupidity allowed me to revel in the fact that their mission had been compromised—that the Jedi were simply luring them into a trap."

The abandoned LiMerge Building had become the assassin's home and training center; The Works and the fringes of the nearby Fobosi district, his nocturnal haunts. Circling him with the cowl of his robe raised over his head, Sidious asked, "The Jedi gained your respect?"

"They might have, had the infiltrators showed any skill. Had I been leading them . . ."

Sidious stopped. "The mission would have been successful? Jedi Knights and Padawans killed; younglings slaughtered."

"I'm certain of it, Master."

"Just you, against the Masters who make up the High Council."

"By hiding and striking I could have killed many."

Plagueis was right, Sidious thought. *I have made him prideful.*

The Yinchorri stratagem had failed, in any case. Additional Jedi had died, but Jedi deaths had never been the primary reason for instigating the crisis. What mattered was that Valorum had triumphed, with some help from Palpatine, it was true, but mostly on his own, by managing to bring Senators Yarua, Tikkes, Farr, and others over to his side and establishing an embargo. But with his political currency spent, Valorum's position was more tenuous than ever. Even a hint of scandal and the Senate would lose what little confidence they had in him.

"You are formidable," Sidious said at last, "but you are not a one-being army, and I've not spent years training you only to have you sacrifice yourself. When I bestowed upon you the title of *Darth,* it was not in reward for your having survived dangerous missions, starvation, and assassin droids, but for your obedience and loyalty. No doubt you will have ample opportunities to demonstrate your superior skill to the Jedi, but bringing down the Order is not your mandate, your hatred of them notwithstanding."

Maul lowered his head, displaying his crown of sharp-tipped horns in their red-and-black field. "Master. As long as those who do derive the joy and satisfaction I would."

"We shall see, my apprentice. But until then, there are matters we need to attend to."

He motioned for Maul to stand and follow him to the holoprojector table and transmission grid—the same ones the Gran had left behind decades before, but fully modernized and enhanced.

"Stand out of view of the cams," Sidious said, indicating a place. "For now, we want to keep you in reserve."

"But—"

"Be patient. You will have a part to play in this."

Sidious settled into a high-backed chair that wrapped around him like a throne and had a remote control built into one of the arms, his thoughts set aswirl by what he was about to do. Had Plagueis felt the enormity of the moment on Naboo all those years before when he had revealed his true self; removed, for the first time, the mask he wore in public? As empowering as it might have been, had the moment also been tainted by a kind of nostalgia; the loss of something so personal, so defining? What had been secret would never be secret again . . .

The comm caught Viceroy Nute Gunray in the midst of eating, and without the ear-flapped tiara and ornate azurestone collar that made him look like a jester. "Greetings, Viceroy," Sidious said.

The nictitating membranes of the Neimoidian's crimson eyes went into spasm, and his mottled muzzle twitched. "What? What? This is a secure address. How did you—"

"Don't bother attempting to trace the origin of this communication," Sidious said, while Gunray's tapered gray fingers flew across the keypad of his holotable. "A trace will only lead you in circles and waste what limited time we have."

"How dare you intrude—"

"Recently, I sent you a gift. A red-spotted pylat."

Gunray stared. "You? You sent it?"

"I trust you had sense enough to have it scanned for monitoring devices."

Gunray whirled to look at something off cam; probably the crested bird itself. "Of course I did. What was your purpose in sending it?" His accent elongated the words and softened the *T* sounds.

"Consider it a token of my appreciation for the unrewarded work you have done for the Trade Federation. The directorate fails to recognize your contributions."

"They—that is, I . . . Why are you hiding inside the cowl of your cloak?"

"It is the clothing of my Order, Viceroy."

"You are a cleric?"

"Do I seem a holy man to you?"

Gunray's expression soured. "I demand to see your face."

"You have yet to earn the privilege of seeing me."

"Privilege? Who do you think you are?"

"Are you certain you want to know?"

"I *demand* to know."

Sidious's smile barely escaped the cowl. "Even better, then. I am a Sith Lord."

There. I said it.

I said it . . .

"Sith Lord?" Gunray repeated.

The response came from deep inside him, from the center of his true being. "You have permission to refer to me as Darth Sidious."

"I've not heard of Darth Sidious."

"Ah, but now that you have, our partnership is forged."

Gunray shook his head. "I am not looking for a partner."

Sidious showed some of his face. "Don't pretend to be content with your position in the Trade Federation, or that you are without aspirations. We are now partners in the future."

Gunray made a hissing sound. "This is a joke. The Sith have been extinct for a thousand years."

"That's precisely what the Republic and the Jedi Order would like you to believe, but we never disappeared. Through the centuries we have taken up just causes and revealed ourselves to select beings like yourself."

Gunray sat back in his chair. "I don't understand. Why me?"

"You and I share an avid interest in where the Republic is headed, and I have deemed it time that we begin to work in concert."

"I won't be part of any covert schemes."

"Truly?" Sidious said. "Do you think that out of millions of influential beings I would choose you without knowing you inside and out? I realize that your voracious desires stem from the cruel conditions of your upbringing—you and your fellow grubs in ruthless competition for limited supplies of fungus. But I understand. We are all shaped by our infantile desires, our longing for affection and attention, our fears of death. And judging by how far you have come, it's clear that you were unrivaled and continue to be. Your years in the Senate, for example. The clandestine meetings in the Claus Building, the Follin Restaurant in the Crimson Corridor, the funds you diverted to Pax Teem and Aks Moe, the secret dealings with Damask Holdings, the assassination of Vidar Kim—"

"Enough! Enough! Do you mean to blackmail me?"

Sidious delayed his reply. "Perhaps you didn't hear me when I spoke of a partnership."

"I heard you. Now tell me what you want of me."

"Nothing more than your cooperation. I will bring about great changes for you, and in exchange you will do the same for me."

Gunray looked worried. "You claim to be a Dark Lord. But how do I know that you are? How do I know you have any ability to help me?"

"I found you a rare bird."

"That hardly validates your claim."

Sidious nodded. "I understand your skepticism. I could, of course, demonstrate my powers. But I'm reluctant to convince you in that way."

Gunray sniffed. "I haven't time for this—"

"Is the pylat nearby?"

"Just behind me," Gunray allowed.

"Show me."

Gunray widened the scope of the holotable's cams to include the bird, perched in a cage that was little more than a circle of precious metal, crowned with a stasis field generator.

"I was concerned, when I extracted him from the jungle habitat, that he would die," Sidious said. "And yet he appears to be at home in his new environment."

"His songs suggest as much," Gunray replied.

"What if I told you that I could reach across space and time and strangle him where he perches?"

Gunray was aghast. "You couldn't. I doubt that even a Jedi—"

"Are you challenging me, Viceroy?"

"Yes," he said abruptly; then, just as quickly: "No—wait!"

Sidious shifted in the chair. "You value the bird—this symbol of wealth."

"I am the envy of my peers for possessing it."

"Would not actual wealth generate even greater envy?"

Gunray grew flustered. "How can I answer, when I know that you might strangle me should I refuse you?"

Sidious loosed an elaborate sigh. "Partners don't strangle each other, Viceroy. I would prefer to earn your trust. Are you agreeable to that?"

"I might be."

"Then here is my first gift to you: the Trade Federation is going to be betrayed. By Naboo, by the Republic, by the members of the directorate. Only you can provide the leadership that will be needed to keep the Federation from splintering. But first we must see to it that you are promoted to the directorate."

"The current directorate would never welcome a Neimoidian."

"Tell me what it would take—" Sidious started, then cut himself off. "No. Never mind. Let me surprise you by arranging a promotion."

"You would do that and ask nothing in return?"

"For the time being. If and when I've earned your full trust, I will expect you to take my suggestions to heart."

"I will. Darth Sidious."

"Then we will speak again soon."

Sidious deactivated the holoprojector and sat in silence.

"There is a world in the Videnda sector called Dorvalla," he said to Maul a long moment later. "You will not have heard of it, but it is a source of lommite ore, which is essential to the production of transparisteel. Two companies—Lommite Limited and InterGalactic Ore—currently control the mining and shipping operations. But for some time the Trade Federation has had its sights on overseeing Dorvalla."

"What is thy bidding, Master?" Maul asked.

"For now, only that you acquaint yourself with Dorvalla, for it may prove the key to ensnaring Gunray in our grasp."

25: THE DISCREET CHARM OF THE MERITOCRACY

A more outlandish quartet hadn't set foot, belly, claw, and jaw on Sojourn in twenty years. A half-breed Theelin female, her Hutt master, his Twi'lek majordomo, and his Chevin chief of security crossed the fort's leaf-litterd courtyard and entered Plagueis's reception room. With the exception of the Theelin, they looked as if they might have wandered in from the greel forests to consort with the creatures that had constructed nests and burrows in the fort's dank corridors and lofty turrets.

Plagueis and 11-4D were waiting just inside the gaping entrance.

"Welcome, Jabba Desilijic Tiure," Plagueis said through his transpirator mask.

Droids had restored some semblance of order to the room and installed tables and chairs. Morning light streamed through square openings high in the wall, and a fire crackled in the stone hearth.

"A pleasure to see you again after so many years, Magister Damask," Jabba said in coarse Basic. The ageless criminal lolled his huge tongue and maneuvered his great slug body onto a low platform the droids had erected. Gazing around, he added, "You and your droid must visit my little place on Tatooine in the Western Dune Sea."

"Someday soon," Plagueis said as he lowered himself into an armchair across from the platform.

Like Toydarians and Yinchorri, Hutts were immune to Force suggestions. Had Jabba known how many of his species Plagueis had experimented on over the decades, he might not have been as sociable, but then the Hutt's own penchant for ruthlessness and torture were legendary. As a tattoo on his arm attested, he cared only for members of his clan. He didn't bother to introduce his subordinates by name, but as was often the case with many of the thugs and ne'er-do-wells with whom he surrounded himself, two of them had reputations that preceded them. The pink-complexioned Twi'lek was Bib Fortuna, a former spice smuggler whose own species had turned its back on him. Tall and red-eyed, he had sharp little teeth and thick, shiny lekku growing from a hairless cranium that looked as if it had been inexpertly stuffed with rocks. The Chevin—a two-meter-high snout that had sprouted arms, legs, and tail—was Ephant Mon. Celebrated as a warrior among his own kind—and mildly Force-sensitive—he wore a blanket someone might have thrown over him to hide his ugliness. Plagueis knew from contacts in the Trade Federation that Mon was involved in a smuggling operation on technophobic Cerea, supplying swoops to a gang of young upstarts.

The Theelin was unknown to Plagueis. Pale and shapely, she had lustrous orange hair and purple beauty marks that ran down her face and neck to disappear beneath a revealing costume.

"Diva Shaliqua," Jabba said when he realized that Plagueis was studying her. "A singer in the band."

"As her name suggests."

"A gift from Ingoda, in place of credits owed to me." Jabba's big eyes settled on the Theelin. "She and Diva Funquita came as a pair, but I made Funquita a present to Gardulla in the hope of smoothing over our lingering rivalry." He grunted. "My first mistake. The second: introducing Shaliqua to Romeo Treblanc, who would move worlds to possess her."

Notorious for his gambling, Treblanc owned the Galaxies Opera House on Coruscant. Why Jabba chose to associate with gamblers and other lowlifes was a mystery to Plagueis. In some ways the Hutt's illicit empire was the inverse of Hego Damask's, where, if nothing else, the criminals were at least politicians, corporate honchos, and financiers. His coming to Sojourn was both uncharacteristic and unexpected.

"Are you here to talk about Treblanc or Gardulla?" Plagueis asked.

Jabba reacted in annoyance. "As always, straight to the heart of the matter. But I can appreciate the fact that you're a busy Muun." He wriggled to adjust his position on the platform. "I know you were instrumental thirty years ago in giving Gardulla the run of Tatooine, as a base for her slavery operations and Podracing events. I've come this far to inform you that Tatooine will soon have a new overseer." He gestured to himself. "Me."

Plagueis said nothing for a long moment. "I was under the impression that Tatooine was already as much yours as Gardulla's."

"Appearances can be deceiving," Jabba said. "I've tried to undermine her influence by fomenting distrust among the so-called Sand People—the Tusken Raiders—but success at chasing her offworld continues to elude me."

Plagueis made an adjustment to the breath mask. "How can I help?"

Jabba appraised him. "I happen to know that Gardulla hasn't been able to make good on the loans you extended. What she earns from events like the Boonta Eve Classic, she loses to gamblers."

"That much is true," Plagueis said. "But what of it?"

"I want you to stop funding her, so I can starve her out."

Plagueis shrugged. "Your information is incomplete, Jabba. I haven't funded her enterprises in a decade."

Jabba balled his hands in anger. "You have influence over members of the Banking Clan and the Trade Federation who are funding her."

Plagueis lifted his head, as if in revelation. "I see. And what can I expect in exchange?"

"To start with, a better percentage of the profits from the races and other enterprises."

Plagueis frowned in disappointment. "You must know that I've no need of credits, Jabba. And you wouldn't have come *this far*, as you say, unless you had learned a few things that might sway me over to your side."

Jabba wriggled, restraining his anger. "In return for your help, I will weaken Black Sun's influence with the Trade Federation Directorate—"

"I need no assistance." Plagueis leaned forward in the armchair. "What do you know that I may not know?"

Jabba inflated his body, then allowed the air to escape him in a protracted, mirthless laugh. "I know something you may not yet know about the Bando Gora."

Plagueis raised himself somewhat in the chair. Hideously masked Bando Gora assassins had become a growing concern in the Outer Rim, posing a problem to the leadership of some of the cartels Plagueis backed. "Now you have my interest, Jabba."

"The cult has a new leader," Jabba went on, happy to have the high ground. "A human female, she has entered into a plan with Gardulla, a Malastare Dug named Sebolto, and a Republic Senator to distribute contaminated death sticks, as a means of supplying the Bando Gora with brain-dead recruits."

Plagueis stretched out with the Force to peer into the Hutt. Jabba wasn't lying. "This human female," he said.

"I've heard rumors."

Again Jabba was telling the truth. "Rumors will suffice for now."

The Hutt rubbed his meaty hands together. "Her name is Komari Vosa, and word has it that she is a former Jedi."

Plagueis knew the name only too well. Some ten years earlier, Komari Vosa had been a Padawan of Master Dooku.

Behind each of the Rotunda's hover platform docking stations extended wedge-shaped office complexes more than half a kilometer in length, where Senators met with one another, entertained guests, and, on rare occasions, carried out the work they had been elected or appointed to perform. Some of the offices were sealed environments, in which the atmospheres of member worlds were replicated; others, especially those belonging to hive species, were staffed by hundreds of beings who performed their duties in cubicles that resembled nectarcomb cells. By comparison, Naboo's was rather prosaic in design and adornment, and yet unrivaled in terms of the number of high-profile visitors it received.

"I'm giving thought to leaving the Order," Master Dooku told Palpatine in the windowless room that was the Senator's private study. "I can no longer abide the decisions of the Council, and I have to be free to speak my mind about the wretched state of the Republic."

Palpatine didn't reply, but thought: *Finally.*

With Darth Maul traveling to Dorvalla on his first mission, Palpatine had been preoccupied all afternoon, and now Dooku's disclosure: long anticipated and yet still something of a surprise.

"This isn't the first time you've been exasperated with the Council," he said carefully, "and it probably won't be the last."

Dooku shook his head firmly. "Never more than this. Even after Galidraan. I've no recourse."

Frigid Galidraan was years behind him, but for Dooku the incident remained an open wound. A local governor had succeeded in luring the Jedi into a conflict with Mandalorian mercenaries that had left eleven Jedi dead and the True Mandalorians—largely innocent of the charges that had been leveled against them—wiped out, save for one. Since then, and on each occasion he and Palpatine had met, Dooku had begun to look less and less like a Jedi Master and more like the noble he would have been on his native Serenno. Meticulously groomed, he carried himself like an aristocrat, affecting tailored tunics and trousers, and a velvety black cloak that gave him a dashing, theatrical look. His slightly curved lightsaber hilt, too, might have been a prop, though he was known to be one of the Order's most skilled duelists. And behind a mask of arrogant civility, Palpatine knew him to be capable of great cruelty.

"By request from the Senate," Dooku went on, "the Council dispatched several Jedi to Baltizaar, and my former Padawan somehow succeeded in accompanying them."

Palpatine nodded soberly. "I know something of that. Baltizaar's Senator petitioned for help in fending off attacks by the Bando Gora."

"Sadistic abductors and assassins," Dooku said in anger. "Military action was called for, not Jedi intercession. But no matter, the Council complied with the request, and now Komari Vosa and the others are believed to be dead."

Palpatine raised an eyebrow. "The young woman who became infatuated with you?"

"The same," Dooku said quietly. "At Galidraan she fought brutally against the Mandalorians, almost as if in an attempt to impress me. As a result I told the Council that she wasn't ready for the trials and Jedi Knighthood. Compounding their initial error in dispatching Jedi, Master Yoda and the rest have refused to send reinforcements to search for survivors."

Palpatine considered it. "If Baltizaar was meant to be another attempt to impress you, all Komari Vosa did was prove that you were right about her all along."

Dooku regarded him. "Perhaps. But the failure is mine." He ran a hand over his short beard. "As skilled as I am with a lightsaber, I've turned out to be an ineffectual teacher. Master Qui-Gon Jinn has become a solitary and secretive rogue. And now Vosa . . ." He snorted. "I declined to be a member of the Council in order to devote myself to diplomacy, and look how that has turned out. The Republic is sliding deeper into chaos."

"You're one man against a galaxy full of scoundrels," Palpatine said.

Dooku's eyes flashed. "One man should be able to make a difference if he is powerful enough."

Palpatine let the silence linger. "You would claim the title of Count of Serenno?"

"By right of birth. My family is agreeable. Now it's simply a matter of informing the High Council."

"Has anyone ever left the Order?"

"Nineteen before me."

"Have you shared your discontent with any of them?"

"Only Master Sifo-Dyas."

"Of course."

Dooku looked up. "He worries that I'm going to do something rash."

"Leaving the Order isn't rash enough?"

"He fears that I will denounce the Council openly, and reveal how divided its members are about answering to the Senate." He looked Palpatine in the eye. "I've half a mind to join your cause."

Palpatine touched his chest. "*My* cause?"

Dooku adopted a sly smile. "I understand politics, my friend. I know that you have to be circumspect about what you say and to whom. But that the disenfranchised worlds of the Outer Rim enjoy any support at all is largely due to you. You speak honestly and you champion the underprivileged, and you may be the only one capable of bringing the Republic back from the brink. Unless, of course, you have been lying to me all these years."

Palpatine made light of the remark. "Perhaps a few lies of omission."

"Those I am willing to forgive," Dooku said, "whether or not we become partners in addition to being allies."

Palpatine interlocked his hands. "It is an interesting notion. We would have to deepen our conversations, become completely honest with each other, bare our innermost thoughts and feelings to determine whether we truly share the same goals."

"I'm being honest when I tell you that the Republic needs to be torn down and built up again from the ground up."

"That is a tall order."

"Tall, indeed."

"It might require a civil war."

"And how far from that are we now?" Dooku fell silent for a moment, then said, "The Senate grapples with trying to solve disputes the Jedi often see firsthand. What laws are enacted only follow from our having brought our lightsabers to bear."

"It was the Jedi who pledged to support the Republic."

"The Order's place in this is a matter Sifo-Dyas and I have discussed endlessly," Dooku snapped. "But the members of the Council are not similarly inclined. They are entrenched in archaic thinking, and slow to embrace change." He paused, and adopted a sinister look. "Don't let yourself be fooled, Palpatine. They see dark times ahead. In fact, they think of little else. That's why they have allowed the Jedi to become involved in parochial conflicts like those at Galidraan, Yinchorr, and Baltizaar, which are like brush fires born of windblown embers from a massive blaze just beyond the horizon. But instead of actually rising up against the corruption in the Republic, perhaps disbanding the Senate entirely for a period of time, they have become fixated on prophecy. They await the coming of a prophesized redeemer who will bring balance to the Force and restore order."

"A redeemer?" Palpatine stared at him in authentic surprise. "You've never alluded to this prophecy."

"Nor would I now if I still thought of myself as loyal to the Order."

"I never considered that the Force needed to be balanced."

Dooku's lip curled. "The Order interprets the prophecy to mean that the dark tide needs to be stemmed."

"You don't accept it?"

Dooku had an answer ready. "Here is the truth of it: the Jedi could fulfill the prophecy on their own, if they were willing to unleash the full powers of the Force."

"The full powers of the Force," Palpatine said. "I'm afraid you've lost me."

Dooku blew out his breath. "Perhaps it's something we can discuss in the future."

"You've made your decision, then?"

Dooku nodded. "If one more Jedi dies because of indolence on the part of the Republic and moral equivocation on the part of the Council, I will leave the Temple and refuse to look back."

No sooner had Dooku left the office than Sidious was donning his cloak and hurrying off to his next appointment. Hailing a sky-cab in Senate Plaza, he instructed the Gran driver to deliver him to Tannik Spaceport.

Relaxing back into the padded seat, he exhaled for what felt like the first time all day. In the space of a standard year he had gone from leading two lives to managing almost half a dozen: apprentice to Plagueis; Master to Maul; distinguished Senator; ally of Supreme Chancellor Valorum; and leader of a growing cabal of conspirators that included Pestage, Doriana, Greejatus—in line to replace him in the Senate—the Force-sensitive human Sim Aloo, intelligence analyst Armand Isard, Eriadu Senator Wilhuff Tarkin, and Umbaran telepath Sly Moore, whom he had made his covert aide.

And leading a double life of his own: Dooku. Carrying out Jedi business while in private moments flirting with the dark side, hungry to bring the full power of the Force to bear in the mundane realm, his slow reorientation a curious inversion of Darth Gravid's, whose similar reach for preeminence had exceeded his grasp.

For the Jedi, Mastery was conferred when one attained a true understanding of the ways of the Force; for the Sith, that level of understanding was merely the beginning. The Jedi Order's homespun cloaks announced: *I want for nothing, because I am clothed in the Force;* the cloaks of the Sith: *I am the light in the dark, the convergence of opposing energies.* And yet, while all Sith Lords were powerful, not all were brilliant or in complete possession of the powers the dark side granted them.

Darth Millennial had rebelled against the teachings of his Master, Darth Cognus, and even Plagueis spoke of having reached a philosophical impasse with his Master, Tenebrous.

A human Sith Lord whose short reign had elapsed some five centuries earlier, Gravid had been persuaded to believe that total commitment to the dark side would sentence the Sith Order to eventual defeat, and so had sought to introduce Jedi selflessness and compassion into his teachings and practice, forgetting that there can be no return to the light for an adept who has entered the dark wood; that the dark side will not surrender one to whom, by mutual agreement, it has staked a claim. Driven increasingly mad by his attempts to straddle the two realms, Gravid became convinced that the only way to safeguard the future of the Sith was to hide or destroy the lore that had been amassed through the generations—the texts, holocrons, and treatises—so that the Sith could fashion a new beginning for themselves that would guarantee success. Barricaded within the walls of a bastion he and his Twi'lek apprentice, Gean, had constructed on Jaguada, he had attempted as much, and was thought to have destroyed more than half the repository of artifacts before Gean, demonstrating consummate will and courage, had managed to penetrate the Force fields Gravid had raised around their stronghold and intercede, killing her Master with her bare hands, though at the cost of her arm, shoulder, and the entire left side of her face and chest.

A Jedi Master of high standing, Dooku possibly already had some theoretical understanding of the dark side; perhaps more, if he had access to Sith Holocrons vaulted within the Temple. He could certainly be a nuisance to the Republic, though hardly an agent of chaos, as Plagueis and Sidious had been. Still, it would be interesting to see just how far Dooku might be willing to go . . .

Palpatine would have to inform Plagueis of their conversation. Or would he? Was an apprentice ever permitted to conceal knowledge from his or her Master?

No. Never. Especially not when there was a chance that Plagueis might learn of Dooku's apostasy on his own, in ways that remained unfathomable.

* * *

Executing a reckless series of maneuvers, the Gran driver had changed lanes and was descending rapidly for Tannik Spaceport—a semicircular docking pad located at the edge of the Manaai district and surrounded on all sides by towering monads. Reserved for low-impact freighters, the port was a haven for drugged and abducted crew members, itinerant workers, and undocumented migrants of diverse species, most of whom were in search of steerage passage to distant worlds.

Glad to be released from the sky-cab, Palpatine edged his way into the crowds and set a course for the headquarters of the Refugee Relief Movement, whose stark offices were tucked under the port's recessed upper level. Halfway to his destination he spied the stout Naboo he had come to see, standing alongside his slender wife and issuing commands to a group of young volunteers. Adopting an expression of good cheer and waving a hand in the air, Palpatine shouted, "Ruwee."

The man swung to the sound of his voice and smiled broadly. "Palpatine!"

President of the RRM, Ruwee Naberrie had a large square head, thin lips, a clean-shaven face, and short hair clipped in high bangs. A onetime mountain man, a builder by trade, and a frequent guest lecturer on microeconomics at Theed University, he was not easily fooled, and his default expression was one of sincerity. The nonprofit organization he directed was devoted to providing aid for Coruscant's billions of lower-tier dwellers.

"What a happy coincidence," Ruwee said, pumping Palpatine's hand. The two Naboo were close in age, but Ruwee was a product of public education rather than the series of private institutions young Palpatine had attended. "You remember Jobal?"

A tall woman with a triangular-shaped face and wide-spaced and compassionate eyes, she was allowing herself to age gracefully, though her long hair was still dark and luxuriant. Married to Ruwee by arrangement, she was every bit as serious as he was, and equally committed to the refugee movement.

"Of course," Palpatine said. Bowing his head, he added, "Madame Naberrie."

She made a move to hug him, then thought better of it and simply smiled in acknowledgment. "How good to see you again, Senator."

Ruwee touched him on the back. "I never had a chance to thank you in person for allowing me to address the Senate about the refugee crisis on Sev Tok."

Palpatine shrugged it off. "It was my honor to be affiliated with such a worthy cause. Speaking of which, Onaconda Farr sends his regards."

"Rodia should be proud of him," Ruwee said. "One of the few in the Senate who recognizes that good fortune should not be taken for granted but should serve as an impetus for bringing comfort to those less fortunate."

Palpatine smiled tightly.

"What brings you to the docks, Senator?" Jobal asked.

"More than coincidence, m'lady. In fact, a matter of utmost urgency that involves your daughter, Padmé."

"She's here," Ruwee said.

Palpatine looked at him. "On Coruscant?"

"Here, at Tannik." He pointed to a nearby dock, where an energetic dark-haired girl was directing an antigrav pallet of foodstuffs into the bay of a waiting freighter. Catching sight of her father, Padmé waved.

"Who is the young man with her?" Palpatine asked.

"Ian Lago," Jobal said.

Palpatine sharpened his vision. "The son of King Veruna's counselor?"

Jobal nodded. "He's become a bit lovesick."

"And Padmé with him?"

"We hope not," Ruwee said. "Ian's a nice boy, but . . . Well, let's just say that Kun Lago would not be happy to learn that his son has been fraternizing with the enemy, so to speak."

Realizing that young Ian was eyeing him with sudden interest, Palpatine returned the look for a moment, then said, "This brings me directly to the point of my visit. As you're no doubt aware, our King has instructed me to support the Trade Federation on the issue of taxation of the free-trade zones."

"Of course he would," Ruwee said with clear disdain. "How otherwise would Veruna continue to line the pockets of his robes with kickbacks."

Palpatine nodded. "You and I and some of the nobles know as much. But now may be the time to let the rest of Naboo in on his secrets."

Jobal's expression soured. "If you're talking about challenging him in the coming election, you're facing a lost cause."

"I beg to disagree, madame," Palpatine said. "With discretion I have already approached several members of the electorate, and they concur that Veruna can be defeated by the right candidate."

When he cut his gaze to Padmé, Ruwee's mouth fell open. "You can't be serious."

"But I am, Ruwee. A member of the Legislative Youth Program at eight years of age; a full Apprentice Legislator at eleven. Her refugee work on Shadda-Bi-Boran. Plus, she enjoys more popular support in Theed than any governor has enjoyed in generations."

Jobal blinked and shook her head in disbelief. "Palpatine, she has only just turned thirteen!"

Palpatine spread his hands. "Naboo has elected younger Queens, m'lady. And hers could be a reign that will last fifty years." He refused to yield to Ruwee or Jobal. "The constitution has a provision that would allow the monarchy to become hereditary for a worthy dynasty. And what more worthy family is there than the Naberries?"

Husband and wife traded looks. "That's very flattering, Senator—" Jobal started to say when Palpatine cut her off.

"The Naboo are exasperated with monarchs like Tapalo and Veruna. Padmé would allow Naboo to reinvent itself."

Ruwee mulled it over momentarily. "Even if Padmé were to entertain the idea, I'm not sure she could be persuaded to support taxation of the trade zones, knowing what that might mean for Naboo and other outlying worlds."

"She wouldn't have to take a stand," Palpatine countered. "She need only campaign against corruption and secret deals, and the embarrassing position in which Veruna has placed Naboo."

Jobal's eyes narrowed in uncertainly. "At the risk of touching on a sore point, Senator, you helped put Veruna on the throne and have been his advocate ever since."

Palpatine shook his head. "Never an advocate. I have always considered myself to be a counterbalance, and in the past few years we've found ourselves on opposite sides of almost every issue, including the library he built and the credits he lavished on creating a space force for

Naboo." He fell silent for a moment, then said, "Trust me, Veruna can be defeated."

Again, Ruwee and Naberrie exchanged worried looks. "We're provincial people, Palpatine," Ruwee said at last. "The world of politics . . . galactic politics, no less . . ."

Palpatine compressed his lips. "I understand. But what compelled the two of you to abandon the mountains for Theed, if not for Padmé and Sola, and the opportunities that might be available to them?"

Palpatine held Ruwee's pensive gaze. *He is beginning to waver.*

"I wouldn't want to put Padmé through this only to see her lose, Palpatine."

Palpatine beamed. "I will work with you to see that that doesn't happen. I don't wish to speak out of turn, but I can almost guarantee the support of the Supreme Chancellor, as well."

"Valorum knows of Padmé?" Jobal asked in delighted surprise.

"Of course he does." Palpatine paused. "Faced with Padmé as competition, perhaps Veruna will see the light and abdicate."

Jobal laughed, then showed Palpatine a serious look. "You have come a long way, Senator."

26: THEIR BASER NATURE

On a clear day, looking northwest across The Works from a debris-strewn room in the circular crown of the LiMerge Building, Maul could just see the elegant centermost spire of the Jedi Temple, poking above the horizon. With his Master en route to Eriadu to attend a trade summit Sidious himself had proposed, the Zabrak had made a habit of climbing to the crown at least once a day and, with electrobinoculars in hand, gazing at the distant spire in the hope of catching sight of a Jedi.

But that hadn't happened.

If any Jedi were present, they would be sitting in contemplation, as Maul knew he should be doing, as well. Or if not meditating, then completing work on the graciously curved speeder bike he had named *Bloodfin* or the droid called C-P3X, or perfecting his skill at using the wrist-mounted projectile launcher known as the lanvarok. Devoting himself to those tasks would have met with more approval from Darth Sidious than Maul's staring at the Temple's fin-ornamented pinnacle and dreaming of the day he could pit himself against a Jedi Master. But ever since his return from Dorvalla several standard weeks earlier, he had been too restless to sit cross-legged on the floor, immersed in the flow of the dark side, or to pore over the probe droid schematics Darth Sidious had furnished before he'd left.

When Maul reflected on the time he had spent on Dorvalla, his thoughts weren't focused on the assassinations he had carried out. He had murdered many in his short life, and there was nothing about the deaths of Patch Bruit, Caba'Zan, and the others involved in the business of mining lommite ore that distinguished them from previous kill-ings. In fact, the miners' carelessness should have condemned them to lingering deaths rather than the quick ends Maul had dispensed. What he remembered instead was the feeling of participation the mission had afforded. Not only had he been able to draw on his talents for stealth, tracking, and combat, but he had used them in a manner that furthered the Sith Grand Plan, as hadn't been the case during his years of training on Orsis, or during the forays Darth Sidious had allowed him to make to other worlds. On his return to Coruscant, the Dark Lord had praised him, which, Maul supposed, should have been reward enough. And might have been, had the mission led to another. But Darth Sidious had excluded him from participating in the Eriadu operation, and had been vague about future plans.

A direct outcome of what Maul had accomplished on Dorvalla, Lommite Limited and InterGalactic Ore had merged and been taken over by the Trade Federation, which in turn had resulted in Nute Gun-ray's promotion to the company's seven-member directorate. In further conversations with the viceroy, Darth Sidious had demanded that the Neimoidians willingly sacrifice one of their Lucrehulk freighters, along with a shipment of aurodium ingots, as a means of funding an Outer Rim insurgent group known as the Nebula Front. Maul had been non-plussed by his Master's decision to reveal himself to the group's leader, as Darth Sidious had done in his initial communication with Gunray; then dismayed to learn that the leader—a human named Havac—had betrayed Darth Sidious by attempting to assassinate Supreme Chancel-lor Valorum on Coruscant. The realization that his Master could be deceived, that he wasn't infallible, had had a curious effect on Maul. It had caused him *unease,* a sudden concern for his Master's safety that had intruded on his ability to still his mind and find reassurance in the dark side. It was not fear—for fear was something alien to Maul's makeup— but a troublesome disquiet. Disquiet for the being he had once tried to kill, and was perhaps *expected to kill.* All these weeks later he would still sometimes spend hours wandering through the LiMerge Building like a house pet picking up on the scent of its owner . . .

When, though, he had expressed a desire to take part in the Eriadu operation, even if that only meant assisting the Neimoidians in pro-curing weapons from the hive species or commencing manufacturing operations on Alaris Prime and other remote worlds, his Master had rejected the idea out of hand.

You have no role in this, he had said, without explanation, and in compensation, Maul surmised, had given him the dark eye schematics.

The rejection, too, had prompted questions of a novel sort. Of all the beings in the galaxy, the Dark Lord had chosen *him* to serve as his apprentice and eventual successor, and yet Darth Sidious had neglected to equip him with the very tools he would need to carry the Sith imperative forward. For all his attempts to familiarize himself with the political landscape and with criminal organizations—some of which were allied to Darth Sidious, others antithetical to his plans— he had a limited understanding of precisely how the galaxy worked. He grasped that the Sith's war was with the Jedi Order rather than the Republic, but he had no real inkling as to how revenge was to be meted out.

What, then, if—beyond contemplation—something untoward should befall his Master? Was there a contingency plan? Unlike Darth Sidious, who masqueraded as Republic Senator Palpatine and debated complex issues in the Senate, Maul lacked a secret identity. With his yellow eyes and horned head a black-and-red mask of arcane sigils, it was all he could do to prowl the fringes of The Works in the dead of night without instilling fear in nearly every being whose gaze he caught.

Maul had expected his life to change when Darth Sidious had relocated him to Coruscant. But in many ways the move struck him as a return to his days as a combat trainee on Orsis, waiting to be allowed to fight, receiving praise and rewards, only to be commanded to train harder. The occasional visits from his Master had allowed him to endure the isolation and superficiality of his existence. Only when his instruction in the Sith arts had begun, had he felt singular, purposeful . . .

But he wasn't entirely without hope.

On occasion Darth Sidious would hint at a mission of utmost importance that they would need to carry out together; one that would call on them to make use of all their powers. He had yet to provide details, even with regard to Maul's studies. But he continued to imply that the mission was looming. And more and more, Maul sensed that it was somehow linked to his Master's homeworld, Naboo.

* * *

His presence requested by King Veruna, Palpatine interrupted his journey to the Eriadu summit to stop at Naboo. The spaceport was crowded with ships of unusual design, and Theed was teeming with citizens who had packed the streets and lanes surrounding Palace Plaza to hear young Padmé Naberrie speak. In stark contrast with the joyous enthusiasm demonstrated by the crowds, and seemingly organized as a kind of counterevent, the palace throne room was the scene of an extravagant fete, attended by the most corrupt of Veruna's supporters in the electorate and several dozen offworlders of dubious character. The announcement of Palpatine's arrival at the room met with hushed innuendos and malicious laughter that continued while he was ushered to a place at the King's table, opposite Veruna and sandwiched between Kun Lago and security chief Magneta.

Motioning with his royal baton for decorum, Veruna greeted Palpatine with an exaggerated smile. "Welcome, Palpatine." Drinking had imparted a slight slur to his speech. Clapping his hands, he added, "Bring wine for Naboo's celebrated Senator."

"Thank you, Majesty," Palpatine said, playing along with Veruna's insincerity. "I've gone without blossom wine for too long."

Veruna pounded a fist on the long wooden table. "Then bring him two goblets, and keep the supply flowing until his thirst is slaked."

Palpatine sat back as servants hurried in to honor Veruna's command. Both ends of the table were anchored by beings he knew by reputation rather than acquaintance. Far to Veruna's right sat Alexi Garyn, head of the Black Sun crime syndicate; and to his left, elevated on durable cushions and drawing smoke from a water pipe, lounged a female Hutt named Gardulla, from Tatooine. Among her retinue of beings were two humanoids whose martial uniforms identified them as members of the Bando Gora terrorist group.

More ammunition for Padmé Naberrie, he thought.

"Tell us, Palpatine," Veruna said, after wiping his mouth on the sleeve of his gaudy robe, "what prompted you to propose this summit on Eriadu?"

Palpatine ignored the goblets of wine. "The summit will provide an opportunity for everyone involved to air their thoughts and grievances regarding taxation of the trade zones."

"I'm certain that your friends in the Trade Federation are very appreciative."

Palpatine waited for the laughter to end, pleased to find that the conversation was headed in the direction he had expected it to go. "Naboo has a great stake in what emerges from the summit, Majesty."

"Ah, then you arranged this for the sake of Naboo." Veruna raised his voice so that everyone at the table could hear. "Palpatine did this out of concern for Naboo!" His expression toughened as he leaned forward. "And no doubt you were thinking of Naboo when you approached the Naberries about having their daughter oppose me in the coming election."

"Think twice before you offer any denials," Magneta told him quietly.

Lago leaned over to add, "My son was present when you tendered the offer."

"With Padmé Naberrie, if I'm not mistaken," Palpatine said in like conspiracy. While Lago was trying to puzzle it out, he looked at Veruna. "We discussed the refugee movement."

The monarch glared at him, then motioned dismissively with his fingertips. "What's done is done. And I'm afraid that includes you, Senator." Gesturing broadly in the direction of Palace Plaza, he said, "Do you really believe that that little political upstart can unseat me? The daughter of mountain peasants?"

Palpatine shrugged. "The crowd she has drawn seems to think so."

"Idealists," Veruna said, sneering. "Regressives. They dream of the Naboo of fifty years ago, but they're not about to have their wish." His finger jabbed the air in front of Palpatine's face. "My first official act following my reelection will be to recall you as Senator." He looked at Lago. "Kun will be Naboo's new representative."

Palpatine frowned in mock disappointment. "Janus Greejatus would be a better choice."

Veruna grew flustered. "A recommendation from you is a condemnation! And I suggest strongly that you remain on Coruscant, because you will no longer be welcome on Naboo." He lowered his voice. "Keep in mind that I have information that can ruin you, Palpatine, in the same way that you, the Naberries, and the rest are attempting to ruin me."

The table fell silent as a squadron of N-1 starfighters shot past the arched windows to disrupt the rally in the plaza.

Palpatine conjured a smile. "The Naboo will be pleased to see that your space force is good for something, Majesty."

Veruna's bloated face flushed. "More than you know. I told you that I meant to end our partnership with the Trade Federation and Hego Damask, and so I shall."

Palpatine glanced at the Hutt and her Bando Gora minions. "With the help of your new partners. And what will you do—chase the Trade Federation's freighters out of the Chommel sector? Challenge Damask openly?"

"Damask has betrayed everyone. Ask Gardulla. Ask Alexi Garyn. The Muun should have learned a lesson thirty years ago from the Gran who targeted him."

Palpatine took secret pleasure in the remark. *And you commit the same egregious blunders they did.*

"What makes you think he didn't?"

Veruna started to speak, but bit back what he had in mind to say and began again. "From this point on, Naboo will manage its own resources. Gardulla and Black Sun will supervise the export of plasma and the import of goods, and the Bando Gora will protect our interests in the space lanes. It's a pity you won't be a part of it."

"A pity to be sure," Palpatine said, rising to his feet. "Until such time as you replace me, Majesty, I will continue to act in Naboo's best interests, at Eriadu and on Coruscant. Should I see Damask, I'll be certain to tell him that he underestimated . . . your ambitions."

Veruna locked eyes with him. "Don't concern yourself unduly, Palpatine. You won't be seeing him again."

The transpirator affixed to his face, Plagueis moved with agile purpose through the stone-cold rooms that had housed twenty years of experiments. Most of the cages and cells were empty now—the captives they had contained, released. He wondered if Sojourn's greel forests would become a kind of laboratory, a great scarlet-wood medium for mutant evolution. OneOne-FourDee shuffled past him on the way to the courtyard, alloy storage boxes piled high in its quartet of appendages.

"Be certain that all the data has been permanently deleted," Plagueis said.

The droid nodded. "I will make certain for the third time, Magister Damask."

"And FourDee, carry my instructions to the Sun Guards that I will contact them on Thyrsus."

"I will see to it, Magister."

Plagueis entered the room that had served as his meditation chamber. Though the high-ceilinged space was already fixed in his memory, he studied the few pieces of furniture in silence, as if searching for some detail that had escaped his notice. His eyes lingered on the small antechamber in which he and Sidious had been sitting when they had brought about the shift, and the strength of that memory was such that he was catapulted into a moment of intense reverie.

For some time he had been aware that Sidious had grown critical of his fixation with unraveling the secrets of life and death. Surely Sidious felt as if Plagueis had made himself too much of a project, often to the neglect of the Grand Plan; that Plagueis had come to place more importance on his own survival than that of the Sith. Meanwhile, to Sidious had fallen the responsibility for arranging and executing the schemes that would place the two of them in power on Coruscant. Sidious directing galactic events in much the same way that Plagueis was overseeing the currents of the dark side. And yet the arrangement was as it should be, for Sidious had a gift for subterfuge that surpassed the talents of any of the Sith Lords who had preceded him, including Bane.

Plagueis found irony in the fact that Sidious had come to feel about him as he himself had felt about Tenebrous at the end of his long apprenticeship. Tenebrous trusted more in Bith science and computer projections than he had in the Sith arts . . . But Plagueis understood, too, that the time had come for him to rejoin the world and stand with Sidious to see this most important phase of the plan to fruition: Palpatine's ascendancy to the chancellorship and the unprecedented appointment of Hego Damask as co-chancellor of the Republic. Ageless Hego

Damask, as it would ultimately emerge. When that was behind them, they could turn to the bigger task of obliterating the Jedi Order.

Master Dooku's dithering over leaving the Order came as no surprise. Yoda had taken Dooku from Serenno, but he had failed to take Serenno from Dooku. Twenty years earlier Plagueis had seen the stirrings of the dark side in him and had attempted since—whenever and wherever possible—to coax more of those latent powers to the surface. At Galidraan, in clandestine partnership with the local governor and members of the Death Watch to lure the Jedi into an ultimately hopeless confrontation with the True Mandalorians; at Yinchorr and Malastare; and most recently, through Sidious's efforts, at Asmeru and Eriadu. Already strong in the Force, trained in combat, and a diplomat, as well, Dooku might have made for a powerful partner under different circumstances. Except for the fact that Dooku, unlike the Dathomiri Zabrak whom Sidious had trained, would never be content to serve as an apprentice or a mere assassin. He would demand to become a true Sith, and that would lead to trouble. A better course of action would be to allow Dooku to find his own way to the dark side—whatever version of it might be accessible to him through study of the Sith Holocrons the Jedi possessed. Better to have him leave the Order of his own accord and become the benevolent spokesperson for the disenfranchised, as one might expect from a being of high status. Yes, better to let him persuade worlds and systems to secede from the Republic and foment a civil war into which the Jedi could be drawn . . .

The sudden blare of klaxons put an abrupt end to his musings.

Time is short.

OneOne-FourDee returned, moving quickly for a droid. "Five battleships have been detected, Magister."

"Ahead of schedule."

"Perhaps your enemies received intelligence that their attack plan had been compromised."

"A sound speculation, FourDee. Is the ship ready?"

"Standing by, Magister."

After a final look around, Plagueis hurried out the gaping door that led to the courtyard, where the sleek starship designed by Rugess Nome and built by Raith Sienar was waiting. Styled loosely after a courier ship that had been commonplace during the ancient Sith Empire, the Infiltrator still looked as if it had flown out of the past. Just under thirty meters in length and shaped like a throwing dart, it had two short wings where fletching feathers might have been, jutting from a round command module and ending in curved radiator fins that enclosed the module parenthetically when deployed. But what made the ship unique was a stygium-crystal-powered cloaking array that occupied much of the long, tapered prow of the fuselage.

As Plagueis entered the cockpit, 11-4D abandoned the single pilot's chair for one of the seats that lined the aft circumference of the module.

"Systems are enabled, Magister."

Folding himself into the swivel chair, Plagueis secured the harness, clamped his hands on the yoke, and raised the ship, which spiraled as it climbed above the towering walls of the old fort before rocketing into Sojourn's opaque sky, invisible to any scanners that might be aimed downside. Already the first energy beams from the enemy flotilla were streaking into the greel forests, hurling vegetation and igniting firestorms. Another extinction for some of the creatures that had been cloned exclusively for the moon, Plagueis thought. A second onslaught of laser beams struck the tower where he had passed so many hours in contemplation, toppling it into the courtyard. Outside the Infiltrator, the air was growing hot and jolting winds were being whipped up by what had been unleashed from above. Far to starboard, starlight glinted off an attack ship that was racing toward the surface.

Ground-based turbolaser batteries began to answer with reciprocating fire, making it appear as if the sky were at war with itself. At the edge of space, short-lived explosions blossomed, as the shields of targeted ships were overwhelmed. But others broke through the barrages, their weapons reducing swaths of forest to ash and blowing huge chunks of rock from the escarpment. The ground shook and great columns of smoke poured upward. One, then another gun emplacement exploded, taking with them an entire wall of the fort.

Plagueis studied the cockpit displays as the Infiltrator continued to gain elevation and velocity, racing through smoke and fleeing clouds.

"Rendezvous coordinates are already programmed into the navicomputer," 11-4D said from behind him. "The comm frequency is also preset."

Plagueis swung to the navicomputer as concussions rocked the ship. He had placed one hand on the device's keyboard when the sky seemed to give birth to a sphere of blinding light. Following a moment of absolute stillness, a cascade of infernal energy descended on what remained of the fort and concentric rings of explosive power radiated outward, leveling everything within a twenty-kilometer radius from ground zero. The Infiltrator was lifted like a bird caught in a thermal, and for a moment all its systems failed.

Plagueis sat in enraged disbelief.

Somehow, Veruna and his cohorts—Gardulla, Black Sun, and the Bando Gora—had gotten their hands on a proscribed nuclear device. None of the Sun Guards could have survived the blast; but then they didn't deserve to. Nuclear weapons were scarce, and the Echani had obviously neglected to check with the few black-market suppliers that had access to them.

A pillar of roiling fire and smoke was clawing into the sky, fanning out in the thinning atmosphere to become a mushroom-shaped cloud. The greel forests were blackened wastelands; the fort was slagged and turned to glass. Deeply moved, Plagueis realized that he hadn't experienced such powerful emotions since he had bid good-bye to Mygeeto so many decades earlier and placed himself in the care of Darth Tenebrous.

Adhering to course, the Infiltrator rose out of the turmoil. Stars winked into visibility, and the fleet ship was suddenly free of the moon's gravity and pulled into the powerful embrace of Sojourn's parent. No sooner had it entered the planet's night side than the comm board issued an urgent tone.

"Magister Damask, we find no trace of your ship on any of our scanners, but we trust that you're out there somewhere."

Plagueis disabled the ship's cloaking device and swiveled to the board. "*Star Jewel*, this is Damask. Your scanners should be able to find us now."

"Affirmative, Magister Damask. You are clear to proceed to Docking Bay Four."

A space cruiser of gargantuan size and ostentatious design could be seen hanging in the middle distance. Shaped like an arrowhead, the vessel was heavily armed and large enough to accommodate half a dozen starfighters. While Plagueis was maneuvering toward it, the comm board's enunciators were rattled by a resonant laugh.

"I hope to persuade you one day to share the secret of your invisible ship, Magister Damask."

"I appreciate your punctuality, Jabba Desilijic Tiure. As I do the advance intelligence that allowed me to avoid being atomized."

"Thus are lasting partnerships solidified, Magister. What is our destination?"

"Coruscant," Plagueis said. "But I've one more favor to ask before we arrive."

"Simply state it, and it will be done."

"Then arrange for communications with Naboo. King Veruna needs to be informed of what he has brought down on himself and his confederates."

Jabba guffawed again. "It will be my pleasure."

27: CALIBRATIONS

Hego Damask didn't simply keep a penthouse on Coruscant; he owned an entire building. While it wasn't as grand as 500 Republica, Kaldani Spires was the Galactic Center's most desired address outside the Senate District. Towering over Monument Plaza, the stately building was as fine an example of Hasennan Period architecture as could be found onworld, and from its uppermost suites residents could see from the peaks of the Manarai Mountains clear to the Western Sea—Coruscant's only instances of naked rock and surface water. A neighborhood for neither politicians nor the newly arrived, the district catered to solid old-money citizenry: financiers, corporate chiefs, industrialists, and bankers.

Damask's residence took up the whole of the Kaldani's summit.

A pair of Sun Guards rode with Palpatine in the private turbolift, only to surrender him to another pair stationed in the penthouse's light-filled atrium. But it was the droid 11-4D that escorted him into Damask's study, which was darkened by tall, brocade curtains and filled with masterpieces of galactic art. The masked Muun himself rose from a plush armchair to greet Palpatine as he was shown into the room.

"Master," Sidious said, interlocking his hands in front of him and bowing his head.

Plagueis lowered his head in a gesture of mutual respect. "Welcome, Darth Sidious. It's good to see you."

As the room was the opposite of the one he had often confined himself to on Sojourn, Plagueis no longer looked like the wide-eyed mystic he had seemed only months earlier. Except for having to wear the breathing device, he struck Palpatine as a slightly older version of the Muun who had visited him on Naboo so many decades before.

The two Sith moved to a sunken area of the room and sat across from each other. Plagueis filled two glasses with clear wine and passed one to his apprentice. He made the act of imbibing through his nasal passages seem almost routine.

"After Sojourn, I find it somewhat dislocating to be back in the greater world."

"Master, I'm sorry I wasn't the first to warn you of the attack," Sidious said. "I didn't think Veruna had the courage to carry out his veiled threats. Perhaps I nudged him too far."

A long moment of silence passed between them.

"What you did and didn't do is immaterial," Plagueis said at last. "Coming when it did, at almost precisely the same time the members of the Trade Federation Directorate were meeting their fates, the attack was the work of the Force, substantiating our ambitions, especially." He took more wine and set the glass down. "I never would have had the heart to destroy Sojourn, though it needed to be done; and so the Force saw to it. The incident reminds us of the need to be prepared for sudden eventualities, whether harmonious or inimical to our plans, and compliant to circumstance."

"And now we are justified in striking back," Sidious said.

"We no longer need to justify our actions to anyone. But bear in mind what I told you long ago: by killing one, we can frighten many."

Sidious nodded. "We owe Jabba a great debt."

"I spoke briefly with Veruna from the Hutt's ship."

Sidious grinned slightly. "I suspected as much when I learned just prior to the summit that he had abdicated, and that Padmé Naberri had been appointed Queen. He has apparently hidden himself away in Naboo's Western Reaches."

"That's not hiding," Plagueis said with a note of menace. "All went well on Eriadu?"

"Better than expected, what with the Jedi running in circles and convinced that Valorum was the target. I savored their dismayed in-credulity on learning that the droids had emptied their weapons on the members of the directorate. In the end, the leaders of the Nebula

Front died, as well, and our friend Wilhuff Tarkin is making matters difficult for Republic investigators. Soon the aurodium stolen from the Trade Federation freighter will be discovered to have been invested in Valorum Shipping and Transport, making it appear that the Supreme Chancellor's push for taxation was motivated by greed and illegal enrichment. He is brought down. Even his power to deploy the Jedi or Judicials will be stripped from him."

Plagueis's eyes narrowed. "And Gunray?"

"Precisely where we want him: leader by default of the Trade Federation, and busy acquiring the droid weapons the Senate will sanction. Where the Neimoidians should be grateful to Senator Palpatine for proposing the summit, they are instead furious. Everything is in place for launching the blockade."

"Almost everything," Plagueis said. "First, there is the matter of our revenge."

"Shall I task Maul to pay Veruna a visit?"

Plagueis shook his head. "I intend to see to him personally. Is the Zabrak—Maul, as you call him—capable of dealing with Alexi Garyn and his Vigos?"

"He will not fail us."

Plagueis considered that for a moment, then said, "The Infiltrator sits under guard at West Championne Starport. Have Pestage transport the ship to the LiMerge Building, so that you can present it as a gift to your apprentice. I will provide you with information about Garyn's current whereabouts."

"That leaves only the Hutt and Bando Gora," Sidious said.

"I have promised Gardulla to Jabba. As for the Bando Gora . . ." Plagueis rose from the chair, walked to the curtained windows, and peered outside. "There is a rumor worth pursuing that Master Dooku's former apprentice, Komari Vosa, is not only alive but the cult's newest leader, and eager to avenge herself on the Jedi Order for having abandoned her and her comrades on Baltizaar."

"Vosa turning to the dark side," Sidious said, as if thinking aloud. "Dooku trained her better than he knows."

"Yes, but she is a fallen Jedi, not a Sith. We will exact revenge on the Bando Gora at another time."

Sidious stood up and joined Plagueis at the parted curtains. "I will inform Viceroy Gunray to prepare his armed ships for relocation to the Naboo system."

In a midlevel hangar in the LiMerge Building, Sidious watched Maul stow the last of his gear and hand-built contrivances aboard the Infiltrator, which, like the Zabrak's speeder bike, now had a name: *Scimitar.* Closing a cargo hatch in the forward portion of the hull, Maul stepped back to admire the ship, then swung to Sidious and genuflected.

"I am not deserving of such a gift, Master."

Sidious glowered. "If you feel that way, then prove your worth to yourself and me by succeeding in your mission."

"I pledge as much."

Sidious watched him carefully. "We need to dismantle the Black Sun criminal cartel. The Vigos had strong ties to some members of the Trade Federation Directorate, and they suspect there was foul play at Eriadu. Right now, the Neimoidians are in their sights, and we can't risk having them interfere with our plans."

He made no mention of Black Sun's complicity in the attack on Sojourn.

Maul nodded. "I understand, Master."

Sidious made a beckoning motion with his hands. "Rise and listen carefully, Darth Maul. Time doesn't permit hunting down Alexi Garyn and his Vigos one by one. Therefore, make Boss Darnada your first victim. You will find the Dug at his deep-space reclamation station. Then jump your ship to Mon Calamari and kill the Vigo called Morn. By then, word of your actions will have reached Garyn, and he will likely summon the remaining seven Vigos to his fortress on Ralltiir. Narees, Mother Dean, Nep Chung, and the rest. You are to contact me when you have verified that they are all in one place." He glanced at the *Scimitar.* "It will be an opportunity to put your probe droids to the test."

A look of eagerness took shape on Maul's fearsome face. Sidious walked to him and placed his hands atop Maul's shoulders. "You will be facing many skilled opponents, my apprentice. Darnada's Twi'lek bodyguard, Sinya; Garyn himself, who has some strength in the Force; and Garyn's chief protector, Mighella, who is a Nightsister and will immediately identify you as a Nightbrother."

Maul scowled. "A Nightsister is not a Sith."

Sidious's eyes narrowed. "As you well know. But as on Dorvalla, take care to leave no witnesses."

Maul showed his sharpened teeth. "It shall be done. And Black Sun will cease to be an impediment."

Sidious nodded. "Then be on your way, Darth Maul. The dark side is with you."

Maul bowed his head and hurried up the rear boarding ramp into the cockpit module. Sidious lingered to watch the ship rise and edge out of the hangar, becoming invisible as it flew over The Works. Through the dark side, he continued to track the *Scimitar* as it angled north toward the Jedi Temple rather than south, and away from the Senate District. Sidious recalled the voyages he had taken ten years earlier to watch Maul fight in gladiatorial matches on Orsis and nearby worlds. Driven to win against all odds, unaffected by pain, daring, and terrifying. An up-and-coming contender at ten years of age and a champion at twelve. Under the markings that masked his face, sleeved his arms, and twisted around his legs and torso, the scars of those battles to the death.

But this one will not be content until he has killed a Jedi Master, Sidious thought.

Assuming that pride didn't defeat him first.

Leaving the hangar space, Sidious made his way to the holoprojector in the building's only refurbished room. What would become of Maul once Palpatine and Damask assumed control of the Republic? he asked himself. As a secret weapon, he would continue to be useful, but could he ever be eased into public life? How would he react to learning that his Master answered to a Master?

With his feet planted on the transmission grid, Sidious sat in the chair that was positioned for the holoprojector's cams, adjusted the controls built into one of the armrests, and raised the cowl of his cloak over his head. For twenty years he had enjoyed living a double life, but now he felt an urge to be known for who he was, and feared for how powerful he could be. He directed his thoughts forward in time, yearning for a clear vision of the future, but none came. Did the dark side blind even its most devoted advocates to what was looming on the horizon? Plagueis had said that they needed to be prepared for sudden eventualities. Was he withholding knowledge of events he knew were imminent?

The Muun's renewed vigor had taken Sidious by surprise. The mere fact that he had escaped the devastation on Sojourn made him seem almost omnipotent. Though even when ensconced in his affluent citadel in the Manarai district, he had yet to relax his vigilance or submit to sleep.

Repressing a sudden feeling of envy, Sidious began to wonder if—blinded by the dark side—he had actually failed to divine Veruna's attack on Sojourn, or if he hadn't allowed himself to divine it.

A touch of his forefinger activated the holoprojector, and moments later a half-sized eidolon of Nute Gunray resolved in midair. As in recent transmissions, the viceroy's Neimoidian underlings, chief litigator Rune Haako, Captain Daultay Dofine, and Deputy Viceroy Hath Monchar were hovering in the background.

"Lord Sidious," Gunray said, with a slight stammer in his voice. "We have been waiting—"

"Do you imagine yourself centermost in my thoughts that I should neglect other matters to communicate with you precisely on time?"

"No, Lord Sidious, I simply meant to say—"

"Are you gratified with your new position, Viceroy?"

"Very gratified. Though I appear to have inherited control of the Trade Federation at a time of crisis."

"Save your whining for another occasion, Viceroy, for matters are about to become worse."

Gunray's nictitating membranes spasmed. "Worse? How can that be?"

"The Republic Senate is on the verge of passing legislation that will enact taxation of the free-trade zones."

"This is an outrage!"

"To be sure. But I warned you that this was coming. Supreme Chancellor Valorum has lost all credibility, and after what occurred at Eriadu, the Senate is determined to weaken the Trade Federation further. King Veruna may have been able to stall the Senate, but he has abdicated, and young Queen Amidala and Naboo's Senator are leading the call for taxation. With the Senate preoccupied, the moment is right for you to begin assembling a fleet of armed freighters to impose a blockade."

"A blockade? Of what system, Lord Sidious?"

"I will inform you in due time." When Gunray didn't respond, Sidious said, "What is it, Viceroy? Across the vastness of space, I can perceive the reeling of your feeble brain."

"Forgive me, Lord Sidious, but, as my advisers have pointed out, the redistribution of our vessels carries with it considerable financial risk. To begin with, there is the cost of fuel. Then, with so many ships allocated to an embargo, a disruption in trade in the Mid and Outer Rims for however long the blockade is maintained. Finally, there is no telling how our investors might react to the news."

Sidious leaned forward. "So this is about credits, is it?"

Gunray's muzzle twitched. "We are, after all, Lord Sidious, a commercial enterprise, not a navy."

Sidious didn't respond immediately. When he did, his voice oozed disgust. "Even after all I have engineered on your behalf you fail to grasp that by allying with me you are investing in the future." He flicked his right hand in dismissal. "But no matter. Does it not occur to you that your most valued investors are in a position to reap great profits from your knowledge of what is about to happen? Would they not profit from learning that the Xi Char, the Geonosians, and other unionized insectoids have turned their pincers and claws to the manufacture of weapons? Might you not balance your precious budget by gaining from other shipping companies what revenue the Trade Federation risks losing?"

Gunray looked uncertain. "We feared that such actions might undermine the element of surprise, Lord Sidious."

"That is the reason for swift action."

Gunray nodded. "I will order a fleet assembled."

Sidious sat back in the chair. "Good. Remember, Viceroy, that what I have delivered to you I can just as easily take away."

Sidious ended the transmission and lowered the cowl.

Was this a vision of the future? A life of micromanaging the affairs of incompetent beings while he and Plagueis set in motion the final phases of the Grand Plan? Or was there perhaps some other way for him to govern, in malevolent satisfaction?

* * *

Even without the drenching rain, the ground would have been soft under Plagueis's booted feet, composed as it was of eons of decayed organic matter. Water dripped from the transpirator mask and the raised hood of his cloak and splashed in the puddles that had formed beneath him. The castle that had once belonged to Veruna's ancestor the Earl of Vis crowned a desolate hill, with no road leading to it and a view in all directions of the rolling, sodden, treeless terrain. Through night-vision electrobinoculars Plagueis studied the scanners that studded the castle's walls and the disposition of the guards, some of whom were keeping dry in the shelter of an arch that crowned an ornate portcullis. Parked near the entrance was a veritable fleet of landspeeders, and off to one side, centered in a circular landing zone, sat a space yacht whose gleaming hull even the torrent couldn't dull. Illumination arrays glowed behind drifting curtains of rain.

Following a deep, fast-moving rivulet, Plagueis descended the hill he had climbed to where he had set his own starship down among a riot of drooping wildflowers and falconberries. OneOne-FourDee was waiting at the foot of the boarding ramp, raindrops pinging on its alloy shell.

"Their scanners may have picked up the ship," Plagueis said.

"Given that all countermeasures were enabled, that seems unlikely, Magister."

"They've flooded the area with light."

"As any vigilant being might on a night such as this."

"A night fit for neither Muun nor shaak."

The droid's photoreceptors tightened their focus on him. "The reference escapes my data bank."

"Seal the ship and remain in the cockpit. If I comm you, reposition the ship above the castle's southwest corner and keep the boarding ramp extended."

"Are you anticipating resistance, Magister?"

"Merely anticipating, FourDee."

"I understand. I would do the same."

"That's comforting to know."

Plagueis fixed the lightsaber hilt to his hip and set out at a fast clip, all but outracing the rain. If the scanners and motion detectors were as precise as they appeared to be, they would find him, though his speed might cause whoever was monitoring the security devices to mistake him for one of the wild, bushy-tailed quadrupeds that inhabited the landscape. He paused at the nebulous edge of the illuminated area to confirm his bearings, then made straight for the castle's ten-meter-high southern wall and leapt to the top without breaking stride. Just as quickly and as effortlessly he dropped into the garden below and sprinted into the shadows cast by an ornamental shrub trimmed to resemble some whimsical beast. Plagueis reasoned that security would be lax inside the manse, but that Veruna's wing of rooms would be outfitted with redundant monitoring devices and perhaps pressure-sensitive floors.

That he hadn't been able to procure an interior plan of the castle was a testament to the self-exiled regent's hypervigilance.

Plagueis moved to a stained-glass window just as two humans were hurrying through a hallway beyond. With rain overflowing a gutter high overhead, he felt as if he were standing behind a waterfall.

"Check on him and report back to me," the female was saying.

Plagueis recognized the voice of security chief Magneta. Sticking close to the outer wall, he paralleled the movement of Magneta's subordinate to the end of the hallway, then through a right-angled turn into a broader hall that led to a control room tucked beneath the sweep of a grand staircase. Plagueis sharpened his auditory senses to hear Magneta's man ask after Veruna, and a human female reply, "Sleeping like a baby."

"Good for him. While the rest of us drown."

"If you're so miserable, Chary," the woman said, "you should consider returning to Theed."

"I'm thinking about it."

"Just don't expect me to follow you."

Plagueis stepped away from the wall to glance at the upper-story windows, all of which were dark, save for an arched opening near the end of the wall. Crouching, he maneuvered through bushes under a series of wide windows, then began to scale the wall, fastened to it like an insect. The tall and narrow target opening turned out to be a fixed pane of thick glass; the source of the light, a pair of photonic sconces that flanked a set of elaborately carved wooden double doors. Peering through the glass, he flicked his fingers at a security cam mounted high on the inner wall and aimed at the doorway, dazzling the mechanism and freezing the image of an unoccupied antechamber. Then, placing his left hand at the center of the glass, he called on the Force, pushing inward on the pane until it broke free of the adhesive weatherseal that held it in place. Telekinetically, he manipulated the intact pane to rest atop a table snugged to the opposite wall of the antechamber, and slipped through the opening. For a long moment he remained on the inner windowsill, waiting for his cloak and boots to dry and studying the patterned floor and double doors for evidence of additional security devices. Satisfied that the stunned cam was all there was, he planted his feet on the floor and walked to the doors, using the Force to trick them into opening just enough to accommodate his passing between them.

The only light in Veruna's enormous bedroom came from a cam similar to the one in the antechamber, and just as easily foiled. The former King himself was sleeping on his back under shimmersilk sheets in the center of a canopied bed large enough to fit half a dozen humans of average size. Plagueis disabled a bedside panel of security alarms, moved an antique chair to the foot of the bed, and switched on a table lamp that supplied dim, yellowish light. Then, sitting down, he roused Veruna from sleep.

The old man woke with a start, blinking in response to the light, then propping himself up against a gathering of pillows to scan the room. His eyes widened in thunderstruck surprise when they found Plagueis seated at the edge of the light's reach.

"Who—"

"Hego Damask, Your Majesty. Beneath this mask my former enemies may as well have fashioned for me."

Since Veruna's eyes couldn't open any wider, his jaw dropped and he flailed for the security control panels, slamming his hand down on the buttons when they didn't respond.

"I've rendered them inoperative," Plagueis explained, "along with the security cams. Just so that you and I could converse without being interrupted."

Veruna swallowed and found his voice. "How did you get past my guards, Damask?"

"We'll come to that in a moment."

"Magne—" Veruna attempted to scream until his voice went mute and he clutched at his throat.

"There will be none of that," Plagueis warned.

"What do you want with me, Damask?" Veruna asked when he could, breathing hard.

"Closure."

Veruna stared at him in disbelief. "You got what you wanted. Isn't it enough that I abdicated?"

"Your abdication would have been enough, had you not tried first to have me killed."

Veruna gritted his teeth. "Everything I built was in jeopardy of being taken from me—even the monarchy! You left me no choice!"

Plagueis stood and reseated himself on the edge of the bed, like some macabre confessor. "I understand. Faced with a similar choice, I might have done the same. The difference is that I would have succeeded where you failed."

"I'll remain here," Veruna said in a grasping way. "I won't cause you or Palpatine any more trouble."

"That's true." Plagueis paused, then said, "Perhaps I should have been more honest with you from the start. I delivered the Trade Federation to you; I put Tapalo, then you on the throne. How did you imagine I came by such power?"

Veruna ran a trembling hand over his thinning hair. "You were born the son of a wealthy Muun, and transformed that wealth into power."

Plagueis made a sound of disappointment. "Have you not yet learned that the galaxy isn't moved by credits alone?"

Veruna gulped and found his voice. "How did you come by such power, Damask?" he asked in a whisper of genuine interest.

"I was shown the way to power by a Bith named Rugess Nome."

"I know the name."

"Yes, but his true name was Darth Tenebrous, and he wore the mantle of the Dark Lord of the Sith. I was at one time his apprentice."

"Sith," Veruna said, as if weakened by the very word.

"Had you known, would you have allied with me?"

Veruna marshaled the strength to shake his head. "Political power is one thing, but what you represent . . ."

Plagueis made his lips a thin line. "I appreciate your honesty, Veruna. Are you beginning to tire of my presence?"

"Not . . . of you," Veruna said, with eyes half closed.

"Let me explain what is happening to you," Plagueis said. "The cells that make up all living things contain within them organelles known as midi-chlorians. They are, in addition to being the basis for life, the elements that enable beings like me to perceive and use the Force. As the result of a lifetime of study, I have learned how to manipulate midi-chlorians, and I have instructed the limited number you possess to return to their source. In plain Basic, Veruna, I am killing you."

Veruna's face was losing color, and his breathing had slowed. "Bring . . . me back. I can still be . . . of service . . . to you . . ."

"But you are, Your Majesty. A celebrated ancient poet once said that every death lessened him, for he considered himself to be a brother to every living being. I, on the other hand, have come to understand that every death I oversee nourishes and *empowers* me, for I am a true Sith."

"No . . . better than . . . an Anzati."

"The brain eaters? What does *better than* mean to those of us who have passed beyond notions of good and evil? Are you better than Bon Tapalo? Are you better than Queen Padmé Amidala? I am the only one fit to answer the question. *Better* are those who do my bidding." Plagueis placed his hand atop Veruna's. "I'll remain with you for a while as you meld with the Force. But at some point, I will have to leave you at the threshold to continue on your own."

"Don't do this . . . Damask. Please . . ."

"I am Darth Plagueis, Veruna. Your shepherd."

As life left Veruna's body, the path he and Plagueis followed wound deeper into darkness and absence. Then Plagueis stopped, overcome by a sudden sense that he had already seen and traveled this path.

Had he? he wondered as Veruna breathed his last.

Or had the Force afforded him a glimpse of the future?

28: CHAIN OF COMMAND

Returned from Ralltiir, Maul sat cross-legged on the floor in the LiMerge Building while Sidious debriefed him. Having just terminated an irritating communication with the Neimoidians, Sidious was in no mood for games.

"The way you make it sound, my apprentice, it seems almost an indignity that none survived to spread the word of your massacre."

"You orders were that none should, Master."

"Yes," Sidious said, continuing to circle him. "And not one of them proved a challenge?"

"No, Master."

"Not Sinya?"

"I decapitated the Twi'lek."

"Not Mighella?"

"My blade halved the Nightsister after she tried to defeat me with summoned Force-lightning."

Sidious paused for a moment. "Not even Garyn?"

"No."

Sidious detected a note of hesitation. "No, what, Darth Maul?"

"I drowned him."

Touching his chin, Sidious stood where the Zabrak could see him.

"Well, someone had to have dealt the wound you suffered to your left hand. Unless, of course, you gave it to yourself."

Maul clenched the black-gloved hand. "There is no pain where strength lies."

"I didn't inquire if the wound hurt. I asked who was responsible."

"Garyn," Maul said quietly.

Sidious feigned surprise. "So he *was* something of a challenge. Being slightly Force-sensitive."

"He was nothing compared with the power of the dark side."

Sidious studied him. "Did you tell him as much, my apprentice? Answer honestly."

"He came to the conclusion."

"He identified you as a Sith. Did he assume, then, that you were a Sith Lord?"

Maul stared at the floor. "I—"

"You revealed that you answer to a Master. Am I correct?"

Maul forced himself to respond. "Yes, Master."

"And perhaps you went so far as to say something about the revenge of the Sith."

"I did, Master."

Sidious approached him, his face contorted in anger. "And if by some marvel Garyn had managed to escape, or even defeat the one-being army that is Darth Maul, what repercussions might we be facing, apprentice?"

"I beg your forgiveness, Master."

"Perhaps you're not worthy of the Infiltrator, after all. The moment you allowed yourself to become distracted, the Black Sun leader cut open your hand."

Maul remained silent.

"I hope you thanked him before you killed him," Sidious went on, "because he taught you a valuable lesson. When you face someone strong in the Force you must remain focused—even when you're convinced that your opponent is incapacitated. Then is not the time to bask in the glory of your victory or draw out the moment. You must deliver a killing strike and be done with it. Reserve your self-praise for after the fact, or you will suffer more than a hand wound."

"I will remember, Master."

The silence attenuated. "I want you to leave Coruscant for the time being."

Maul looked up in alarm.

"Take the Infiltrator and your combat droids and return to your former home. There, train and meditate until I recall you."

"My lord, I beg—"

Sidious held up his hands. "Enough! You executed the mission well, and I am pleased. Now learn from your mistake."

Maul rose slowly, bowed his head once, and headed for the hangar. Watching him leave, Sidious examined the nature of his unease.

Might he, in a similar situation, have given in to an urge to gloat and reveal his true identity?

Had Plagueis done so before killing Veruna? Had he felt compelled to come out from behind his mask? To be *honest*?

Or was Maul's revelation to Garyn nothing more than a symptom of the dark side's growing impatience, and its demand for full disclosure?

"Black Sun is in utter disorder," Palpatine told Hego Damask as they strolled among the sightseers that crowded Monument Plaza. Hundreds were clustered around the summit of Umate, which jutted from the center of the bowl-shaped park, and mixed-being groups of others were trailing tour guides toward the old Senate agora or the Galactic Museum. "Prince Xixor and Sise Fromm will inherit the dregs."

"Again, the Zabrak proves his value," Damask said. "You trained him well."

"Perhaps not well enough," Palpatine said after a moment. "While I was questioning him about a wound he received, he confessed to having divulged his identity to Alexi Garyn."

Angling his masked face away from Palpatine, Damask said, "Garyn is dead. What does it matter now?"

The Muun's flippant tone put Palpatine further on edge, but his composure held.

"This may be the last time I'm permitted to appear in public without armed escort," he said in a casual way. "When Queen Amidala informed me of Veruna's unexpected death, she mentioned that her new chief of security—a man named Panaka—will be taking unprecedented steps to ensure the safety of all Naboo diplomats. The Queen, for example, is to be surrounded by a clutch of handmaidens, all of whom resemble her to some extent."

"And you're be to chaperoned at all times?" Damask asked. "That won't do."

"I'll convince Panaka otherwise."

They stopped to watch a group of younglings at play under one of the plaza's banners. Plagueis indicated a nearby bench, but Palpatine's disquiet wouldn't allow him to sit.

"Did the Queen express any concern about the presence of so many Trade Federation freighters?"

Palpatine shook his head. "The fleet is holding at the edge of the system, awaiting word from me to jump to Naboo. As angry as Gunray is about the taxation legislation, I had to convince him that Naboo is significant enough to ensure galactic interest in the blockade. I assured him that Amidala will not allow her people to suffer, and that before a month has elapsed she will sign a treaty that will make Naboo and Naboo's plasma property of the Trade Federation."

The transpirator concealed Damask's smile, but it was clear that he liked what he heard. "While Valorum dithers, Senator Palpatine garners the sympathy of the electorate." He tracked Palpatine. "Is it not a measure of our success that we can award worlds as if they were mere business contracts?"

A group of well-dressed Twi'leks sauntered by, gaping at Palpatine in recognition. That he should openly fraternize with a Muun was an indication of the power and influence of both beings.

It was Damask who had stressed the importance of their being seen together in public; and so, in the weeks since the Muun had arrived on Coruscant, they had dined on several occasions at the Manarai and other exclusive restaurants, and had attended recitals at both the Coruscant and Galaxies operas. Most recently they had been present at an elite gathering in 500 Republica, hosted by Senator Orn Free Taa, at which Plagueis had overheard the Rutian Twi'lek discussing plans to nominate Palpatine for the chancellorship. Next on their busy agenda was a political rally scheduled to take place on Coruscant's Perlemian Orbital Facility, where potential candidates for the office of Supreme Chancellor would have a chance to mingle with corporation executives, lobbyists, campaigners, and even some Jedi Masters.

"A blockade followed by an actual invasion isn't likely to win the Trade Federation any new allies," Damask was saying. "But if nothing else we'll be able to assess the performance of Gunray's droid army and make adjustments as necessary."

"Through their own carelessness, the Neimoidians managed to compromise their secret foundries on Eos and Alaris Prime," Palpatine said, letting some of his exasperation show.

Damask eyed him. "For the moment, they have what they need. The acquisition of Naboo will demonstrate the failings of diplomacy, and prompt a sense of militancy among the Jedi." Keeping his gaze fixed on Palpatine, he added, "In preparation for the coming war, we will relocate Baktoid Armor to Geonosis. Even then, however, we can't equip our allies with sufficient weapons to secure a quick victory. A drawn-out conflict will ensure a galaxy pounded to a pulp and eager to embrace us."

Palpatine finally sat down. "We still need to raise an army for the Jedi to command. But one that answers ultimately to the Supreme Chancellor."

"A grown army could be designed to do just that," Damask said.

Palpatine considered it. "It sounds too simple. Jedi are not easily taken by surprise. Honed for warfare, they will be even more difficult to ensnare."

"At the end of a long war, perhaps? With victory in sight?"

"To achieve that, both sides would have to be managed." Palpatine blew out his breath. "Even if a surprise attack could be launched, not every Jedi would be in the field."

"Only those suitable for combat would need concern us."

Palpatine broke a long silence. "The Kaminoan cloners failed you once."

Damask acknowledged the statement with a nod. "Because I gave them a Yinchorri template. They told me then that your species might be easier to replicate."

"You'll contact them again?"

"This army must not be traced to us. But there is someone I might be able to persuade to place the initial order."

Palpatine waited, but Damask had nothing to add. The fact that he had said as much about the matter as he intended to say brought Palpatine full-circle to consternation. Abruptly, he stood and paced away from the bench.

"Instruct the Neimoidians to launch the blockade," Damask said to his back. "It's important that events be set in motion before the orbital facility congress." When Palpatine didn't respond, Plagueis stood and followed him. "What's troubling you, Sidious? Perhaps you feel that you've become nothing more than a messenger."

Palpatine whirled on him. "Yes, at times. But I know my place, and am content with it."

"What, then, has whipped you to a froth?"

"The Neimoidians," Palpatine said with sudden conviction. "In addition to Gunray, I have been dealing with three others: Haako, Daultay, and Monchar."

"I know Monchar slightly," Damask said. "He maintains a suite in the Kaldani Spires."

"He was absent when I last spoke with Gunray."

Suspicion bloomed in the Muun's eyes, and he hissed, "Where were they, then?"

"Aboard their flagship. Gunray claimed that Monchar had taken ill as a result of rich food."

"But you know better."

Palpatine nodded. "The sniveling toady knows about the blockade. I suspect that he's on the loose, and out for profit."

Damask's eyes flashed yellow. "This is what happens when beings are promoted beyond their level of competence!"

Palpatine tensed in anger.

"Not you," Damask said quickly. "Gunray and his ilk! The Force harrows and penalizes us for consorting with those too ignorant to appreciate and execute our designs!"

Palpatine took comfort in the fact that even Plagueis had his limits. "I failed to heed your words about sudden reversals."

Damask frowned at him, then relaxed. "I ignore my own advice. The blockade must wait."

"I will recall Maul," Palpatine said.

* * *

Two weeks after the Neimoidian's unannounced disappearance from the flagship *Saak'ak,* Plagueis and Sidious knew only that Darth Maul had succeeded in tracking down and killing Hath Monchar—though not without wide-ranging collateral damage—and that Maul had piloted the stealth Infiltrator to a docking station linked by a series of zero-g air locks to the Perlemian Orbital Facility's principal reception dome, a grand enclosure that looked out on a sweep of Coruscant and the stars beyond, and was designed to feel more like a garden in space than a sterile conference hall. Just then the dome was filled with Senators and judges, corporate leaders and ambassadors, power brokers and media pundits, and contingents of Senate Guards and Jedi.

"Why did you order him to come here, of all places?" Damask asked Palpatine during a respite from the handshaking, casual conversation, and forced conviviality. Dressed in their finest robes, they were standing near a back-lighted waterfall, nodding to passing beings, even as the two of them conspired. "He has cut a swath of destruction through the Crimson Corridor and killed two Jedi, along with beings of a dozen species, including a Hutt. We can't trust that someone isn't on his scent—if not Jedi then perhaps law enforcement personnel. If by some fluke he were to be apprehended, he has the skill to scramble the minds of ordinary beings, but not to cloak himself from a Jedi. Both our existence and our plans for the blockade could be endangered."

"Jedi were on his scent," Palpatine explained. "That's precisely why I ordered him offworld."

Damask started to respond, but stopped himself and began again. "He is in possession of this holocron Monchar recorded?"

Palpatine nodded. "I instructed Pestage to clear a route through a seldom-used docking bay. I merely have to rendezvous with Maul at the prearranged time and place."

Damask still wasn't convinced. The Monchar affair had almost ended in catastrophe. It was as if the Force, so often compared to a current, had been diverted into a sheer canyon and twisted back on itself to generate treacherous eddies and hydraulics. "Why not simply have him surrender the crystal to Pestage?" he asked at last.

"We don't know what other sensitive data the holocron might contain."

Damask exhaled forcefully through the mask. "I trust that at least you instructed him not to be seen." He glanced around him. "A tattooed Zabrak enrobed in head-to-toe black would certainly stand out among this crowd."

Palpatine couldn't argue the point. Off to one side of them stood Senator Bail Antilles and his aides. A Prince on his homeworld of Alderaan and chair of the Senate's Internal Activities Committee, the handsome, dark-haired Antilles was surrounded by a crowd that included Core World Senators and businessbeings, all of whom had pledged to support him in the coming election, and Jedi Master Jorus C'baoth, who had been enlisted to arbitrate a dispute among some of Alderaan's royal houses. An arrogant, wild-eyed human, C'baoth was cut from the same cloth as Dooku, whose absence from the political gathering had been noted by many. Antilles had been the Sith's pawn in bringing to the fore accusations of wrongdoing on the part of Valorum during the Eriadu crisis, but the notoriety he had gained as a result—in the Senate and in the media—had bolstered his campaign and made him the current top candidate for the chancellorship.

No Jedi had attached themselves to Ainlee Teem, who was also within view. But the Malastare Gran was widely popular on many Mid and Outer Rim worlds, and enjoyed the support of Senator Lott Dod, of the Trade Federation, and Shu Mai, of the Commerce Guild.

At the center of the domed hall stood Valorum and Sei Taria, who was as media-savvy as she was lovely. Though ineligible for reelection, recently stripped of some of his Senatorial powers, and frequently engaged in defending himself against accusations by the Ethics Committee, Valorum had managed to make himself the center of attention, due to the presence of Masters Yoda, Mace Windu, and Adi Gallia among his followers. Merely by standing with the Supreme Chancellor, the Jedi were sending a message that they would continue to support him for the remainder of his term of office, the calumny of illegal enrichment notwithstanding.

With the Trade Federation fleet still holding in the Chommell sector, and without a besieged world to generate sympathy and support for his nomination, Palpatine might have been just one more potential nominee—but for the company of Hego Damask; Banking Clan co-chairman San Hill; recently appointed Senate Vice Chairman Mas

Amedda; and Senator Orn Free Taa, a moving target for Antilles's investigation into corruption and now ostracized by the Rim Faction for backing Palpatine.

"It's almost time," Palpatine said. He indicated a gardened area of dwarf trees and shrubs close to where Ainlee Teem was conferring with a handful of Senators. "I'll trade quips with the Gran, then find some pretext to excuse myself."

Damask grunted noncommittally. "My own target is in sight, in any case."

Without further word the two separated, Damask weaving his way through the crowd toward a grim-faced, bearded human Jedi who was standing apart from everyone, observing the scene.

"Master Sifo-Dyas," he called.

The topknotted Jedi turned and, recognizing him, nodded in greeting. "Magister Damask."

"I hope I'm not intruding."

Sifo-Dyas shook his head, his gaze fixed on the breath mask. "No, I was . . ." He exhaled and began again, adjusting his stance. "Until your recent arrival on Coruscant, I was under the impression that you had retired."

Damask loosed an exaggerated sigh. "It is not in a Muun's blood to retire. I work now with only a few powerful but largely invisible clients."

The Jedi lifted a graying eyebrow. "It seems I can't view a news holo that doesn't feature you and Senator Palpatine, who is anything but invisible."

"To my thinking, he is the only one capable of rescuing the Republic from the brink."

Sifo-Dyas grunted. "To remain untouched by scandal for twenty years is in itself extraordinary. So perhaps you're right."

Damask waited a moment, then said, "I have never forgotten our discussion on Serenno."

"What discussion was that, Magister?"

"We spoke at some length of threats that were assailing the Republic even then."

Sifo-Dyas grew pensive. "I have some vague recollection."

"Well, what with assassinations, taxation of the free-trade zones, posturing by the Trade Federation, and accusations of political impropriety, the conversation has been much on my mind of late. Fractiousness, factionalism, intersystem conflicts . . . Even in this hall the Jedi appear to be divided in their loyalties. Master C'baoth here, Masters Yoda and Gallia there, and yet no sign of Master Dooku."

Sifo-Dyas said nothing.

"Master Jedi, I want to share with you a suspicion I've been carrying like a burden." Damask paused. "I have reason to suspect that the Trade Federation has secretly been procuring more weapons than anyone realizes."

Sifo-Dyas's forehead furrowed. "Do you have evidence of this?"

"No hard evidence. But my business demands a thorough knowledge of the investment markets. Also, my clients sometimes reveal information to me in private."

"Then you're breaking confidentiality by coming to me with this."

"I am. But only because I believe so strongly that what was once speculation is now fact. To go further, I predict that a civil war is brewing. I give the Republic fifteen years at the most. Soon we'll see disgruntled star systems begin to secede. They will lack only a strong, charismatic leader to unite them." He fell briefly silent before adding: "I will be blunt with you, Master Sifo-Dyas: the Republic will be vulnerable. The Jedi will be too few to turn the tide. A military needs to be created now, while there's still a chance."

Sifo-Dyas folded his arms across his chest. "I encourage you to share this with Supreme Chancellor Valorum, or even Senator Palpatine, Magister."

"I intend to. But even under Chancellor Valorum's watch this Senate will not overturn the Reformation Act. Too many Senators have a financial stake in galactic war. They are heavily invested in corporations that will grow fat on profits from weapons and reconstruction. War will be beneficial for an economy they now view as stagnant."

"Are you willing to state this in front of an investigatory committee?"

Damask frowned with his eyes. "You have to understand that many of these corporations are owned and operated by my clients."

A dark look came over the Jedi's face. "You have read my thoughts,

Magister. I have also sensed that war is imminent. I've confessed as much to Master Yoda and others, but to no avail. They give all appearances of being unconcerned. Or preoccupied. I'm no longer sure."

"Master Dooku, as well?"

Sifo-Dyas sniffed. "Unfortunately, Magister, Dooku's recent statements about Republic discord and our Order's 'self-righteousness' have only added to my concern."

"You said that you have some vague recall of our conversation on Serenno. Do you remember my mentioning a group of gifted cloners?"

"I'm sorry, I do not."

"They are native to an extragalactic world called Kamino. I have on occasion done business with them on behalf of clients who desire cloned creatures, or require cloned laborers capable of working in harsh environments."

The Jedi shook his head in uncertainty. "What does this have to do with anything?"

"I believe that the Kaminoans could be induced to grow and train a cloned army."

Sifo-Dyas took a long moment to reply. "You said yourself that the Republic would never sanction an army."

"The Republic needn't know," Damask said cautiously. "Neither would the Jedi Order have to know. It would be an army that might never have to be used, and yet be available in reserve should need ever arise."

"Who in their right mind would fund an army that might never be used?"

"I would," Damask said. "Along with some of my associates in the Banking Clan—and in conjunction with contacts in Rothana Heavy Engineering, which would supply the ships, armaments, and other matériel."

Sifo-Dyas fixed him with a look. "Come to the point, Magister."

"The Kaminoans will not create an army for me, but they would do so for the Jedi Order. They have been fascinated by the Jedi for millennia."

Sifo-Dyas's dark brown eyes widened. "You're not proposing cloning Jedi—"

"No. I have been assured that such a thing is impossible, in any case. But I have also been assured that a human army a million strong could be ready for deployment in as few as ten years."

"You're suggesting that I circumvent the High Council."

"I suppose I am. The Kaminoans need only a modest down payment, which I could provide to you through untraceable accounts I maintain in Outer Rim banks."

Again, the Jedi remained silent for a long moment. "I need time to consider this."

"Of course you do," Damask said. "And when you've reached a decision, you can contact me at my residence downside."

Sifo-Dyas nodded in glum introspection, and Damask spun on his heel and disappeared into the crowd. Palpatine was just returning to the place where they had been standing earlier, his eyes and his movements suggesting unusual excitement.

"You have the holocron?" Damask said as he approached.

"Yes, but not from Maul."

Damask waited for an explanation.

"It was dropped into my hand by none other than the information broker Maul had been pursuing and thought dead—Lorn Pavan. The fact that Pavan's right hand had been cleanly and recently amputated told me at once that the two fought in one of the air locks."

"This Pavan defeated Maul?"

Palpatine shook his head. "But I suspect that Pavan somehow managed to outwit him and take him by surprise."

"Incredible," Damask said, astonished that events could become even more convoluted. "Then Pavan must know what the holocron contains."

"I'm supposed to deliver it to the Jedi," Palpatine said with obvious amusement; and looking around, added, "Perhaps to Yoda or Windu . . ."

"Pavan," Damask snapped.

Palpatine squared his shoulders. "Pestage and Doriana are escorting him downside, where he'll receive medical attention, maybe even a new hand, and a comfortable hotel suite in which to spend the final day of his life."

"A reward we should withhold from Maul, but probably won't."

Damask glanced at Palpatine. "In any event, it wasn't Pavan who handed you the holocron. It was delivered by the dark side."

Palpatine thought about it for a moment. "And Sifo-Dyas? Will he do it?"

"Even if he decides against it, there may be a way to place the order in his name. But the Force tells me that he will do it."

"That will make him a potential danger to us."

Damask nodded. "But it won't matter. We have become invincible."

This will never do, Palpatine thought as he sat opposite Valorum in the Supreme Chancellor's cloudcutting office in the Senate Building, listening to him drone on about his troubles with the Ethics Committee.

The view through the large triangular windows was pleasant enough, but the office was far too small. Worse, it felt more like a relic from a bygone age rather than a nerve center for the New Order. No amount of remodeling could transform it into the space Palpatine imagined for himself. Perhaps a new building was required; an annex of sorts or, better still, an executive office building—if only to grant those who would work there the illusion that their pitiful efforts mattered . . .

"The deeper my lawyers and accountants pursue this matter, the more dead ends they encounter," Valorum was saying. Dark circles underscored his eyes, and his hands were trembling slightly. "The aurodium ingots the Nebula Front stole from the Trade Federation freighter were converted to credits, which were used to finance their operations on Asmeru and Eriadu. But the ingots themselves moved through a series of specious banks and other financial institutions, and were ultimately invested in Valorum Shipping by unknown parties. I say *unknown* because the beings listed as investors appear never to have existed."

"Baffling," Palpatine said, drawing out the word. "I don't know what to think."

A week had passed since the Perlemian political gathering. Lorn Pavan was dead by Maul's lightsaber, a day before an artificial hand was to have been grafted to the information broker's stub of forearm. *Cost cutting,* Plagueis had remarked at the time.

Valorum was resting his head in his hands. "That someone or some organization engineered this to cripple me is beyond doubt. The question of why anyone—even my most stalwart detractors in the Senate—would essentially discard tens of millions of credits to achieve this in the final months of my term is inexplicable." He raised his face to Palpatine. "My immediate predecessors were bold, and they knew how to manage the Senate. I believed I could bring something different to the office. A quieter diplomacy; one informed by the Force, and by the ideals of the Jedi Order."

Palpatine suppressed an urge to leap across the desk and strangle him.

"I realize that I've made some poor decisions. But has any chancellor in the past century had to face more challenges than I have? Has any chancellor had to deal with a more corrupt and self-serving Senate, or more megalomaniacal corporations?" Valorum closed his eyes and exhaled. "Whoever is behind this machination wants nothing more than to destroy my legacy entirely; to make the name Valorum seem a stain on history . . ."

"Then we must double our efforts to exonerate you," Palpatine said.

Valorum laughed without amusement. "I'm useless to the Republic if we can't. Until the matter is resolved, I'm prohibited from sanctioning the use of Jedi or Judicials to intervene in disputes. I'm not permitted to convene special sessions without the express consent of this new vice chancellor, Mas Amedda, who blocks my every proposal and venerates procedure as if it were holy text."

"Deception begins with bureaucracy," Palpatine said.

Silent for a moment, Valorum adopted an expression of resolve. "I'm not without ideas."

He tapped a touch screen built into his desk, and a large data display resolved above the holoprojector. Rising from his chair, he indicated a graph on which several dozen corporations were listed.

"One might assume—in light of the accusations stacked against me—that my family's concern on Eriadu would suffer a sudden decline in the market. But precisely the opposite is happening. Credits have been flowing into Valorum Shipping at an unparalleled rate, and to several other shipping and transport concerns, as well—many of them based in the Outer Rim. And that's not all."

His hands returned to the touch screen, and a second graph took shape alongside the first. "Investments in minor suppliers of plasma and alternative energy conglomerates have increased threefold. But most important, a surge has occurred in the military supply sector, with astonishing growth in Baktoid Armor Workshop, Haor Chall Engineering, the Colicoid Creation Nest, and similar providers."

Palpatine, despite himself, was impressed. "What do these data suggest?"

"That some nefarious business is unfolding under our very noses. That even the scandal in which I'm embroiled may be part of a larger plan."

Palpatine was about to respond when the voice of Valorum's personal secretary issued from the intercom.

"Supreme Chancellor, I apologize for interrupting, but we have received an urgent transmission from Queen Amidala, of Naboo."

"The Queen!" Palpatine said with theatrical surprise.

"Can you direct the transmission to my office?" Valorum said.

"Our comm techs are telling me that the signal is very weak, but that they will do their best."

Palpatine and Valorum turned to the office holoprojector table and waited. Within moments a noisy, fluctuating 3-D image of Naboo's pale-faced teenage queen appeared.

"Supreme Chancellor Valorum," she said. "We bring news of a grave development on our homeworld. Without warning, the Neimoidian faction of the Trade Federation has initiated a blockade. Their massive freighters encircle our world, and no ships are permitted to arrive or depart."

Palpatine and Valorum exchanged stunned looks.

How perfectly she plays her part, Palpatine thought. Sitting on her throne like some costumed and overly made-up animatronic doll. The stately pose, the uninflected voice, long-bearded adviser Sio Bibble standing to one side, dark-complected security chief Panaka to the other . . .

"Your Highness, have the Neimoidians communicated any demands?" Valorum asked as the blue-tinged image flickered, stabilized, and flickered again.

"Viceroy Gunray states that the blockade has been launched in protest of the Senate's decision to tax shipping in the free-trade zones. He assures that any attempts to break the embargo will meet with deadly force. Unless the new regulations are rescinded, he is prepared to see everyone on Naboo starve."

Valorum clenched his hands. "Your Majesty, Senator Palpatine is here with me."

Neither Amidala's expression nor her flat tone of voice wavered. "Senator Palpatine, we are pleased that you are able to hear this news firsthand."

"Your Highness," Palpatine said, stepping into view of the holoprojector cams and inclining his head. "I will contact the Trade Federation delegates immediately and demand that this blockade be terminated."

"Demands may not be enough to sway them, Senator. Naboo requests that the Republic intervene in this matter as quickly as possible."

"And it will, Your Highness," Valorum said all too quickly. "I will convene a special session . . . I pledge that Naboo will have my undivided attention."

Amidala nodded. "You have shown us much courtesy in the past, Supreme Chancellor. We trust that you will do everything in your power, as you are our only hope."

The transmission ended abruptly.

"The face of this nefarious business reveals itself," Palpatine said.

Valorum returned to his desk and sat. "I give you my word—for your help during the Yinchorri Crisis and for so many years of friendship—that this situation will not stand. Though my hands be bound, I will find some way to resolve this."

"I know that you will try, Supreme Chancellor."

Valorum took a deep breath. "One word of advice, Palpatine. Prepare to be thrust into the spotlight."

29: THE FORCE STRIKES BACK

Though the blockade of Naboo had been launched in direct defiance of Republic law—as much a protest against taxation as it was a challenge to the jurisdiction of the Jedi—it failed to achieve the immediate effect Plagueis and Sidious had anticipated. Far from the Core, Naboo hadn't been invaded, and no important beings had died, as had occurred during the Yinchorri Crisis and at the summit on Eriadu. Thus the blockade was viewed by many as little more than saber rattling by the vexed Trade Federation; an inconvenience to those worlds that relied on the consortium for goods; the latest in a series of confrontations to expose the incompetence of a hopelessly splintered Senate.

Nevertheless, the two Sith had worked tirelessly to make the most of Naboo's predicament to secure support among Palpatine's peers, and ensure not only that his name would be placed in nomination, but that he could win if nominated. Equally important, they had to make certain that Palpatine could marshal enough votes in the Senate to ratify his decision to appoint Hego Damask co-chancellor.

For a change, Damask had taken the lead—making the rounds, making promises, calling in long-overdue favors and debts—while Palpatine, for appearances' sake, made several futile attempts to meet privately with Trade Federation representative Lott Dod. Pestage, Doriana, Janus Greejatus, Armand Isard, and others were also busy behind the scenes, planting incriminating evidence where necessary, and seeing to it that instances of graft were made public.

Their joint efforts did not constitute a political campaign so much as an exercise in elaborate subterfuge.

"Bail Antilles remains the front-runner," Plagueis told Sidious when he arrived at the Muun's penthouse. "Ironically, the crisis at Naboo has drawn the Core Worlds into a tighter circle. Where Antilles has always been in danger of being dismissed as the candidate most likely to follow in Valorum's footsteps, he is suddenly the darling of those advocating for strong, central authority."

"He can be undermined," Sidious said. "What about Teem?"

"In addition to the Trade Federation, Teem now has the backing of the Corporate Policy League."

Sidious remained indifferent. "The Senate is not ready to elect a militant, much less a militant Gran. Embracing the support of the CPL is equivalent to promising the repeal of anti-slavery restrictions."

Plagueis's frustration was evident, even if his frown was hidden. "Interest in Naboo is already beginning to wane, and with it the sympathy vote we counted on."

Sidious had his mouth open to respond when his comlink chimed, and he held the device to his ear.

Plagueis watched him closely.

"That is most welcome news," Sidious said into the device, as if in a daze. "I didn't expect this . . . A good choice, I think . . . I am certain of it, Supreme Chancellor . . . Yes, I'm sure she meant every word of it."

"What now?" Plagueis asked the moment Palpatine broke the connection.

Sidious shook his head in disbelief. "Valorum somehow managed to persuade the Council to send two Jedi to Naboo."

Despite all his talk about invincibility, Plagueis looked confounded. "Without Senate approval? He tightens the noose around his own neck!"

"And ours," Sidious said, "if the Neimoidians panic and decide to admit the truth about the blockade."

Plagueis paced away from him in anger. "He must have approached the High Council in secret. Otherwise, Mas Amedda would have apprised us."

Sidious followed the Muun's nervous movements. "Dooku mentioned that the Council would continue to support him."

"Did Valorum say which Jedi were sent?"

"Qui-Gon Jinn and his Padawan, Obi-Wan Kenobi."

Plagueis came to an abrupt halt. "Worse news yet. I have met Qui-Gon, and he is nothing like some of the others Dooku trained."

"They are a pesky duo," Sidious said. "The nemesis of the Nebula Front at Dorvalla, Asmeru, and on Eriadu."

"Then Gunray and his sycophants stand no chance against them."

Sidious had an answer ready. "Two lone Jedi are no match for thousands of battle droids and droidekas. I will order Gunray to kill them."

"And we will have another Yinchorr, and the added danger of Gunray divulging our actions, past and present." Plagueis thought for a moment. "Qui-Gon will evade detection by the droids and wreak slow but inevitable havoc on the flagship."

"Then I will command Gunray to launch the invasion ahead of schedule. Protecting the Naboo will become the immediate concern, as opposed to arresting the Neimoidians. Gunray may balk at the idea, but I will assure him that the Republic will not intervene."

Plagueis agreed. "Amedda can deny any request Valorum makes to convene the Senate in special session. Still . . ."

They regarded each other in stony silence; then Sidious nodded.

"I will see to it that Maul is ready."

Plagueis pressed his hands together. "It is the will of the dark side that we finally reveal ourselves," he said in a solemn voice.

It certainly wasn't that he didn't trust Darth Sidious. But Plagueis had never observed Maul at close range, and he was curious about Sidious's relationship with him. He knew that they had seldom met outside The Works, let alone walked together on a balcony of one of Coruscant's most stylish monads in the dead of night, wrapped in their cowled cloaks. But it was only fitting that they should finally do so. With 11-4D close at hand, Plagueis stood observing the two of them from afar, his presence in the Force minimized.

The invasion and occupation of Naboo were proceeding on schedule, and the swamps were being searched in an effort to locate and isolate the principal underwater habitats of the planet's indigenous Gungans, before they could pose a threat. But the two Jedi, Queen

Amidala, and her retinue of body doubles and guards had succeeded in blasting their way through the blockade. With Maul's help, counterfeit messages from the Queen's adviser Sio Bibble had been transmitted to the missing starship, and one transmission had returned a faint connection trace to the Hutt-owned world of Tatooine. On learning as much, Plagueis had considered asking Jabba to apprehend the Queen, but not for long, out of concern for what the dark side might demand of him in return.

"Tatooine is sparsely populated," 11-4D said, repeating what the Dathomiri Zabrak was saying to Sidious. "If the trace was correct, I will find them quickly, Master."

"Go on," Plagueis said quietly.

"In reply, Sidious is instructing Maul to make the Jedi his first priority. Once Qui-Gon and Obi-Wan are disposed of, Maul is to return Queen Amidala to Naboo and force her to sign a treaty that cedes control of the planet and its plasma reserves to the Trade Federation."

The droid paused, then added, "Maul says, 'At last we reveal ourselves to the Jedi. At last we will have revenge.'"

In the distance, Sidious turned to Maul.

FourDee sharpened its auditory inputs. "Sidious says: 'You have been well trained, my young apprentice. They will be no match for you.'"

The words stirred deep misgiving in Plagueis and he stretched out with the Force, attuned to its swirling currents. Momentarily, the gates that obscured the future parted and he had a glimpse of events to come, or events that might come.

Either way, he was not encouraged.

Had he and Sidious misunderstood? Would it be better to abort the plan and trust that Palpatine would be elected even without having Naboo fall to the Trade Federation? Once the Jedi learned of the existence of one Sith, would they launch an intense hunt for the other?

Sidious had formed an almost filial bond with Maul. Attached to the present, he failed to grasp the truth: that this was the last time he and his apprentice might see each other in the flesh.

* * *

Events were converging rapidly.

Unexpected obstacles notwithstanding, Maul's tracking skills had led him to the missing Queen. But he had failed in his mission. Despite a brief confrontation with Qui-Gon Jinn, the Jedi Master and his party had managed a second successful escape. The Zabrak hadn't been killed, as Plagueis had initially feared, but his crimson blade had identified him as a Sith, and now the Jedi, Amidala, and her retinue of guards and handmaidens were inbound to Coruscant in the Queen's reflective starship. Sidious had ordered Maul to go to Naboo to oversee the Neimoidian occupation.

"Pestage and Doriana have put a plan in place that will weaken the campaigns of your chief rivals," Plagueis was saying as he and Palpatine hurried toward the skyhopper that would carry them to the antigrav platform on which the Royal Starship had been cleared to land. "Coruscant will soon know that Senator Ainlee Teem has been protecting a Dug who is deeply involved with Gardulla the Hutt and the Bando Gora's death stick distribution network."

"Another favor from Jabba?" Sidious asked.

"The Hutt has become an ally," Plagueis said.

"With Black Sun headless, he'll have free rein over the spice trade."

"For a time," Plagueis said. "The information about Senator Teem has been sent to Antilles, who has been trying for years to have him removed from the Senate. When the corruption inquest is announced, Teem's support will disappear. And so will support for Antilles, whose ambitions have blinded him to the fact that no one in the Senate wants an overzealous reformer in the chancellorship. The Rim Faction will then flock to you, in the hope of being able to manipulate you, and the humancentric Core Faction will back you because you're one of their own."

Sidious regarded him. "Were it not for you—"

Plagueis waved him silent and came to a sudden halt.

Sidious walked a few more steps and turned to him. "You're not going to accompany me to greet the Queen?"

"No. The Jedi are still with her, and our joint presence might allow them to sense our leanings."

"You're right, of course."

"There's one more issue," Plagueis said. "The Naboo crisis has finally caught the fancy of Coruscant. If we could force a similar crisis in the Senate, your election would be guaranteed."

Sidious thought about it. "There may be a way." He looked hard at Plagueis. "The call for a vote of no-confidence in Valorum."

"If you—"

"Not me," Sidious cut him off. "Queen Amidala. I will fill her head with doubts about Valorum's inability to resolve the crisis and fears of what Trade Federation rule would mean for Naboo. Then I will take her to the Senate so that she can see for herself how untenable the situation has become."

"Grand theater," Plagueis mused. "She'll not only call for a vote of no-confidence. She'll flee home to be with her people."

"Where we wanted her to begin with."

"I trust that the food is better than the view," Dooku remarked without humor as he joined Palpatine at a window-side table in Mok's Cheap Eats the following day. A small establishment catering to factory personnel, it overlooked the heart of The Works.

"The Senate is studying plans to develop housing projects in the flatlands."

Dooku frowned in revulsion. "Why not simply build over a radioactive waste dump?"

"Where there are credits to be made, the lives of ordinary citizens are of little consequence."

Dooku cocked an eyebrow. "I hope you'll put a stop to it."

"I'd prefer The Works to remain unchanged for a time."

Dooku waved off a waiter and regarded Palpatine with interest. "So, a blockade prevents you from going to Naboo, and what happens but Naboo comes to you. Quite a piece of magic."

Palpatine showed him a thin smile. "Yes, my Queen has arrived."

"Your Queen," Dooku said, tugging at his short beard. "And from all I hear you may soon be her Supreme Chancellor."

Palpatine shrugged off the remark, then adopted a more serious look. "That is, however, part of the reason behind my asking you to meet me here."

"Worried that you won't receive Jedi backing if you're seen with me in the usual places?"

"Nothing of the sort. But *if* I am elected, and *if* you and I are going to begin to work together, it behooves us to give all appearances of being on opposite sides."

Dooku folded his arms and stared. "Work together in what capacity?"

"That remains to be seen. But our common goal would be to return the Republic to what it once was by tearing it down."

Dooku didn't say anything for a long moment, and when he spoke it was as if he were assembling his thoughts on the fly. "With perhaps your homeworld as the spark that touches off a conflagration? Clearly the crisis has benefited you politically, and that fact alone has certain beings wondering." He scanned Palpatine's face. "Under normal circumstances, the Council wouldn't have subverted the authority of the Senate by honoring Valorum's request to send Jedi to Naboo. But for Yoda, Mace Windu, and the rest, Valorum is a known quantity, whereas Senators Antilles and Teem and you have yet to disclose your true agendas. Take you, for instance. Most are aware that you are a career politician, and that you've managed thus far to avoid imbroglios. But what does anyone know about you beyond your voting record, or the fact that you reside in Five Hundred Republica? We all think that there's much more to you than meets the eye, as it were; something about you that has yet to be uncovered."

Instead of speaking directly to Dooku's point, Palpatine said, "I was as surprised as anyone to learn that Master Qui-Gon and Obi-Wan Kenobi were sent to Naboo."

"Surprised, of course. But pleased?"

"Naboo is my homeworld. I want to see the crisis resolved as quickly as possible."

"Do you?"

Palpatine held his look. "I begin to wonder what may have prompted your confrontational mood. But for the sake of argument, let us say that I feel no shame in taking full advantage of the crisis. Would that cause you to distance yourself from me?"

Dooku smiled with his eyes, but not in mirth. "On the contrary, as you say. Since I'm interested in learning more about the possibility of an alliance."

Palpatine adopted a hooded look. "You're resolved to leave the Order?"

"Even more than when we last spoke."

"Because of the Council's decision to intervene at Naboo?"

"I can forgive them that. The blockade has to be broken. But something else has occurred." Dooku chose his next words carefully. "Qui-Gon returned from Tatooine with a former slave boy. According to the boy's mother, the boy had no father."

"A clone?" Palpatine asked uncertainly.

"Not a clone," Dooku said. "Perhaps conceived by the Force. As Qui-Gon believes."

Palpatine's head snapped back: "You don't sit on the Council. How do you know this?"

"I have my ways."

"Does this have something to do with the prophecy you spoke of?"

"Everything. Qui-Gon believes that the boy—Anakin is his name— stands at the center of a vergence in the Force, and believes further that his finding him was the will of the Force. Blood tests were apparently performed, and the boy's concentration of midi-chlorians is unprecedented."

"Do you believe that he is the prophesied one?"

"The Chosen One," Dooku amended. "No. But Qui-Gon accepts it as fact, and the Council is willing to have him tested."

"What is known about this Anakin?"

"Very little, except for the fact that he was born into slavery nine years ago and was, until recently, along with his mother, the property of Gardulla the Hutt, then a Toydarian junk dealer." Dooku smirked. "Also that he won the Boonta Eve Classic Podrace."

Palpatine had stopped listening.

Nine years old . . . Conceived by the Force . . . Is it possible . . .

His thoughts rewound at frantic speed: to the landing platform on which he and Valorum had welcomed Amidala and her group. Actually not Amidala, but one of her look-alikes. But the sandy-haired boy, this Anakin, swathed in filthy clothing, had been there, along with a Gungan and the two Jedi. Anakin had spent the night in a tiny room in his apartment suite.

And I sensed nothing *about him.*

"Qui-Gon is rash," Dooku was saying. "Despite his fixation with the living Force, he demonstrates his own contradictions by being a true believer in the prophecy—a foretelling more in line with the unifying Force."

"Nine years old," Palpatine said when he could. "Surely too old to be trained."

"If the Council shows any sense."

"And what will become of the boy then?"

Dooku's shoulders heaved. "Though no longer a slave, he will probably be sent to rejoin his mother on Tatooine."

"I understand your disillusionment," Palpatine said.

Dooku shook his head. "I haven't told you all of it. As if the announcement of having found the Chosen One wasn't enough, Qui-Gon discovered that the Trade Federation may have had the help of powerful allies in planning and executing the blockade of Naboo."

Palpatine sat straighter in his chair. "What allies?"

"On Tatooine, Qui-Gon dueled with an assassin who is well trained in the Jedi arts. But he dismissed the idea that the assassin is some rogue Jedi. He is convinced that the warrior is a Sith."

Ignoring the reactions of apprehensive residents and wary security personnel, Plagueis hastened along a plush corridor in 500 Republica toward Palpatine's suite of crimson rooms. He had planned to be at the Senate Building to hear Amidala's call for a vote of no-confidence in Valorum, which would strike the first death knell for the Republic. At the last moment, however, Palpatine had contacted him to recount a conversation he had had with Dooku. The fact that Qui-Gon Jinn had identified Maul as a Sith was to be expected; but Dooku's news about a human boy at the center of a vergence of the Force had come as a shock. More, Qui-Gon saw the boy as the Jedi's prophesied Chosen One!

He had to see this Anakin Skywalker for himself; had to sense him for himself. He had to know if the Force had struck back again, nine years earlier, by conceiving a human being to restore balance to the galaxy.

Plagueis came to a halt at the entry to Palpatine's apartment. Eventually one of Queen Amidala's near-identical handmaidens came to the door, a vision in a dark cowled robe. Her eyes fixed on the breath mask.

"I'm sorry, sir," she said, "Senator Palpatine is not here."

"I know," Plagueis said. "I'm here to speak with a guest of the Senator. A young human boy."

Her eyes remained glued on the mask. "I'm not permitted—"

Damask motioned swiftly with his left hand, compelling her to answer him. "You have my permission to speak."

"I have your permission," she said in a distracted voice.

"Now where is the boy?"

"Anakin, you mean."

"Anakin, yes," he said in a rush. "He's the one. Fetch him—now!"

"You just missed him, sir," the handmaiden said.

Plagueis peered past her into Palpatine's suite. "Missed him?" He straightened in anger. "Where is he?"

"Jedi Master Qui-Gon Jinn came to collect him, sir. I suspect that you can find him at the Jedi Temple."

Plagueis fell back a step, his thoughts reeling.

There was still a chance that the Council would decide that Anakin was too old to be trained as a Jedi. That way, assuming he was returned to Tatooine . . .

But if not . . . If Qui-Gon managed to sway the Council Masters, and they reneged on their own dictates . . .

Plagueis ran a hand over his forehead. *Are we undone?* he thought. *Have you undone us?*

30: TAKING THE FUTURE FROM THE NOW

Magister Damask was still unnerved when he arrived at the Senate Building and hurried through its maze of corridors and turbolifts to reach Naboo's station on time for the event.

During a recess that ensued after the call for a vote of no-confidence, Queen Amidala and the pair of retainers she had arrived with had decided to return to 500 Republica. But Panaka was there, in his brown leather cap and jerkin, along with Sate Pestage and Kinman Doriana. With scarcely a word of acknowledgment, Plagueis edged past the three men to join Palpatine on the hover platform.

"Did you speak with him?" Palpatine asked, while the voice of the Senator from Kuat boomed through the Rotunda's speakers.

The Muun shook his head in anger. "Qui-Gon had already been there. They've gone to the Temple."

"There's still a chance—"

"Yes," Damask said. "But if the boy's midi-chlorian concentrations are as high as Dooku hinted they are, then the Jedi aren't likely to allow him to escape their clutches."

"High midi-chlorian counts don't always equate to Force talents. You told me yourself."

"That's not what concerns me," Damask said, but he went no further. Gesturing broadly, he asked, "Where do we stand?"

"Antilles was placed into nomination by Com Fordox. Teem, by Edcel Bar Gan."

"Traitors," Damask seethed. "Fordox and Bar Gan."

Palpatine was about to reply when the voice of Mas Amedda filled the Rotunda. "The Senate recognizes Senator Orn Free Taa of Ryloth," the Chagrian said from the podium. Sei Taria was there, as well, but Valorum—all but ousted from power—had either disappeared or was seated out of sight.

The big blue Twi'lek stood proudly in the bow of the platform as it floated toward the center of the Rotunda, flanked by hovercams. In the curved rear of the platform were Free Taa's consort, a petite red-skinned Twi'lek, and Ryloth's co-Senator and death stick distributor, Connus Trell.

"Ryloth is proud to place into nomination one who has not only devoted twenty years of unflagging service to the Republic while managing to steer a gallant course through the storms that continue to lash this body, but whose homeworld has become the latest target of corporate greed and corruption. Beings of all species and all worlds, I nominate Senate Palpatine of Naboo."

Cheers and applause rang out from nearly every sector of the hall, growing louder and more enthusiastic as Naboo's platform detached from the docking station and hovered to join those of Alderaan and Malastare.

"You've done it, Darth Plagueis," Palpatine said quietly and without a glance.

"Not yet," came the reply. "I will not rest until I'm certain of a *win*."

It was late in the evening when Plagueis made his way onto a public observatory that provided a vantage on the proprietary arabesque of a landing platform on which Queen Amidala's Royal Starship basked in the ambient light.

With the cowl of his hood raised, he moved to one of the stationary macrobinocular posts and pressed his eyes to the cushioned eye grips. Qui-Gon Jinn, Obi-Wan Kenobi, and the boy had arrived at the platform in a Jedi ship; Amidala, her handmaidens and guards, and a loose-limbed Gungan in an open-topped hemispherical air taxi. Just then the latter group was ascending the starship's boarding ramp, but Qui-Gon and the round-faced desert urchin had stopped short of the ship to speak about something.

What? Plagueis asked himself. *What topic has summoned such an earnest look to Qui-Gon's face, and such confused urgency in the boy?*

Lifting his face from the macrobinoculars, he stretched out with the Force and fell victim to an assault of perplexing images: ferocious battles in deep space; the clashing of lightsabers; partitions of radiant light; a black-helmeted cyborg rising from a table . . . By the time his gaze had returned to the platform, Qui-Gon and the boy had disappeared.

Trying desperately to make some sense of the images granted him by the Force, he stood motionless, watching the starship lift from the platform and climb into the night.

He fought to repress the truth.

The boy would change the course of history.

Unless . . .

Maul had to kill Qui-Gon, to keep the boy from being trained. *Qui-Gon was the key to everything.*

Plagueis and Sidious spent the day before the Senate vote in the LiMerge Building, communicating with Maul and Gunray and seeing to other matters. Early reports from Naboo indicated that Amidala was more daring than either of them had anticipated. She had engineered a reconciliation between the Naboo and the Gungans, and had persuaded the latter to assemble an army in the swamps. Initially, Sidious had forbidden Maul and the Neimoidians to take action. The last thing the Sith needed was to have Amidala emerge as the hero of their manufactured drama. But when the Gungan army had commenced a march on the city of Theed, he had no choice but to order Gunray to repel the attack and slaughter everyone.

Plagueis neither offered advice nor contradicted the commands, even though he knew that the battle was lost and that the boy would not die.

Instead he arranged for a conference comm with the leaders of the Commerce Guild, the Techno Union, the Corporate Alliance, and others, telling them that, despite the legality of the blockade, the Trade Federation had brought doom upon itself.

"Pay heed to the way the Republic and the Jedi Order deal with them," Hego Damask told his holo-audience. "The Federation will be dismantled, and the precedent will be set. Unless you take steps to begin a slow, carefully planned withdrawal from the Senate, taking your home and client systems with you, you, too, risk becoming the property of the Republic."

As daylight was fading over The Works, Sate Pestage informed them that Senators Teem and Antilles were crippled, and that some of Coruscant's political oddsmakers were now giving Palpatine the edge in the election.

That left only one piece of business to finalize.

Attend the opera.

Suspended like a scintillating ornament from a bracket of roadways and pedestrian ramps, Galaxies Opera was owned by notorious gambler and playboy Romeo Treblanc, and designed to function as an alternative to the stuffy Coruscant Opera, which for decades had been patronized by House Valorum and other wealthy Core lineages. With the Senate scheduled to convene in extraordinary session the following morning, excitement gripped Coruscant, and in celebration of the possibility that the election of a new Supreme Chancellor might usher in an era of positive change, half the Senate had turned out. Never had so much veda cloth, brocart, and shimmersilk graced the lavish carpets that led to the front doors; and never had such a diverse assortment of Coruscanti spilled from the taxis and limos that delivered them: patricians and doyennes, tycoons and philanthropists, pundits and patrons, lotharios and ingénues, gangsters and their molls . . . many clothed in costumes as ostentatious as those worn by the performers on the stage.

Valorum had declined to appear, but both Ainlee Teem and Bail Antilles were among the thousands streaming in to enjoy the debut performance of a new work by a Mon Calamari mastermind. Only Palpatine and Damask, however, were personally welcomed by Treblanc—Palpatine wrapped in a dark cloak, and the Muun in deep green, with matching bonnet and a breather mask that left part of his hoary jaw exposed.

"Word has it that he lost a fortune at the Boonta Eve Podrace," Damask said when they were out of Treblanc's earshot.

"The event Anakin won," Palpatine said.

Damask stopped short in surprise, and turned to Palpatine for explanation.

"He captured first place."

Damask absorbed the news in brooding silence, then muttered, "The boy's actions already echo across the stars."

A Nautolan female escorted them to a private box on the third tier, close to the stage, their appearance prompting applause from some of the beings seated below, rumormongering by others.

The lights dimmed and the performance began. Watery metaphors alternated with symbol-laden projections. The experimental nature of the work seemed to enhance an atmosphere of expectation that hung over the audience. Their thoughts elsewhere, the two secret Sith sat in respectful silence, as if hypnotized.

During intermission, the crowd filed into the lobby for refreshments. Discreetly, Damask sipped from a goblet of wine while distinguished beings approached Palpatine to wish him good fortune in the coming election. Other celebrated beings gawked at Damask from a polite distance; it was as if some long-sought phantom had become flesh and blood for the evening. Holocams grabbed images of the pair for media outlets. Damask ingested a second goblet of wine while the lights flickered, announcing the end of the intermission. Pestage had assured him that some of Palpatine's opponents in the Senate would be waylaid; others, rendered too drunk or drugged to attend the morning session. None would die, but several might have to be threatened. And yet, Damask continued to fret over the outcome . . .

Following the performance, he and Palpatine joined a select group of politicians that included Orn Free Taa and Mas Amedda for a late dinner in a private room in the Manarai.

Then they retired to Damask's penthouse.

Plagueis had given the Sun Guards the night off, and the only other intelligence in the sprawling apartment was the droid 11-4D, their servant for the occasion, pouring wine into expensive glassware as they removed their cloaks.

"Sullustan," Plagueis said, holding the glass up to the light and swirling its claret contents. "More than half a century old."

"A toast, then," Sidious said. "To the culmination of decades of brilliant planning and execution."

"And to the new meaning we will tomorrow impart to the Rule of Two."

They drained their glasses, and 11-4D immediately refilled them.

"Only you could have brought this to fruition, Darth Plagueis," Sidious said, settling into a chair. "I will endeavor to live up your expectations and fulfill my responsibility."

Plagueis took the compliment in stride, neither haughty nor embarrassed. "With my guidance and your charisma, we will soon be in a position to initiate the final act of the Grand Plan." Making himself more comfortable on the couch, he signaled for 11-4D to open a second bottle of the vintage. "Have you given thought to what you will say tomorrow?"

"I have prepared some remarks," Sidious said. "Shall I spoil the surprise?"

"Why not."

Sidious took a moment to compose himself. "To begin, I thought I would say, that, while we in the Senate have managed to keep the Republic intact for a thousand years, we would never have been able to do so without the assistance of a few beings, largely invisible to the public eye, whose accomplishments now need to be brought into the light of day."

Plagueis smiled. "I'm pleased. Go on."

Speaking in a low monotone, Sidious said, "Hego Damask is one of those beings. It was Hego Damask who was responsible for overseeing development of the Republic Reserve Administration and for providing financial support for the Resettlement Acts that enabled beings to blaze new hyperspace routes to the outlying systems and colonize distant worlds."

"That will come as a revelation to some."

"In a similar fashion, it was Hego Damask who transformed the Trade Federation—"

"No, no," Plagueis interrupted. "Now is not the time to mention the Trade Federation."

"I thought—"

"I don't see any problem with calling attention to the arrangements

James Luceno

er and close, and his breathing slowed. In twenty years of
had to contend with Plagueis in a state of sleep, the tran-
:d repeatedly in adjustment, almost as if in panic.

ters distant, Sidious came to a halt, gazing at Plagueis
oment, as though making up his mind about something.
ig out his breath, he set his own glass down and reached
he had draped over a chair. Swirling it around himself, he
e door, only to stop shortly before he reached it. Turning
g out with the Force, he glanced around the room, as one
a memory in the mind. Briefly his gaze fell on the droid,
hotoreceptors whirring to regard him in evident curiosity.
sinister purpose contorted Sidious's face.
s eyes darted around the room, and the dark side whis-

on assured, the Sun Guards absent, Plagueis unsuspecting and

loved in a blur.
from his fingertips, a web of blue lightning ground it-
Muun's breathing device. Plagueis's eyes snapped open,
thering in him like a storm, but he stopped short of de-
self. This being who had survived assassinations and killed
ponents merely gazed at Sidious, until it struck him that
challenging him! Confident that he couldn't be killed, and
t he was slowly suffocating, he might have been simply ex-
with himself, actually courting death to put it in its place.
y taken aback, Sidious stood absolutely still. Was Plagueis
led as to believe that he had achieved immortality?
tion lingered for only a moment, then Sidious unleashed
le of lightning, drawing more deeply on the dark side than

over the second part of the speech, shall we," he said,
his tousled cloak. "You useless old fool."
narl, he threw the cloak back behind his shoulders and
rd Plagueis, planting his palms on the low table that was
d with spilled wine.
Hego Damask as Darth Plagueis who came to Naboo, de-
suck the planet dry of plasma and set the Trade Federa-

I facilitated between the Republic
Techno Union. But we must take c

"Of course," Sidious said, as if cl
of my head."

"Try a different approach."

So Sidious did.

And as the night wore on, he cc
touching on Damask's childhood or
ask's contributions to the InterGala
as co-chair. Wineglass in hand, Sidio
often vacillating between confidence
Plagueis voiced satisfaction with ev
Sidious to save his energy for the m
was too wound up to heed the advice
the remarks and the emphasis he gave

The droid brought out a third, the
wine.

Pleasantly intoxicated, Plagueis, v
than to revel in the sweet taste of vic
collaborator's performance exhausting,
to close his eyes and drift into imaginir
Rotunda; the looks of surprise, astoni
faces of the gathered Senators; his lor
the shadows; his ascension to galactic p

Unfortunately, Sidious wouldn't let l

"That's enough for now," Plagueis tri
probably return home and get at least a

"Just one more time—from the begir

"The beginning?"

"Lord Plagueis, you said you wouldn'
ter of fact."

"So it is, and so I shall, Darth Sidious.

"Then let us celebrate that, as well."
"Fill our glasses, droid."

With dreamy weariness beginning to g
Plagueis could do to lift the glass to his nc
drink down than it tipped over, saturating

began to fli
never havin
spirator clic

A few i
for a long
Then, blov
for the clo
started for
and stretcl
might to
its glowin

A look
Again,
pered:

Your e
asleep . . .

And h
Crack
self on t
the Forc
fending
countles
Plagueis
in denia
perimer
Momer
so self-c

The
another
he ever

"Le
smoot

Wit
leaned
now p

"It
termi

tion up as its overseers. It was Hego Damask as Plagueis who then set his sights on a seemingly confused young man and, with meticulous skill, manipulated him into committing patricide, matricide, fratricide. Darth Plagueis who took him as an apprentice, sharing some of his knowledge but withholding his most powerful secrets, denying the apprentice his wishes as a means of controlling him, instilling in him a sense of murderous rage, and turning him to the dark side."

Sidious stood to his full height, glaring.

"It was Plagueis who criticized the early efforts of his apprentice, and who once choked him in a demonstration of his superiority.

"Plagueis, who denigrated him in private for hiring an inept assassin to carry out the murder of Senator Kim—and yet who allowed himself to be tricked by the Gran and nearly killed by mercenaries.

"Plagueis, who turned away from the Grand Plan to focus entirely on himself, in an egotistical quest for immortality.

"Plagueis who had the temerity to criticize his apprentice for having inculcated too much pride in the assassin *he* had trained.

"Plagueis who attempted to turn his equally powerful apprentice into a messenger and mere intermediary.

"And Plagueis who watched in secret while his apprentice tasked their true intermediary to reveal the reborn Sith to the galaxy."

Sidious paused, then, in derision, added, "Plagueis the Wise, who in his time truly was, except at the end, trusting that the Rule of Two had been superseded, and failed to realize that he would not be excused from it. Plagueis the Wise, who forged the most powerful Sith Lord the galaxy has ever known, and yet who forgot to leave a place for himself; whose pride never allowed him to question that he would no longer be needed."

Still struggling for breath, Plagueis managed to stand, but only to collapse back onto the couch, knocking a statue from its perch. Sidious moved in, his hands upraised to deliver another bolt, his expression arctic enough to chill the room. A Force storm gathered over the couch, spreading out in concentric rings, to wash over Sidious and hurl objects to all corners. In the center of it, Plagueis's form became anamorphic, then resumed shape as the storm began to wane.

Sidious's eyes bored into the Muun's.

"How often you said that the old order of Bane had ended with the death of your Master. An apprentice no longer needs to be stronger, you told me, merely more clever. The era of keeping score, suspicion, and betrayal was over. Strength is not in the flesh but in the Force."

He laughed. "You lost the game on the very first day you chose to train me to rule by your side—or better still, under your thumb. Teacher, yes, and for that I will be eternally grateful. But Master—*never.*"

Sidious peered at Plagueis through the Force. "Oh, yes, by all means gather your midi-chlorians, Plagueis." He held his thumb and forefinger close together. "Try to keep yourself alive while I choke the life out of you."

Plagueis gulped for air and lifted an arm toward him.

"There's the rub, you see," Sidious said in a philosophical tone. "All the ones you experimented on, killed, and brought back to life'. . . They were little more than toys. Now, though, you get to experience it from their side, and look what you discover: in a body that is being denied air, in which even the Force is failing, your own midi-chlorians can't accomplish what you're asking of them."

Hatred stained Sidious's eyes.

"I could save you, of course. Return you from the brink, as you did Venamis. I could retask your body to repair the damage already done to your lungs, your hearts, your aged brain. But I'll do no such thing. The idea here is not to drag you back at the last moment, but to bring you to death's door and shove you through to the other side."

Sidious sighed. "A tragedy, really, for one so wise. One who could oversee the lives and deaths of all beings, except himself."

The Muun's eyes had begun to bulge; his pale flesh, to turn cyanotic.

"You may be wondering: when did he begin to change?

"The truth is that I haven't changed. As we have clouded the minds of the Jedi, I clouded yours. Never once did I have any intention of sharing power with you. I needed to learn from you; no more, no less. To learn all of your secrets, which I trusted you would eventually reveal. But what made you think that I would need you after that? Vanity, perhaps; your sense of self-importance. You've been nothing more than a pawn in a game played by a genuine Master.

"The Sith'ari."

A cruel laugh escaped him.

"Reflect back on even the past few years—assuming you have the capacity. Yinchorr, Dorvalla, Eriadu, Maul, the Neimoidians, Naboo, an army of clones, the fallen Jedi Dooku . . . You think these were your ideas, when in fact they were mine, cleverly suggested to you so that you could feed them back to me. You were far too trusting, Plagueis. No true Sith can ever really care about another. This has always been known. There is no way but my way."

Sidious's eyes narrowed. "Are you still with me, Plagueis? Yes, I detect that you are—though barely.

"A few final words, then.

"I could have let you die in the Fobosi district, but I couldn't allow that to happen when there was still so much I didn't know; so many powers that remained just outside my reach. And as it happened, I acted wisely in rescuing you. Otherwise how could I be standing here and you be dying? I actually thought you would die on Sojourn—and you would have if the Hutt hadn't tipped you off to Veruna's scheme.

"And yet that also turned out for the best, for even after all you taught me, I might not have been able to take the final steps to the chancellorship without your help in manipulating the Senate and bringing into play your various and sundry allies. If it's any consolation, I'm being honest when I say that I could not have succeeded without you. But now that we've won the race, I've no need for a *co*-chancellor. Your presence, much less your unnecessary counsel, would only confuse matters. I have Maul to do what the risk of discovery might not allow me to do, while I execute the rest of the Grand Plan: growing an army, fomenting rebellion and fabricating intergalactic war, corralling the Jedi and catching them unawares . . .

"Rest easy in your grave, Plagueis. In the end, I will be proclaimed Emperor. The Sith will have had their revenge, and I will rule the galaxy."

Plagueis slid to the floor and rolled facedown. Death rattled his lungs and he died.

OneOne-FourDee started to approach, but Sidious motioned for it to stop.

"We're going to have to find you a new home and a new body, droid."

OneOne-FourDee looked once at the Muun, then at Sidious. "Yes, Master Palpatine."

Sidious moved to the window, then turned to regard the murder scene. Hego Damask would appear to have died because of a malfunction of the breathing apparatus. He would have the droid alert the medtechs. But no autopsy would be performed, and no inquest would follow. Holos of their appearance at the Galaxies Opera would run on the HoloNet, and pundits would weigh in. Senator Palpatine might garner even greater sympathy; his delight in being elected to the chancellorship diminished by the sudden death of a powerful financial ally.

Sidious moved back into the room to take a closer look at Plagueis. Then, after a long moment, he returned to the window and pulled the drapes aside.

His spirit soared, but briefly.

Something was shading his sense of triumph: a vague awareness of a power greater than himself. Was it Plagueis reaching out from the far side of death to vex him? Or was the feeling a mere consequence of apotheosis?

Outside, the summits of the tallest buildings were gilded by the first rays of daylight.

EPILOGUE

Palpatine's election to the chancellorship dominated the HoloNet. It was far from a landslide victory, but he won by a wider margin than even the oddsmakers had predicted, due in part to the unexplained absence of several of his key opponents. With two Supreme Court judges and Vice Chancellor Mas Amedda presiding, he took the oath of office atop the Senate Podium, after Valorum had shaken his hand and disappeared down the turbolift that led to the preparation room far below. In his address he pledged to return the Republic to its former glory and to purge the Senate of corrupt practices. No one paid much attention, since every Supreme Chancellor for the past two hundred years had made the same promises.

Pundits, however, were quick to weigh in on what the election might mean for the immediate future. The fact that Naboo had managed to defeat the Trade Federation without the aid of mercenaries or Republic intervention had many beings wondering whether planets might follow Naboo in establishing their own militaries and challenging the power of the galactic consortiums. How might the events of Naboo shape the new Supreme Chancellor's policies toward the Corporate Alliance and other cartels? Would legislation regarding taxation of the free-trade zones and the legality of droid armies be reexamined? Would harsher enforcement lead eventually to the cartels' secession from the Republic? And might entire systems end up joining the exodus?

With so much attention being focused on the election, stories that might otherwise have been viewed as significant escaped notice. One such story was the unexpected death of reclusive Muun financier Hego Damask. Hastily prepared obituaries contained the few facts about his life that were public knowledge but scarcely touched on the behind-the-scenes role he had played in shaping the history of the Republic. Members of the InterGalactic Banking Clan were refusing to release any information about the funeral or about the disposition of Damask's substantial holdings on Muunilinst and dozens of other worlds. Off the record, beings remarked that the intricacies of the Muun's business concerns might take decades to unravel.

With the Battle of Naboo concluded—*lost,* in his estimation—Palpatine had no time to bask in adulation or celebrate his win. His first order of business, indeed his first official duty, was to travel to his homeworld to congratulate Queen Amidala and her new allies, the Gungans, on their surprise victory.

It wasn't until he arrived in Theed and learned of Darth Maul's defeat at the hands of the Jedi in a power-generator station that he understood in part the reason for the sense of loss and profound solitude he had experienced following the murder of Plagueis. He could have pressed one of the other Jedi who had arrived on Naboo for information as to how Maul had managed to kill a master sword fighter only to be overcome by a lesser one, but he didn't want to know, and as a result be able to imagine the contest. Still, it gave him great pleasure to stand among Yoda, Mace Windu, and other Masters and watch Qui-Gon Jinn's body reduced to ash, knowing that the Jedi was just the first casualty in a war that had been declared but not yet begun; one in which ten thousand Jedi would follow Qui-Gon to the grave . . .

That Plagueis's death and Maul's defeat had occurred in relative simultaneity could only have been the will of the dark side of the Force, as was the fact that, until such time as he took and trained a new apprentice, Palpatine was now the galaxy's sole Sith Lord.

Disappointment also attended the fact that the droid army of the Trade Federation had been so easily vanquished by a handful of Naboo and an army of primitives. But Anakin Skywalker was the larger issue.

No one could argue that he had shown remarkable courage and Force ability in destroying the Trade Federation's Droid Control Ship.

As Plagueis had said: *Already his actions begin to echo across the stars.*

"What is this place?" Dooku asked after Palpatine had welcomed him into the LiMerge Building.

"An old factory. It was owned by Hego Damask, but he deeded it to me before he died."

Dooku's brow wrinkled. "For what purpose?"

"He thought I might have some use for it in jump-starting a plan of urban revitalization."

Back on Coruscant for a little over a month, Palpatine was wearing a cowled cloak closed at the neck by a Sith clasp, ostensibly as protection against acid-laden rain that was falling in The Works. Dooku was dressed as a civilian, in tight-fitting trousers and a smart cape.

The former Jedi regarded the factory's enormous main room. "No Senate Guards?"

"They're within comm range should I need them."

"I would have thought you at least wanted me to see your new office," Dooku said, brushing beads of water from his shoulder. "Then I recalled what you said last time we spoke, about our not being seen together in public."

Palpatine waved negligently. "The office is temporary. One more suited to the position is already in the planning stages."

Side by side, they began to walk through the room. "So you've hooked them already," Dooku said.

Palpatine feigned a look of innocence. "Not at all. The Appropriations Committee approached me with the idea of constructing a dome near the Senate Building that will also serve as a docking facility."

"You appear to be very pleased with the idea."

"Most pleased."

Dooku stopped to study him. "Your truer nature begins to reveal itself, I think." When Palpatine made no response, he added, "Congratulations, by the way, on Naboo's defeat of the Trade Federation. An odd series of events, wouldn't you agree?"

Palpatine nodded and resumed a measured pace. "Everyone involved—including me—underestimated the abilities of our Queen. It pained me to learn that Master Qui-Gon had been killed." He paused momentarily. "Was it his death that firmed your decision to leave the Order?"

"To a degree," Dooku said, scowling. "I've learned recently that another of my Padawans—Komari Vosa—is alive."

"I hope that's some consolation," Palpatine started to say.

"It isn't, as she is said to be leading the Bando Gora." Dooku looked at him. "She could be a danger to the Republic, Supreme Chancellor."

"Then thank you for the warning. How did the Council react to your departure?"

"Not well. They demanded more explanation than I was willing to provide."

"And Master Sifo-Dyas?"

Dooku frowned. "He knew that my leaving was simply a matter of time. Although he did say something I found to be rather curious. He said that if I had any designs on instigating dissent, he would be one step ahead of me."

Palpatine shook his head in confusion. "Are you planning to instigate dissent?"

Dooku smiled faintly. "My first order of business is to reclaim my title."

"Count Dooku," Palpatine said, assessing the sound of it. "Somehow it suits you better than Master Dooku."

"I'm tempted to adopt a new name altogether."

"A new beginning."

"Perhaps I should do as you've done."

"As I've done?" Palpatine said.

"Call myself Dooku, as you retitled yourself Palpatine."

"I see. Well, what meaning is conveyed by a name, in any case?" Again, he paused for a long moment. "I understand that Qui-Gon fell to a lightsaber."

Dooku's head snapped around. "The same Sith he confronted on Tatooine. The Council is hoping that Gunray can shed some light on the matter once the trial is under way."

"I wouldn't put much faith in that. Does the Council know anything at all?"

"Not even his Sith name," Dooku said. "But they know that there is another."

"How could they?"

"In theory, when the Sith went into hiding one thousand years ago, they vowed that there should be only two of them at any given time—one Master, one apprentice, through the generations."

"Was this one who killed Qui-Gon the apprentice or the Master?"

Dooku looked at him as they walked. "My every instinct tells me that he was the apprentice. Obi-Wan suspects as much, as well, based on the Zabrak's behavior. The Council is being more circumspect, but naturally they want the other one found." He fell silent, then added, "The Sith deliberately revealed himself on Tatooine and on Naboo. More than disclosing their alliance with the Trade Federation, he did so to send a message to the Jedi. It amounts to a declaration of war."

Palpatine came to a stop at a broken window that overlooked the rain-drenched Works. "How would one even begin to know where to look for this other Sith?"

"I'm not sure," Dooku said, coming abreast of him. "Several crises of the past decade bear the signature of a more sinister intelligence than those who planned and perpetrated the events. Yinchorr, for example; but especially Eriadu and the assassination of the Trade Federation leadership. Clearly, certain beings have dealt with the Sith—perhaps without realizing it—and some may be dealing with the surviving one currently. Now that I'm no longer a Jedi, there may be a way for me to extract information from the crime cartels and other organizations. Eventually I will find him—or her—and with any fortune before the Jedi do."

"To avenge the death of Master Qui-Gon," Palpatine said, nodding, and aware that Dooku was staring at him intently.

"The thought preoccupied me for some time, but no longer."

Palpatine turned his head slightly. "Then why seek this one?"

"Because I suspect that Naboo was only the beginning—a kind of opening salvo. The Sith want to see the Republic brought down. Much as you and I do."

Palpatine didn't respond for a long moment. "But to ally with a Sith . . ."

"For many, they are the embodiment of pure evil, but the Council knows differently. What separates a Sith from a Jedi is the way each approaches the Force. The Jedi Order has placed limits on itself, but the Sith have never shied from incorporating the power of the dark side to accomplish their goals."

"You wish to learn the secrets of the dark side?"

"I confess that I do."

Palpatine restrained an impulse to reveal his true identity. Dooku was strong in the Force, and might simply be attempting to draw him out. On the other hand . . .

"Something tells me that this hidden Sith may eventually find his way to you," he said at last. "And if and when he or she does, I hope that the alliance you forge will help us restore order to the galaxy."

Sate Pestage showed Obi-Wan Kenobi and his young Padawan, Anakin Skywalker, into Palpatine's temporary office in the Senate Building. Both Jedi were wearing light-colored tunics, brown robes, and tall boots. Facsimiles of each other.

"Thank you both for accepting my invitation," Palpatine said, coming out from behind a broad, burnished desk to welcome them. "Sit please, both of you," he added, gesturing to chairs that faced the desk and the large window behind it.

Anakin had nearly seated himself when Obi-Wan chastised him with a shake of his head.

"Thank you, Supreme Chancellor," the short-bearded Jedi said, "but we'll stand." He folded his hands in front of him and waited for Anakin to join him before saying: "We realize that your time is valuable."

Returned to his armchair, Palpatine smiled receptively. "Not too valuable to spend with two of the people who saved the life of my Queen and rescued my homeworld from the clutches of the Trade Federation." He kept his eyes on Obi-Wan. "I am sorry for the loss of Qui-Gon Jinn, Master Obi-Wan."

The Jedi nodded in gratitude, then said: "I have only recently been named a Jedi Knight, Supreme Chancellor."

Palpatine adopted a look of surprise. "And already you've been appointed a learner. Qui-Gon must have trained you brilliantly."

Again, Obi-Wan nodded. "He was an inspired teacher."

Palpatine firmed his lips and shook his head. "Such a waste of a life . . ." His cut his gaze to Anakin. "I didn't have an opportunity on Naboo to thank you, young Skywalker. Your actions were nothing less than extraordinary. May the Force ever be as strong with you."

"Thank you, sir," Anakin said in a quiet voice.

Palpatine interlinked the fingers of his hands. "I'm told that you grew up on Tatooine. I visited there, many years ago."

Anakin's eyes narrowed for the briefest moment. "I did, sir, but I'm not supposed to talk about that."

Palpatine watched him glance up at Obi-Wan. "And why is that?"

"My mother—"

"Anakin," Obi-Wan snapped in reprimand.

Palpatine reclined slightly, studying the two of them. Obi-Wan seemed not to have noticed the fury simmering in the boy, but for an instant Palpatine perceived a touch of his younger self in Skywalker. The need to challenge authority; the gift for masking his emotions. The yet-unrecognized *power.*

"I apologize if I've stirred something between you," he said after a moment.

Clearly uncomfortable, Obi-Wan shifted in place. "The Jedi are trained to live in the moment, Supreme Chancellor. Our upbringings have little to do with our lives in the Force."

Palpatine furrowed his brow. "Easy for an infant, I'm certain, but for a young boy . . ." He interrupted himself with a negligent gesture. "Well, who am I to pass judgment on the tenets of your Order, when the Jedi have kept peace in the Republic for one thousand years."

Obi-Wan said nothing in a definite way.

"But tell me, Padawan Skywalker, how it feels to have become a member of such a revered group."

"It's like a dream come true, sir," Anakin said in genuine sincerity.

"A dream come true . . . Then you've long thought about the Jedi Order and about the Force."

Anakin nodded. "I've always wanted to bring justice—"

"It's not for you to decide your destiny, Anakin," Obi-Wan said. "The Force will guide you."

Palpatine smiled inwardly. *Guide you to me, young Skywalker.*

Dooku had talent, and could be a powerful placeholder. But this seemingly guiless pleasant-faced boy, this *Forceful* boy, was the one he would take as his appretice, and use to execute the final stage of the Grand Plan. Let Obi-Wan instruct him in the ways of the Force, and let Skywalker grow embittered over the next decade as his mother aged in slavery, the galaxy deteriorated around him, and his fellow Jedi fell to inextricable conflicts. He was too young to be trained in the ways of the Sith, in any case, but he was the perfect age to bond with a father figure who would listen to all his troubles and coax him inexorably over to the dark side.

"As I told you on Naboo, Anakin," he said finally, "we will continue to follow your career with great interest."

And assure that it culminates in the ruination of the Jedi Order and the reascendancy of the Sith!

About the Author

JAMES LUCENO is the *New York Times* bestselling author of the *Star Wars* novels *Dark Lord: The Rise of Darth Vader, Cloak of Deception,* and *Labyrinth of Evil,* as well as the *New Jedi Order* novels *Agents of Chaos I: Hero's Trial* and *Agents of Chaos II: Jedi Eclipse, The Unifying Force,* and the eBook *Darth Maul: Saboteur.* He lives in Annapolis, Maryland, with his wife and youngest child.

The galaxy has always been a dangerous place, but for the most famous singer in the universe, Javul Charn, it's become downright deadly: murder is stalking her tour. What she needs is protection.

What she gets is Dash Rendar.

Between the discovery of dead bodies in a cargo hold and an attack by an unidentified warship, Black Sun intimidation and Imperial scrutiny, it's up to Dash and co-pilot Eaden Vrill to try to understand who is terrorizing Javul's tour and why.

SHADOW GAMES

A *Star Wars* Thriller

by

Michael Reaves and Maya Kaathryn Bohnhoff

In Stores Now

"Corellian ale. And by the way—you know anyone with an empty cargo bay who might be looking for a quick score?" Dash's gaze was still roaming the crowded room.

Chal, setting Dash's ale before him, harned and moaned to the effect that he just might at that. It was a good thing, Dash reflected, that over the years he had picked up enough of the big furry bipeds' language to gather the gist of their statements—mostly, anyway. He could still get tripped up by the inflection. Shyriiwook was a tonal language, which meant intonation contour was vitally important. Depending on the phonology, the same phrase could mean either "You honor me with your presence" or "You smell like a dead dewback."

He understood the Wookiee's statement well enough, accompanied as it was with the jerk of a shaggy head toward the nether regions of the cantina. "Really?" He brightened. "Where?"

In answer Chalmun pointed to a small cubicle on the other side of the bandstand and closest to the rear exit. There was but one table in it and he could see nothing of the individual sitting in it, save for a hand gripping a mug. Several empties already cluttered the tabletop.

"Thanks, Chal." He lifted his ale and, sipping it, headed for the corner booth. He could've sworn he heard a smothered chuckle from behind him, but when he peered back over his shoulder the big guy was busily serving drinks.

Just shy of the doorway he bumped into a Kubaz who was nattering at the band to set up faster and begin playing immediately, if not sooner. Dash staggered back a few steps, amazingly spilling none of his ale. Hence the smile he showed his potential mark when he slipped into the cubicle was genuine.

Genuine or not, it faded just inside the doorway. "Sith spit! *You*."

Han Solo looked up from his drink, his eyes coming into relatively quick focus on Dash's face. "Oh, *nice*. Is that any way to greet an old friend, old friend?"

"Old *friend*? You're kidding me, right? I've heard all the trash you've been talking about me and my ship up and down the space lanes. I seem to recall that the last time we met, you took a swing at my head."

"Hey, I was a little drunk. Okay?"

Dash considered the number of empty glasses on the tabletop. "Not like now, huh?"

"No, I'm not drunk. Yet. But give me some time and I'll manage."

Frowning, Dash sidled into the booth and sat down. "What's up? And where's Chewie?" An uneasy thought made him sit up straighter. "Nothing's happened to Chewie?"

Han waved a dismissive hand. "Not unless you consider fatherhood something. He's back on Kashyyyk with Malla and their new baby boy."

"Yeah? What'd they name the kid?"

"Lumpawarrump," said Han with some difficulty.

"Lumpa . . . Lumpa—?"

"Yeah, that's usually as far as I get, too."

"So Chewbacca's home with the family and you're hanging out at Chal's drinking yourself under a table?"

Han gave him a fierce look. "I'm relash—re*lax*ing."

"Is that what you humans call it? I had wondered." Eaden Vrill stood in the cubicle doorway, thumbs tucked into his weapons belt.

Han smiled broadly. "Vrill, old buddy! Good to see you. Still hanging around with losers, I see."

"So it would seem." Eaden tilted his head toward Dash. "Luck?"

"None . . . unless . . ." Dash regarded Han speculatively. When Solo was this cocky, it usually meant he'd scored some profits. If that were the case, maybe he could be induced to part with a few. Maybe just enough for Dash to complete repairs on *Outrider* and avoid having to hire another ship.

"Luck with what?" asked Han.

"I don't suppose you could see your way clear to lend me a few credits, old friend."

Han poked a finger into his right ear and wiggled it. "Wait a minute, I can't have heard that right. You're asking me for a favor? No—better yet—you're asking me for money? Oh, *that's* rich."

Dash grabbed hold of his temper with both hands. "Can we be serious for just a moment? The *Outrider* is out of commission and I've got a whole lot of cargo sitting in the hold needing pretty desperately to get to Nal Hutta."

"Huh. What's wrong with the old boat?"

"Blown hyperdrives."

"Both of 'em? How'd you manage that?"

"We ran into Imperials on the Kessel Run. Almost got blasted out of space, then almost ran into a planetoid, then almost got sucked into the Maw. We fried our primary and secondary drives getting out again."

Han sat up straighter and leaned toward Dash across the table. "You're messing with my head." He glanced up at Eaden. "Isn't he? He's joking, right?"

"If only. We nearly perished."

Han leaned back in his seat again, taking a slug of his drink. "I guess you're lucky to be here then, aren't you?"

"Sure. Except that I've got a ship that can't fly and a cargo to get to Nal Hutta with no way to get it there." Dash leaned forward, elbows on the table, trying to look earnest. His mom had always fallen for his earnest look. "I just need enough to get the drive up and running . . ."

"Even at Kerlew's best prices that's gonna come to quite a pile of credits. More than I've got. You think I'd be sittin' here if I had a commishun—com-*miss*-ion?"

Unfortunately, Dash's mom was unique.

"Just a few credits to—"

Eaden made a sound like steam venting, then said, "If I may: We have a cargo. Han has a ship. The purchaser has the credits we need so that *we* can have a ship. Again."

Dash looked at Han. Han looked at Dash. It fried Dash's circuits to have to hire Han Solo, of all the people in the galaxy, to take his load to Nal Hutta, but—

Han's slow smile was crooked. "Sounds like you need me."

Dash came to his feet fast enough to reach orbit. "Forget it! I don't need—" He felt a heavy hand fall on his shoulder.

"Pride rises before disaster falls," said the Nautolan philosophically. Then he addressed Solo. "What percentage would you charge to take a full hold to Nal Hutta . . . and a few items to Nar Shaddaa as well?"

Han considered. "Forty percent."

Now Dash leapt to his feet, fists on the table. "That's piracy!"

"It's business."

"It's space lane robbery! It's—ow!" Eaden's fingers had tightened on Dash's shoulder in painful warning.

"Twenty percent," said the Nautolan calmly.

"I should strangle you with your own tentacles," Dash muttered.

"Thirty-five," said Han.

Dash exploded anew. "We almost *died* for that cargo! We dodged Imperial ordnance for that cargo! We flew into the sucking *Maw* for that cargo! In other words, Han, *old friend,* we did all the hard work!"

Han made his eyes as wide and innocent as possible and shrugged eloquently. "All right. All right. Ice it, okay? Always was a sucker for a sob story. Thirty. And I off-load everything on Nar Shaddaa."

"Twenty-five," said Eaden. "And you deliver to Nal Hutta."

"Hey, I could be putting my life on the line going back to Nal Hutta right now. Things are kind of tense there, case you hadn't noticed— what with the assassinations and all. And I hear Jabba's in a bad mood. Something about a dropped spice shipment." Han scraped at a smudge on his glass. "Twenty-seven."

"Done," said Eaden and pushed Dash inexorably back into his seat. Dash slumped, defeated.

Han smiled broadly. "Great. Where's the old *Outrigger* stashed?"

Dash ground his teeth audibly. "It's *Outrider*. The usual place—Bay Ninety-two. How soon can you leave?"

"As soon as you can shift the load."

"As soon as *we* shift it?"

Han slid out of the booth and stood, polishing off his drink. "Sure. If you'd been able to do thirty percent on the cut I'd've been happy to help with the cargo transfer, but I don't have a first mate right now and you do. So if you don't mind, I'll just go and prep the *Falcon.* Your hold's full, is it?"

"Yeah."

"No problem. The *Falcon*'ll take that on with room to spare. See you at the docks in a few, boys." Han sketched a salute at Dash, returned Eaden's attenuated bow, and left, whistling.

Dash watched him go, then tilted his head back to look up at Eaden. "Gotta admire your nerve, Eaden. I'd've caved at thirty."

"Which is why we have our respective roles. I knew he would go lower." He flexed a couple of his head-tresses to emphasize the point.

"I thought you said that empathy trick doesn't always work out of water."

Eaden gave the Nautolan version of a shrug—a lifting of side locks. "What can I say? It was a good hair day."

About the Type

This book was set in Galliard, a typeface designed by Matthew Carter for the Mergenthaler Linotype Company in 1978. Galliard is based on the sixteenth-century typefaces of Robert Granjon.